ZERO™ **Vol.3** —
“Tenderness of Wolves”

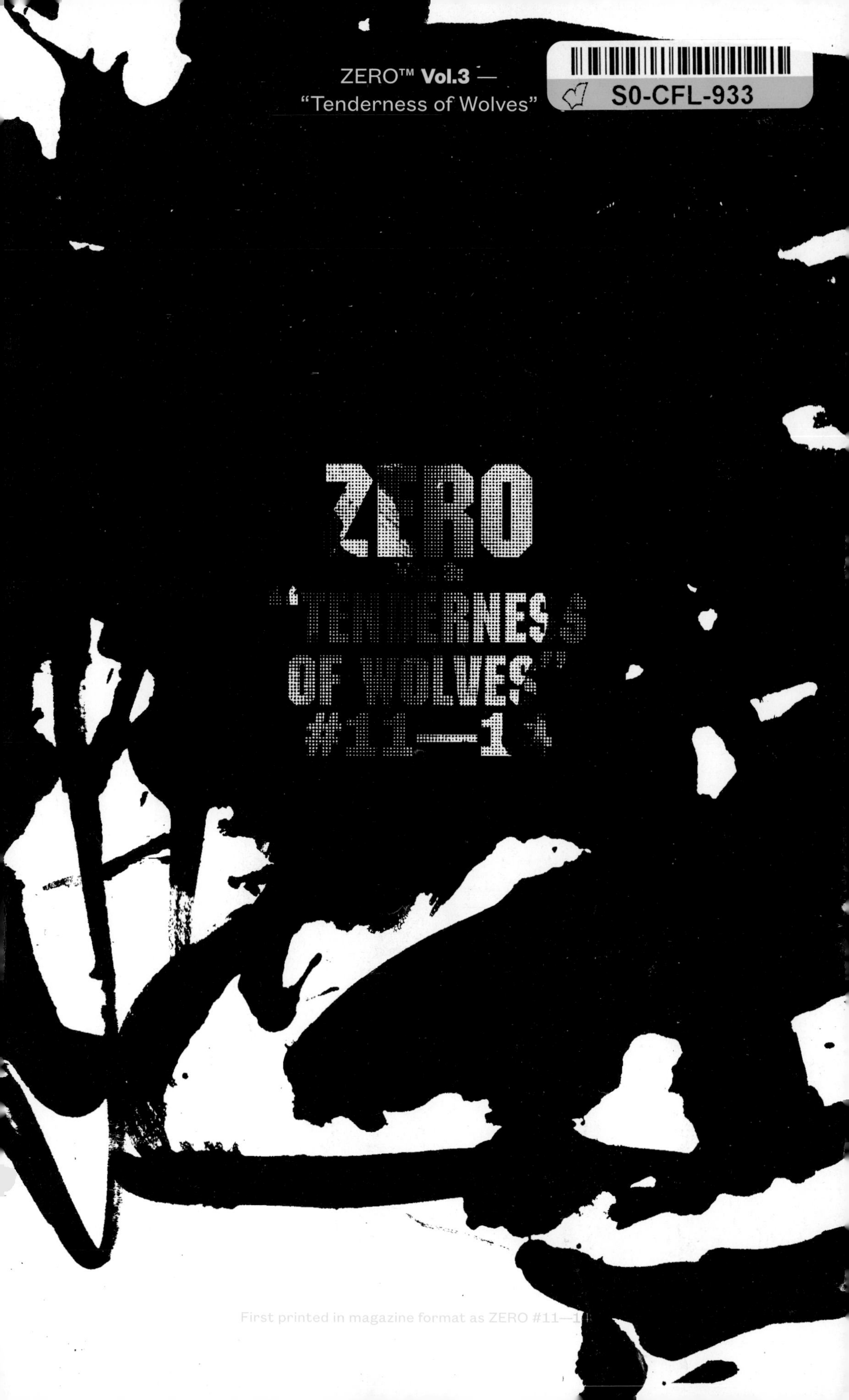
ZERO
“TENDERNESS
OF WOLVES”
#11—14

First printed in magazine format as ZERO #11—1

ZERO™
Vol. 3: #11–14 "TENDERNESS OF WOLVES"

Written by
Ales KOT

Designed by
Tom MULLER

Illustrated by
Ricardo Lopez ORTIZ
Adam GORHAM
Alberto PONTICELLI
Marek OLEKSICKI

Colored by
Jordie BELLAIRE

Lettered by
Clayton COWLES

Collection designed by
Tom MULLER

Original cover design, graphics and colors
by Tom Muller, with Ricardo Lopez Ortiz,
Adam Gorham, Alberto Ponticelli,
Marek Oleksicki, Sarah Horrocks,
and Tonči Zonjić.

Image Comics, Inc.

Robert Kirkman — Chief Operating Officer
Erik Larsen — Chief Financial Officer
Todd McFarlane — President
Marc Silvestri — Chief Executive Officer
Jim Valentino — Vice-President

Eric Stephenson — Publisher
Ron Richards — Director of Business Development
Jennifer de Guzman — Director of Trade Book Sales
Kat Salazar — Director of PR & Marketing
Corey Murphy — Director of Retail Sales
Jeremy Sullivan — Director of Digital Sales
Emilio Bautista — Sales Assistant
Branwyn Bigglestone — Senior Accounts Manager
Emily Miller — Accounts Manager
Jessica Ambriz — Administrative Assistant
Tyler Shainline — Events Coordinator
David Brothers — Content Manager
Jonathan Chan — Production Manager
Drew Gill — Art Director
Meredith Wallace — Print Manager
Addison Duke — Production Artist
Vincent Kukua — Production Artist
Tricia Ramos — Production Assistant

ZERO VOL. 3. First Printing. February 2015. Published
by Image Comics, Inc. Office of publication: 2001
Center Street, Sixth Floor, Berkeley, CA 94704.
Copyright © 2014 ALES KOT. All rights reserved. ZERO™
(including all prominent characters featured herein),
its logo and all character likenesses are trademarks of
Ales Kot, unless otherwise noted. Image Comics® and
its logos are registered trademarks of Image Comics,
Inc. No part of this publication may be reproduced or
transmitted, in any form or by any means (except for short
excerpts for review purposes) without the express written
permission of Image Comics, Inc. All names, characters,
events, and locales in this publication are entirely
fictional. Any resemblance to actual living persons
(living or dead), events or places, without satiric intent,
is coincidental. First printed in single magazine form
as ZERO #11-14 by Image Comics, Inc. Printed in the USA.
For information regarding the CPSIA on this printed
material call: 203-595-3636 and provide reference
RICH - 605763. For international rights contact:
foreignlicensing@imagecomics.com
ISBN: 978-1-63215-252-7

CHAPTER 11

KILL SHOT

Illustrated by Ricardo Lopez Ortiz

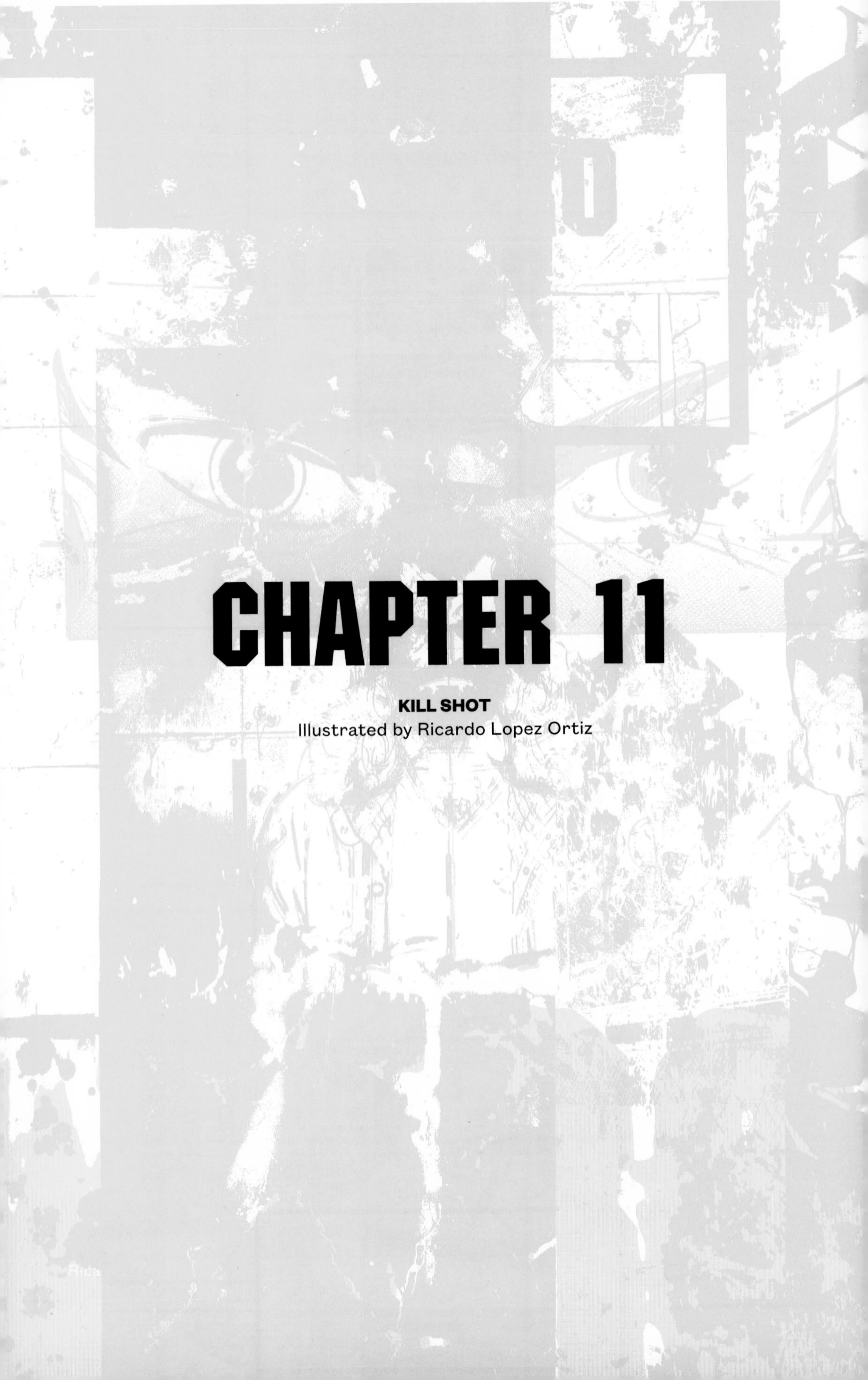

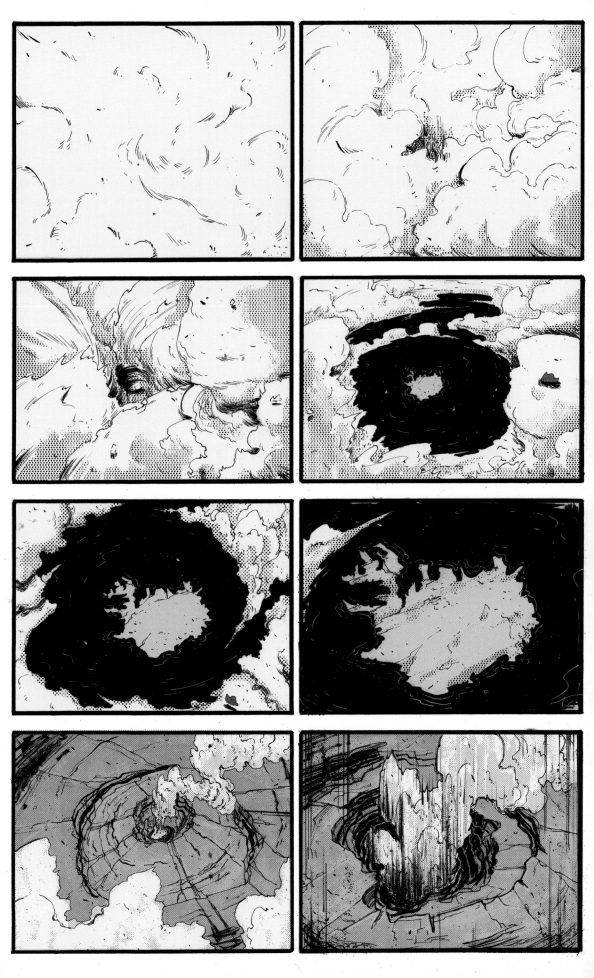

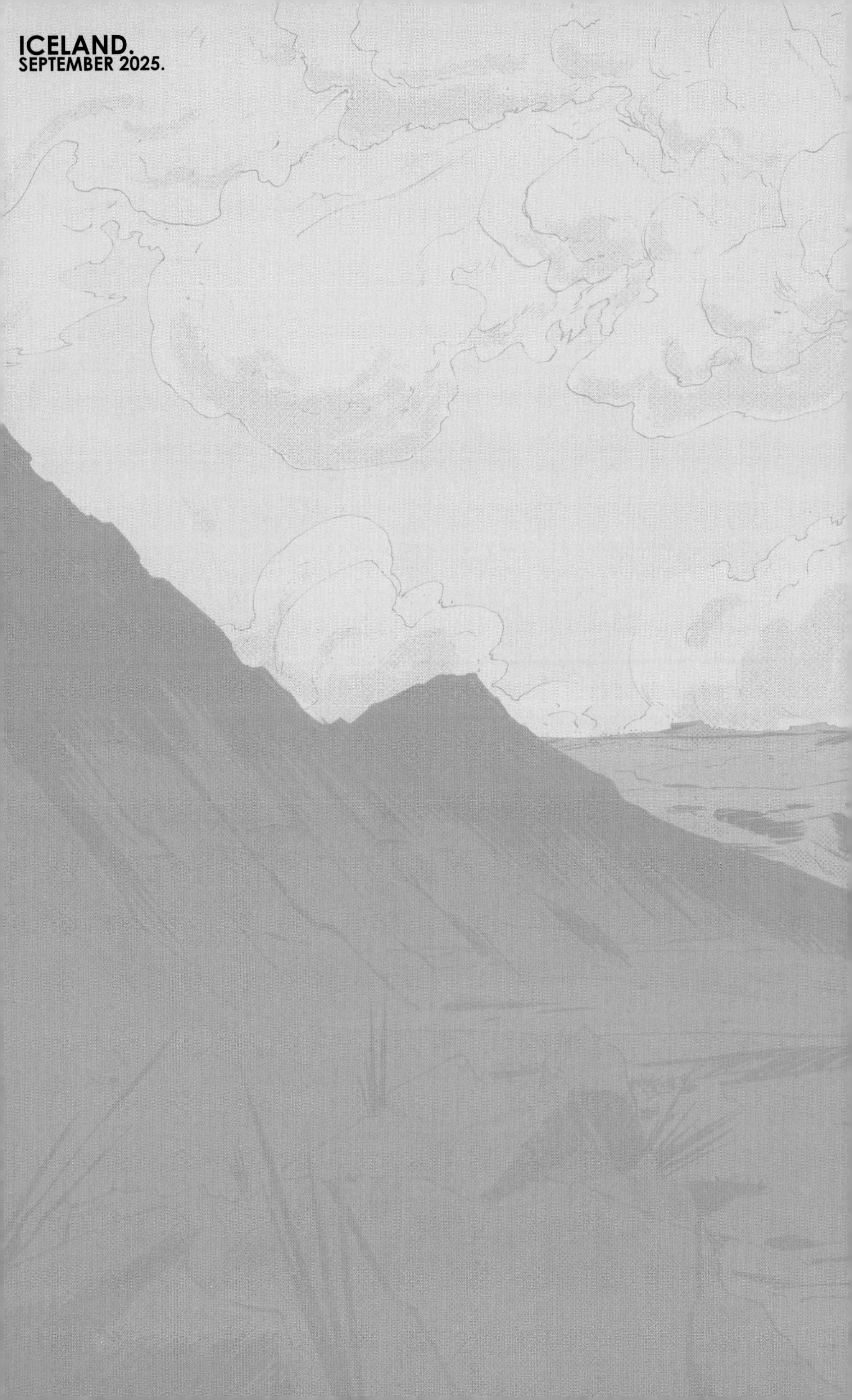
ICELAND.
SEPTEMBER 2025.

DAY ONE

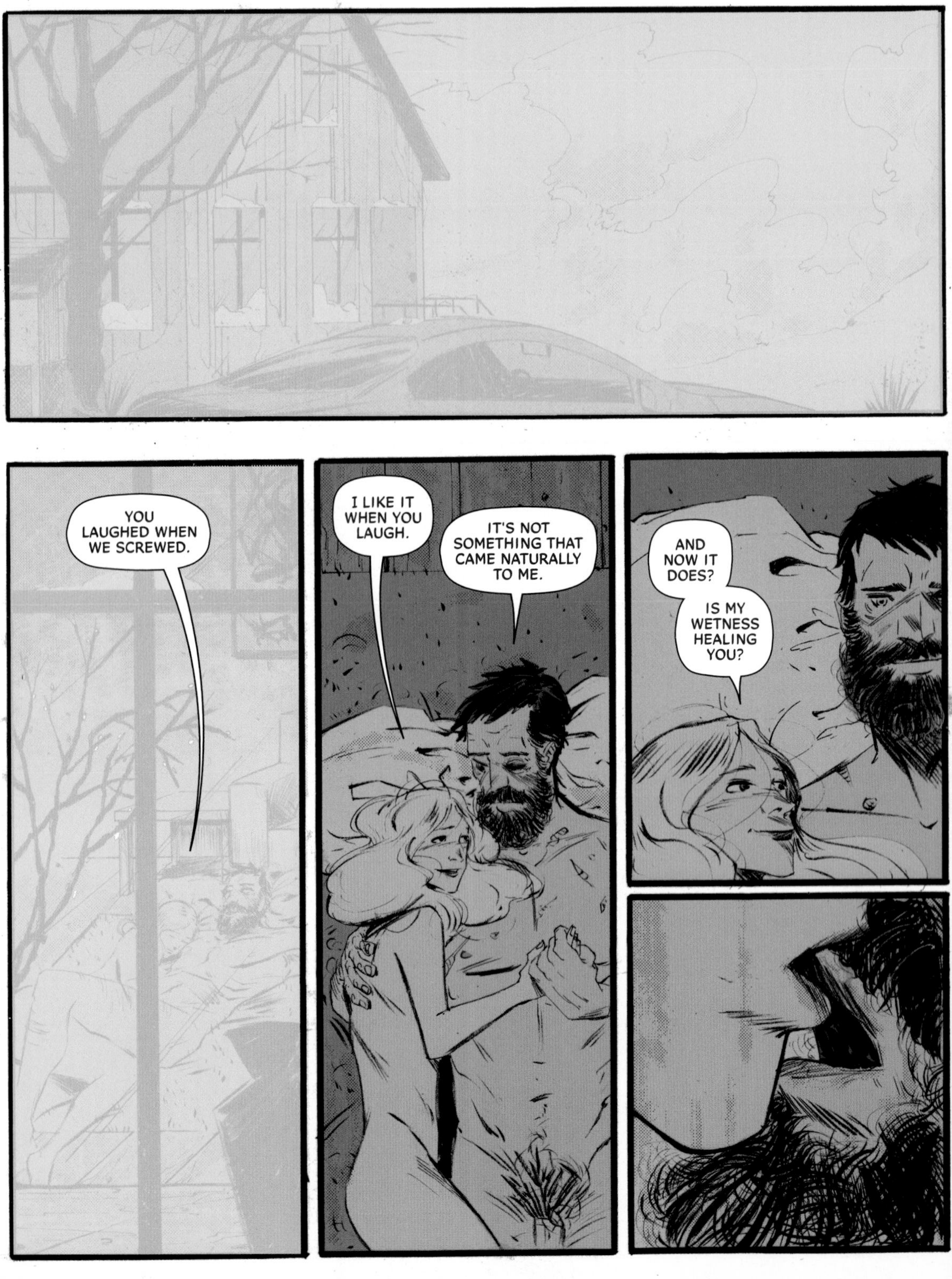
YOU LAUGHED WHEN WE SCREWED.
I LIKE IT WHEN YOU LAUGH.
IT'S NOT SOMETHING THAT CAME NATURALLY TO ME.
AND NOW IT DOES?
IS MY WETNESS HEALING YOU?

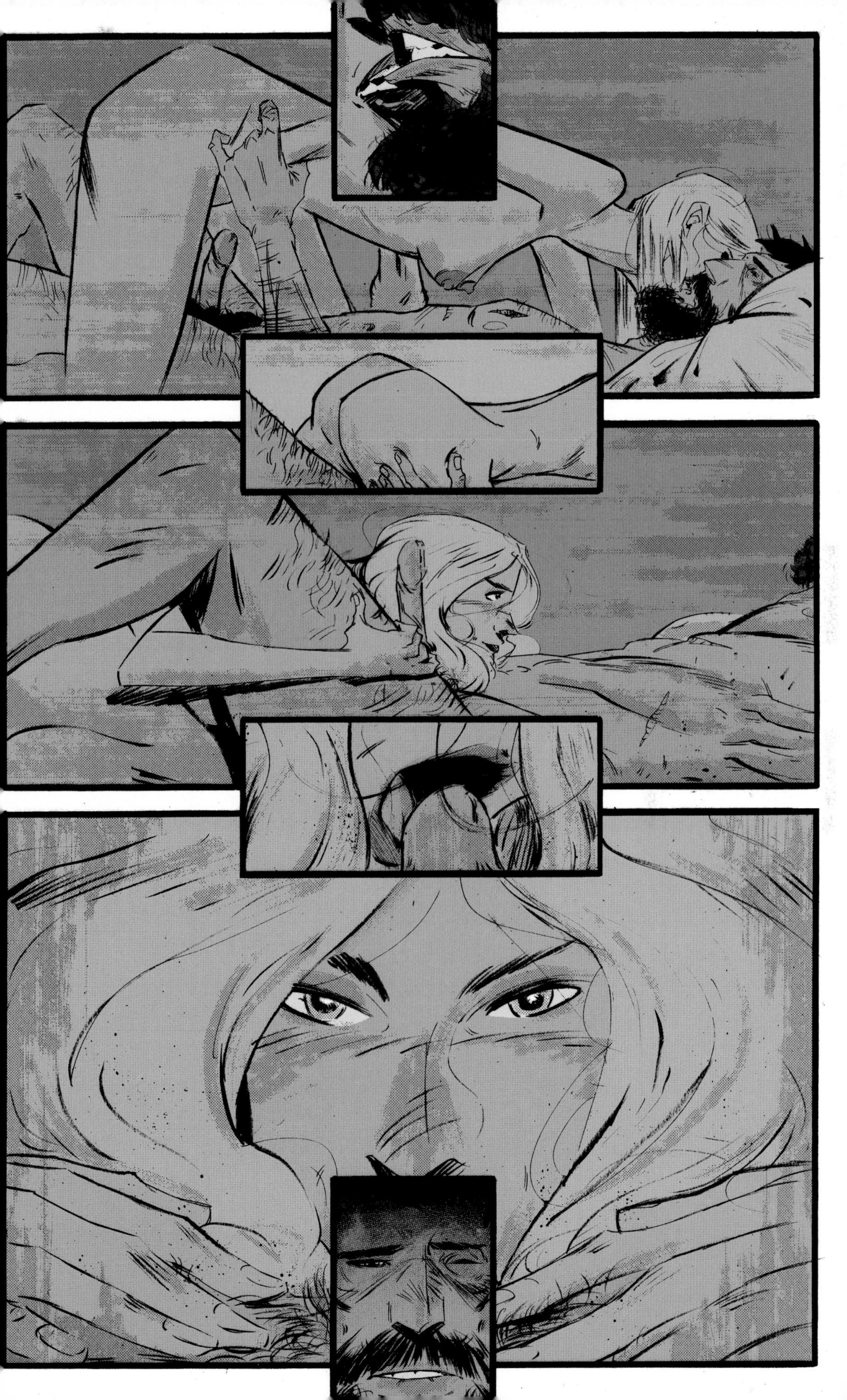

DAY TWO

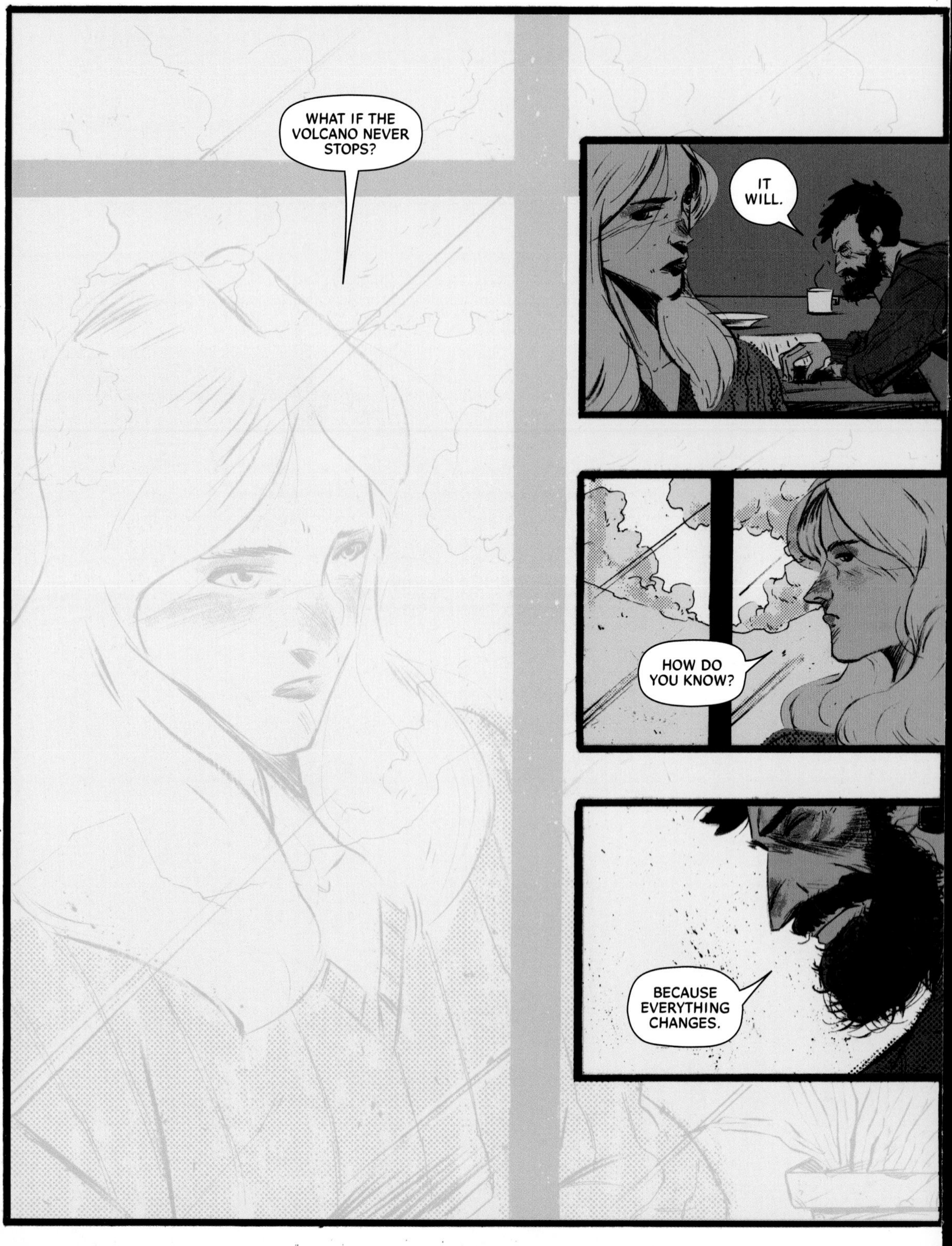

WHAT IF THE VOLCANO NEVER STOPS?
IT WILL.
HOW DO YOU KNOW?
BECAUSE EVERYTHING CHANGES.

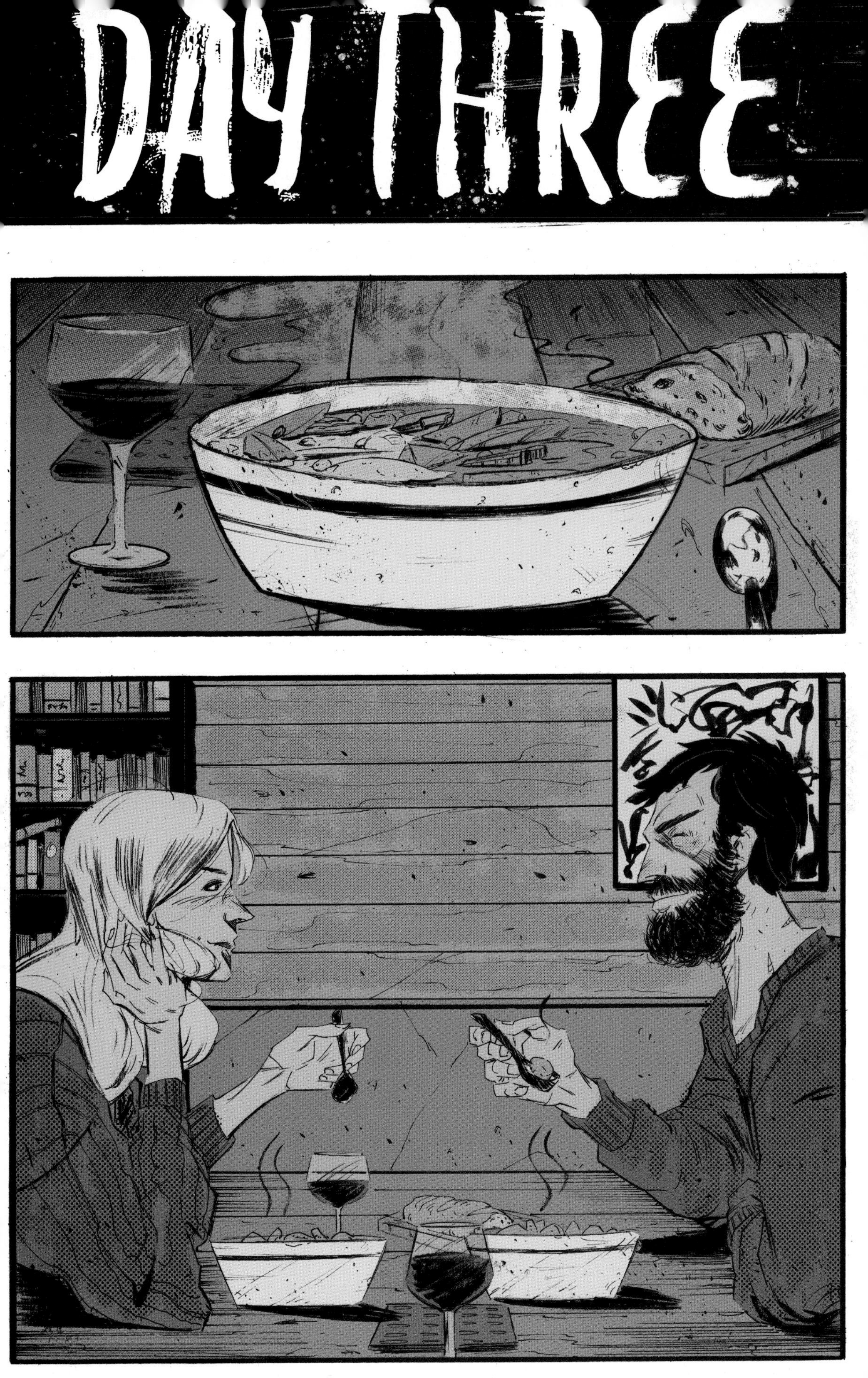
DAY THREE

DAY FOUR

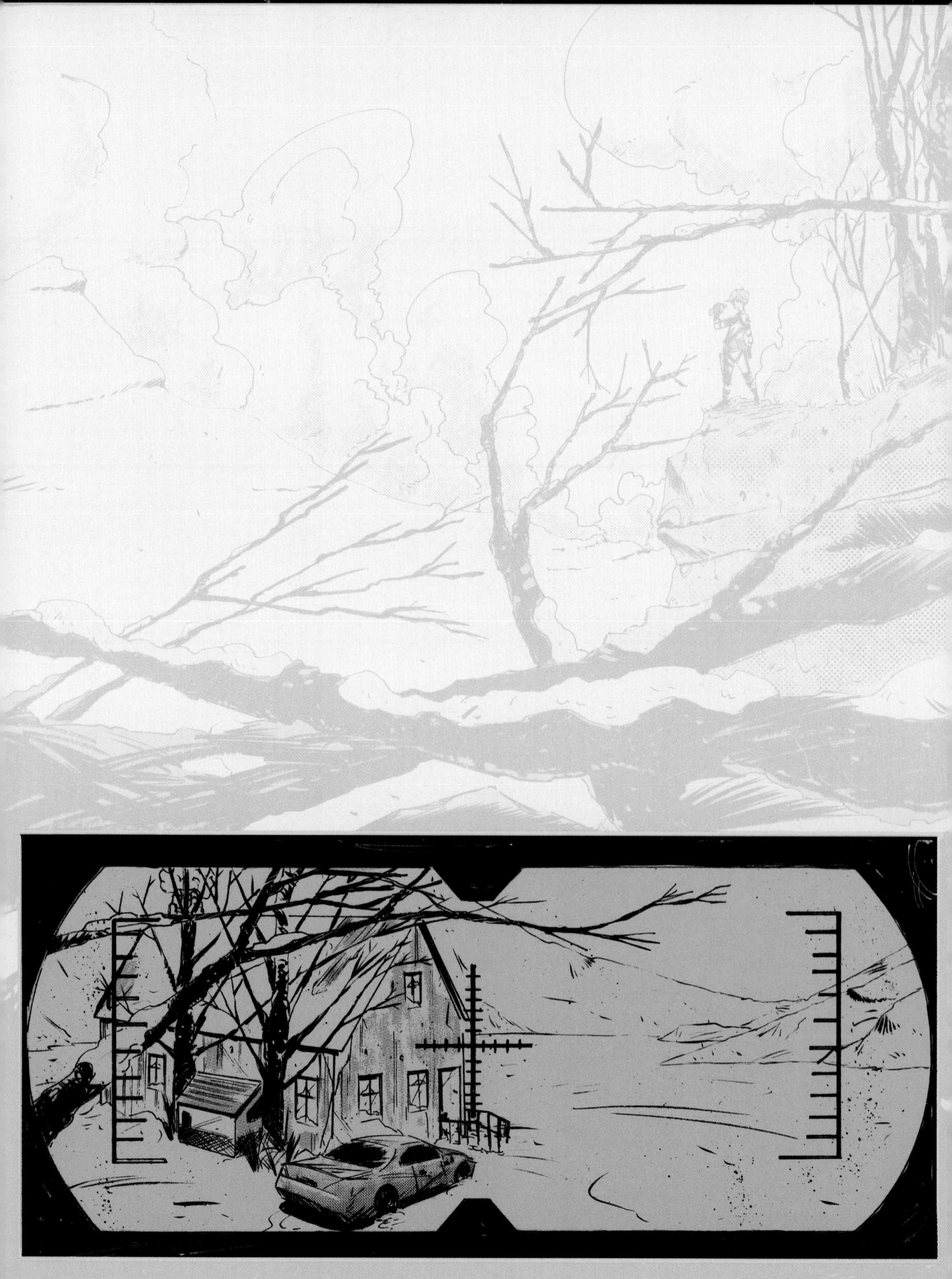

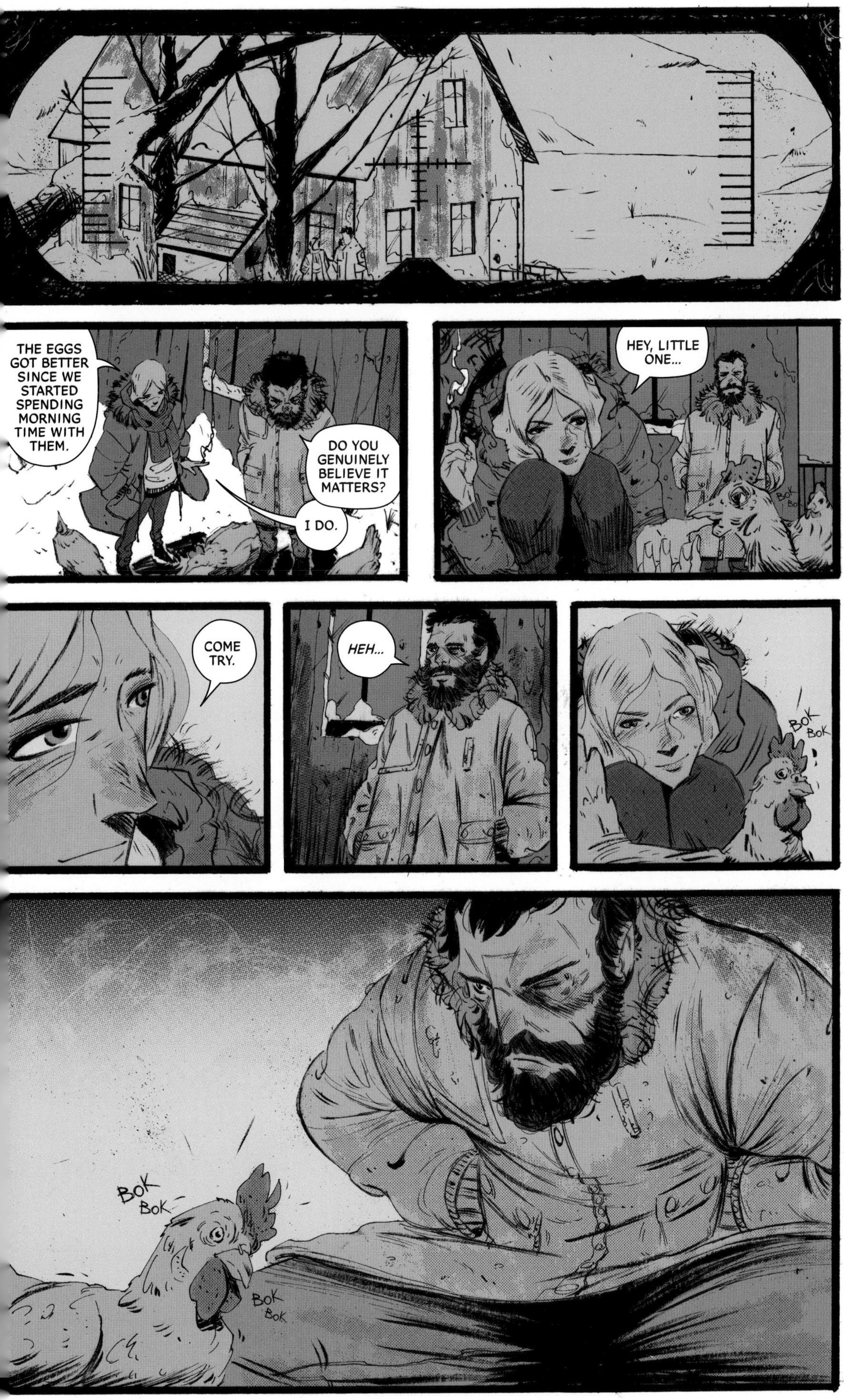
THE EGGS GOT BETTER SINCE WE STARTED SPENDING MORNING TIME WITH THEM.
DO YOU GENUINELY BELIEVE IT MATTERS?
I DO.
HEY, LITTLE ONE...
BOK BOK
COME TRY.
HEH...
BOK BOK
BOK BOK
BOK BOK

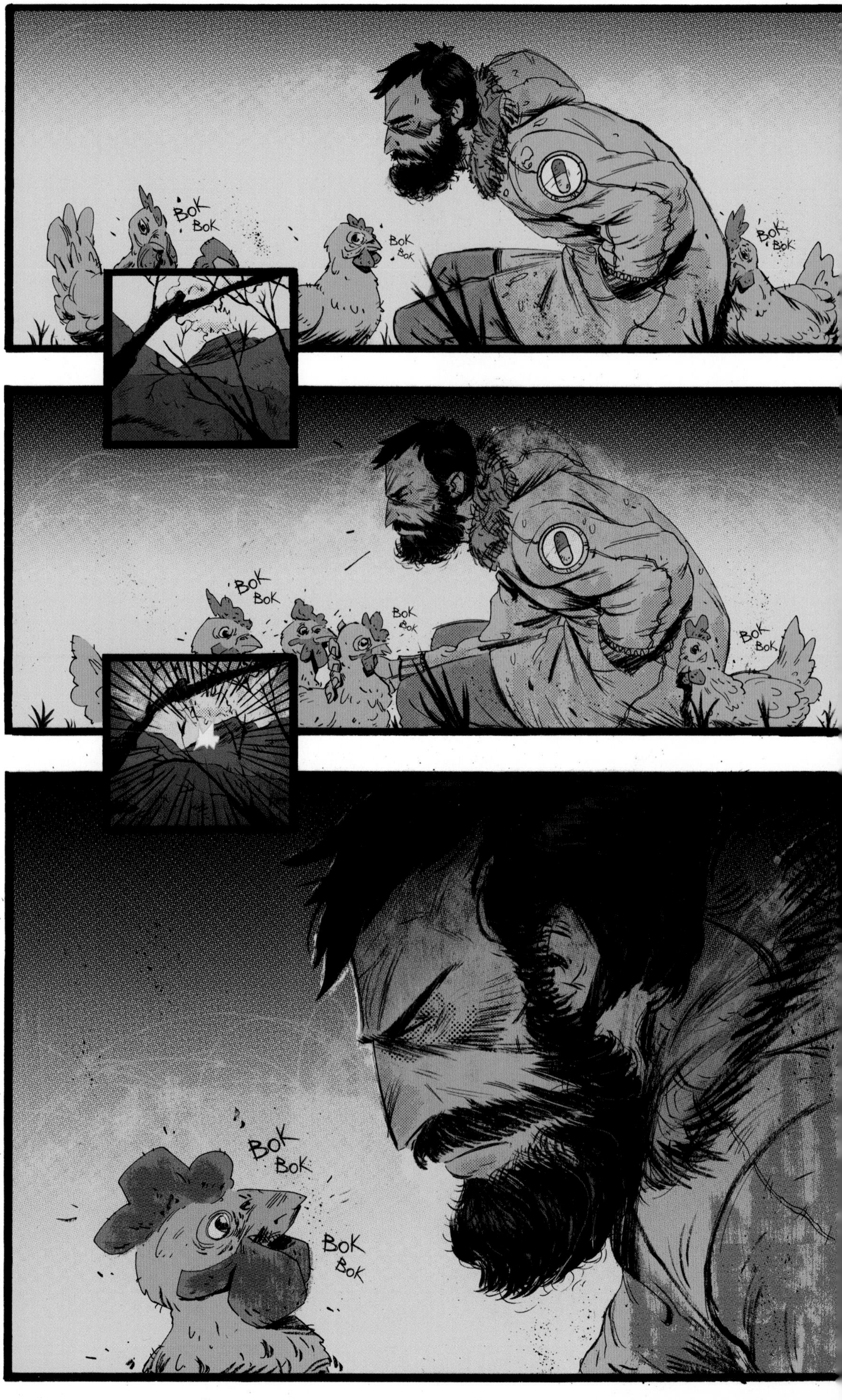
BOK
BOK
BOK
BOK
BOK
BOK
BOK
BOK
BOK
BOK
BOK
BOK
BOK
BOK
BOK
BOK

DAY FIVE

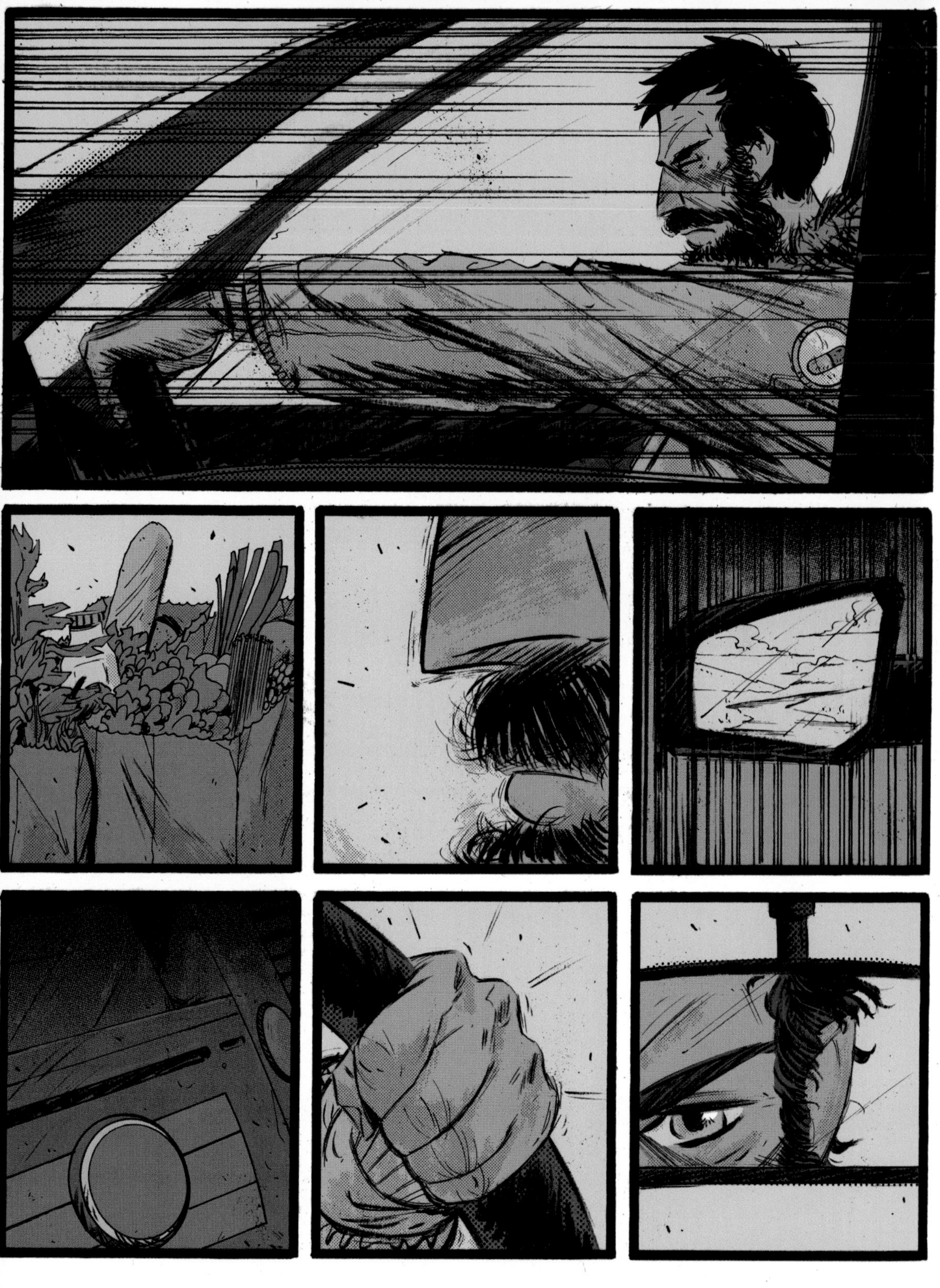

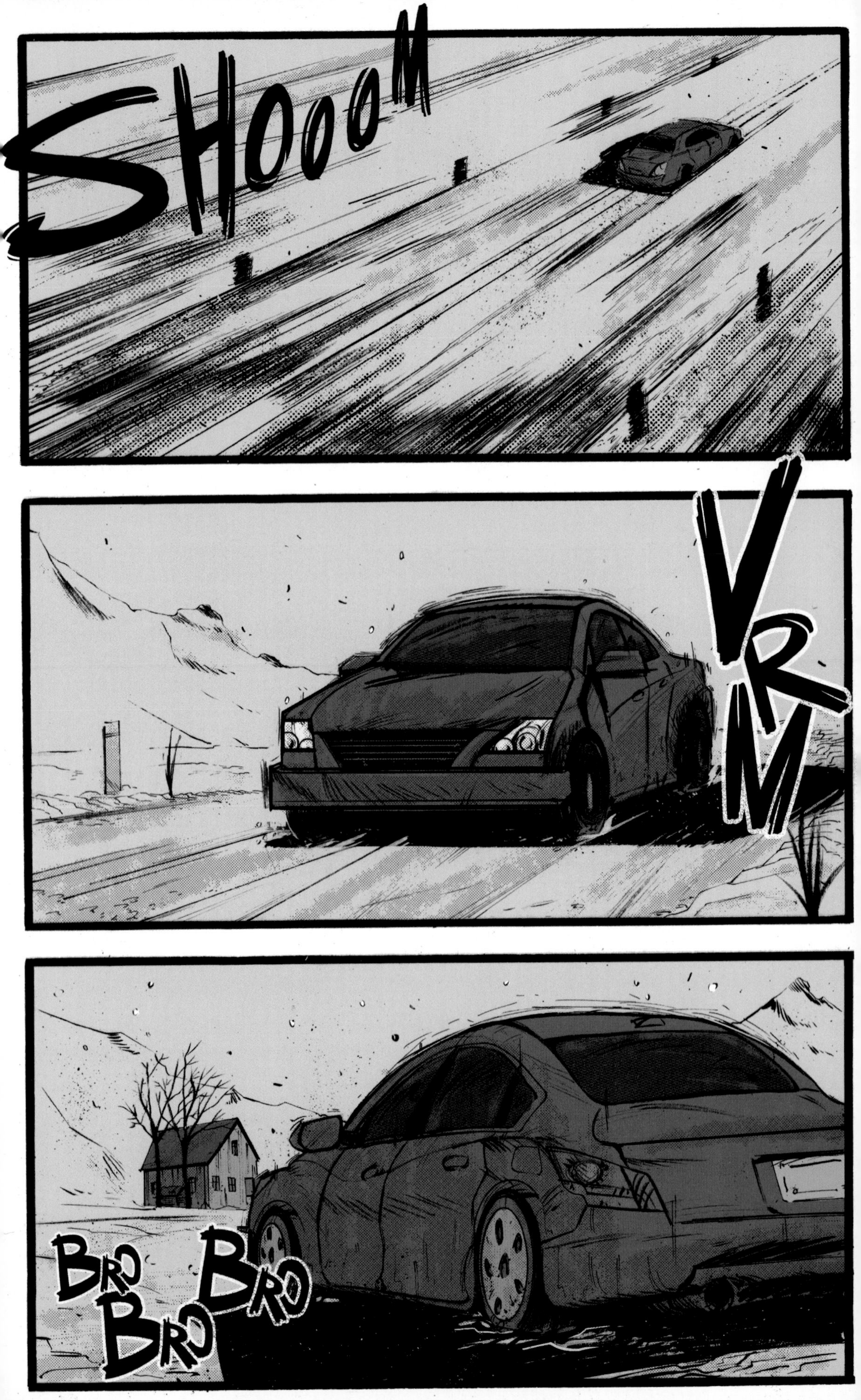
SHOOOM
VRM
BRO BRO
BRO BRO

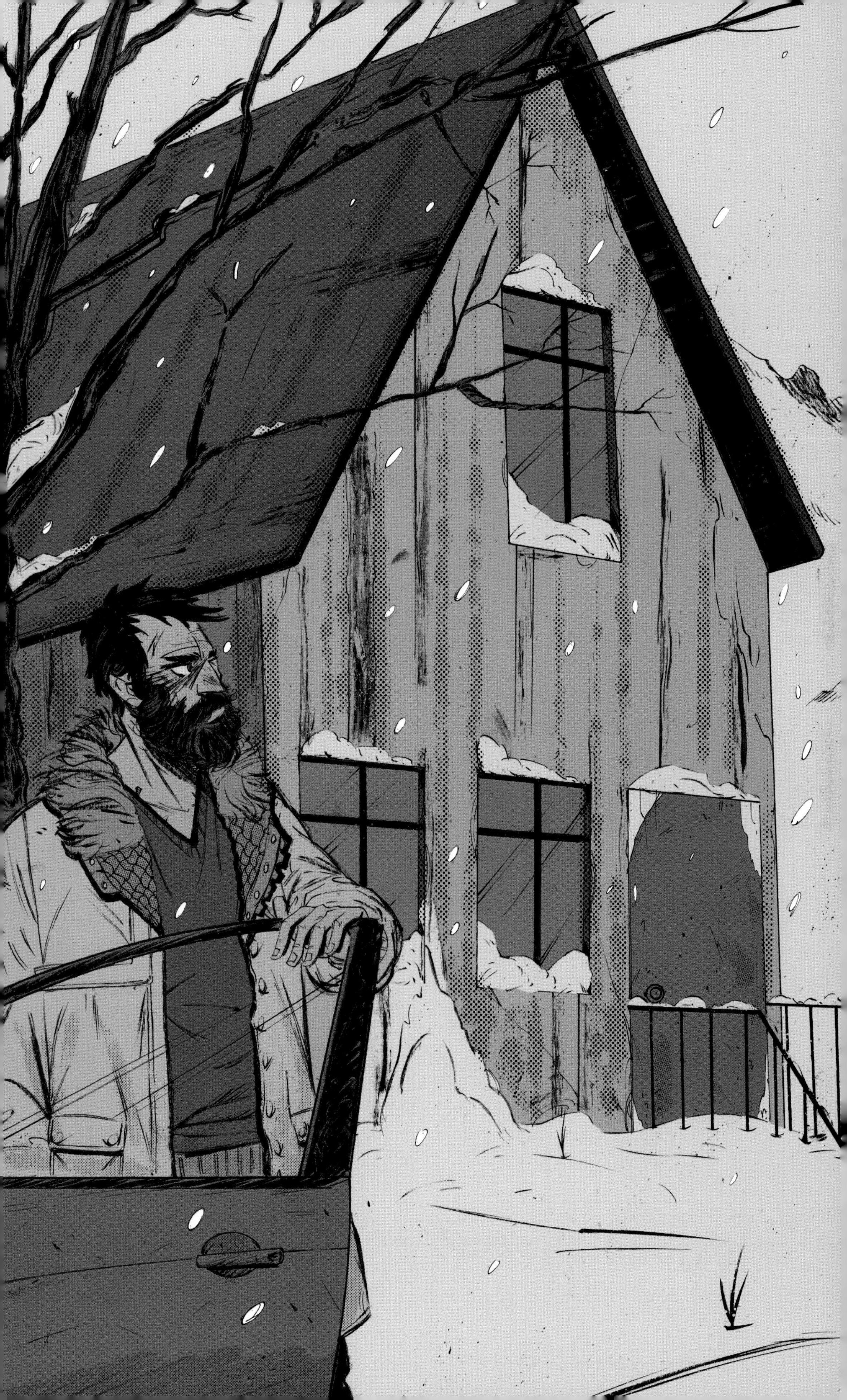

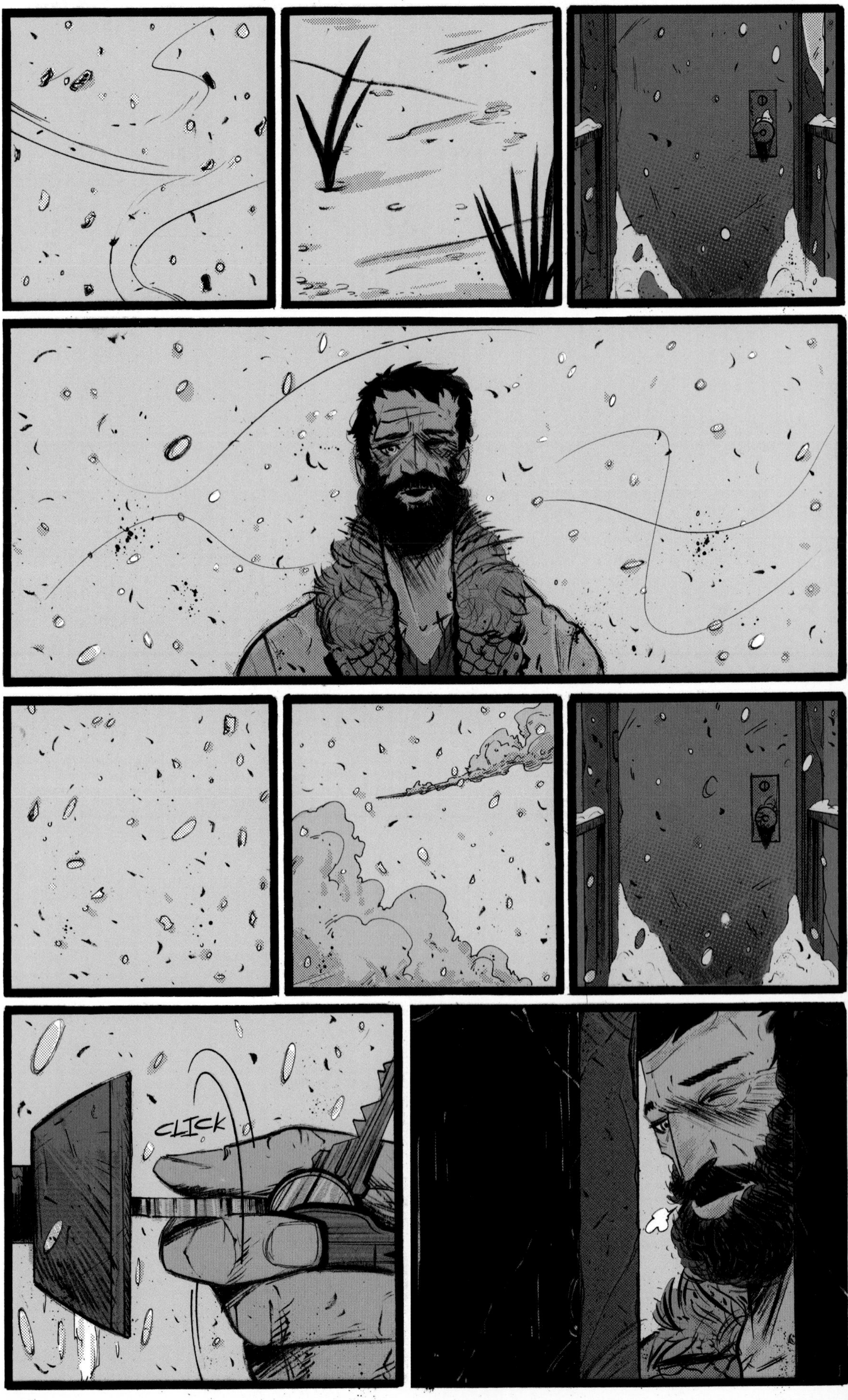
CLICK

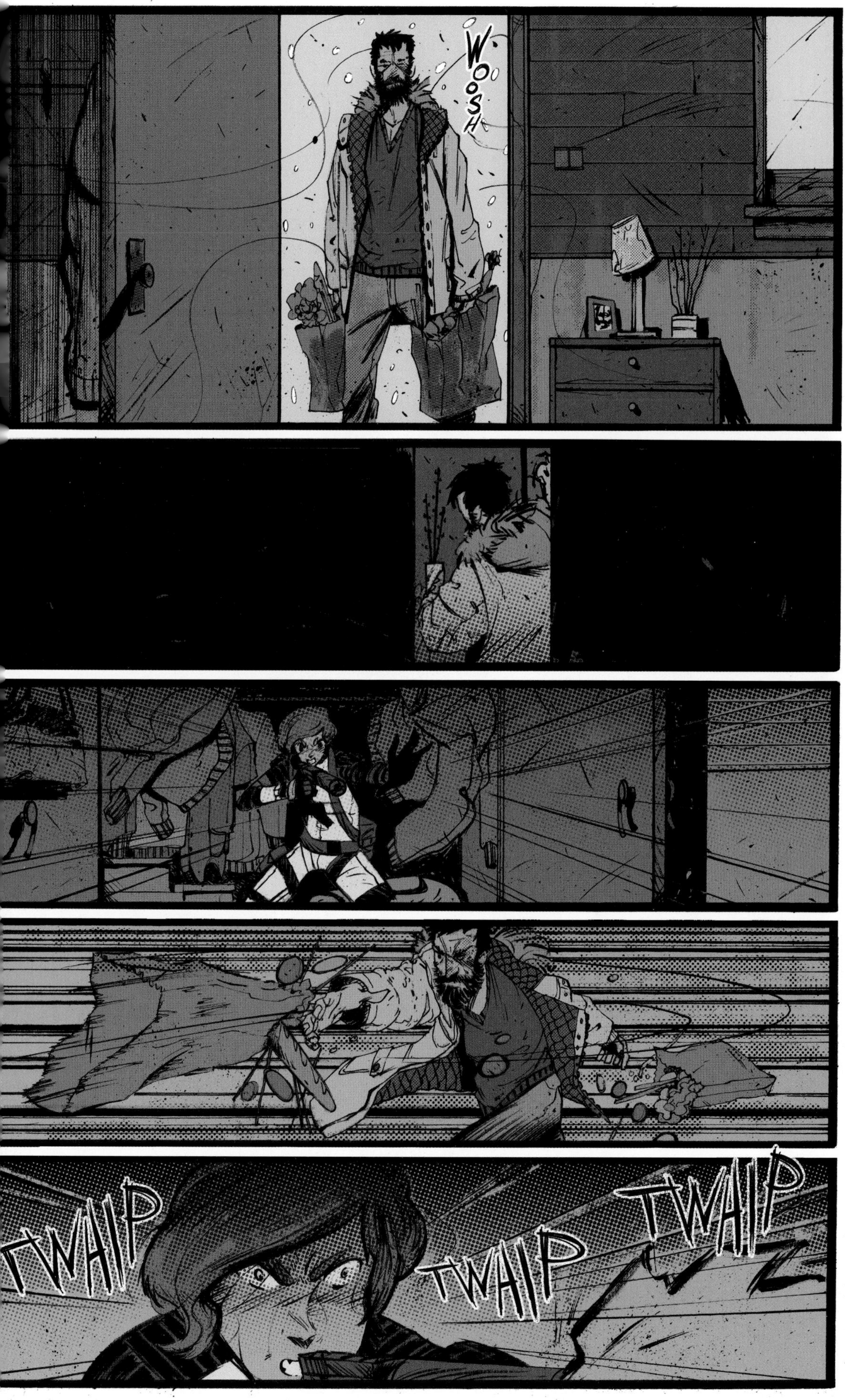
WOOSH
TWAIP
TWAIP
TWAIP

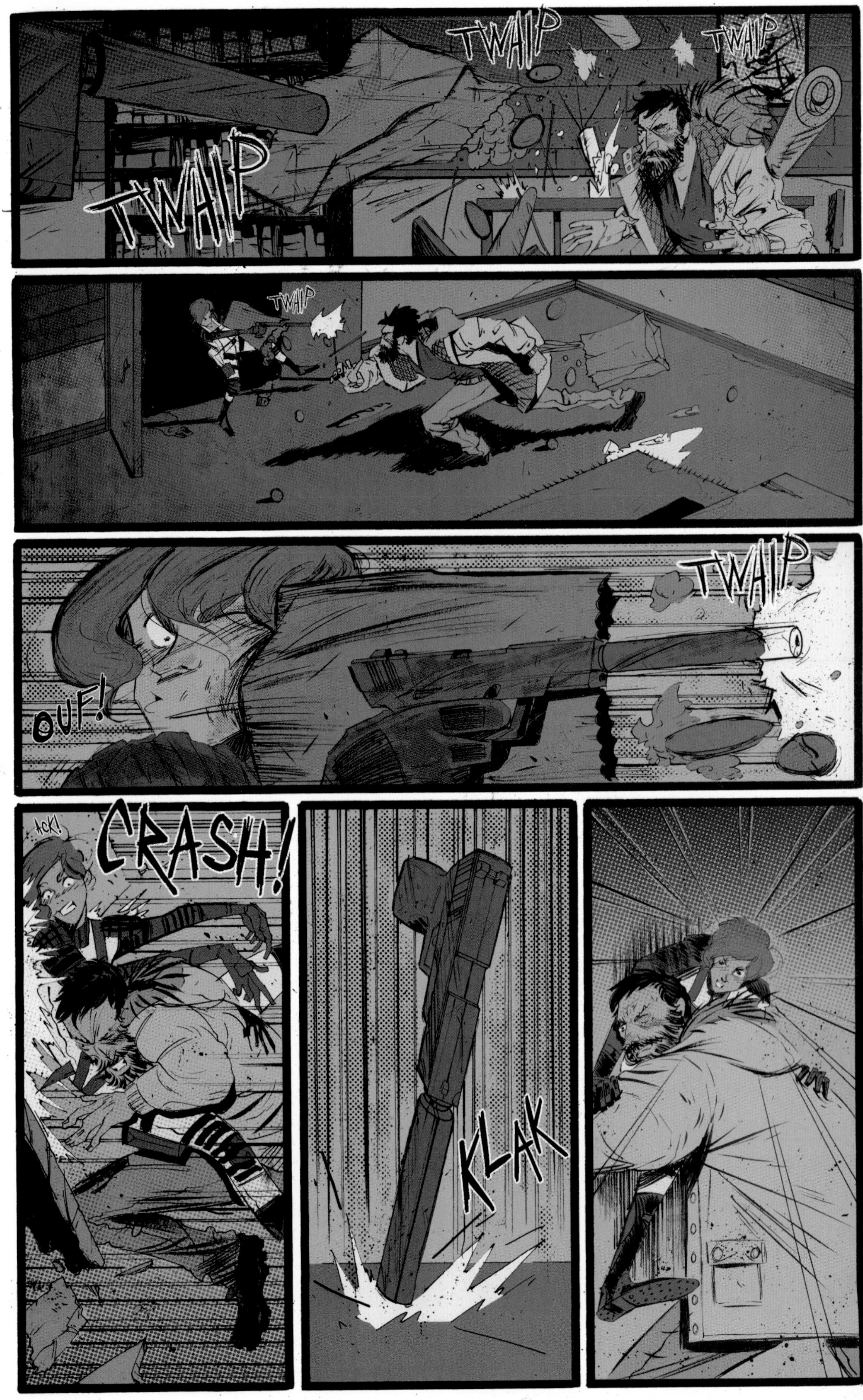
TWAIP
TWAIP
TWAIP
TWAIP
TWAIP
OUF!
ACK!
CRASH!
KLAK

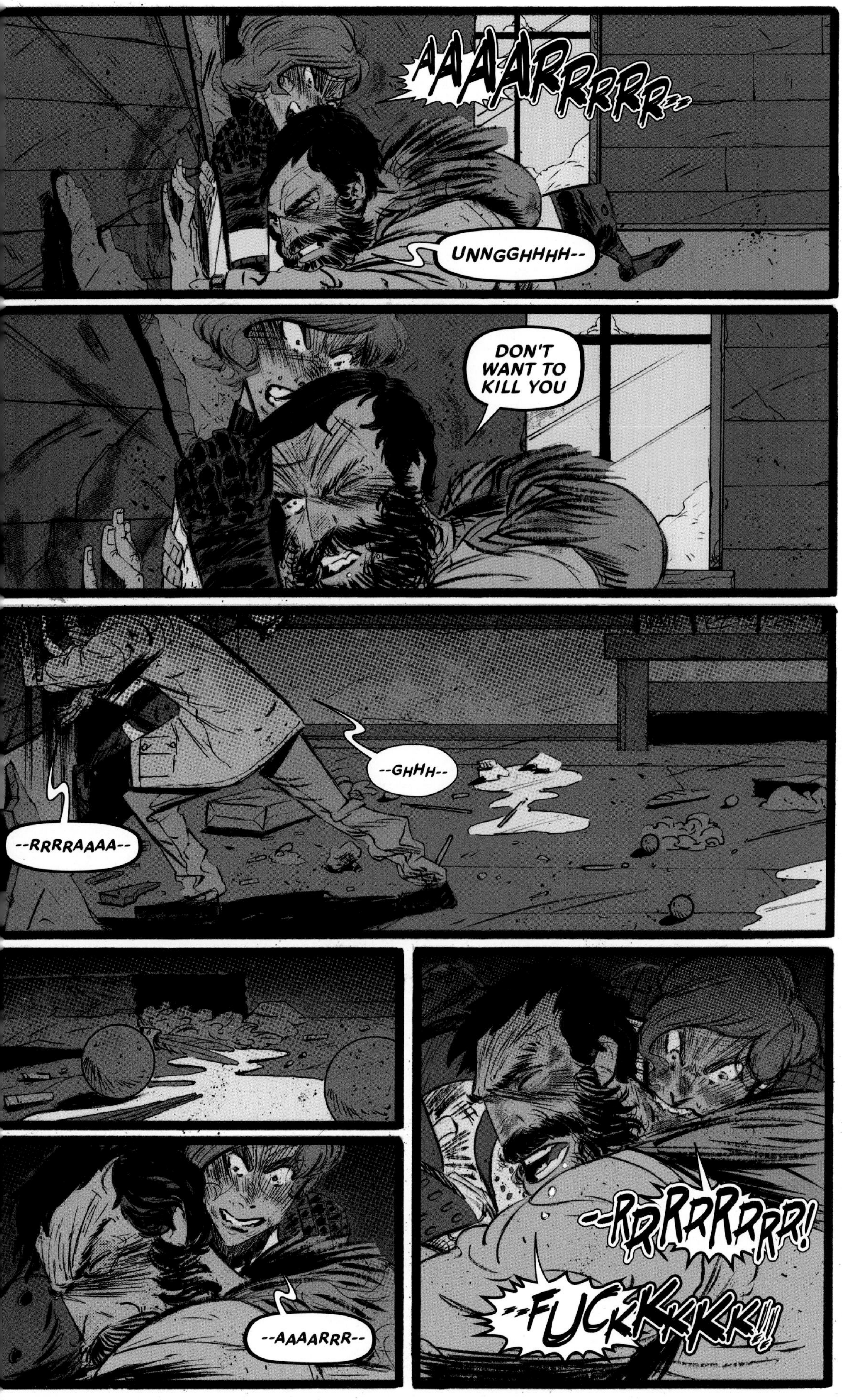
AAAARRRRR--
UNNGGHHHH--
DON'T WANT TO KILL YOU
--GHHH--
--RRRRAAAA--
--AAAARRR--
--RRRRRRRR!
--FUCKKKKK!!!

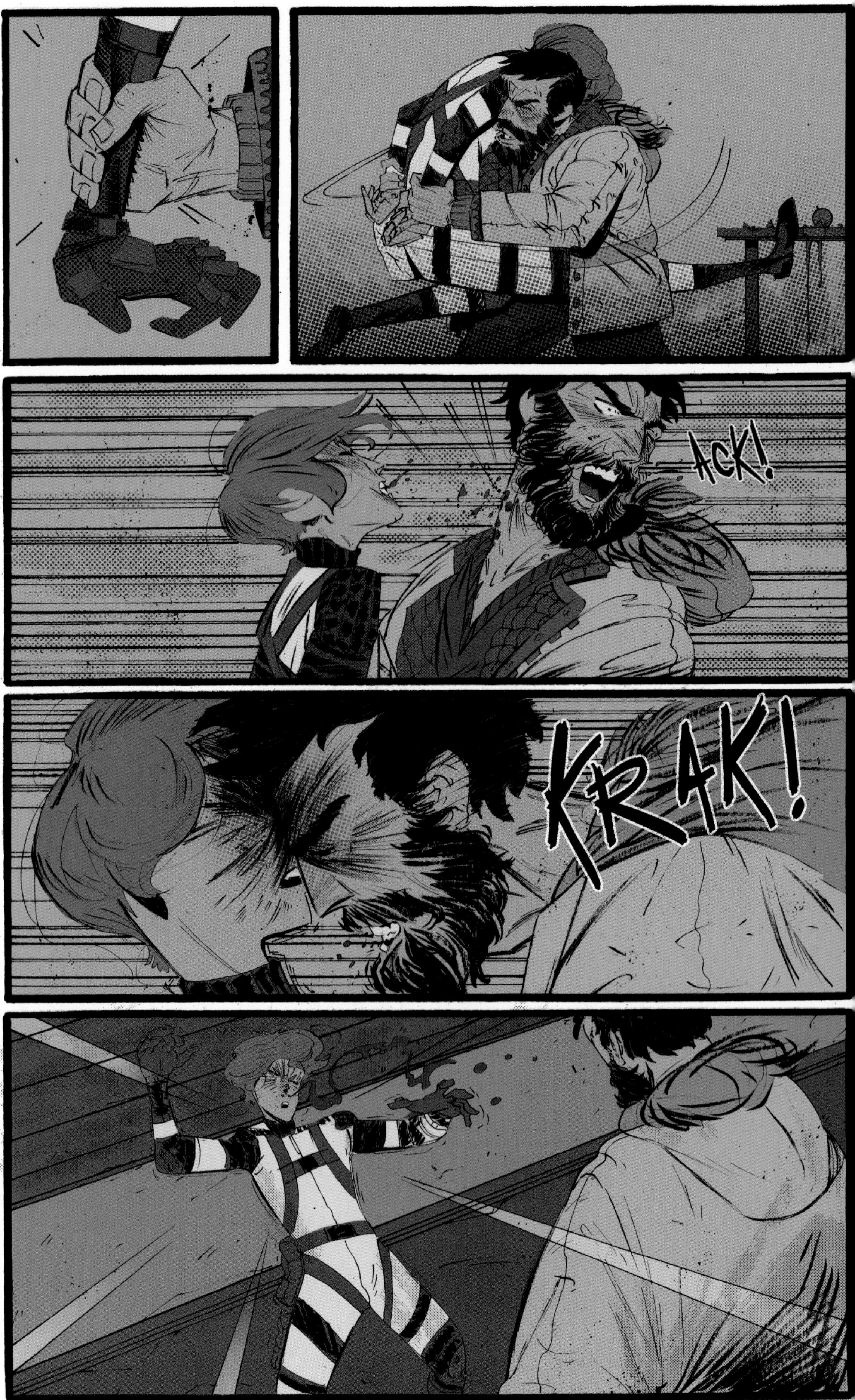
ACK!
KRAK!

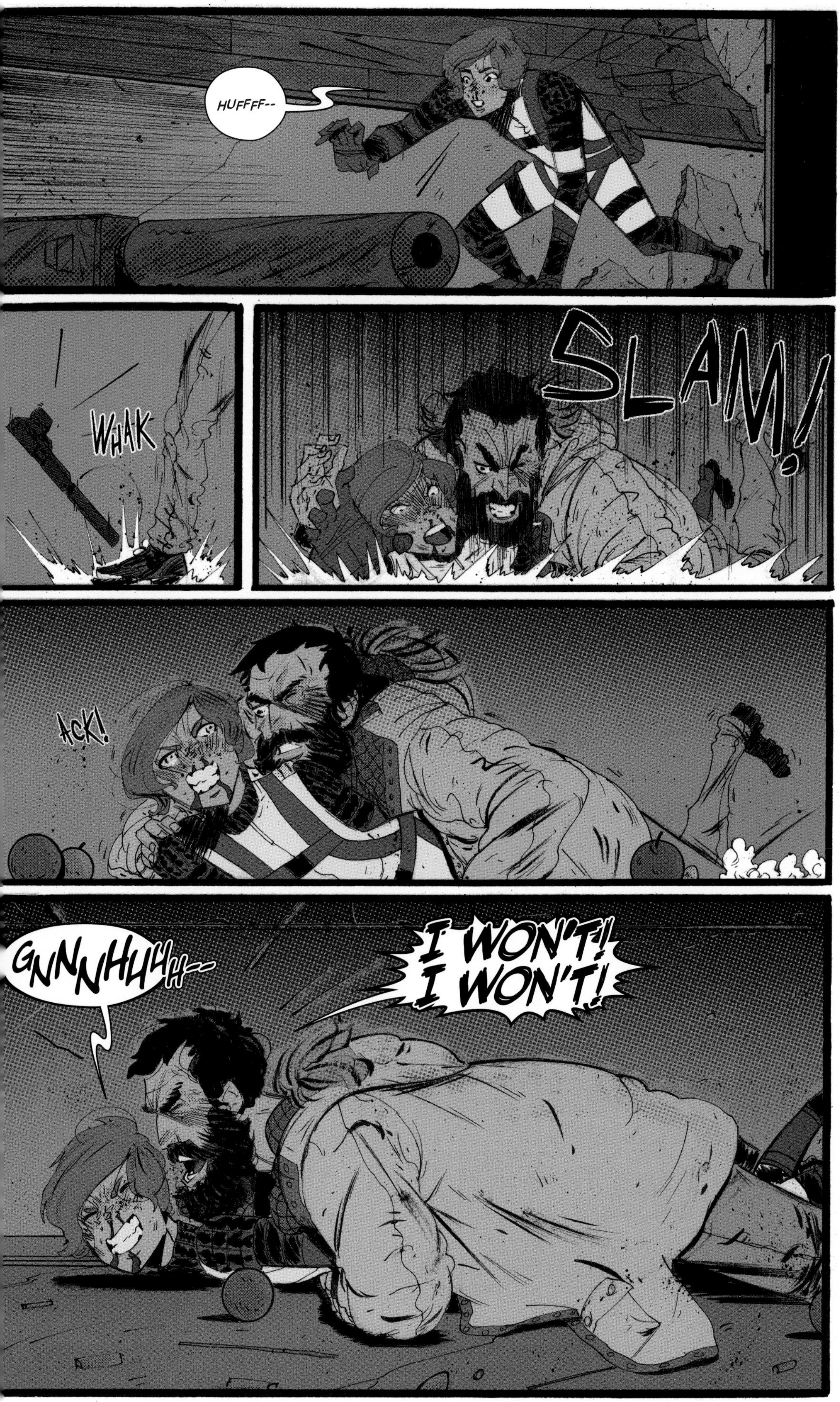
HUFFFF--
WHAK
SLAM!
ACK!
GNNNHUUHH--
I WON'T! I WON'T!

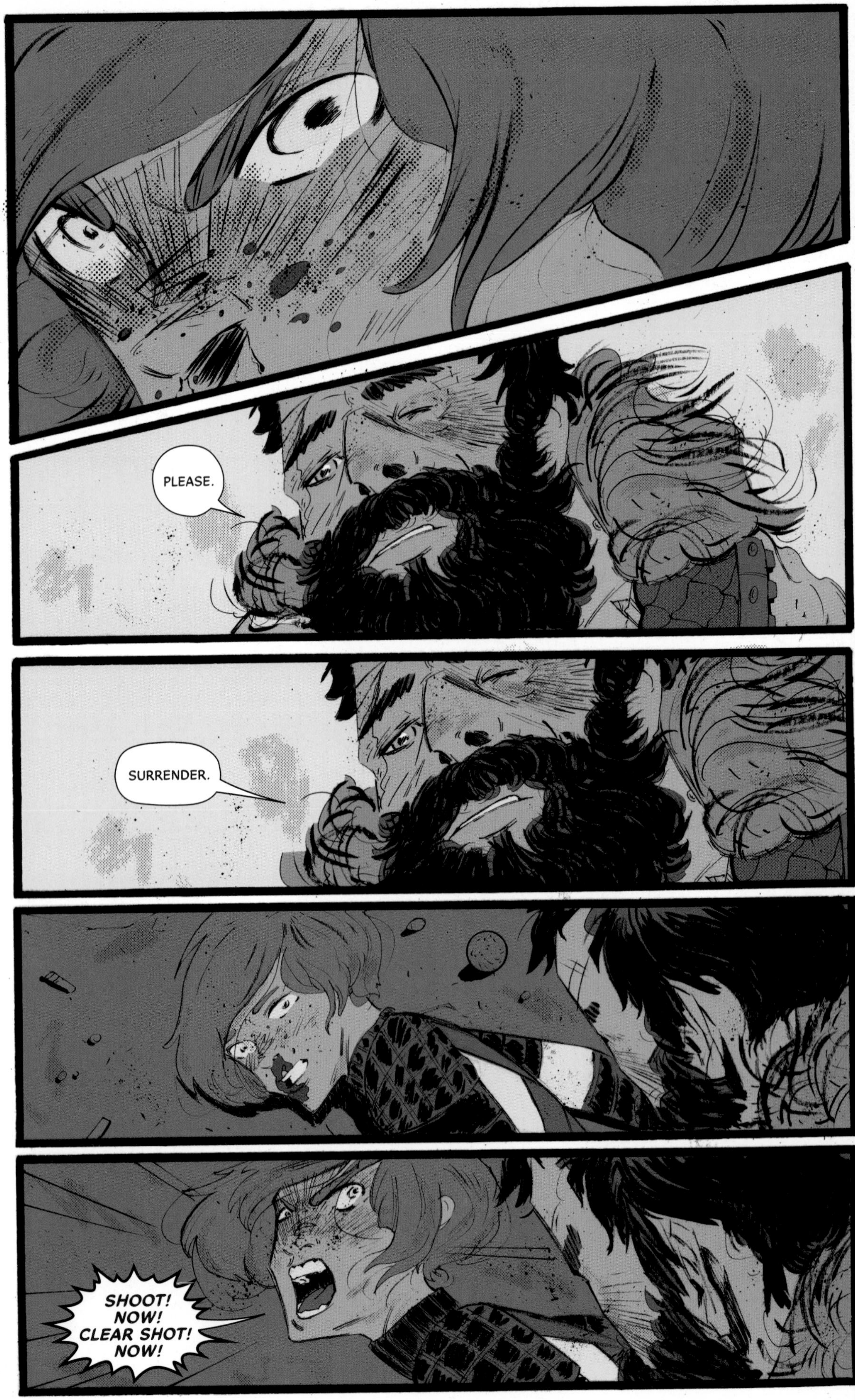
PLEASE.
SURRENDER.
SHOOT! NOW! CLEAR SHOT! NOW!

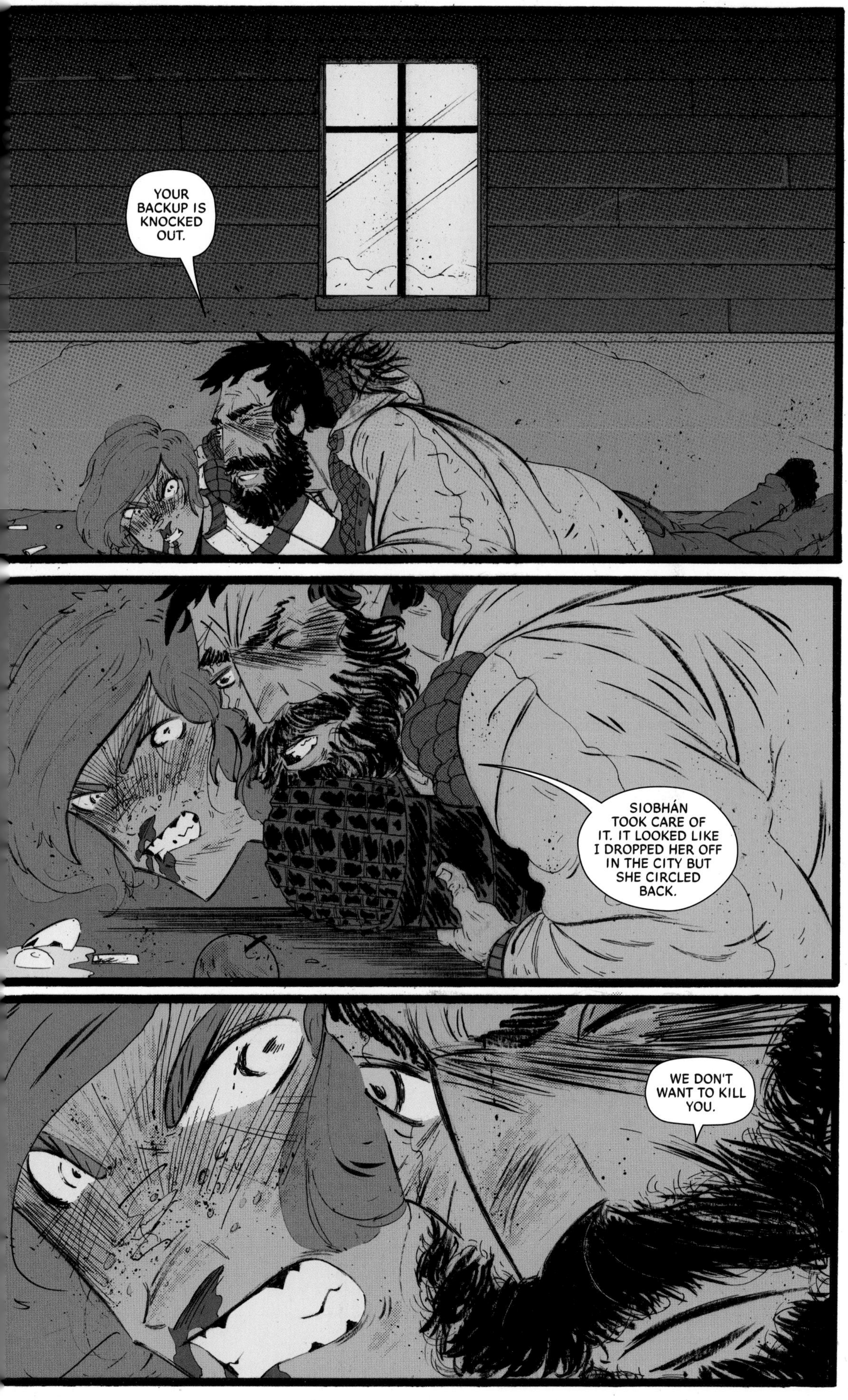
YOUR BACKUP IS KNOCKED OUT.
SIOBHÁN TOOK CARE OF IT. IT LOOKED LIKE I DROPPED HER OFF IN THE CITY BUT SHE CIRCLED BACK.
WE DON'T WANT TO KILL YOU.

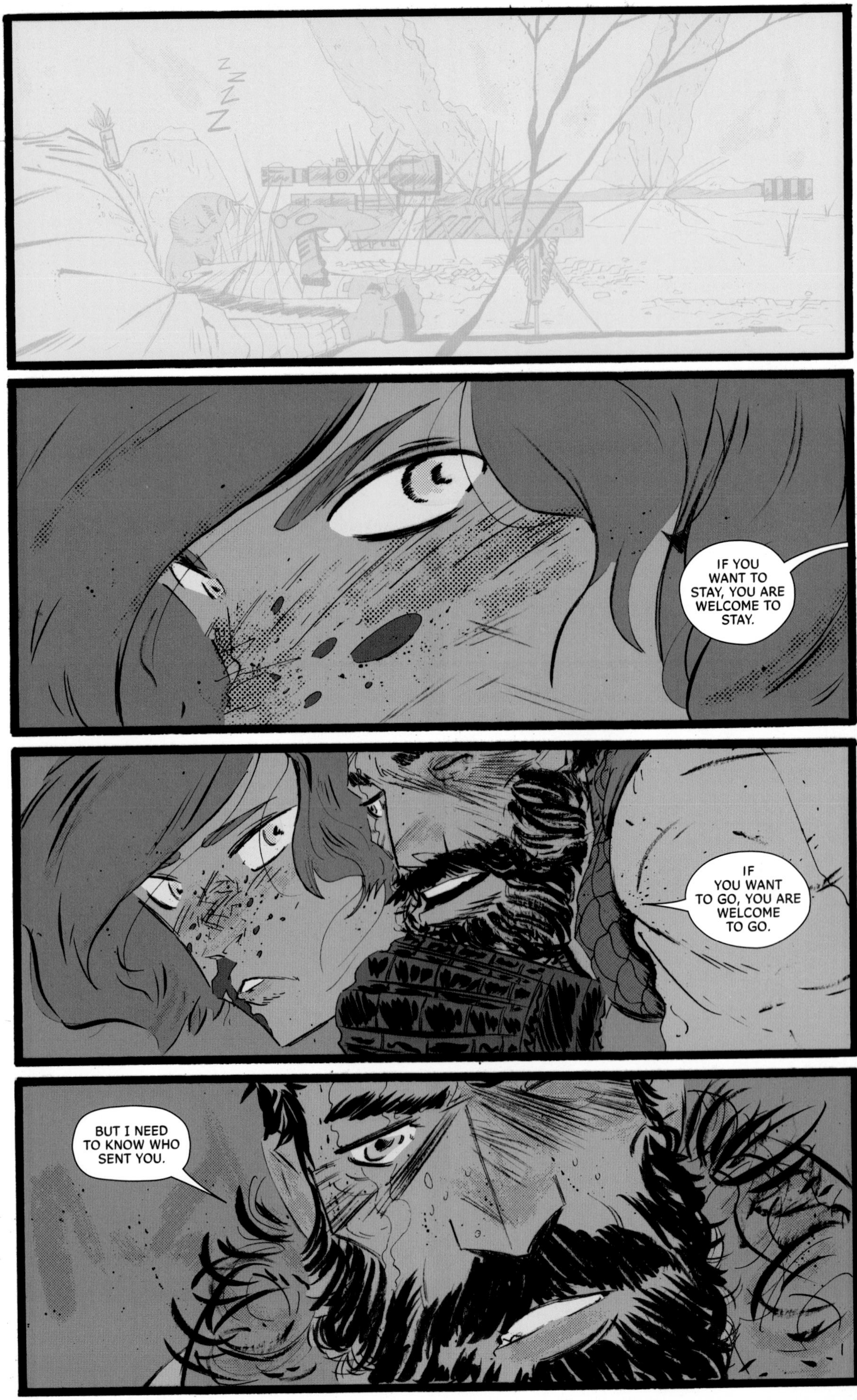
ZZZZ
IF YOU WANT TO STAY, YOU ARE WELCOME TO STAY.
IF YOU WANT TO GO, YOU ARE WELCOME TO GO.
BUT I NEED TO KNOW WHO SENT YOU.

DAY SIX
BZZZ
BZZZ
CLICK
EDWARD.

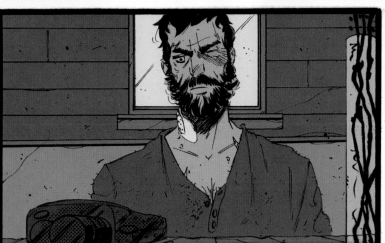

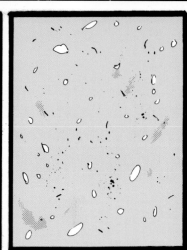

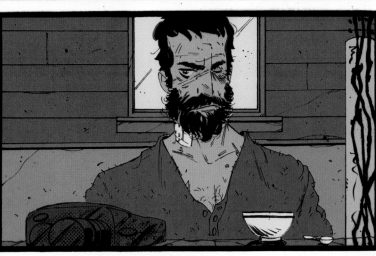

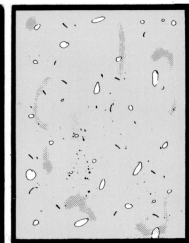

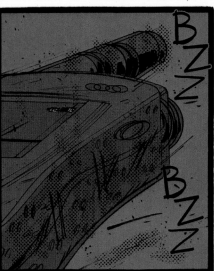

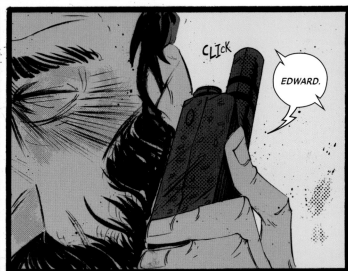

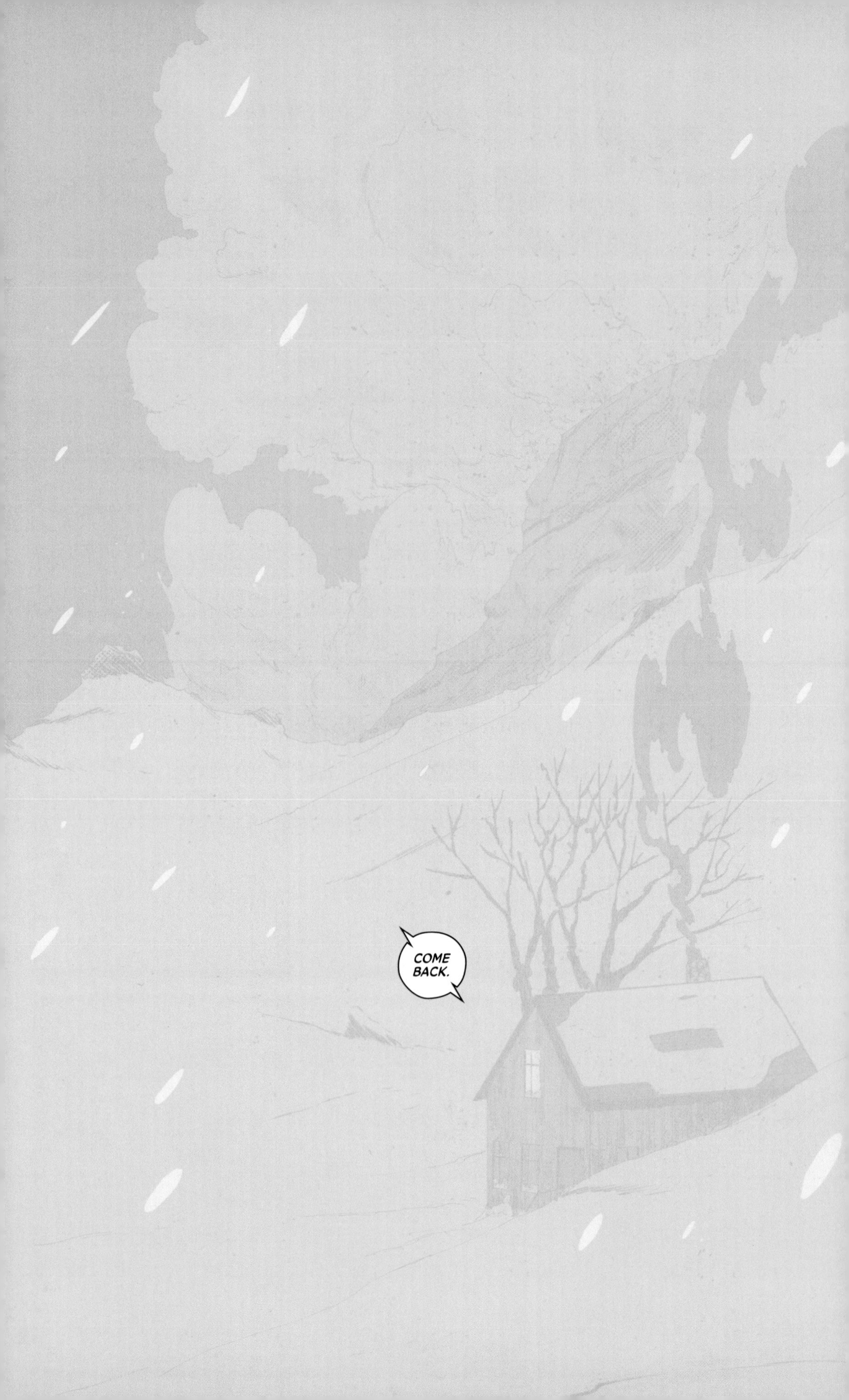
COME BACK.

TRANSCRIPT FOR: COOKE, SARA
DATE: 28-09-2025
PLACE: LOCAL MARKET (SPECIFICS IN SECTION D)

1 ZERO: HOW ABOUT THESE?

2 PENN: I LIKE THEM. CAN YOU GO GET SOME FISH, PLEASE? I'LL BE WITH YOU IN A MINUTE.

3 ZERO: SURE. WHY?

4 PENN: WHY WHAT?

5 ZERO: WHY DO YOU WANT TO BE ALONE?

6 PENN: OH, IT'S NOT THAT. I JUST WANT TO--

7 PENN: --ARE YOU FEELING ANXIETY?

8 ZERO: YES. YES, I THINK.

9 PENN: DO YOU FEEL IT?

10 ZERO: I'M NOT SURE. I THINK SO?

11 PENN: OKAY. I'LL TELL YOU WHAT. THE ONLY REASON I WANT YOU TO GO BUY FISH IS BECAUSE I WANT TO BUY YOU A SURPRISE.

12 PENN: DO YOU UNDERSTAND?

13 ZERO: I AM SORRY.

14 PENN: THERE'S NOTHING TO BE SORRY ABOUT. IT'S OKAY.

15 ZERO: I WAS AFRAID YOU WOULD JUST VANISH IN THE CROWD. I DON'T KNOW WHY.

16 PENN: I LOVE YOU. IF I VANISH IN THE CROWD, KNOW THAT I INTEND TO COME BACK TO YOU.

17 PENN: I LOVE YOU.

18 ZERO: I LOVE YOU.

19 PENN: GOOD. NOW GO GET THE FISH.

TRANSCRIPT FOR: COOKE, SARA
DATE: 28-09-2025
PLACE: COTTAGE

1 PENN: WOULD YOU LIKE TO WATCH A MOVIE TONIGHT?

2 ZERO: I LIKE THAT IDEA.

3 PENN: HOW ABOUT...'THE MIRROR?'

4 ZERO: WHAT IS IT ABOUT?

5 ZERO: WAIT...

6 ZERO: DON'T TELL ME. YES. I WANT TO BE SURPRISED.

7 PENN: SURPRISED? THAT'S EASY, CONSIDERING YOU STARTED WATCHING MOVIES THREE YEARS AGO...

8 PENN: IT'S BY THIS FANTASTIC DIRECTOR, ANDREI TARKOVSKY. DO YOU REMEMBER WHEN WE WATCHED 'STALKER?'

9 ZERO: I...I THINK SO. 'THE ZONE?'

10 PENN: YOU REMEMBER!

\---

TRANSCRIPT FOR: COOKE, SARA
DATE: 28-09-2025
PLACE: COTTAGE

ZERO: FEELING BETTER?

PENN: MUCH BETTER.

PENN: OH. MY. GODDESS.

PENN: MY LEGS. STILL. SHAKING.

ZERO: MY JAW HURTS

TRANSCRIPT FOR: COOKE, SARA
DATE: 29-09-2025
PLACE: COTTAGE

1 PENN: IT'S TRUE – WE CAN COMMUNICATE BRAIN-TO-BRAIN.
THE RESEARCHERS PROVED IT A LONG TIME AGO. NEUROSCIENTISTS AND
2 ROBOTICS ENGINEERS.

3 ZERO: HOW SO?

4 PENN: THEY USED INTERNET-LINKED ELECTROENCEPHALOGRAM AND TRANSCRAN—TRANSCRANIAL! I REMEMBERED! TRANSCRANIAL MAGNETIC STIMULATION. AND WHAT THEY BASICALLY DID IS THEY CREATED BRAIN-TO-BRAIN TRANSMISSION THAT WAS COMPLETELY COMPUTER-MEDIATED BETWEEN SCALPS OF TWO PEOPLE, EACH ONE IN A DIFFERENT COUNTRY.

5 ZERO: SO THE PEOPLE SAID SOME WORDS AND THE OTHERS HEARD THE WORDS?

6 PENN: WELL, THE WORDS THEY SAID WERE TRANSLATED INTO BINARY BY THE ENCEPHALOGRAM. THEN THE COMPUTER-TO-BRAIN INTERFACE TRANSMITTED THE MESSAGE TO THE RECEIVER'S BRAIN—WOULD YOU LIKE MORE TEA?

7 ZERO: YES, PLEASE. A COOKIE?

8 PENN: I'LL SAVE IT FOR LATER. SO THE MESSAGE IS TRANSMITTED TO THE RECEIVER'S BRAIN THROUGH BRAIN STIMULATION. THE RECEIVER EXPERIENCES THEM AS FLASHES OF LIGHT, AND THOSE FLASHES OF LIGHT APPEAR IN NUMERICAL SEQUENCES, SO THE RECEIVER CAN DECODE THE SEQUENCES. THAT WAY HE OR SHE READS THE MESSAGE.

PENN: ISN'T IT AMAZING?

9

ZERO: IT IS.

10

ZERO: I SAW A WHALE THE OTHER DAY.

11

PENN: UM.

12

PENN: YOU HEARD EVERYTHING I JUST TOLD YOU, RIGHT?

13

ZERO: I MOST CERTAINLY DID, MY LADY.

14

PENN: THEN READ MY MIND.

15

--LAUGHTER--

16

CHAPTER 12

FAMILY REUNION

Illustrated by Adam Gorham

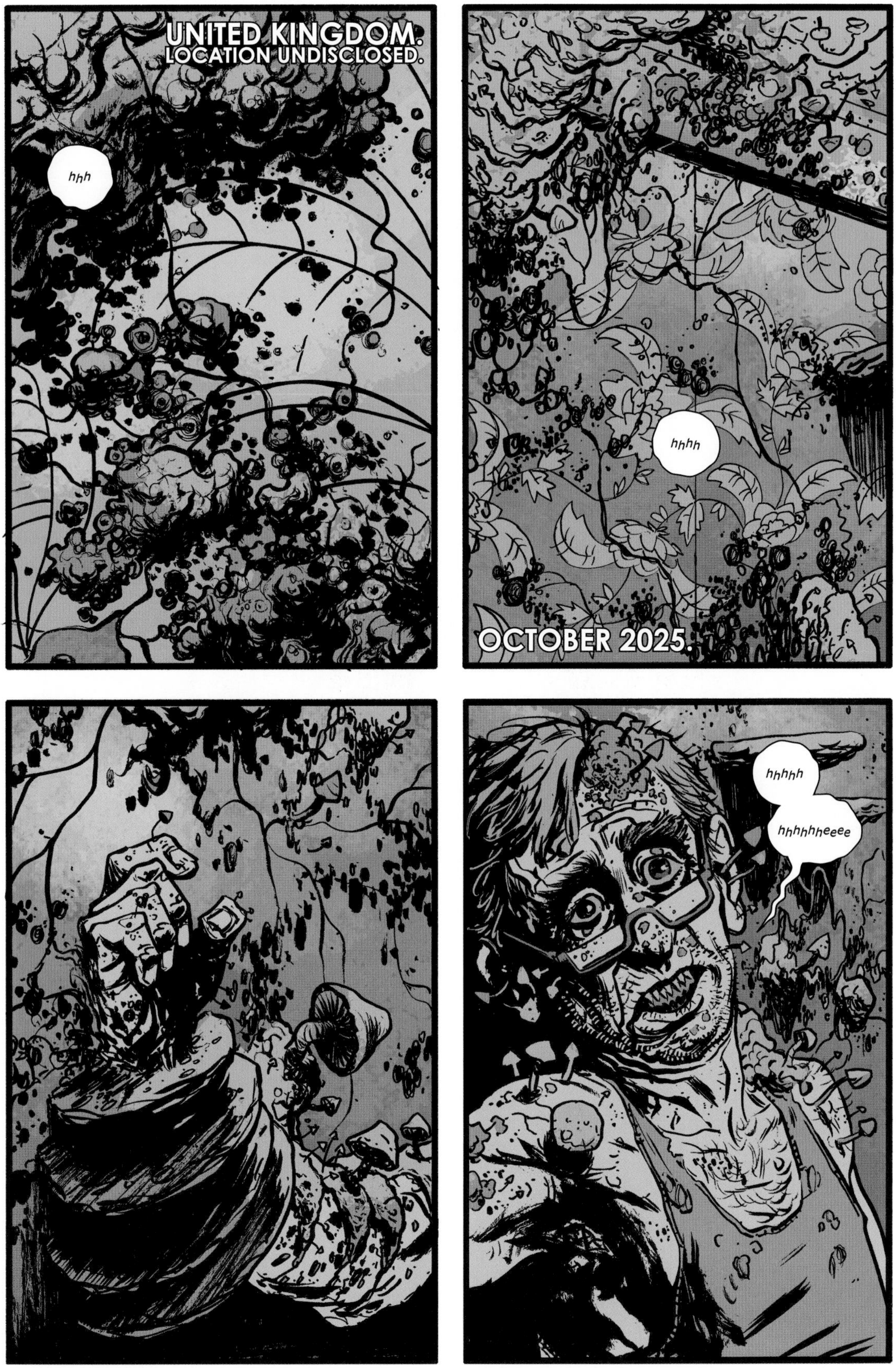
UNITED KINGDOM.
LOCATION UNDISCLOSED.
hhh
hhhh
OCTOBER 2025.
hhhhh
hhhhhheeee

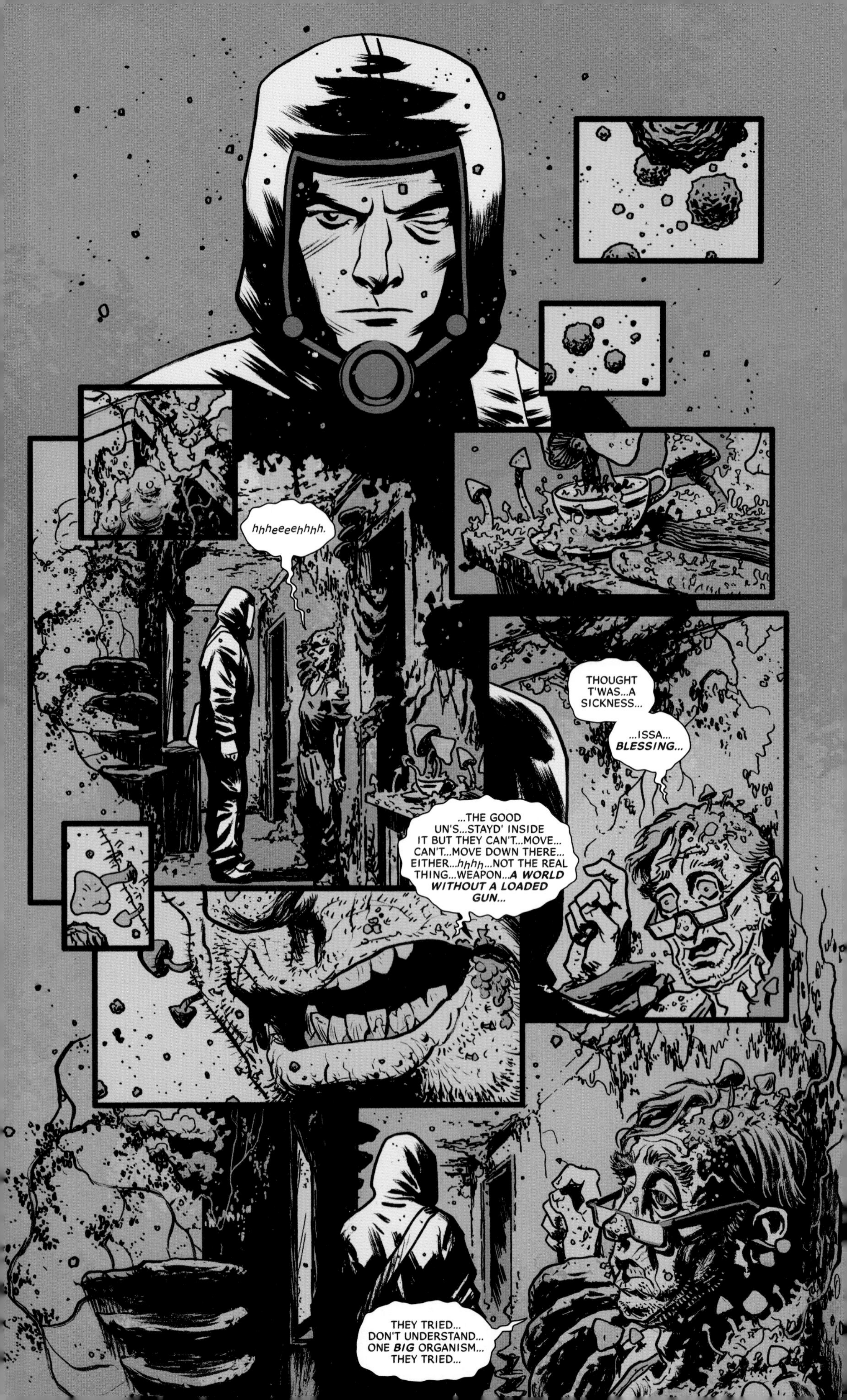
hhheeeehhhh.
THOUGHT T'WAS...A SICKNESS...
...ISSA... BLESSING...
...THE GOOD UN'S...STAYD' INSIDE IT BUT THEY CAN'T...MOVE... CAN'T...MOVE DOWN THERE... EITHER...hhhh...NOT THE REAL THING...WEAPON...A WORLD WITHOUT A LOADED GUN...
THEY TRIED... DON'T UNDERSTAND... ONE BIG ORGANISM... THEY TRIED...

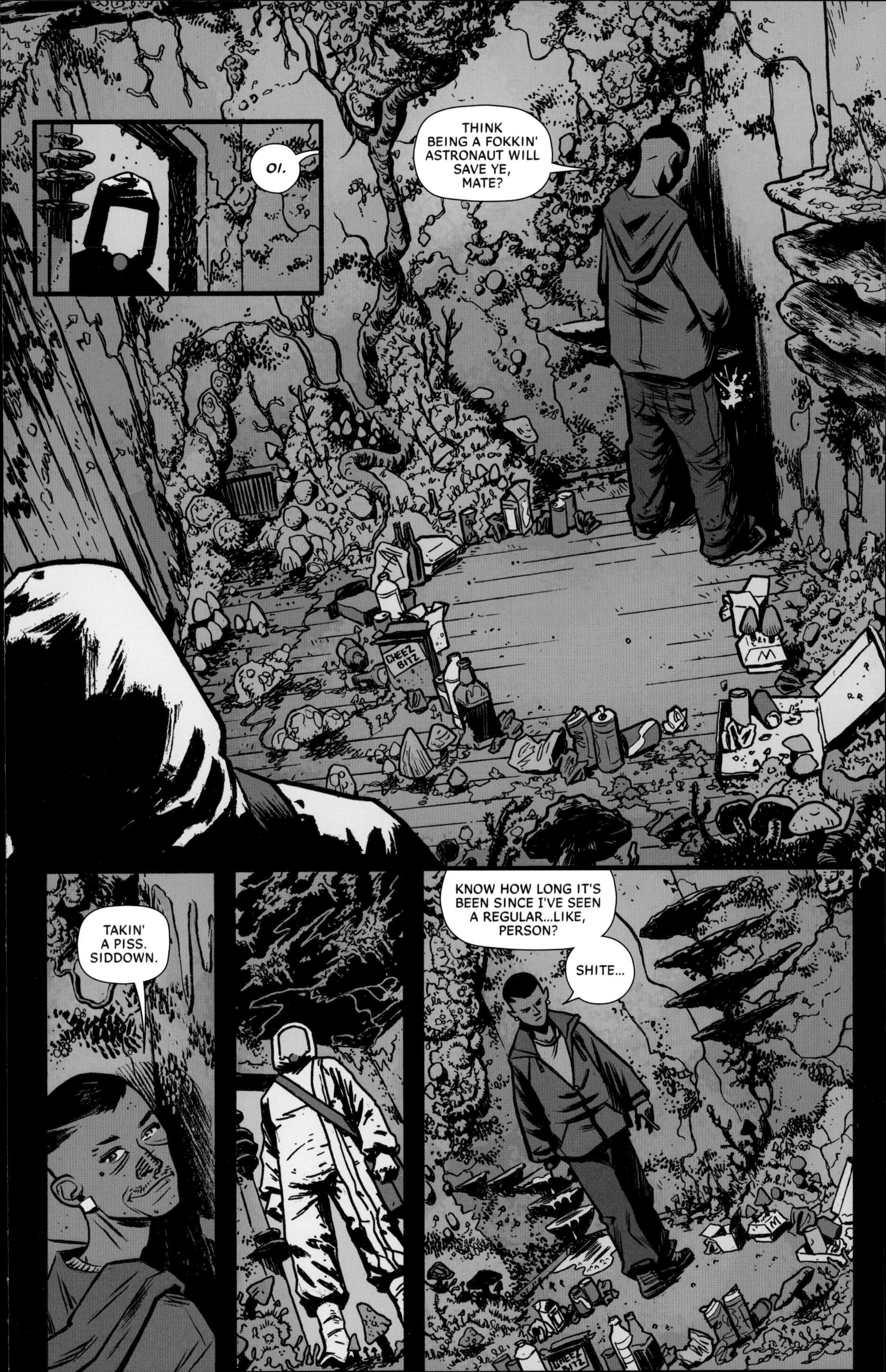
OI.
THINK BEING A FOKKIN' ASTRONAUT WILL SAVE YE, MATE?
TAKIN' A PISS. SIDDOWN.
KNOW HOW LONG IT'S BEEN SINCE I'VE SEEN A REGULAR...LIKE, PERSON?
SHITE...
CHEEZ BITZ

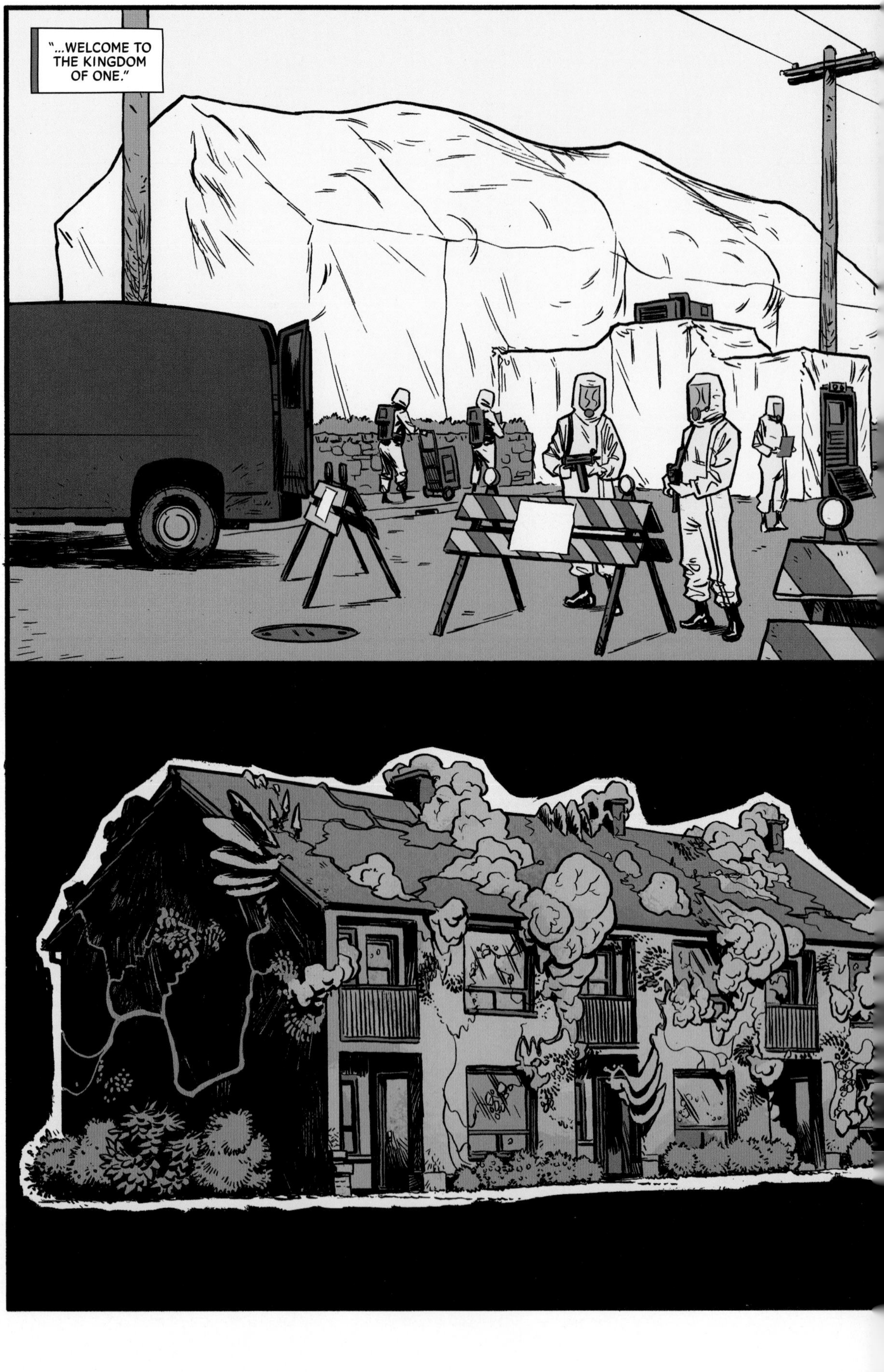
"...WELCOME TO THE KINGDOM OF ONE."

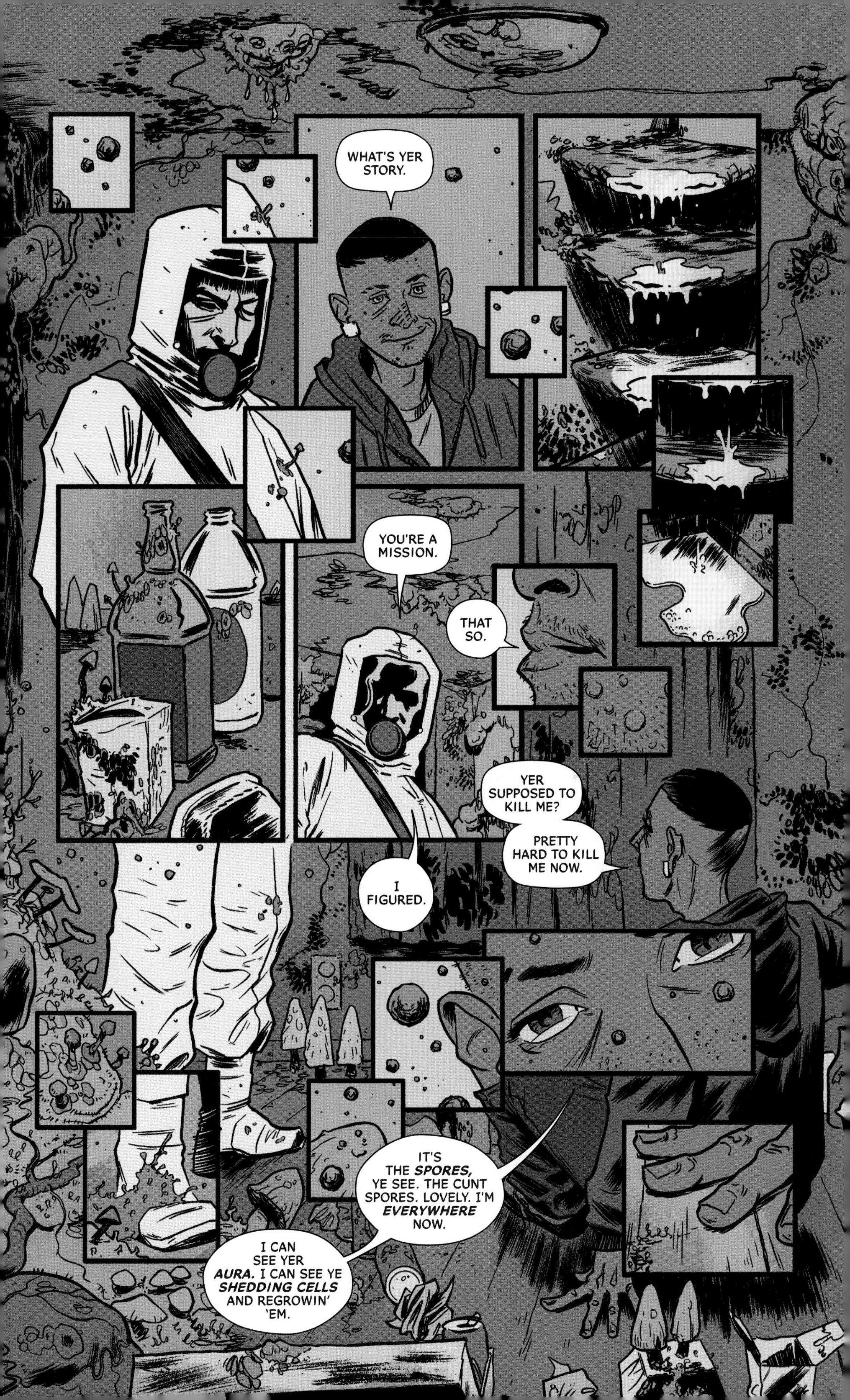
WHAT'S YER STORY.
YOU'RE A MISSION.
THAT SO.
YER SUPPOSED TO KILL ME?
PRETTY HARD TO KILL ME NOW.
I FIGURED.
IT'S THE SPORES, YE SEE. THE CUNT SPORES. LOVELY. I'M EVERYWHERE NOW.
I CAN SEE YER AURA. I CAN SEE YE SHEDDING CELLS AND REGROWIN' 'EM.

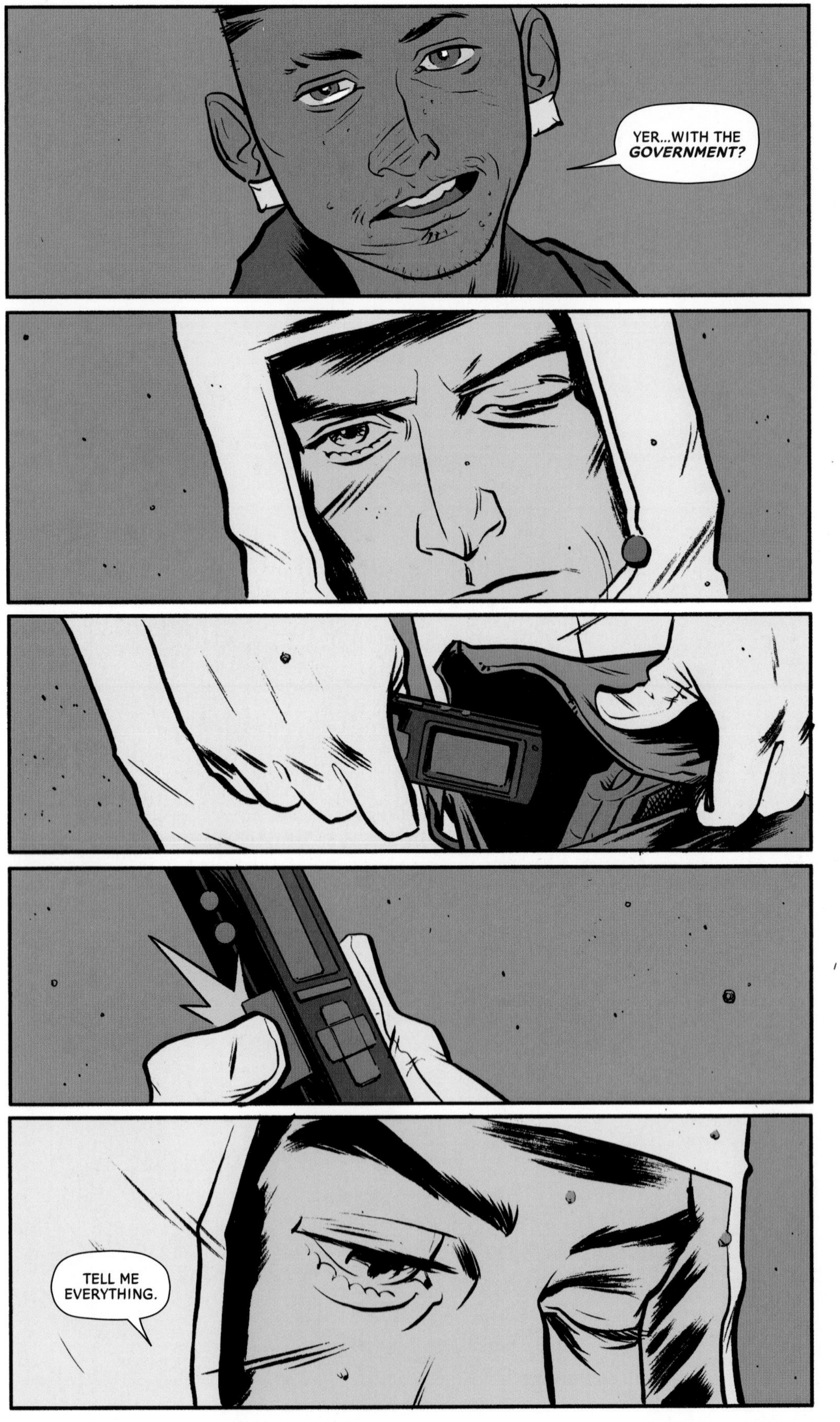
YER...WITH THE *GOVERNMENT?*
TELL ME EVERYTHING.

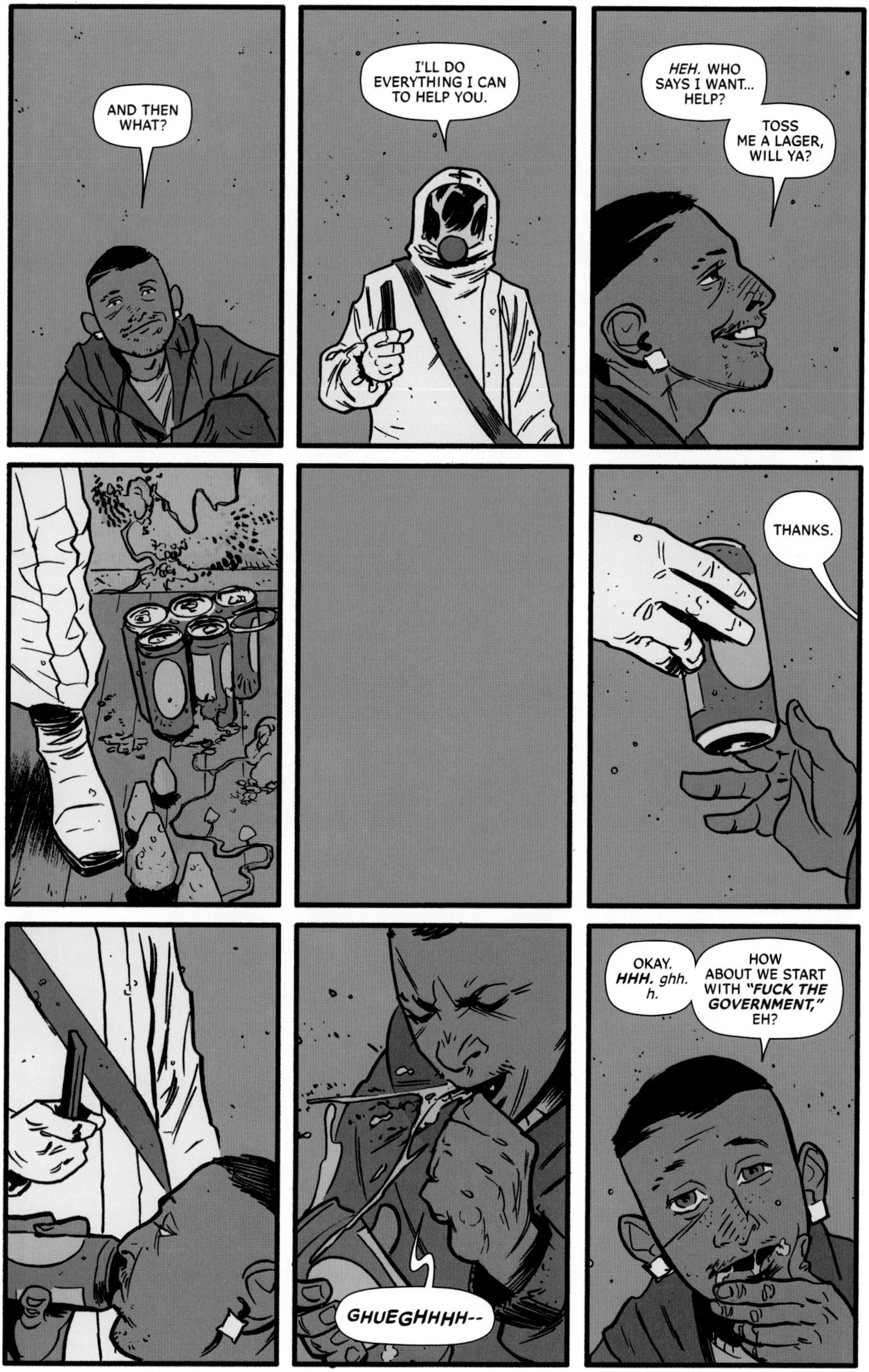
AND THEN WHAT?
I'LL DO EVERYTHING I CAN TO HELP YOU.
HEH. WHO SAYS I WANT... HELP?
TOSS ME A LAGER, WILL YA?
THANKS.
GHUEGHHHH--
OKAY. HHH. ghh. h.
HOW ABOUT WE START WITH "FUCK THE GOVERNMENT," EH?

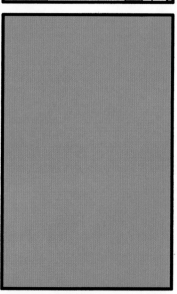

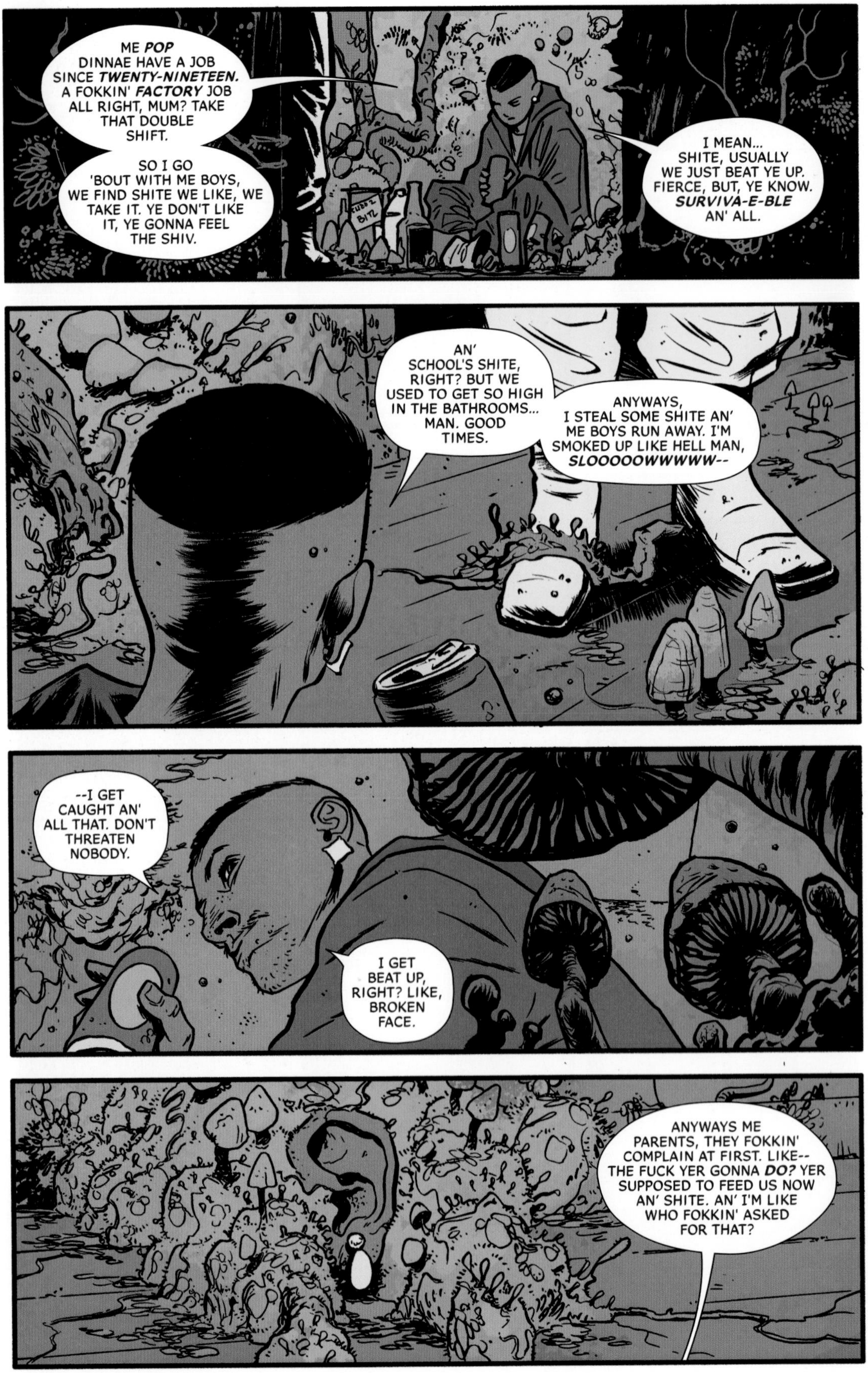

ME *POP* DINNAE HAVE A JOB SINCE *TWENTY-NINETEEN.* A FOKKIN' *FACTORY* JOB ALL RIGHT, MUM? TAKE THAT DOUBLE SHIFT.
SO I GO 'BOUT WITH ME BOYS, WE FIND SHITE WE LIKE, WE TAKE IT. YE DON'T LIKE IT, YE GONNA FEEL THE SHIV.
I MEAN... SHITE, USUALLY WE JUST BEAT YE UP. FIERCE, BUT, YE KNOW. *SURVIVA-E-BLE* AN' ALL.
AN' SCHOOL'S SHITE, RIGHT? BUT WE USED TO GET SO HIGH IN THE BATHROOMS... MAN. GOOD TIMES.
ANYWAYS, I STEAL SOME SHITE AN' ME BOYS RUN AWAY. I'M SMOKED UP LIKE HELL MAN, *SLOOOOOWWWWW--*
--I GET CAUGHT AN' ALL THAT. DON'T THREATEN NOBODY.
I GET BEAT UP, RIGHT? LIKE, BROKEN FACE.
ANYWAYS ME PARENTS, THEY FOKKIN' COMPLAIN AT FIRST. LIKE-- THE FUCK YER GONNA *DO?* YER SUPPOSED TO FEED US NOW AN' SHITE. AN' I'M LIKE WHO FOKKIN' ASKED FOR THAT?

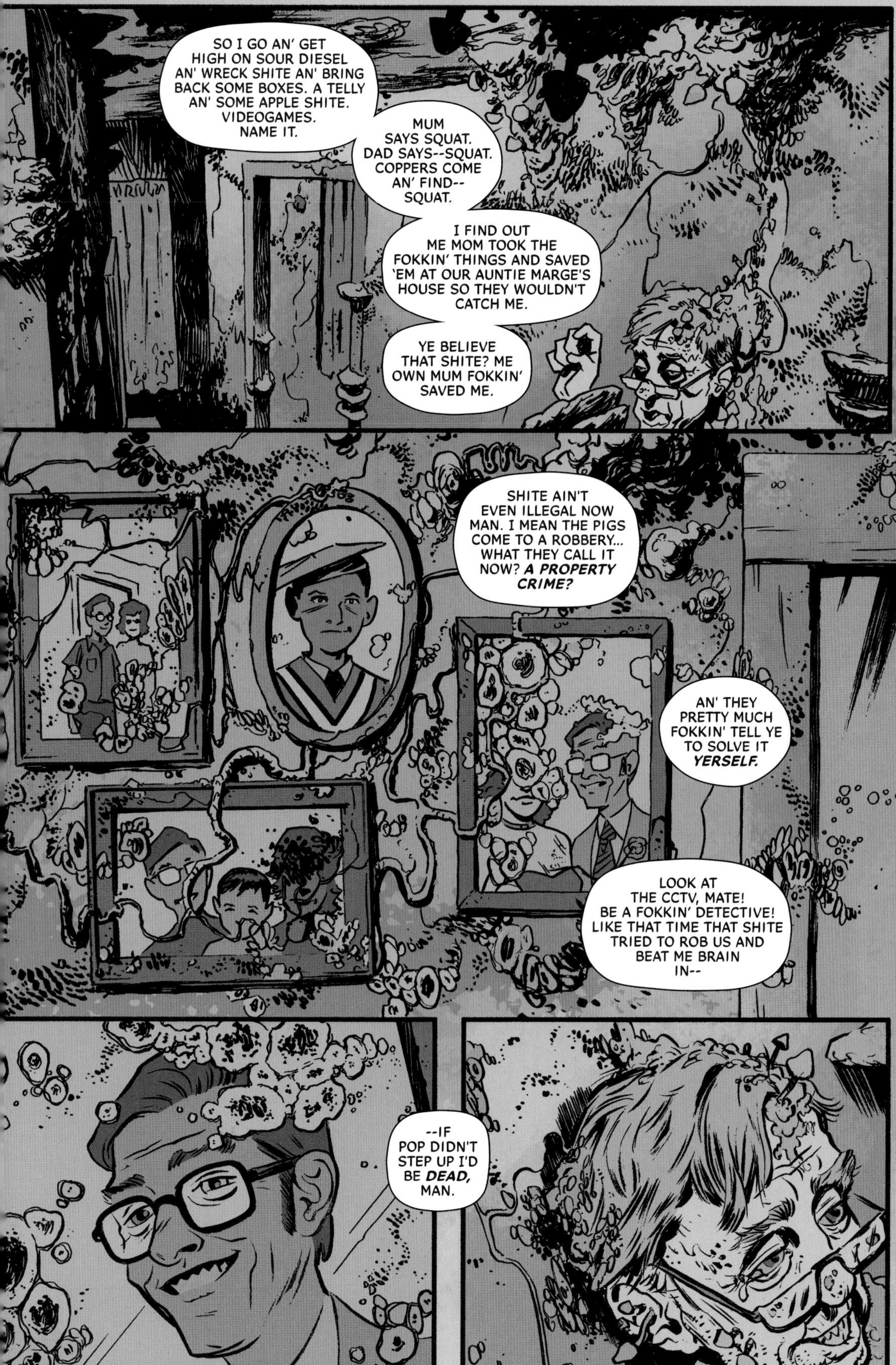
SO I GO AN' GET HIGH ON SOUR DIESEL AN' WRECK SHITE AN' BRING BACK SOME BOXES. A TELLY AN' SOME APPLE SHITE. VIDEOGAMES. NAME IT.
MUM SAYS SQUAT. DAD SAYS--SQUAT. COPPERS COME AN' FIND--SQUAT.
I FIND OUT ME MOM TOOK THE FOKKIN' THINGS AND SAVED 'EM AT OUR AUNTIE MARGE'S HOUSE SO THEY WOULDN'T CATCH ME.
YE BELIEVE THAT SHITE? ME OWN MUM FOKKIN' SAVED ME.
SHITE AIN'T EVEN ILLEGAL NOW MAN. I MEAN THE PIGS COME TO A ROBBERY... WHAT THEY CALL IT NOW? *A PROPERTY CRIME?*
AN' THEY PRETTY MUCH FOKKIN' TELL YE TO SOLVE IT *YERSELF.*
LOOK AT THE CCTV, MATE! BE A FOKKIN' DETECTIVE! LIKE THAT TIME THAT SHITE TRIED TO ROB US AND BEAT ME BRAIN IN--
--IF POP DIDN'T STEP UP I'D BE *DEAD,* MAN.

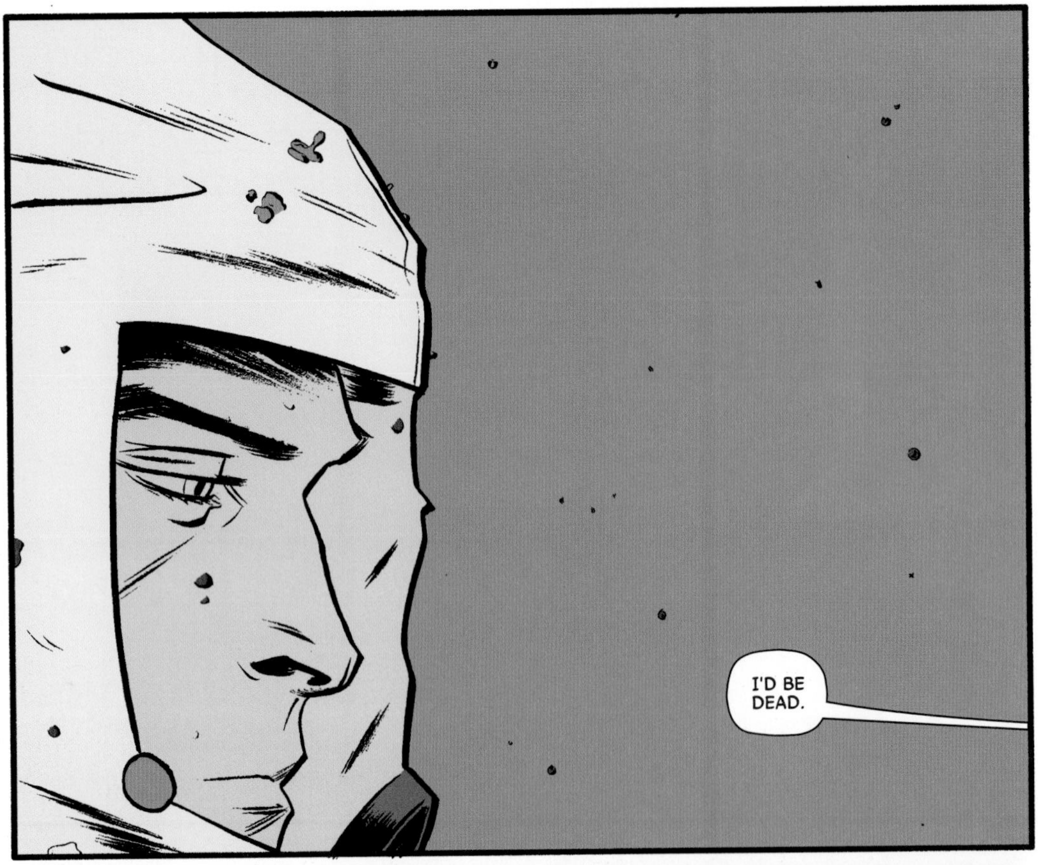
I'D BE DEAD.

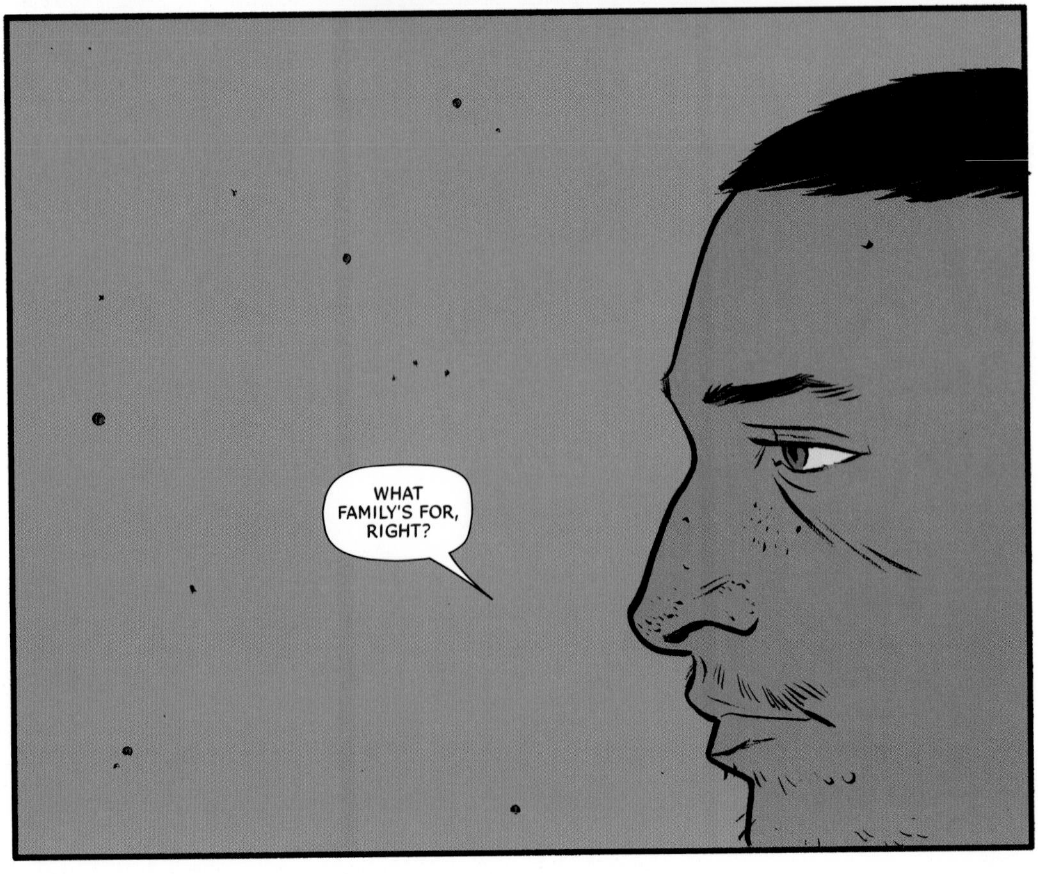
WHAT FAMILY'S FOR, RIGHT?

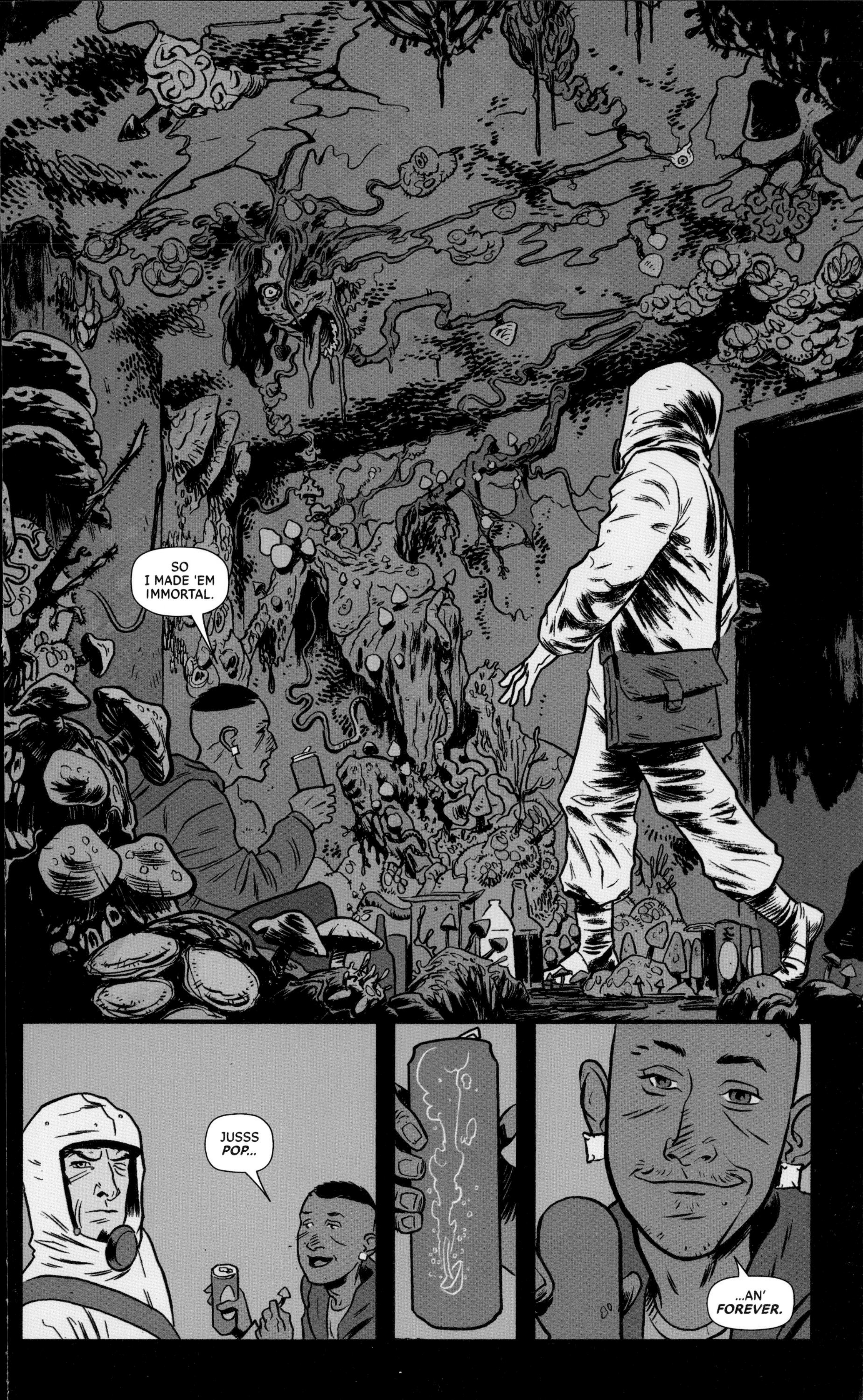
SO
I MADE 'EM
IMMORTAL.
JUSSS
POP...
...AN'
FOREVER.

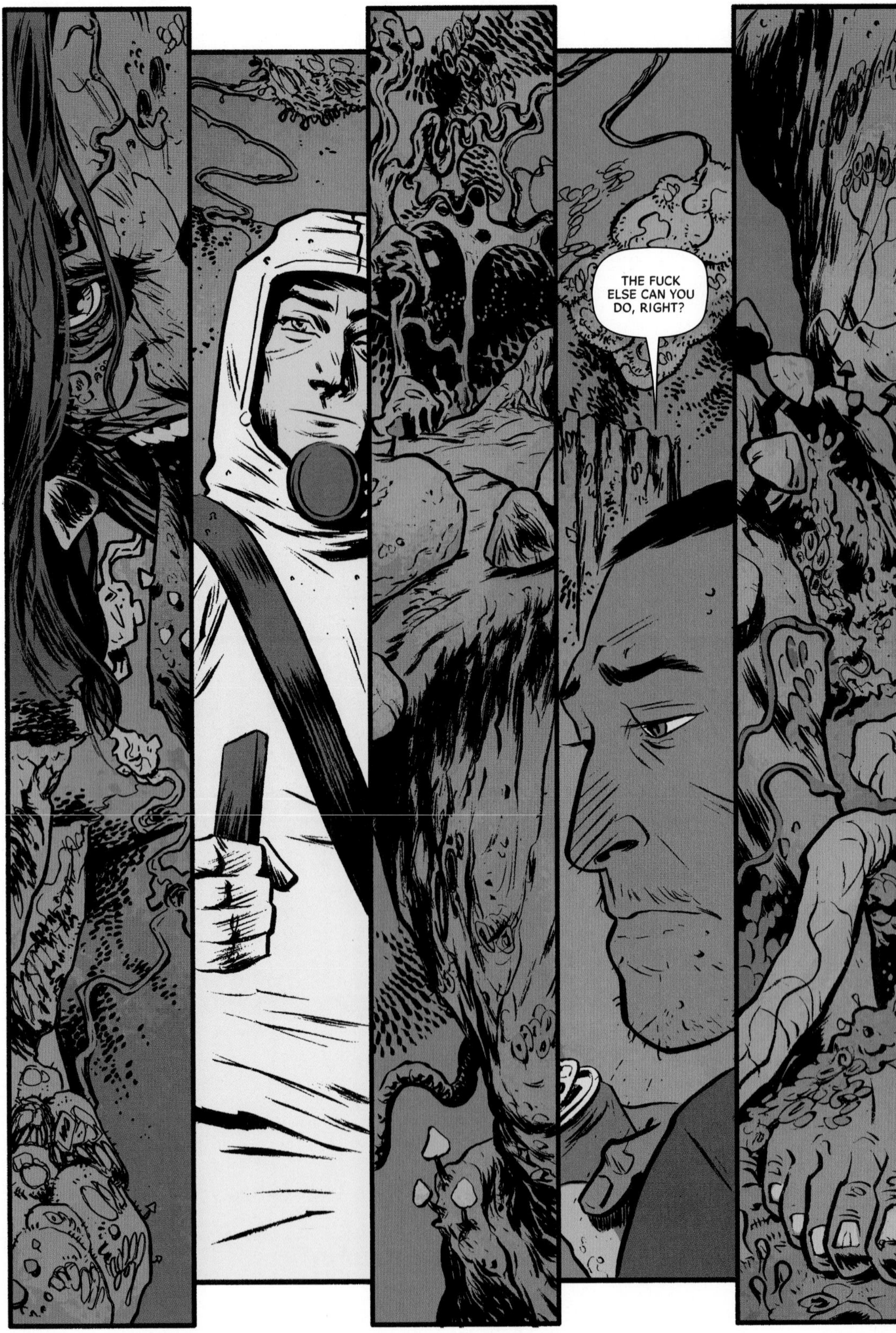
THE FUCK ELSE CAN YOU DO, RIGHT?

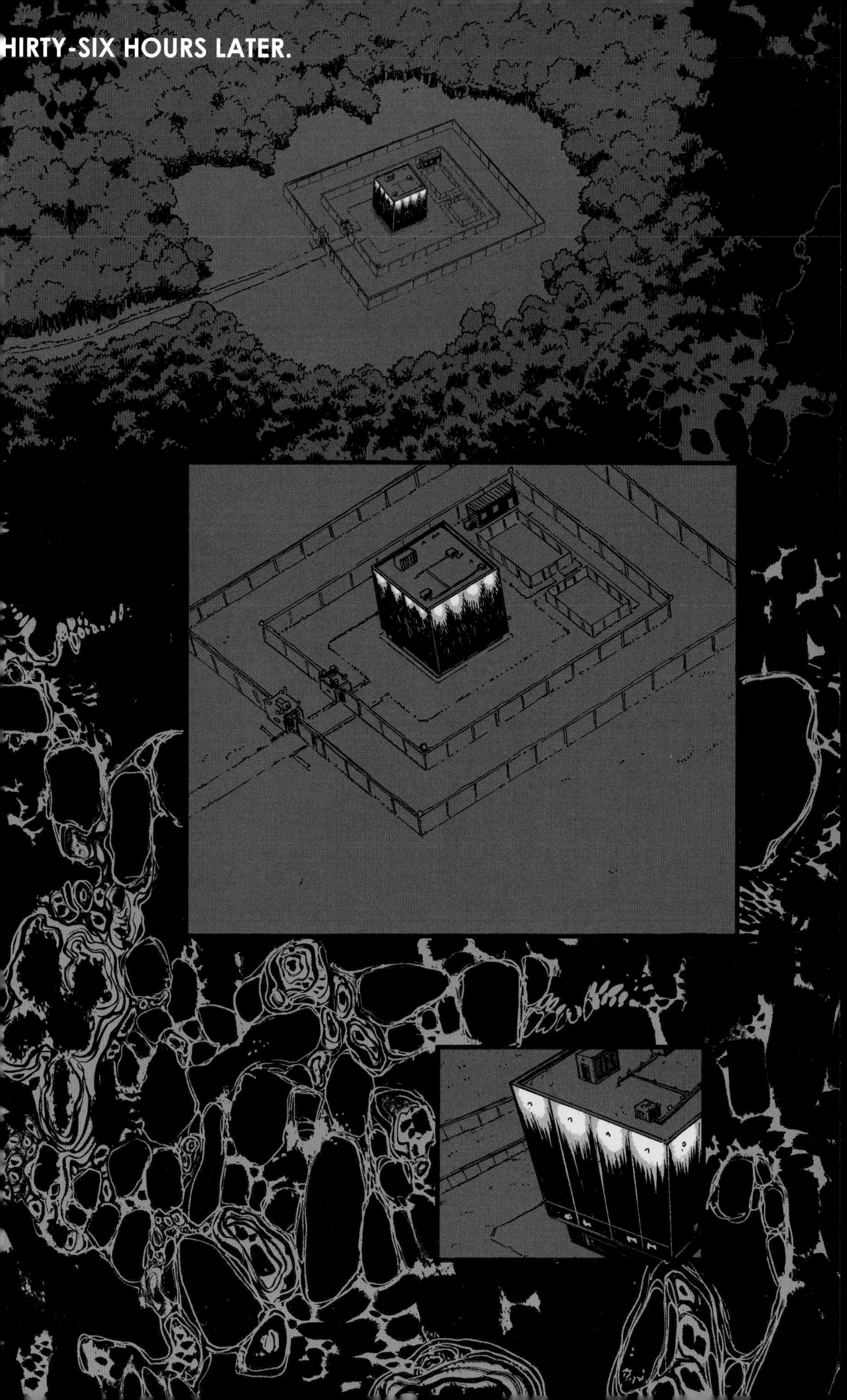
HIRTY-SIX HOURS LATER.

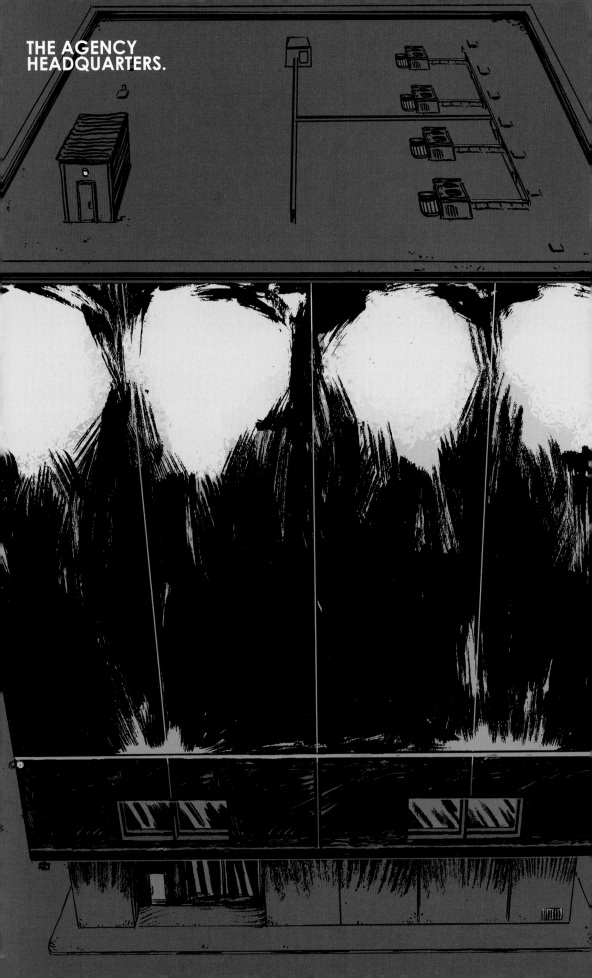

THE AGENCY
HEADQUARTERS.

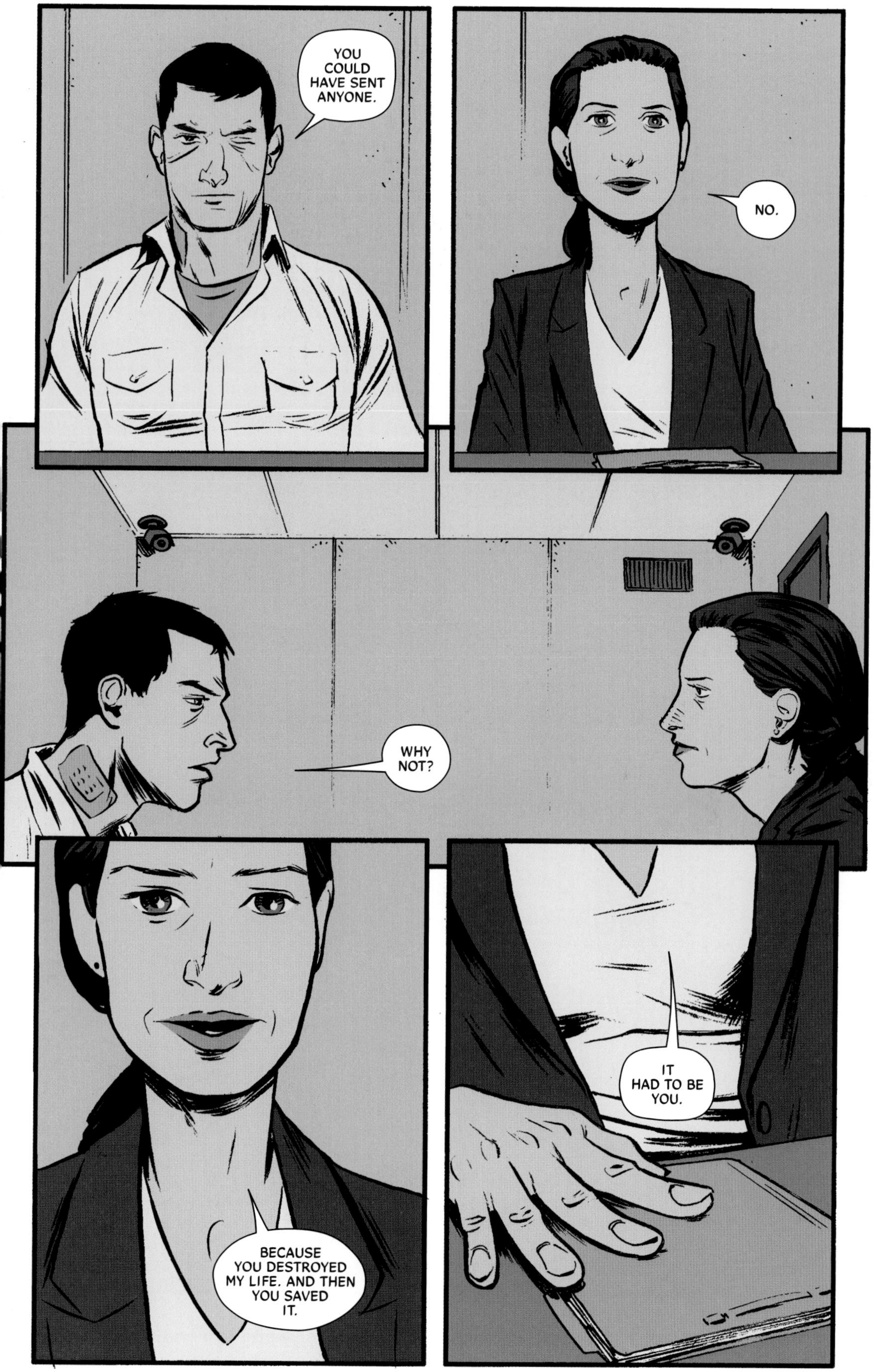
YOU COULD HAVE SENT ANYONE.
NO.
WHY NOT?
BECAUSE YOU DESTROYED MY LIFE. AND THEN YOU SAVED IT.
IT HAD TO BE YOU.

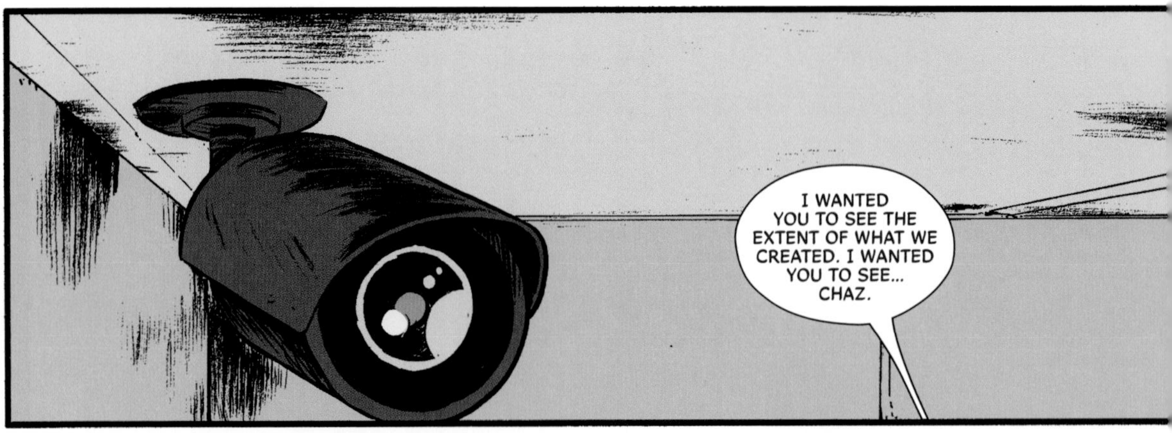
I WANTED YOU TO SEE THE EXTENT OF WHAT WE CREATED. I WANTED YOU TO SEE... CHAZ.

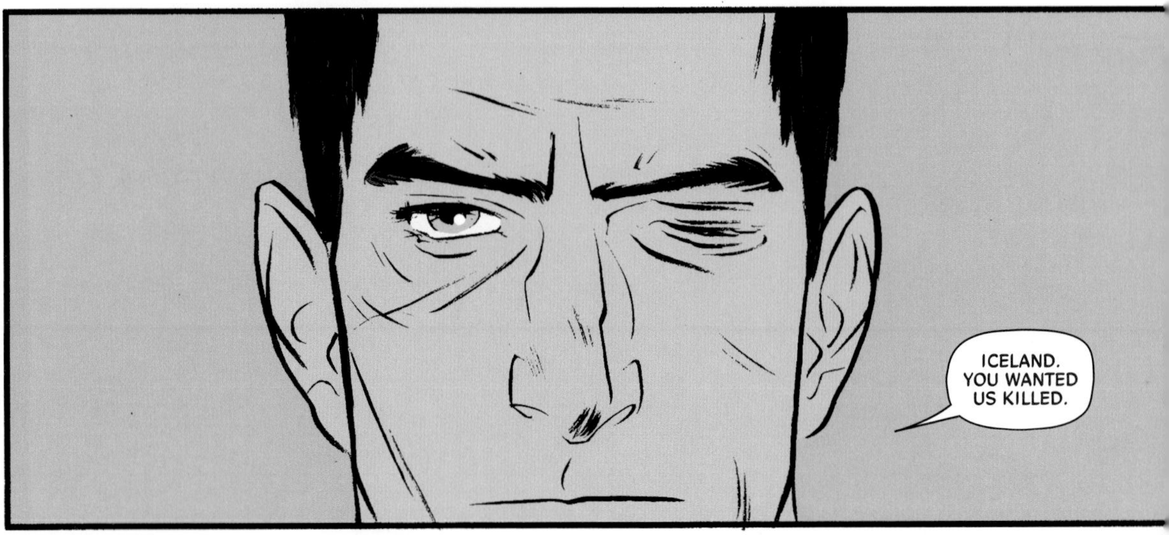
ICELAND. YOU WANTED US KILLED.

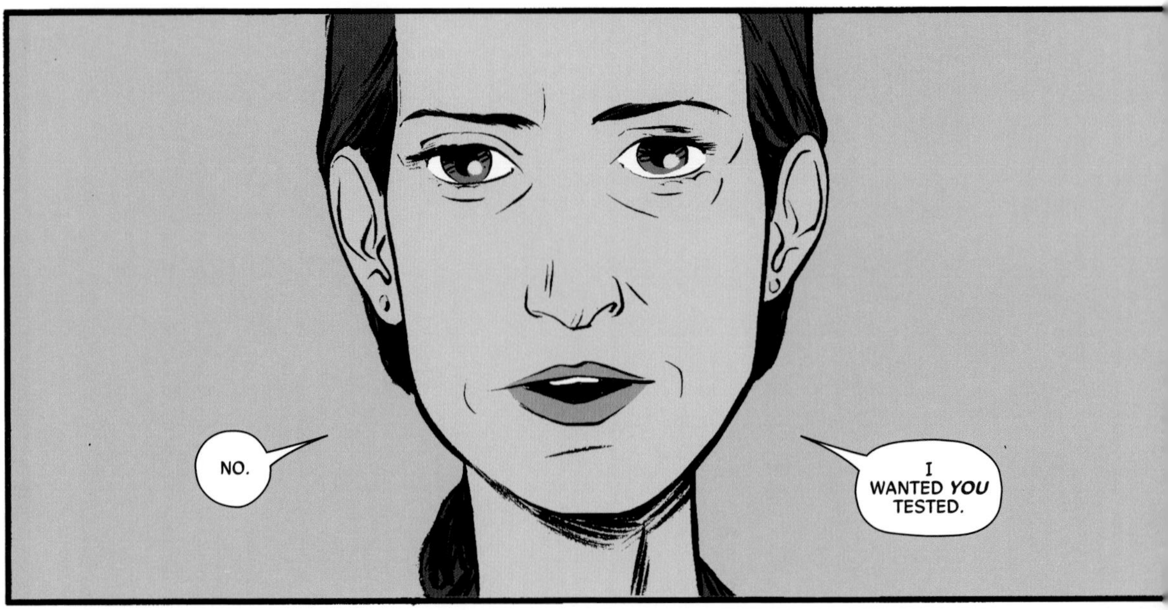
NO.
I WANTED *YOU* TESTED.

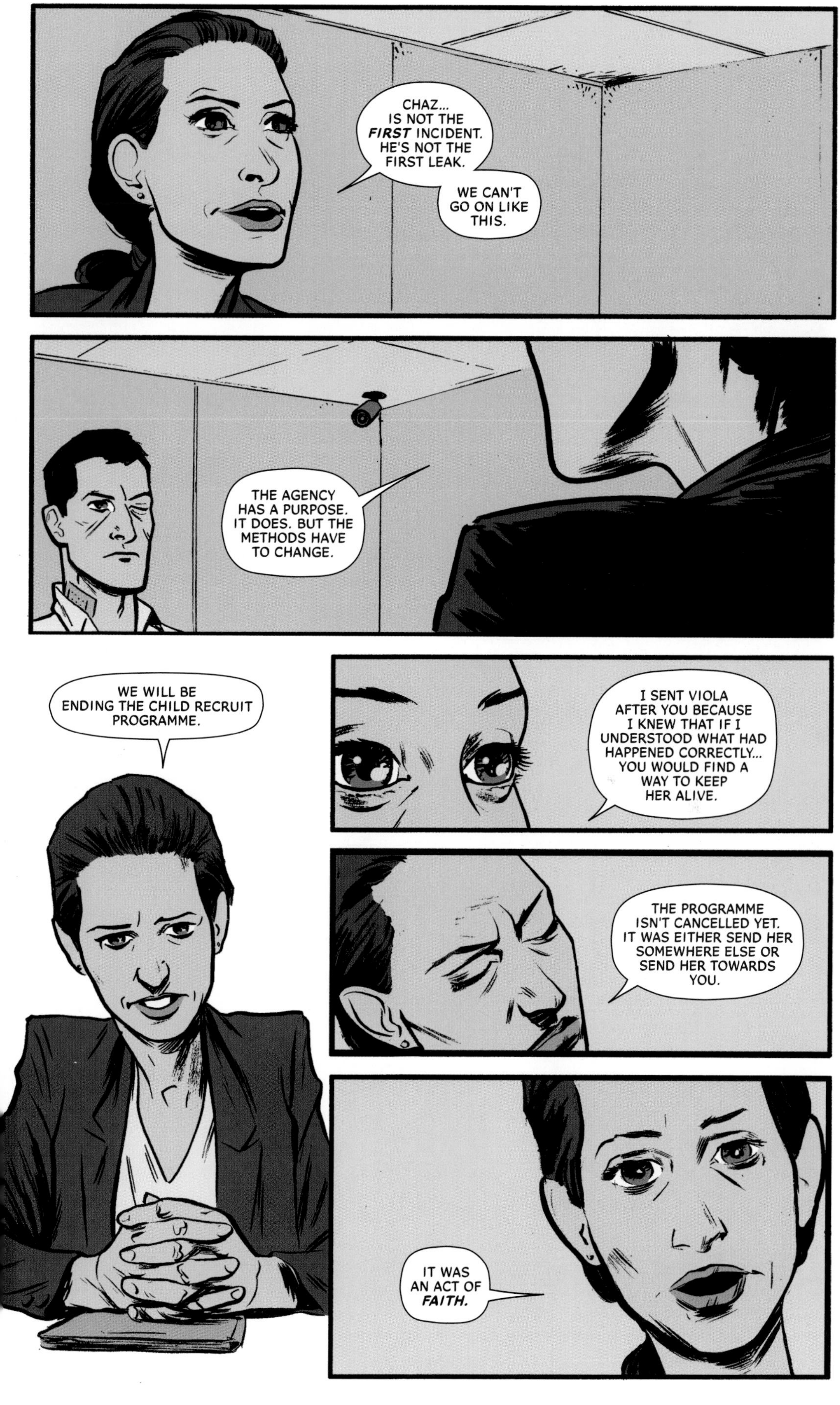
CHAZ... IS NOT THE *FIRST* INCIDENT. HE'S NOT THE FIRST LEAK.
WE CAN'T GO ON LIKE THIS.
THE AGENCY HAS A PURPOSE. IT DOES. BUT THE METHODS HAVE TO CHANGE.
WE WILL BE ENDING THE CHILD RECRUIT PROGRAMME.
I SENT VIOLA AFTER YOU BECAUSE I KNEW THAT IF I UNDERSTOOD WHAT HAD HAPPENED CORRECTLY... YOU WOULD FIND A WAY TO KEEP HER ALIVE.
THE PROGRAMME ISN'T CANCELLED YET. IT WAS EITHER SEND HER SOMEWHERE ELSE OR SEND HER TOWARDS YOU.
IT WAS AN ACT OF *FAITH.*

WHY SEND HER WITH THE BACKUP?

I COULDN'T CHANGE THE PROTOCOL, SO I MADE SURE THE BACKUP WAS ONE OF THE PEOPLE WHO WERE SPYING ON ME FOR THE HIGHER-UPS.

NICE OF YOU TO NOT KILL HIM, BY THE WAY.

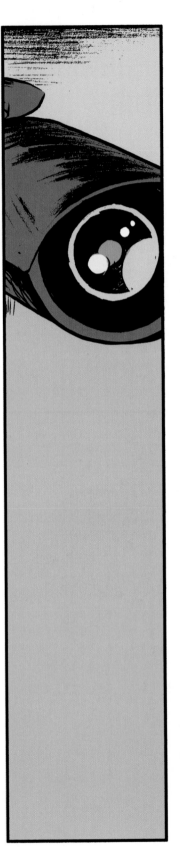

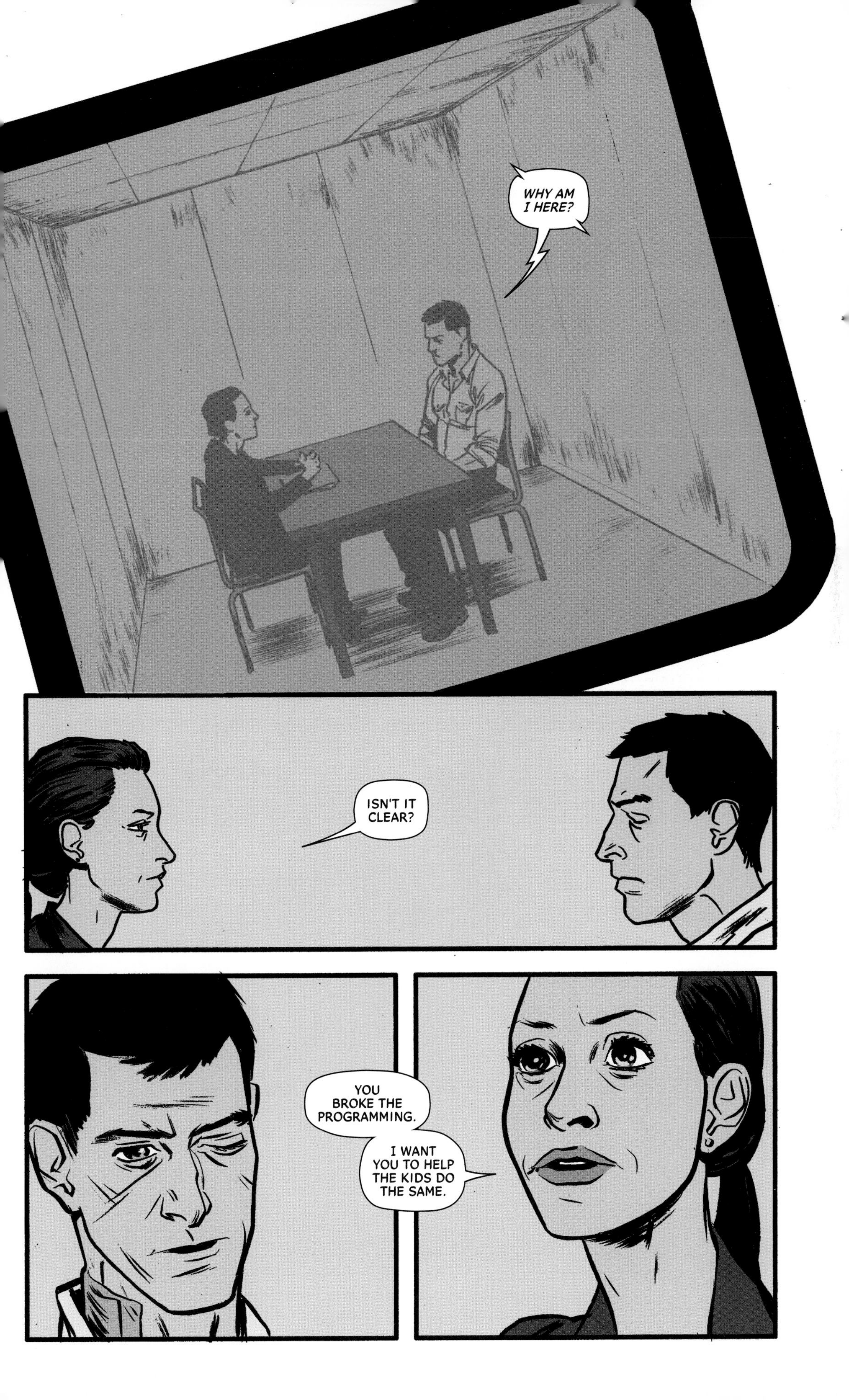
WHY AM I HERE?
ISN'T IT CLEAR?
YOU BROKE THE PROGRAMMING.
I WANT YOU TO HELP THE KIDS DO THE SAME.

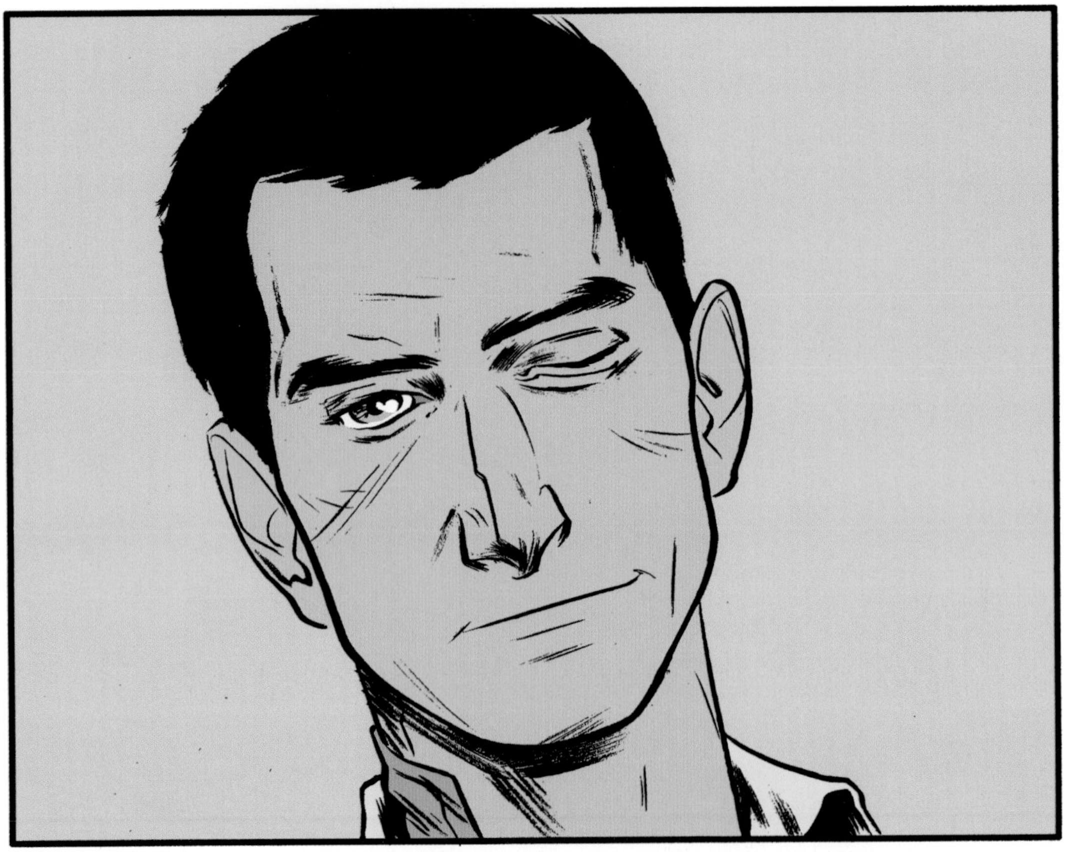

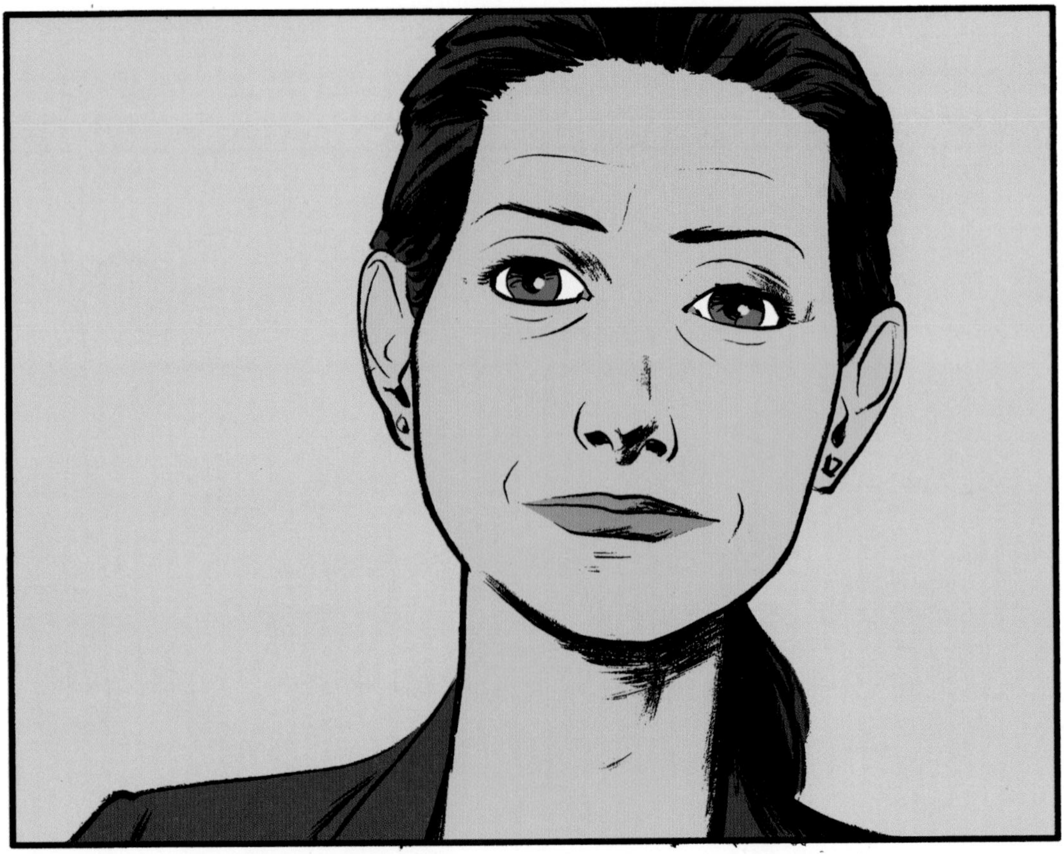

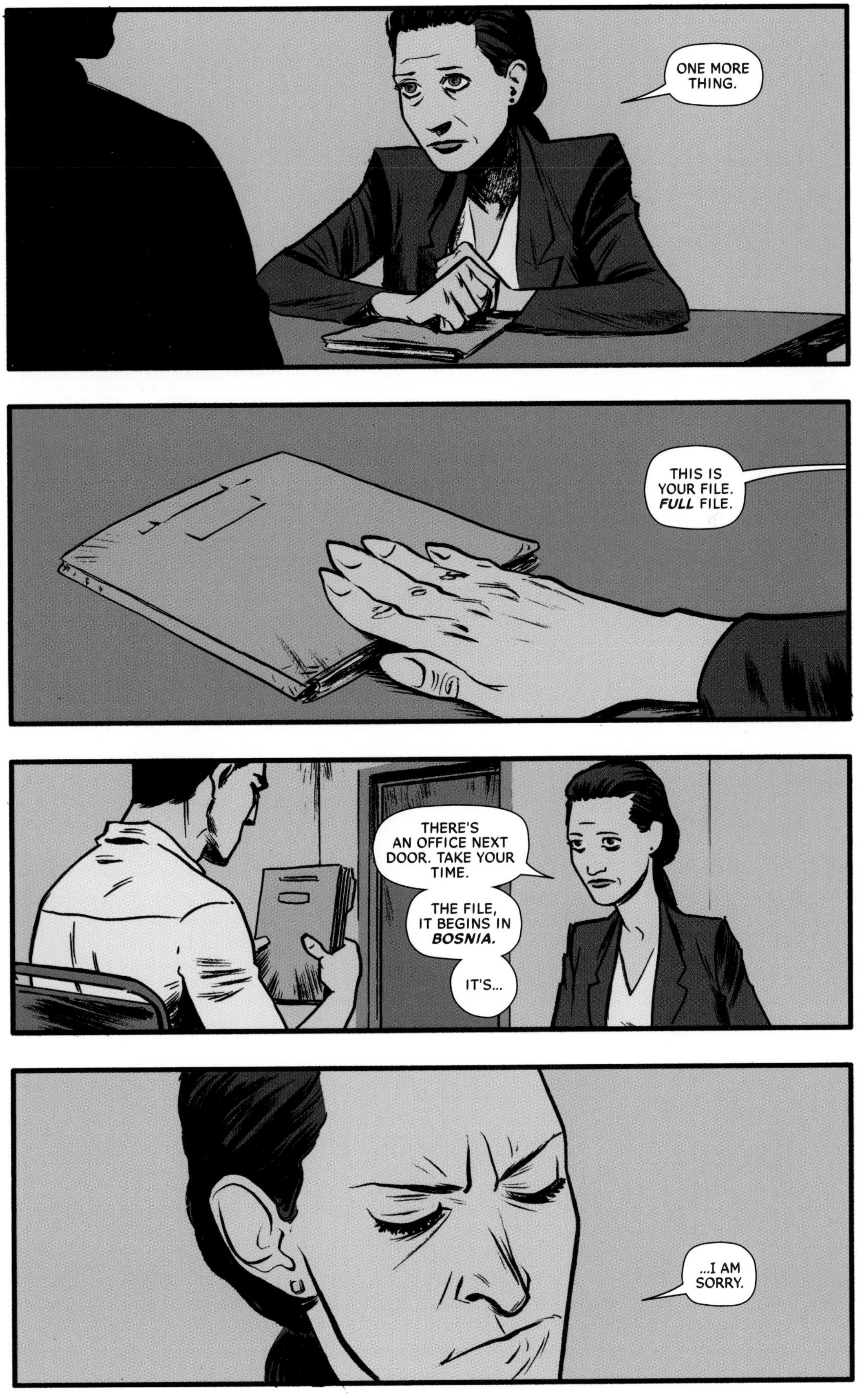
ONE MORE THING.
THIS IS YOUR FILE. *FULL* FILE.
THERE'S AN OFFICE NEXT DOOR. TAKE YOUR TIME.
THE FILE, IT BEGINS IN *BOSNIA.*
IT'S...
...I AM SORRY.

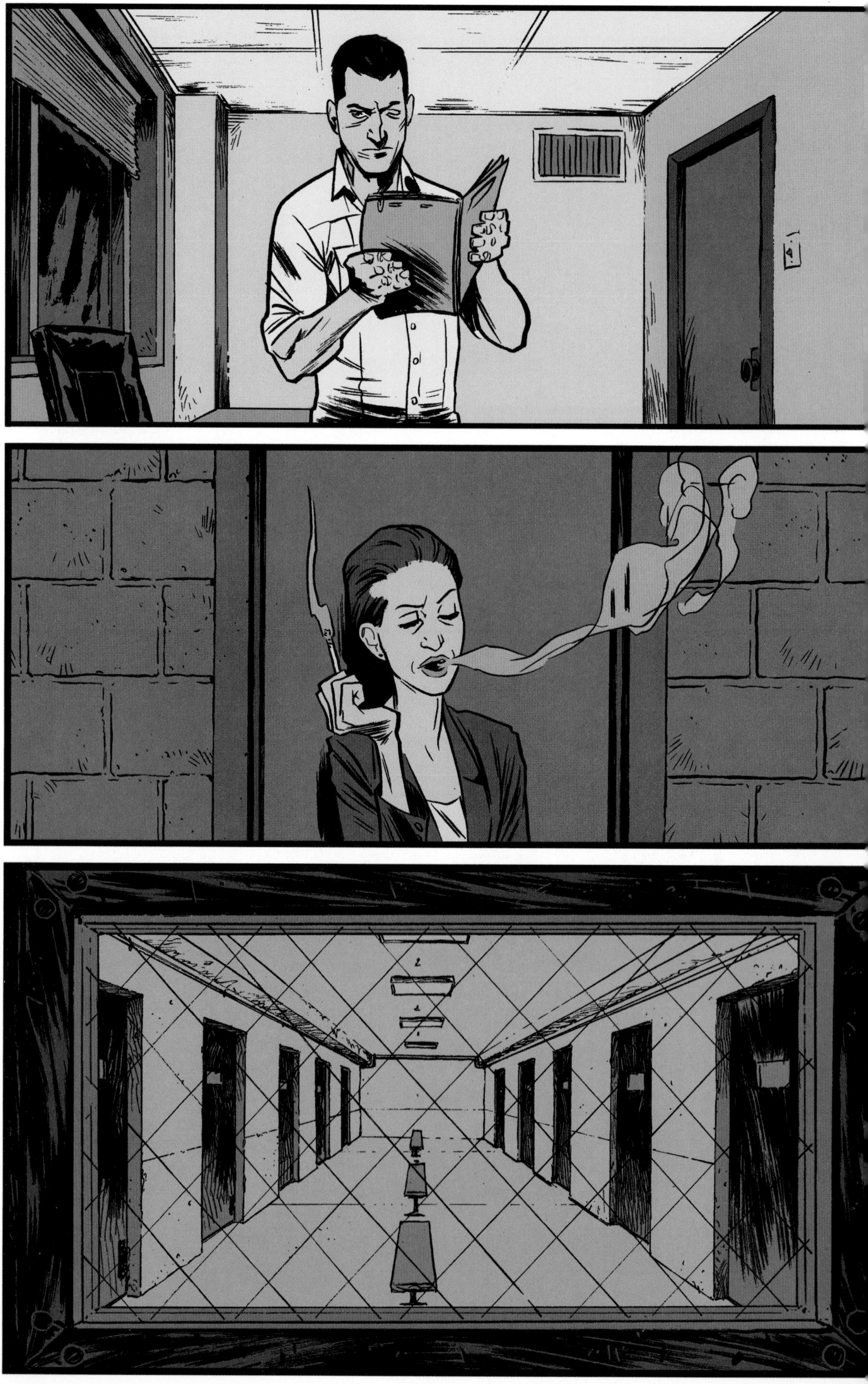

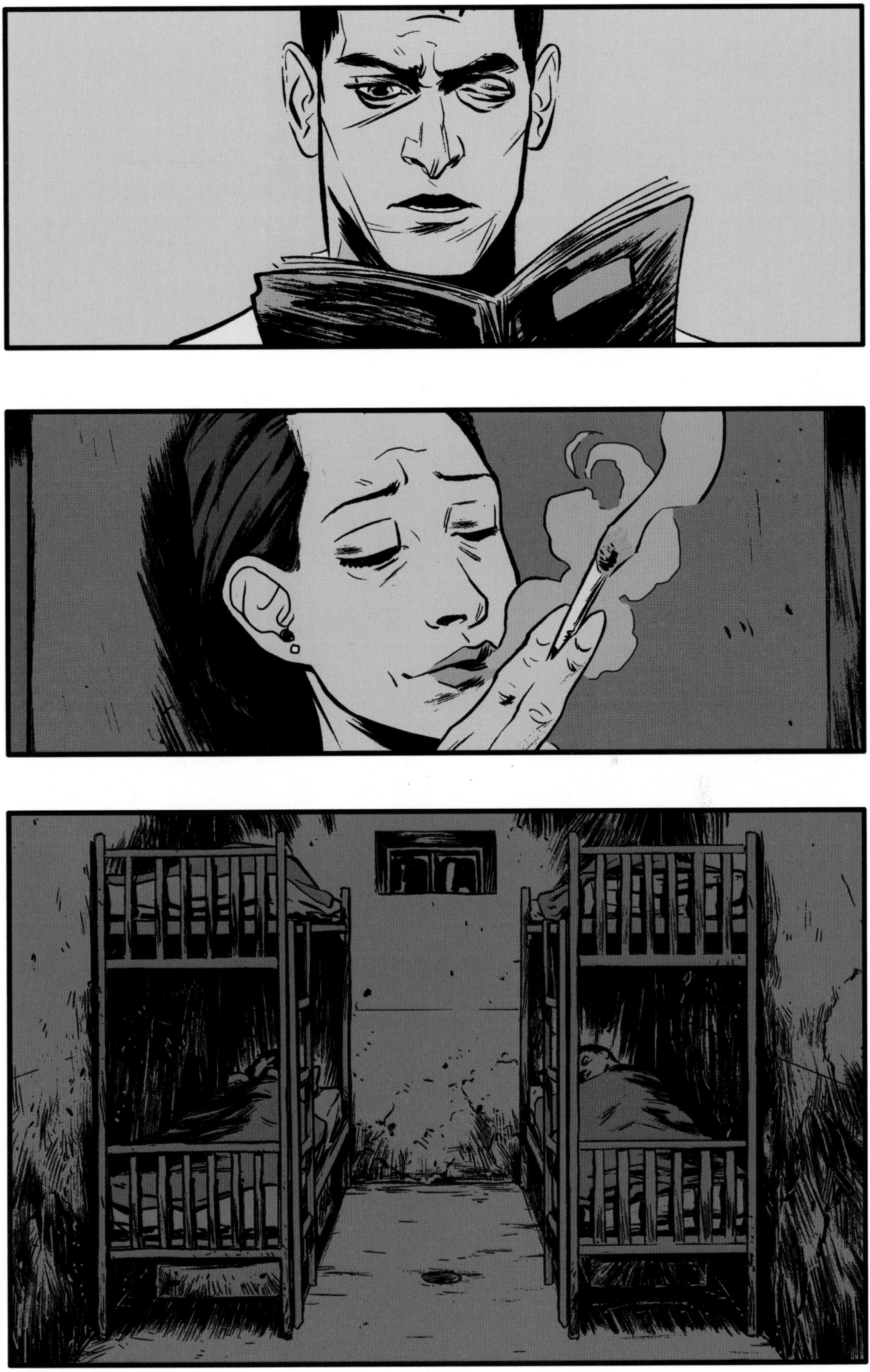

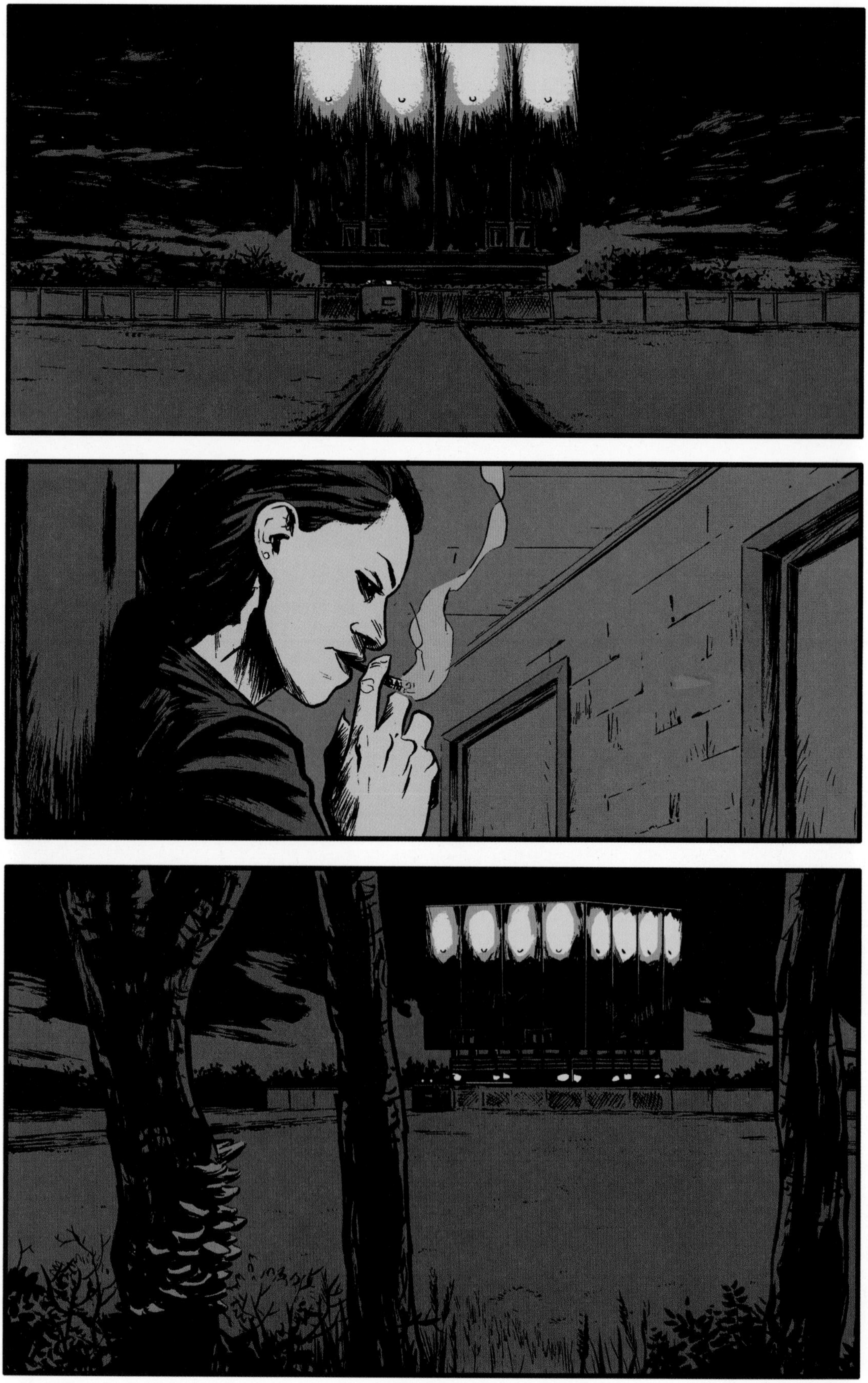

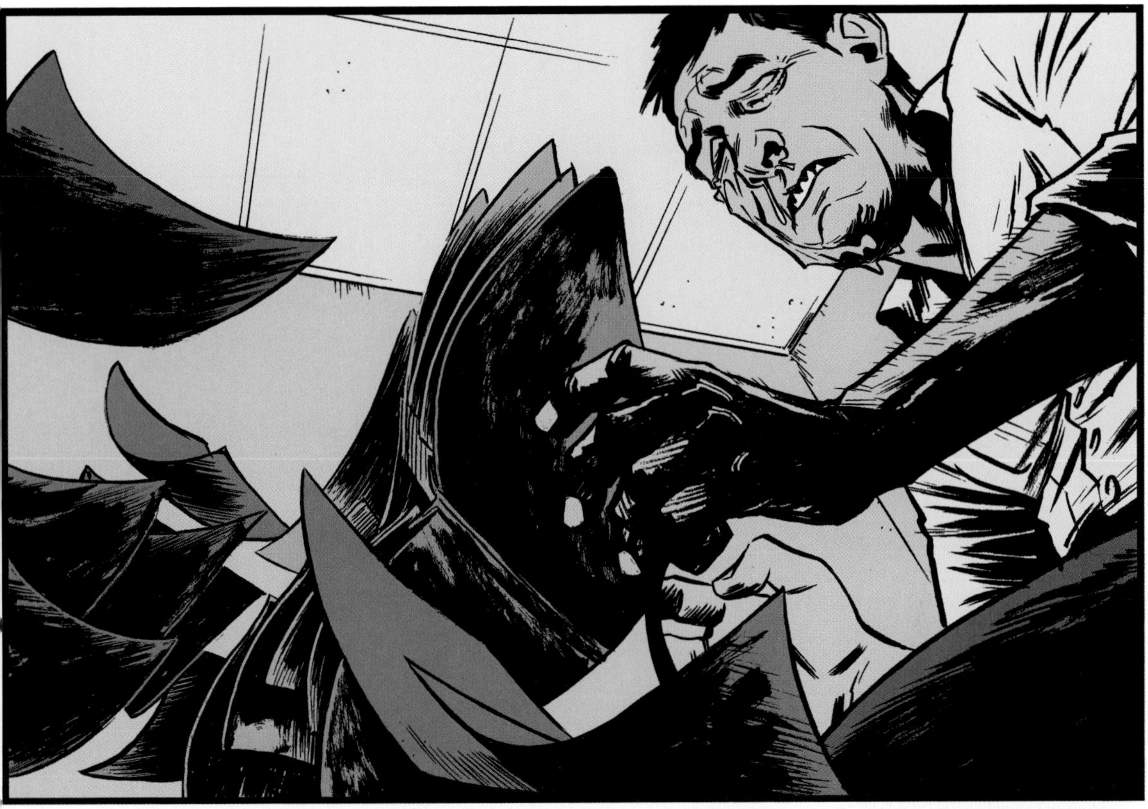

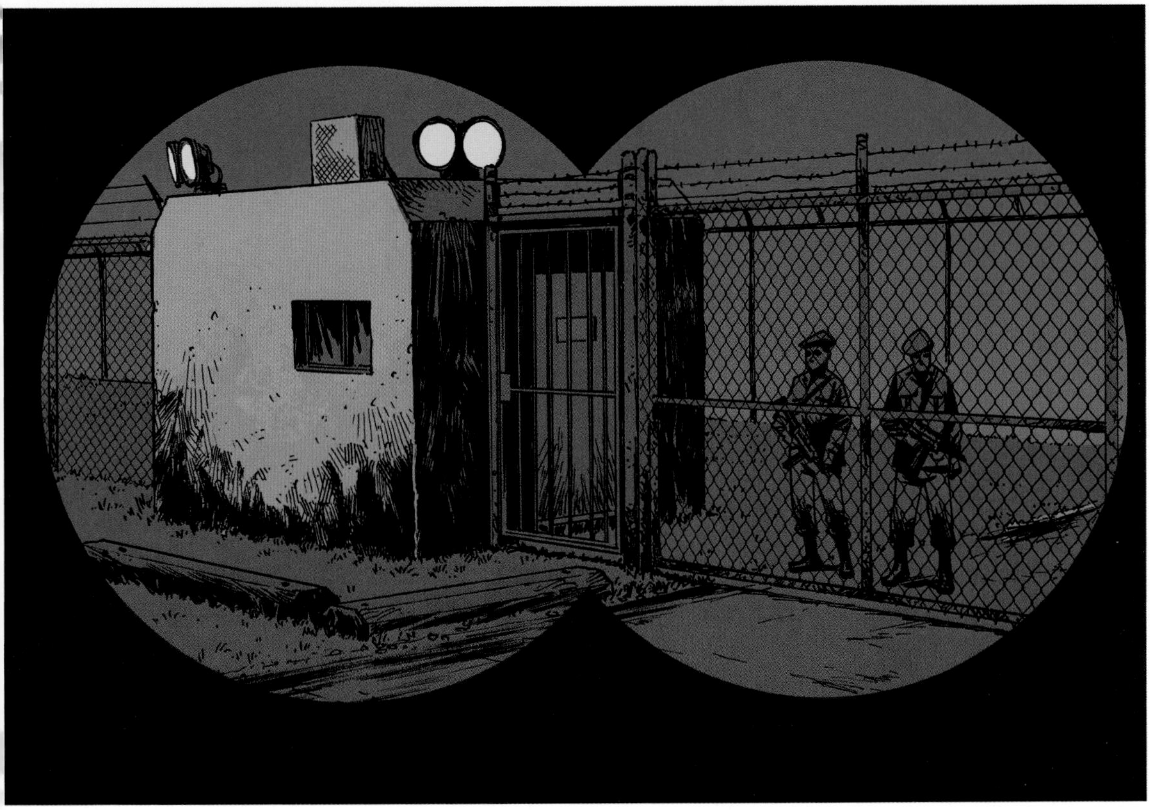

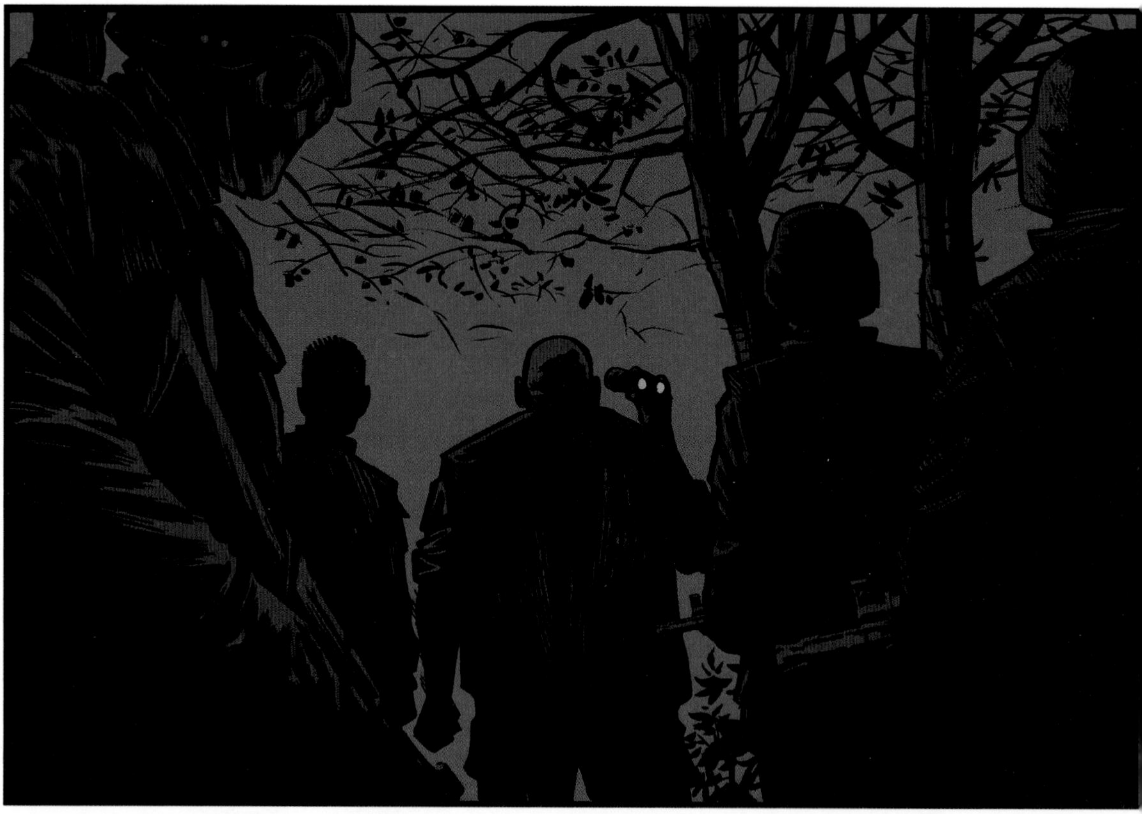

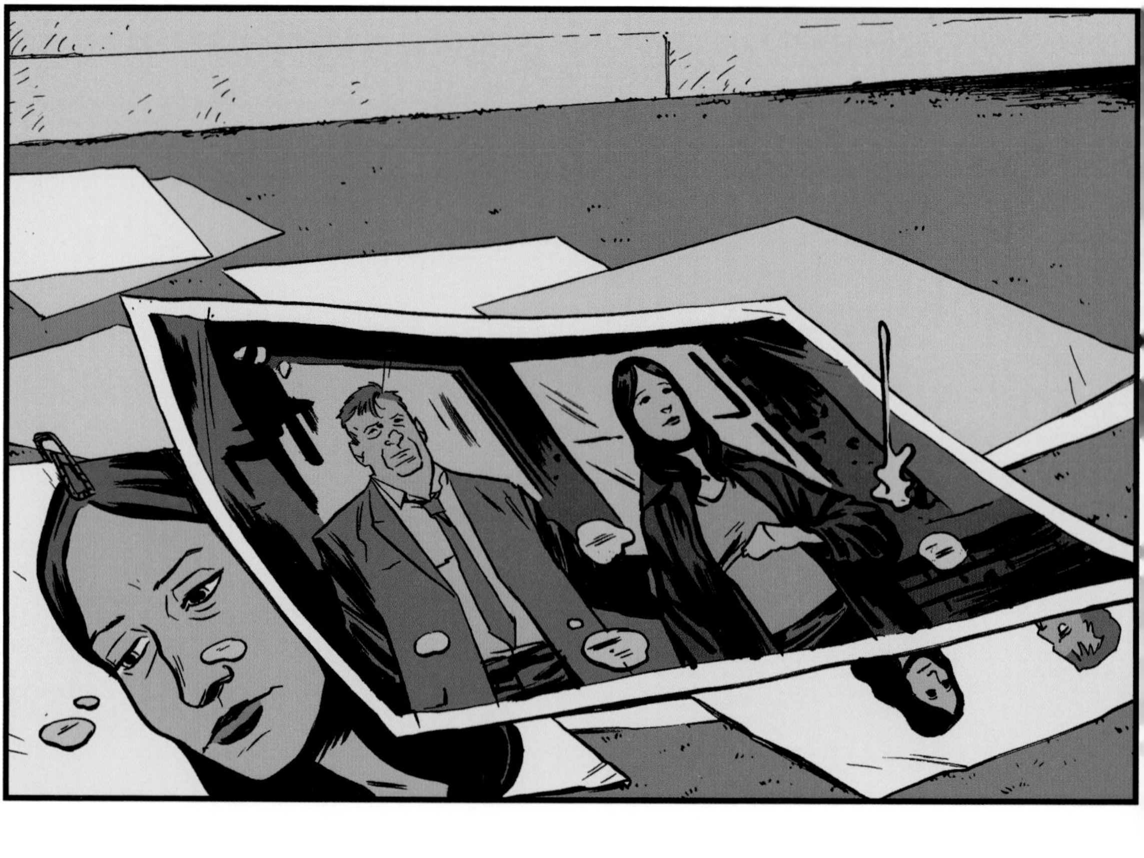

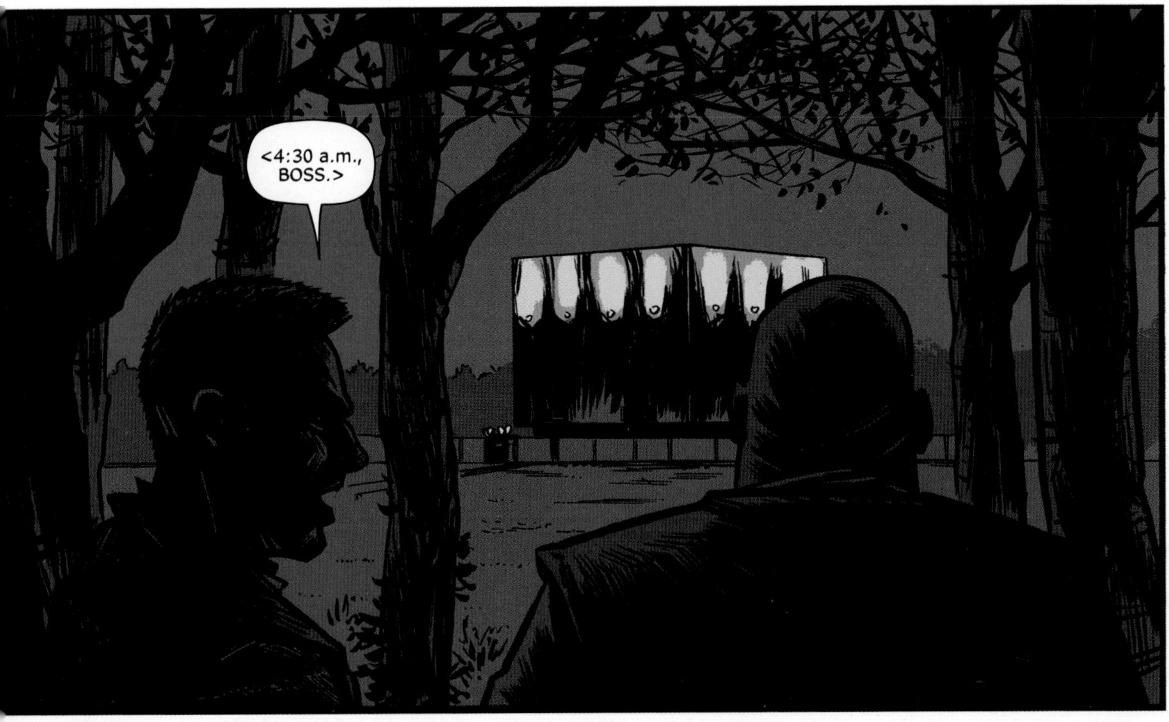
<4:30 a.m., BOSS.>

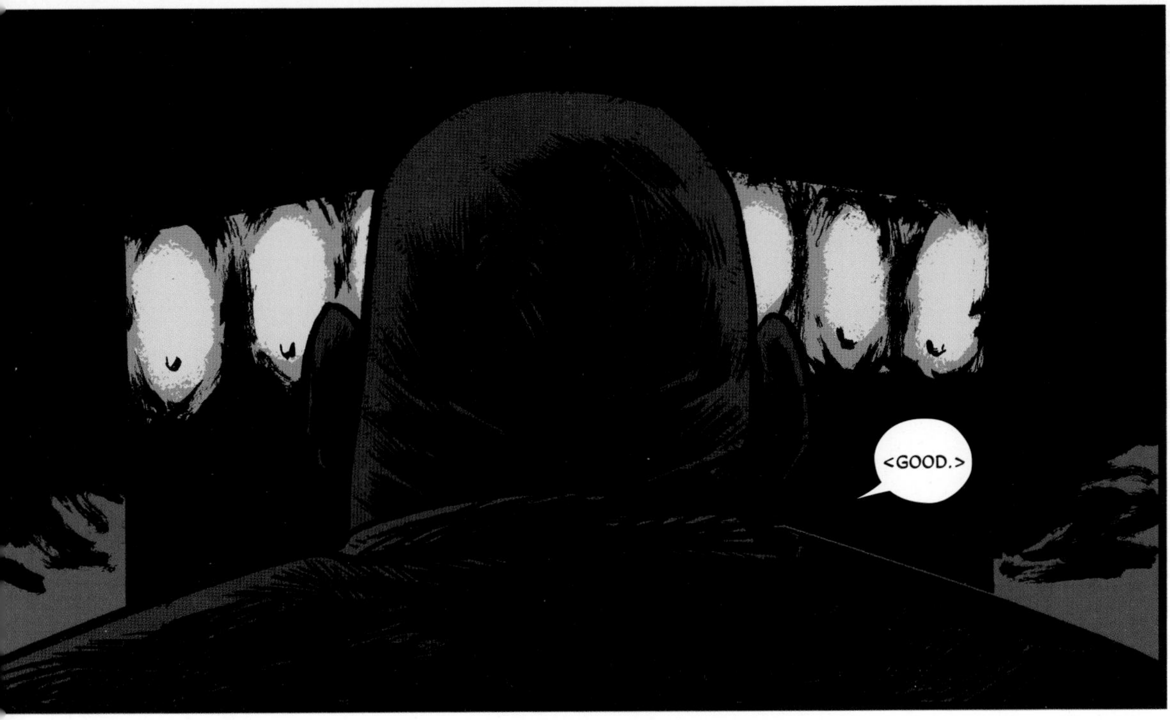
<GOOD.>

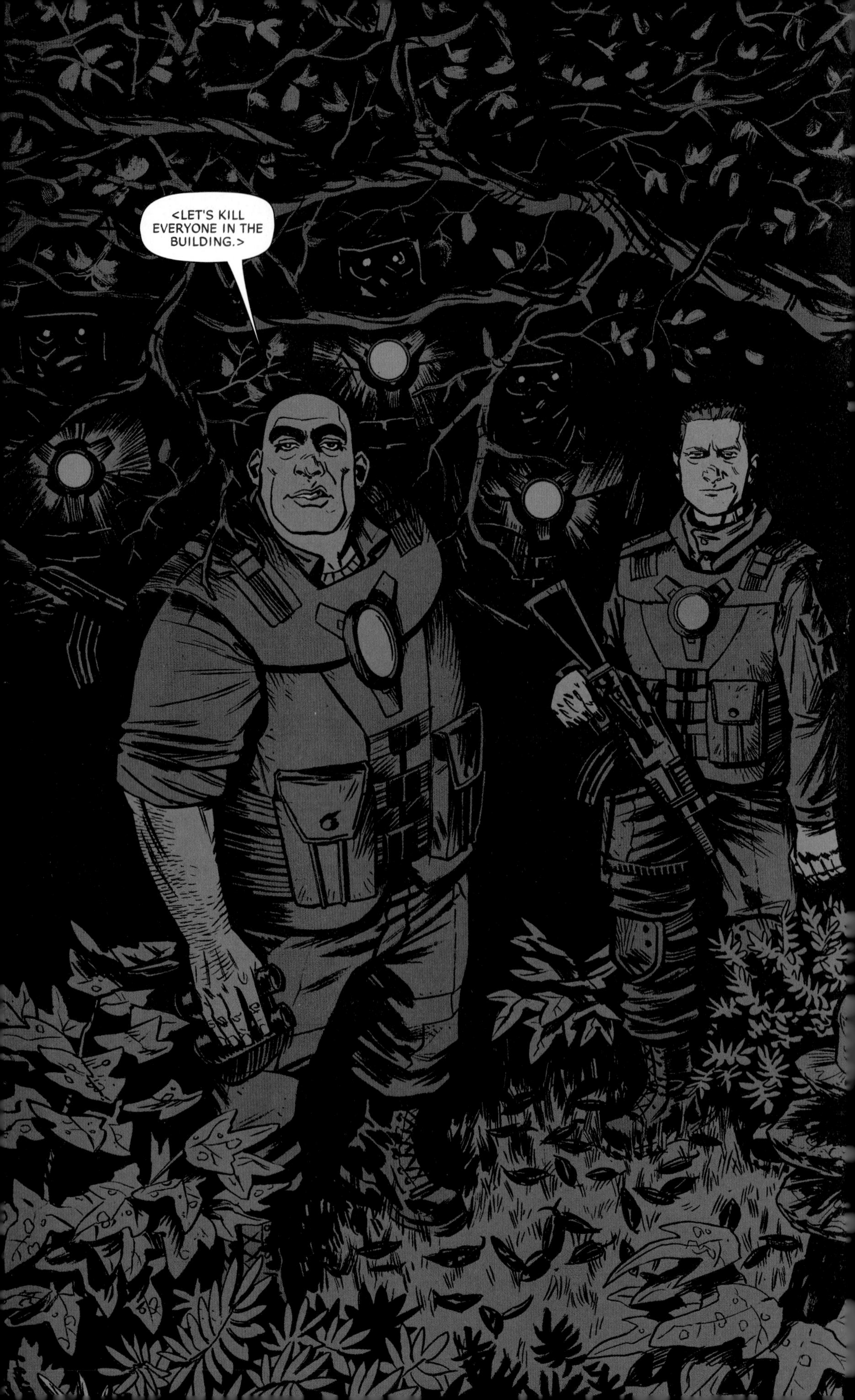
<LET'S KILL EVERYONE IN THE BUILDING.>

CHAPTER 13

FAREWELL
Illustrated by Alberto Ponticelli

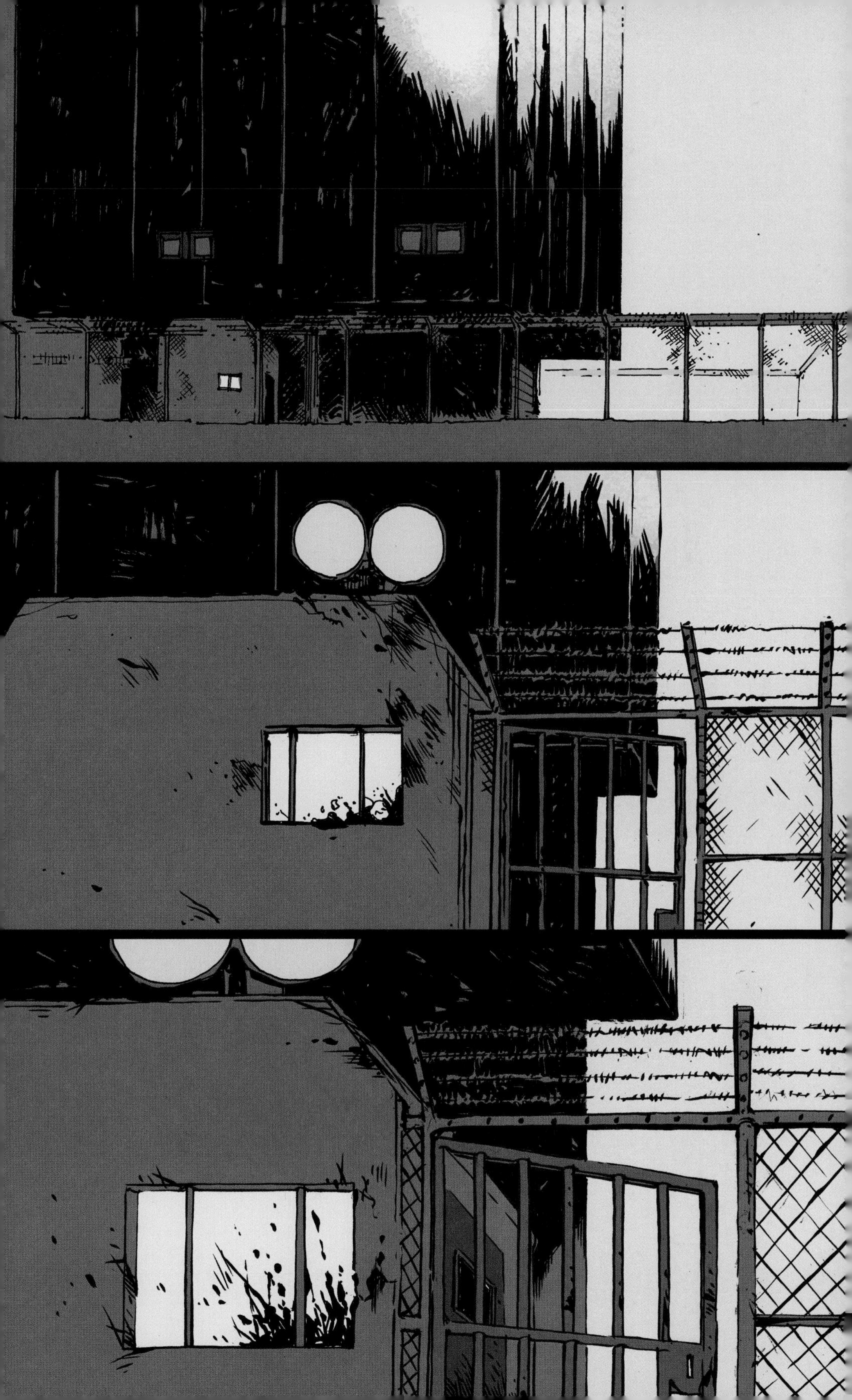

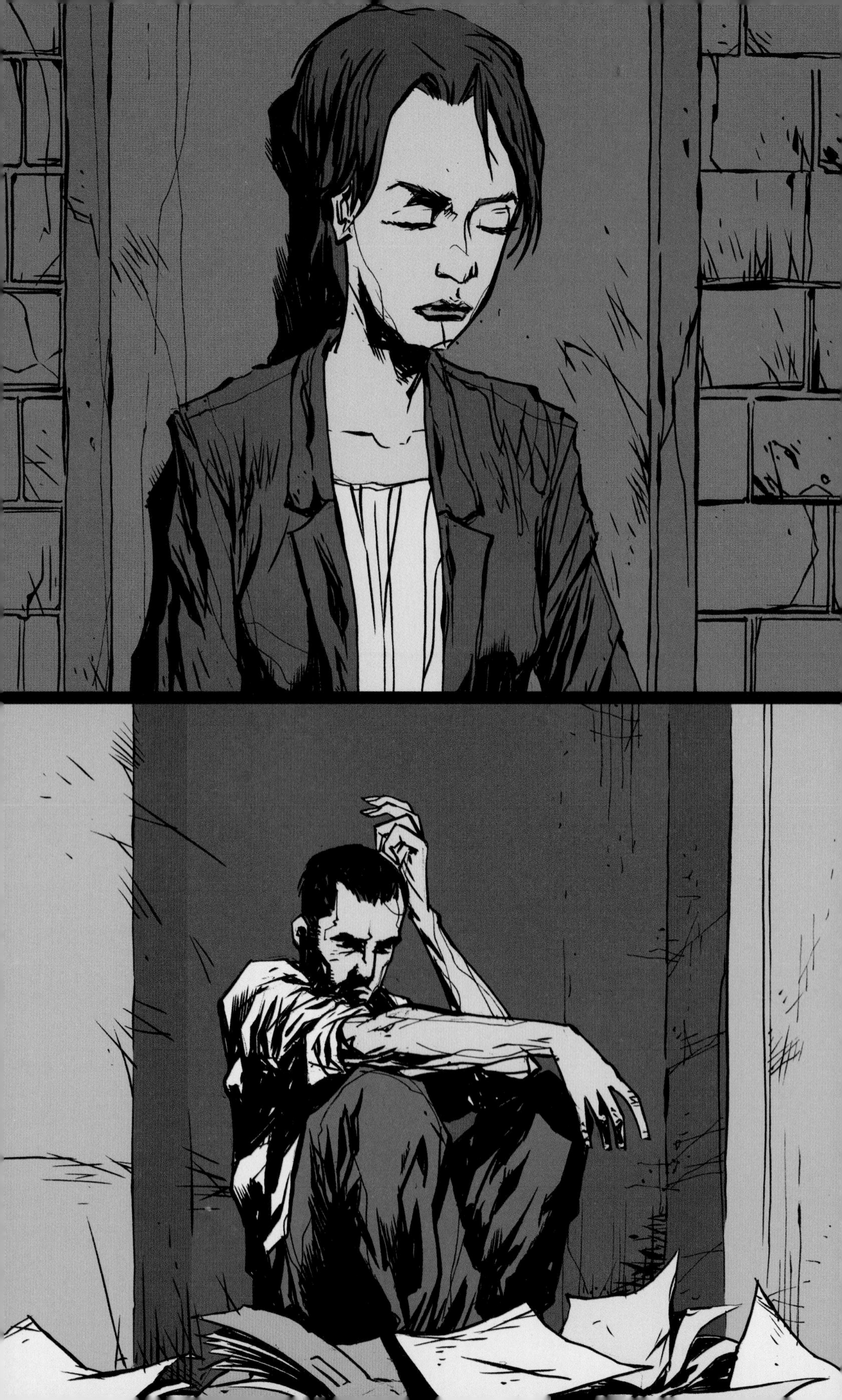

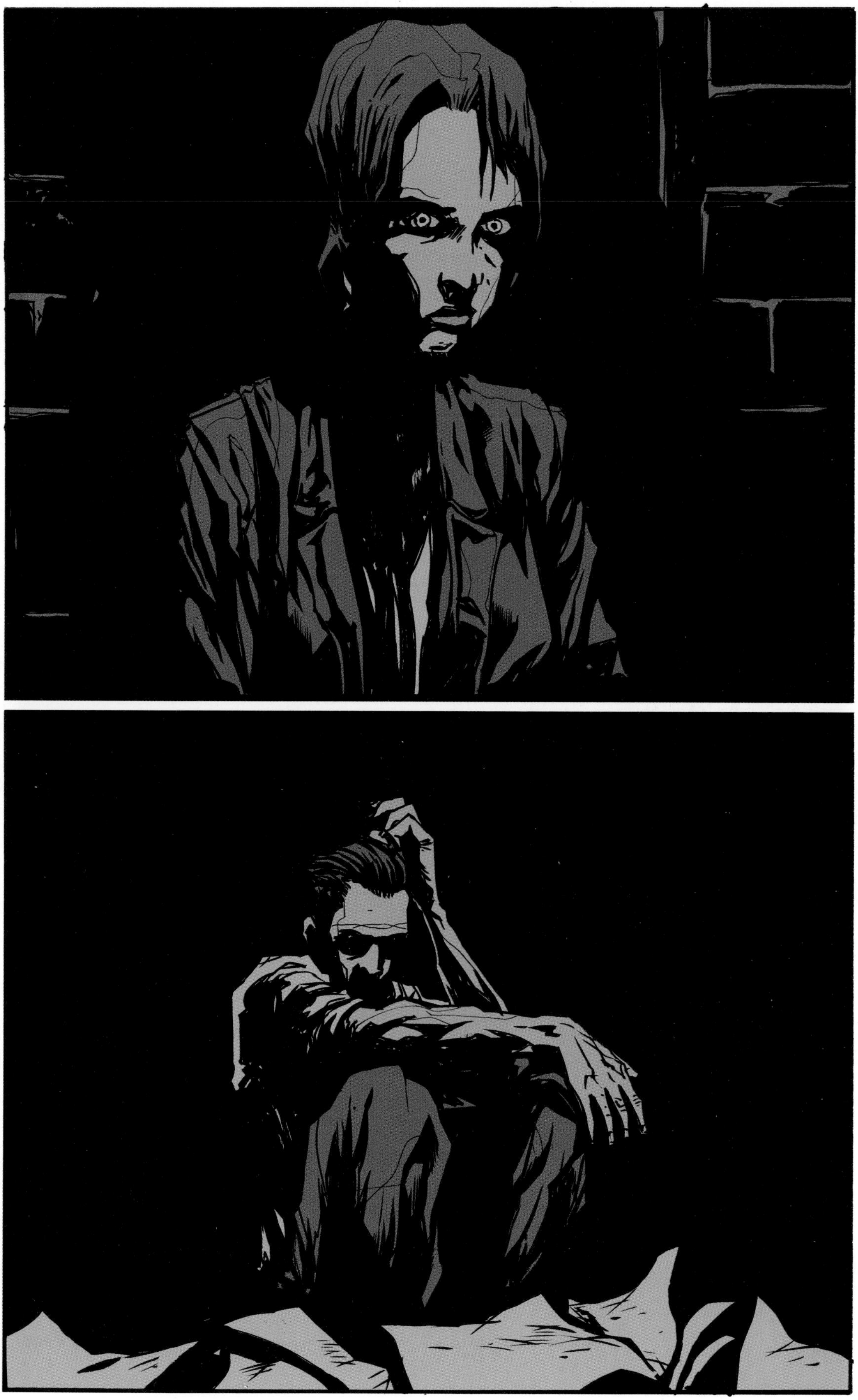

GRABOVSKY?

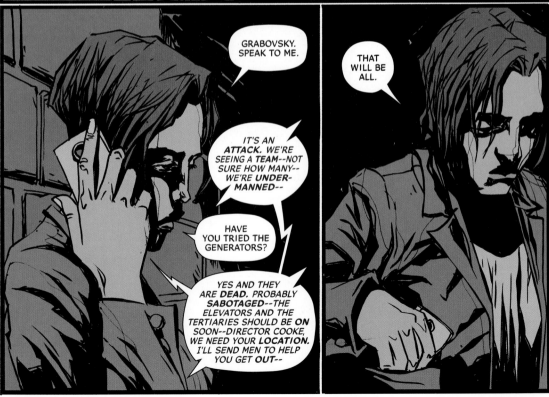

GRABOVSKY. SPEAK TO ME.

THAT WILL BE ALL.

IT'S AN **ATTACK**. WE'RE SEEING A **TEAM**--NOT SURE HOW MANY-- WE'RE **UNDER-MANNED**--

HAVE YOU TRIED THE GENERATORS?

YES AND THEY ARE **DEAD**. PROBABLY **SABOTAGED**--THE ELEVATORS AND THE TERTIARIES SHOULD BE **ON** SOON--DIRECTOR COOKE, WE NEED YOUR **LOCATION**. I'LL SEND MEN TO HELP YOU GET **OUT**--

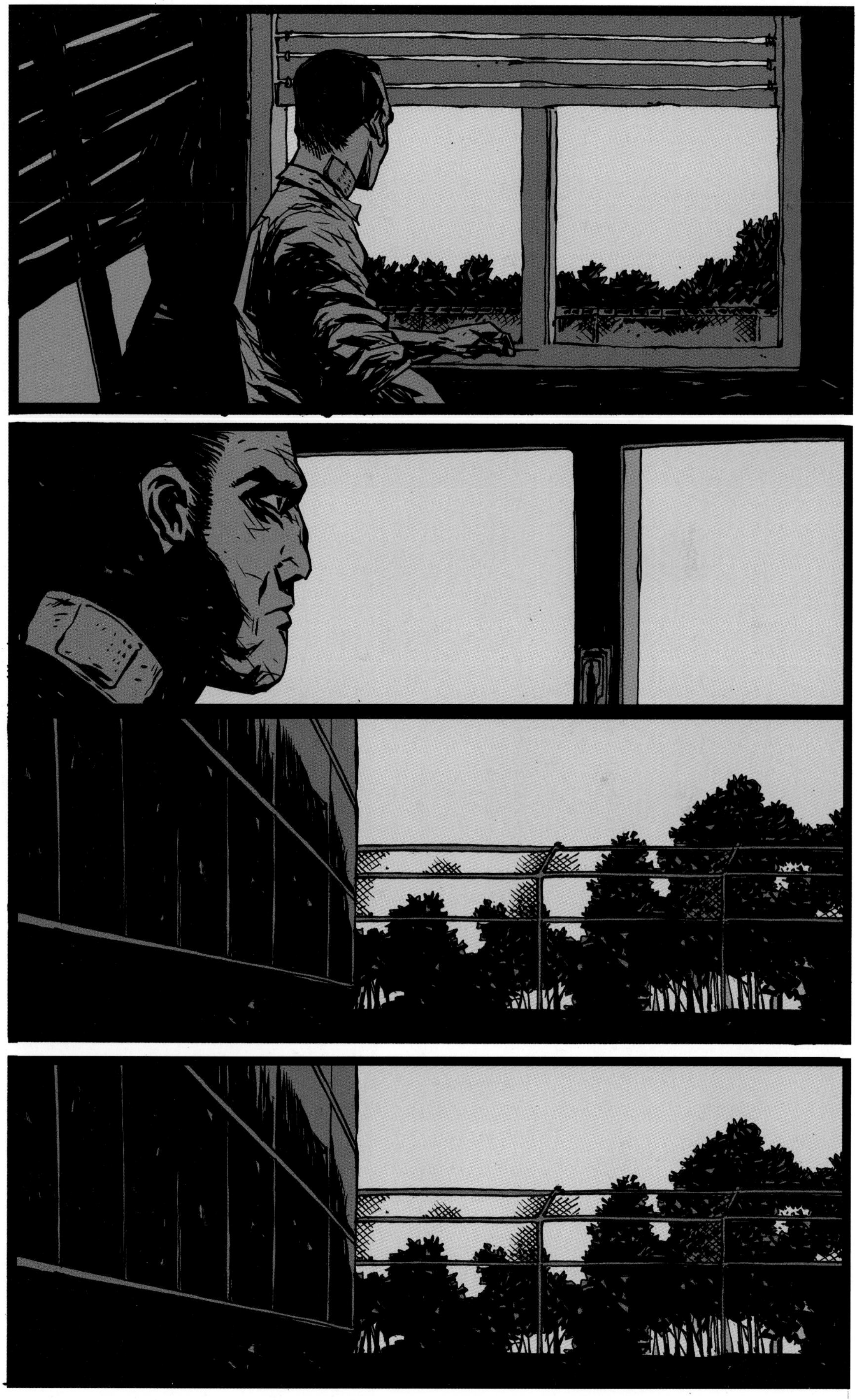

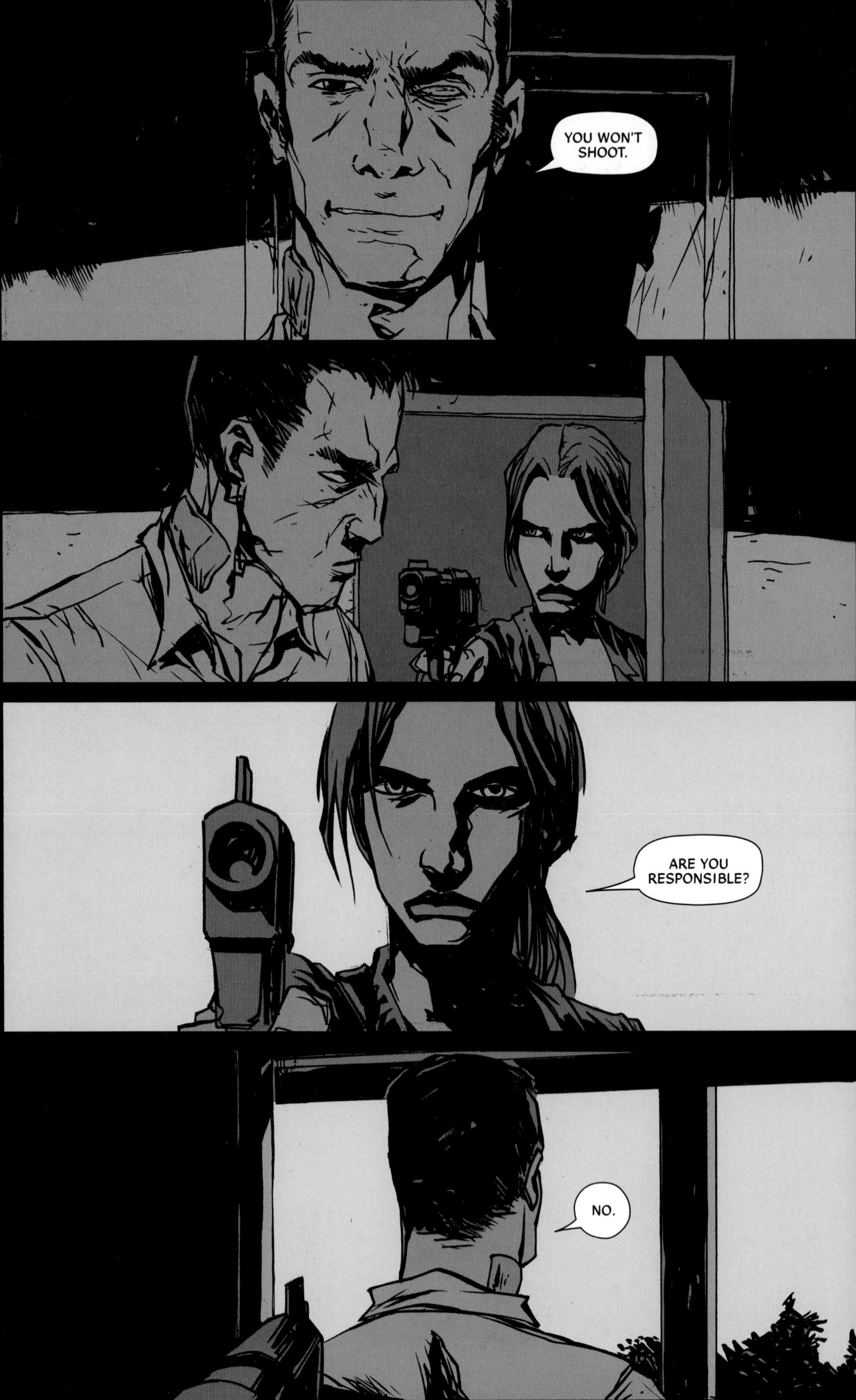
YOU WON'T SHOOT.
ARE YOU RESPONSIBLE?
NO.

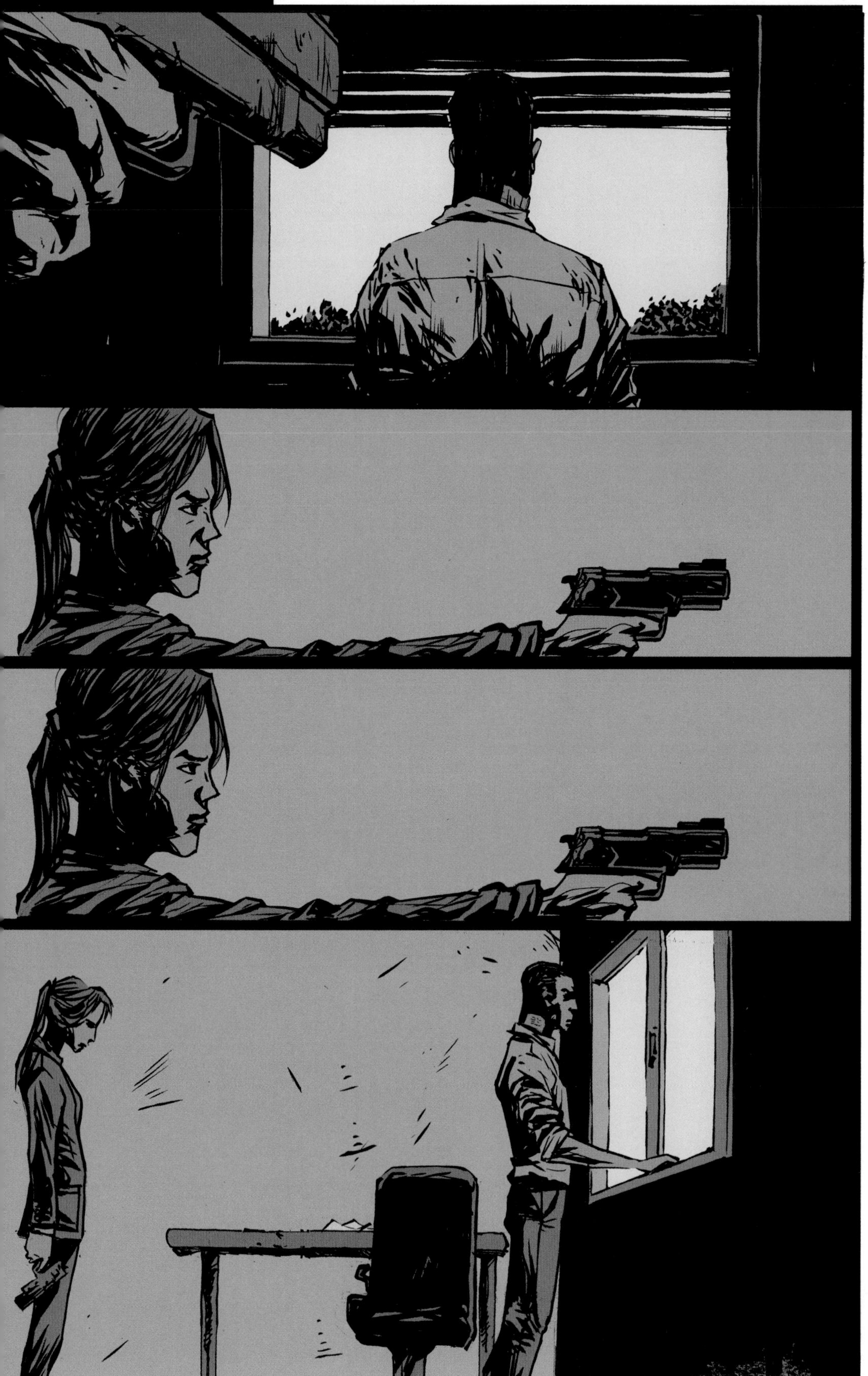

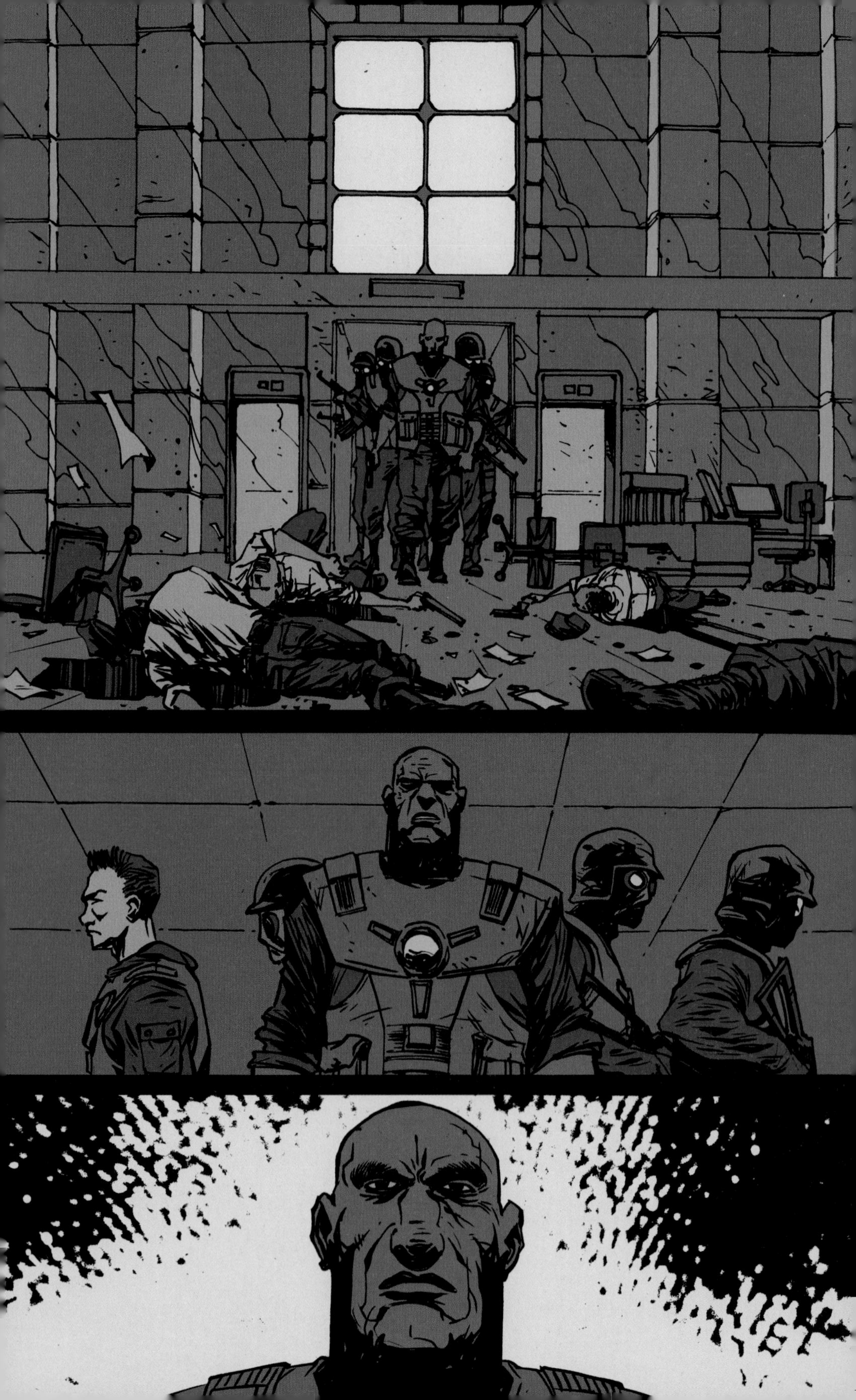

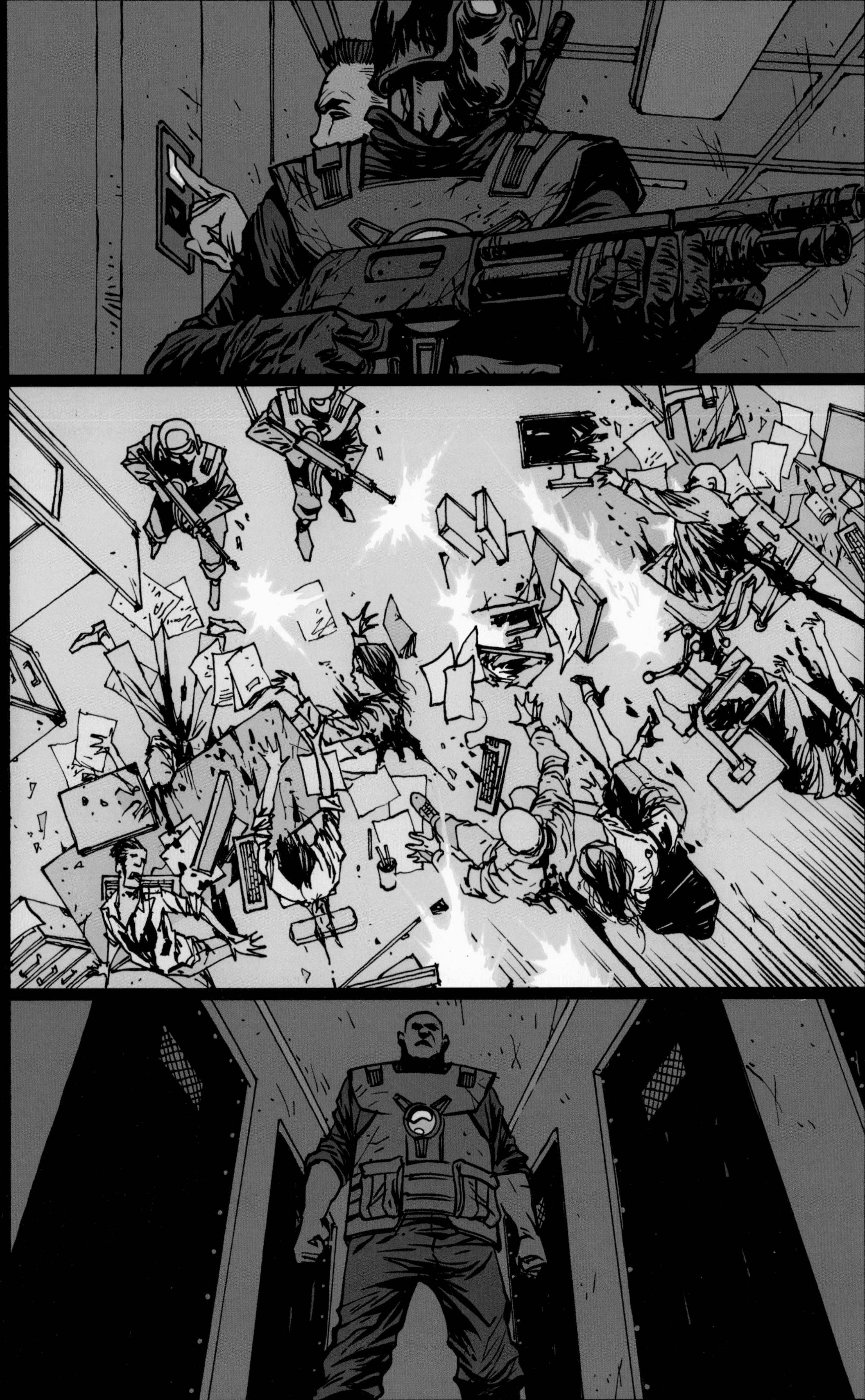

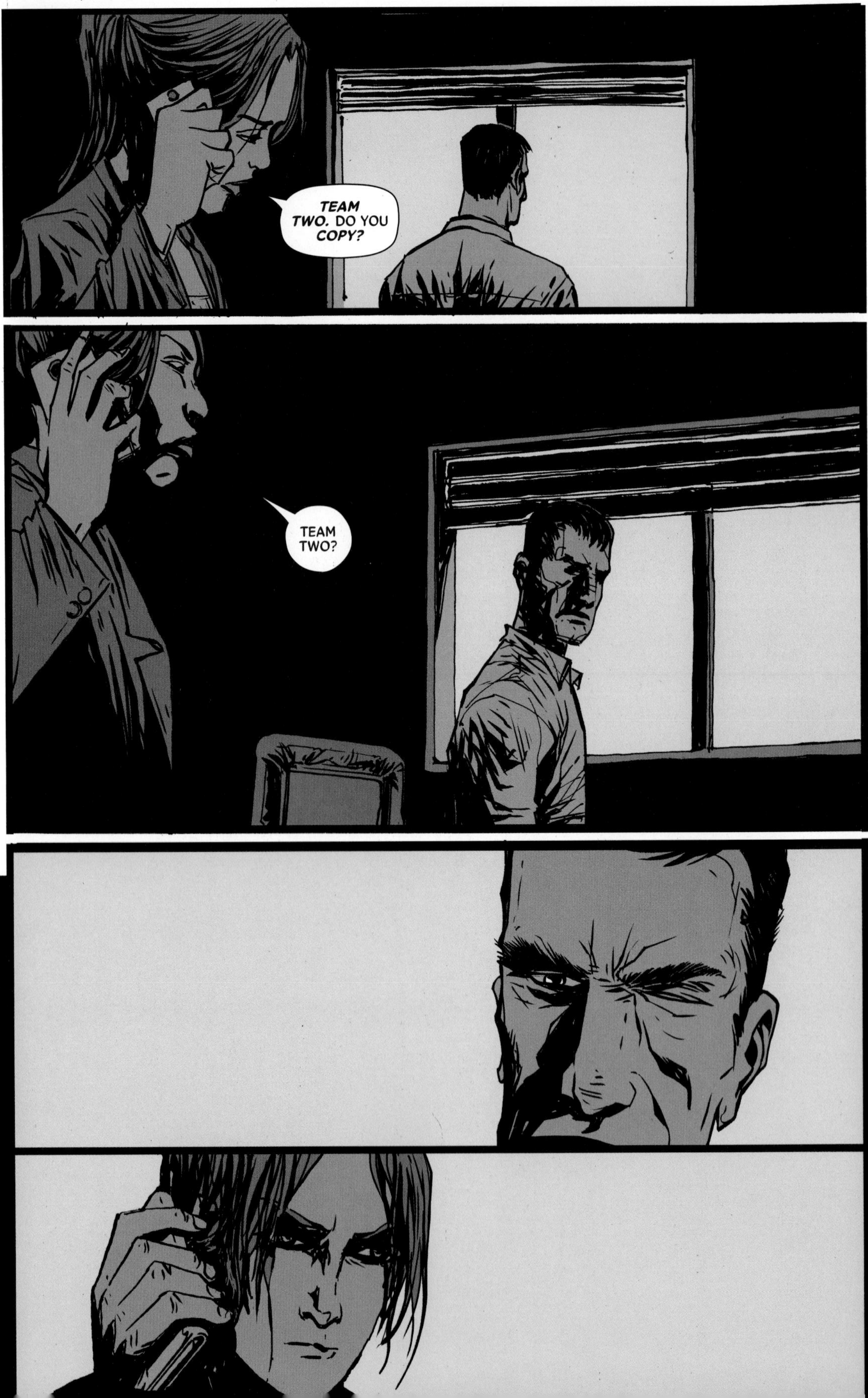
TEAM TWO. DO YOU COPY?
TEAM TWO?

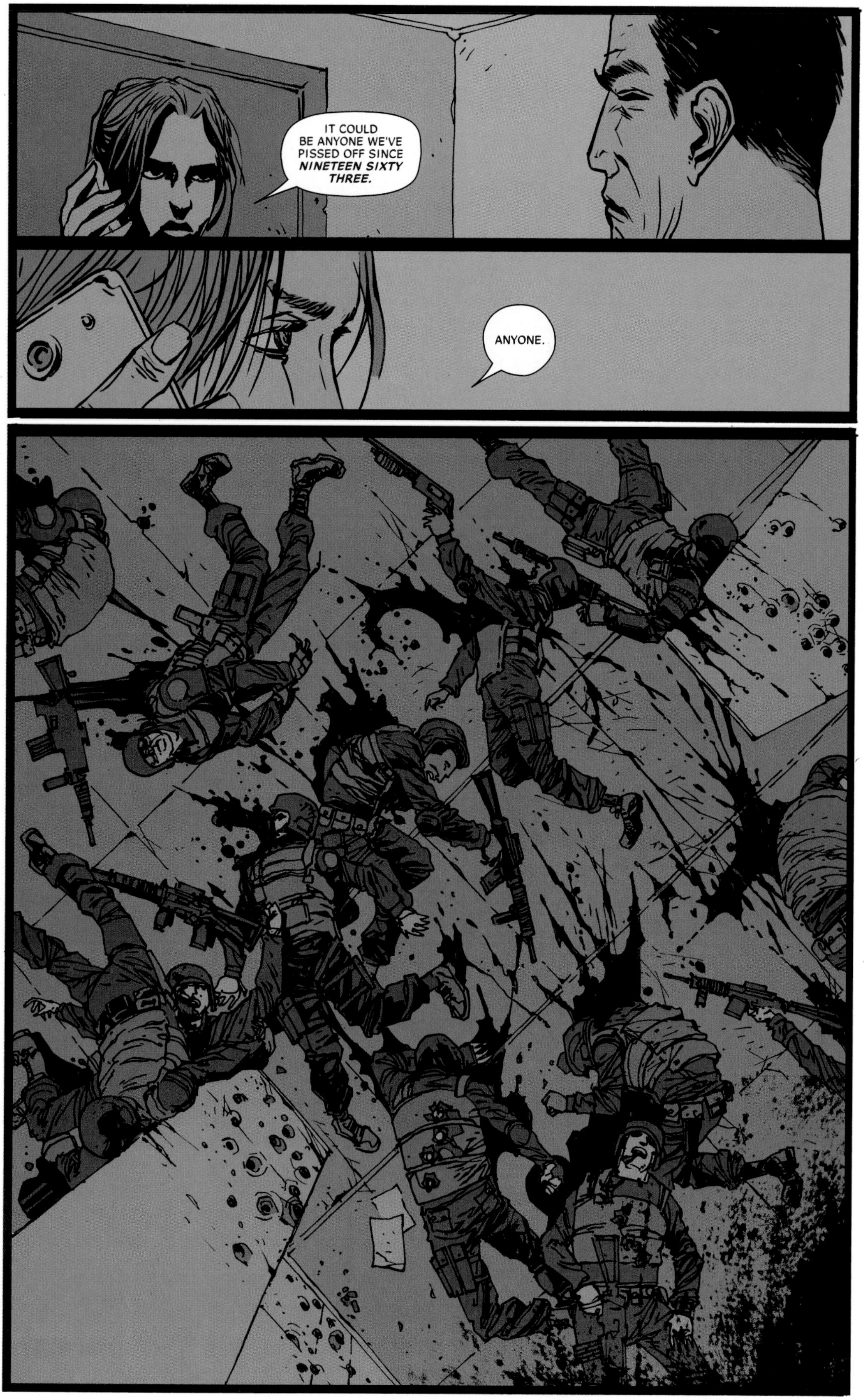
IT COULD BE ANYONE WE'VE PISSED OFF SINCE ***NINETEEN SIXTY THREE.***
ANYONE.

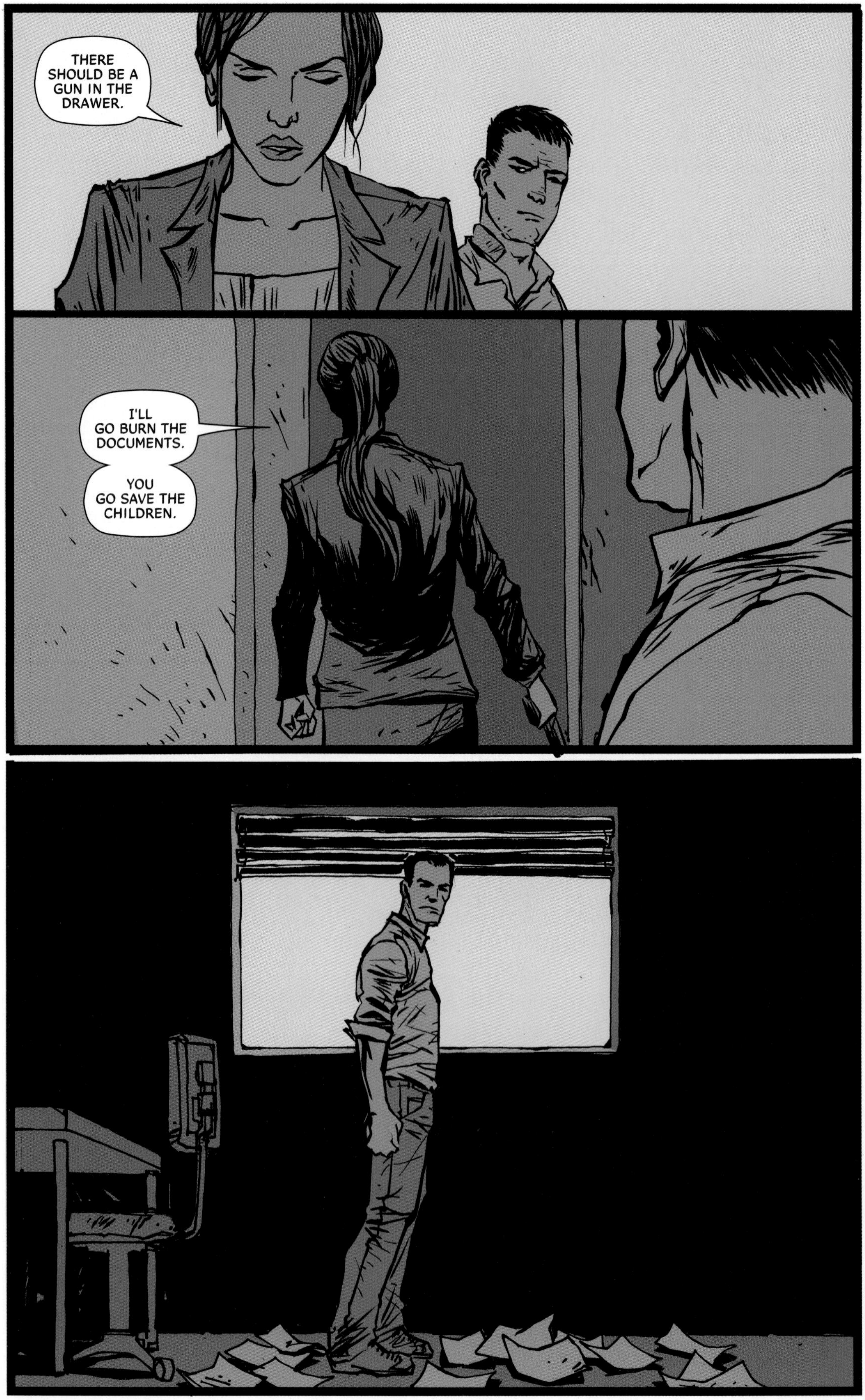
THERE SHOULD BE A GUN IN THE DRAWER.
I'LL GO BURN THE DOCUMENTS.
YOU GO SAVE THE CHILDREN.

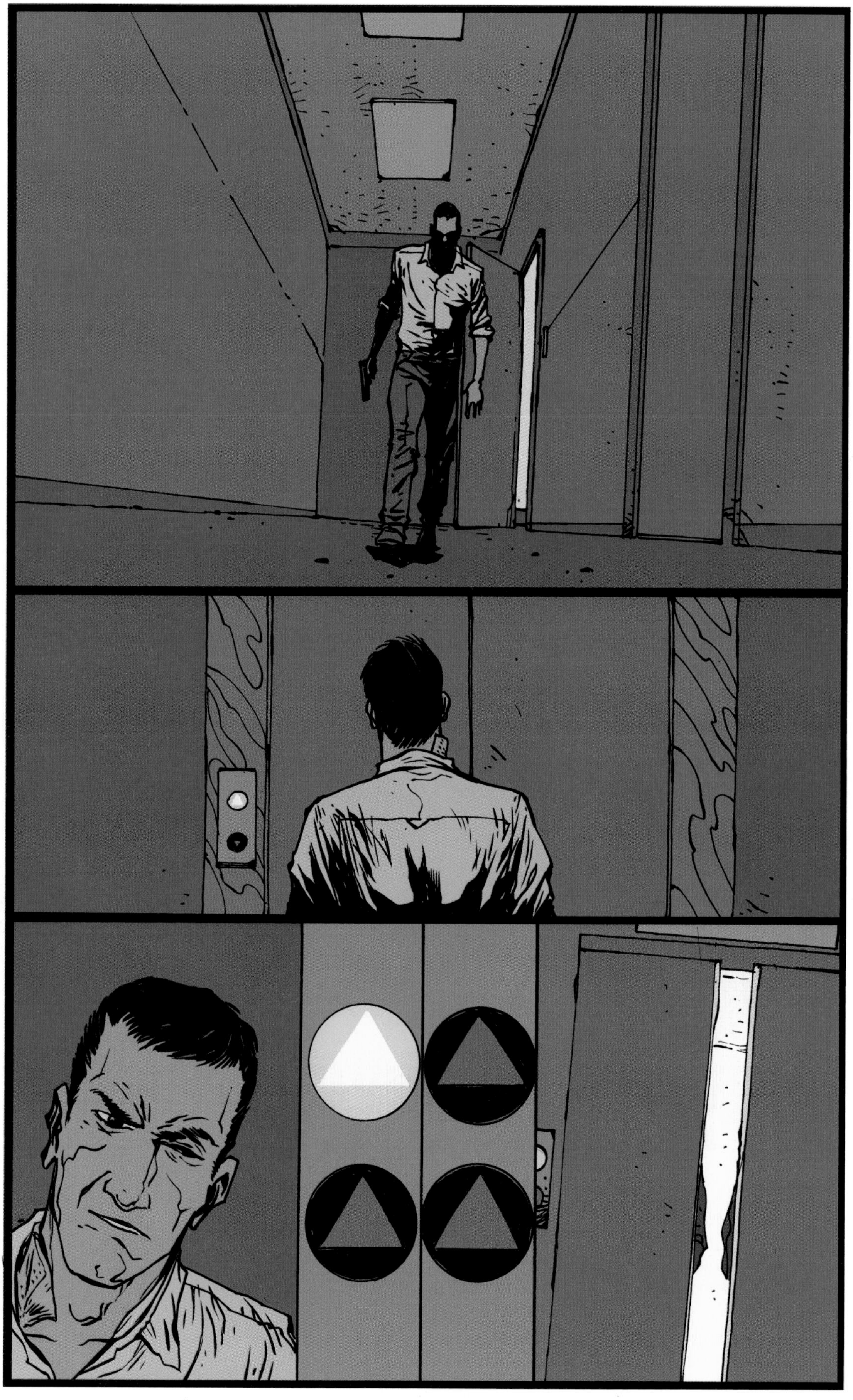

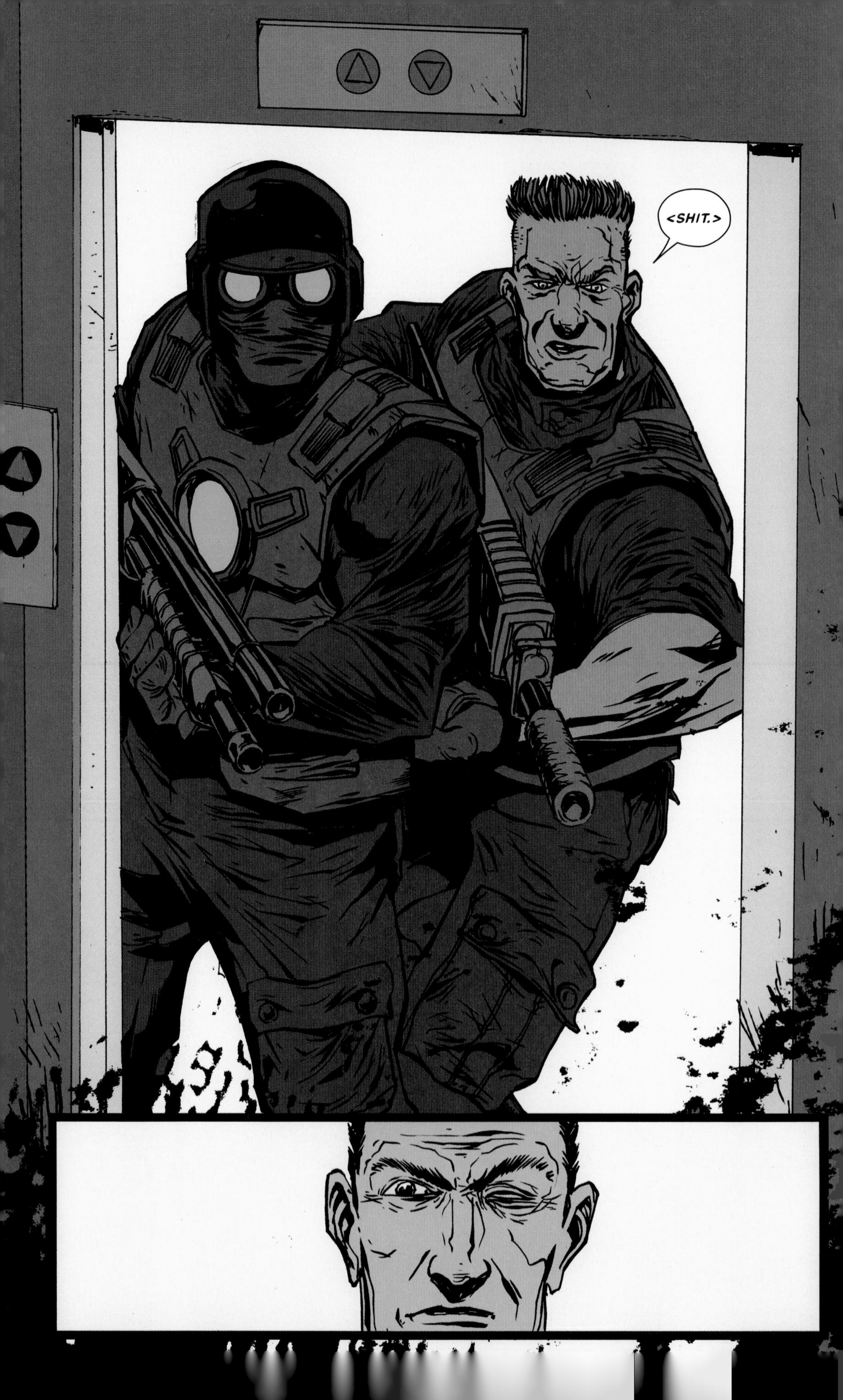
<SHIT.>

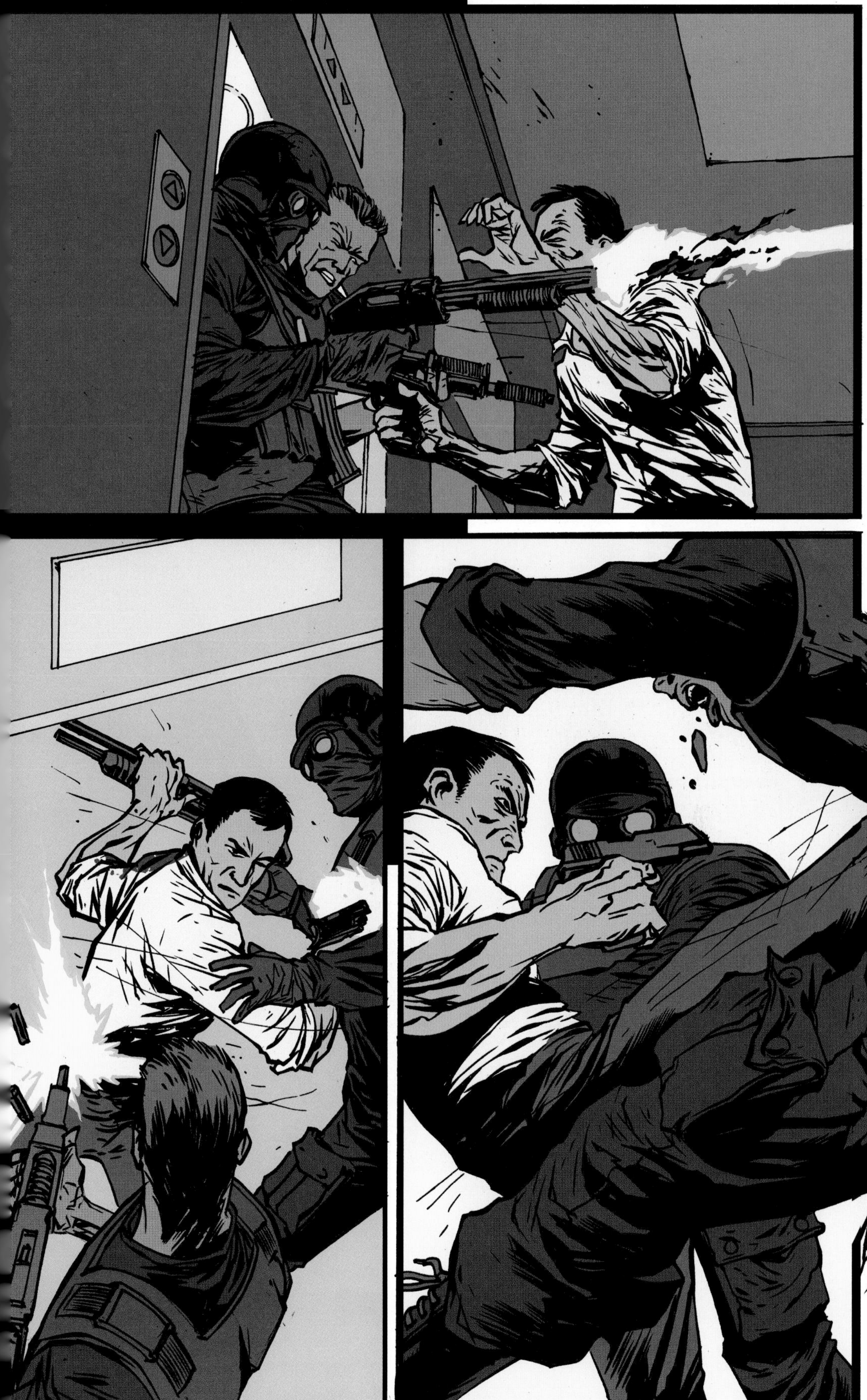

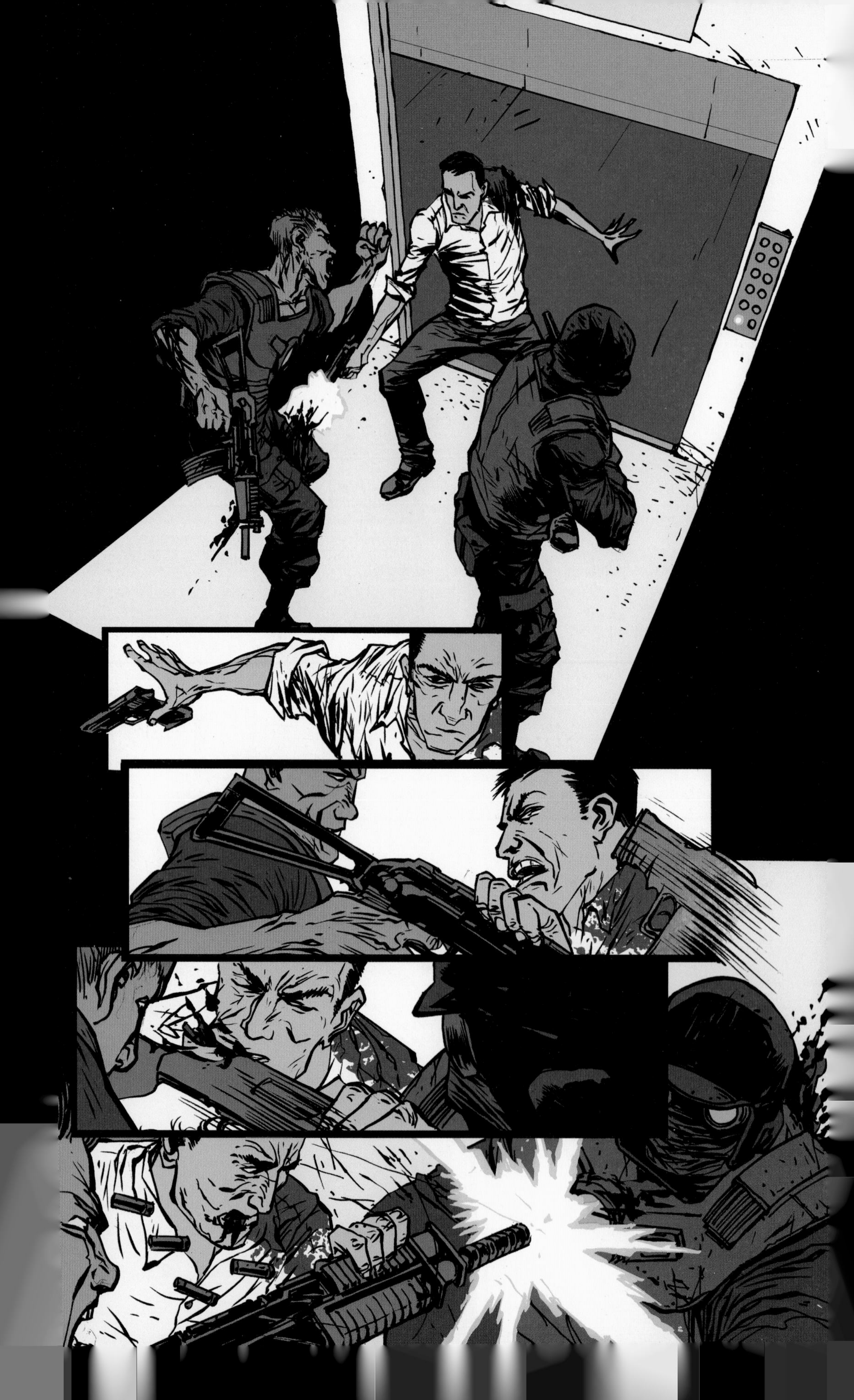

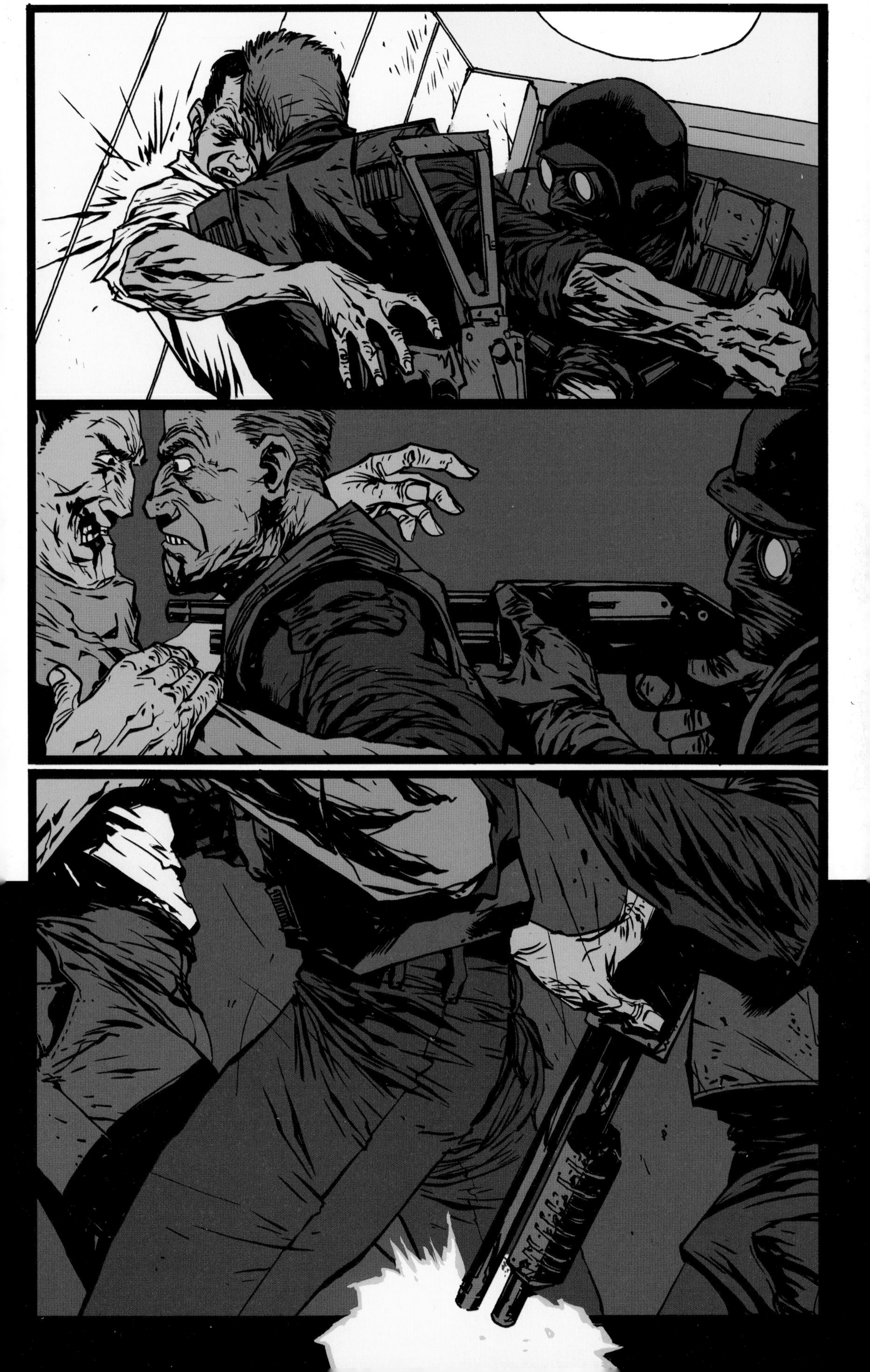

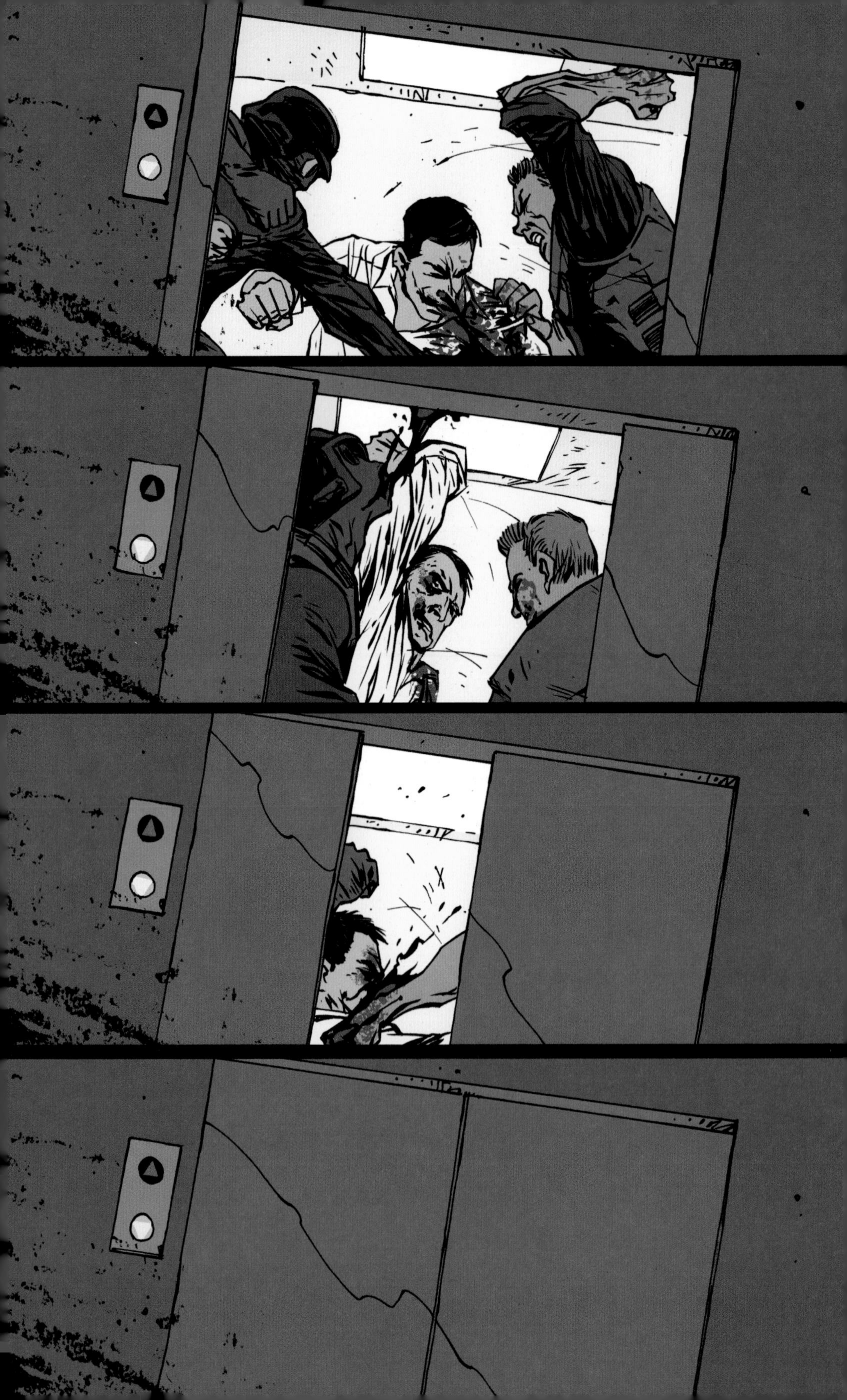

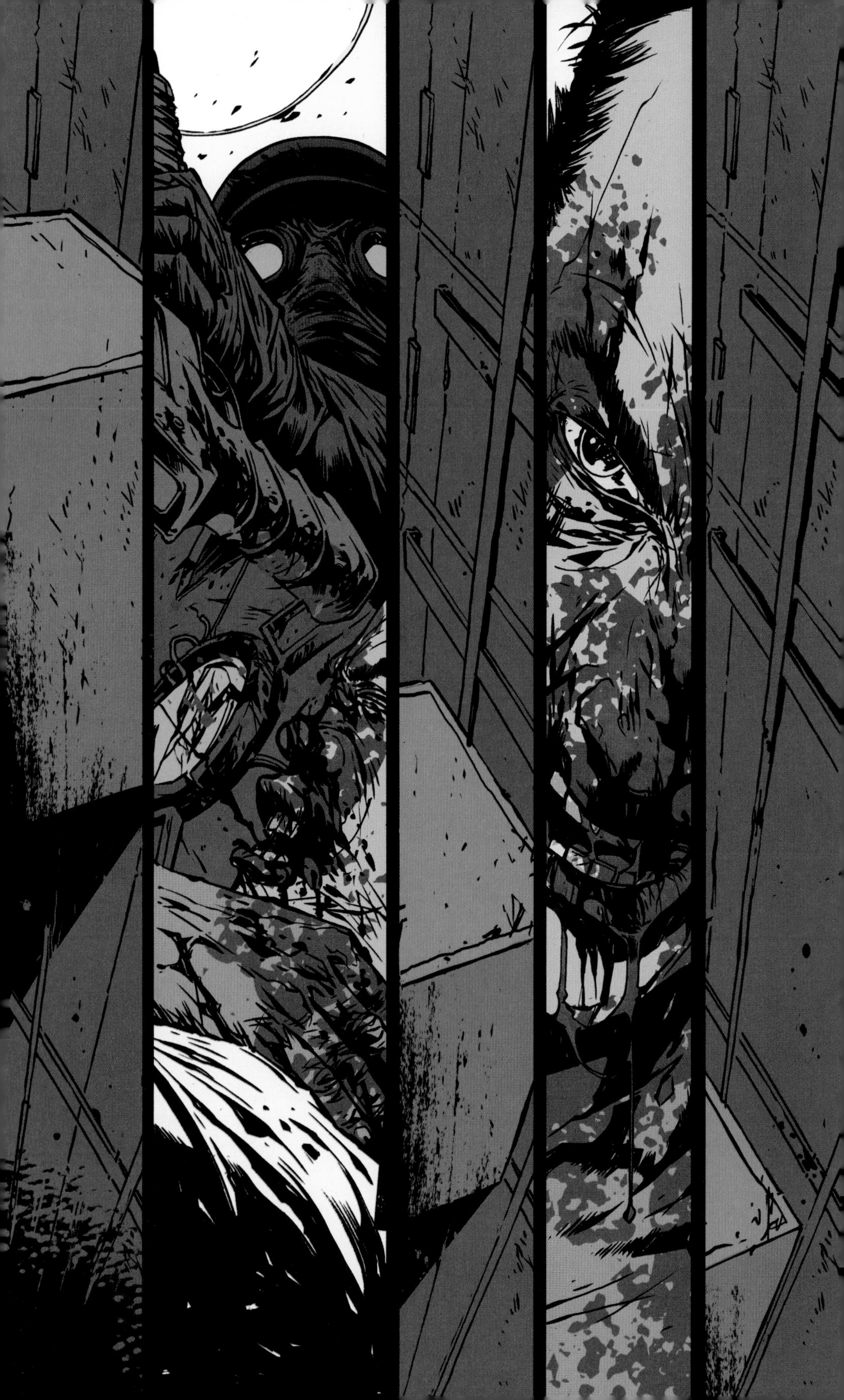

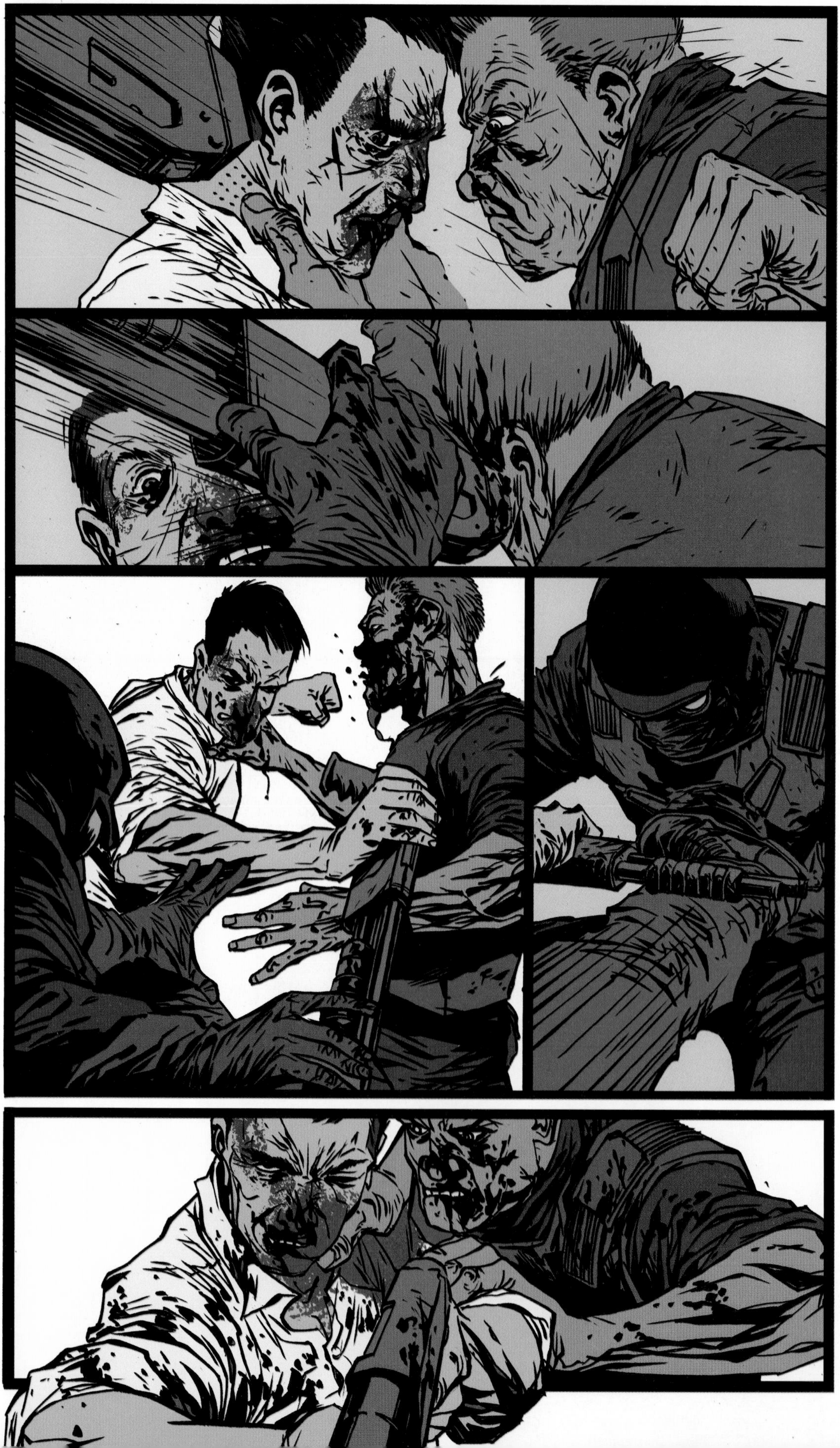

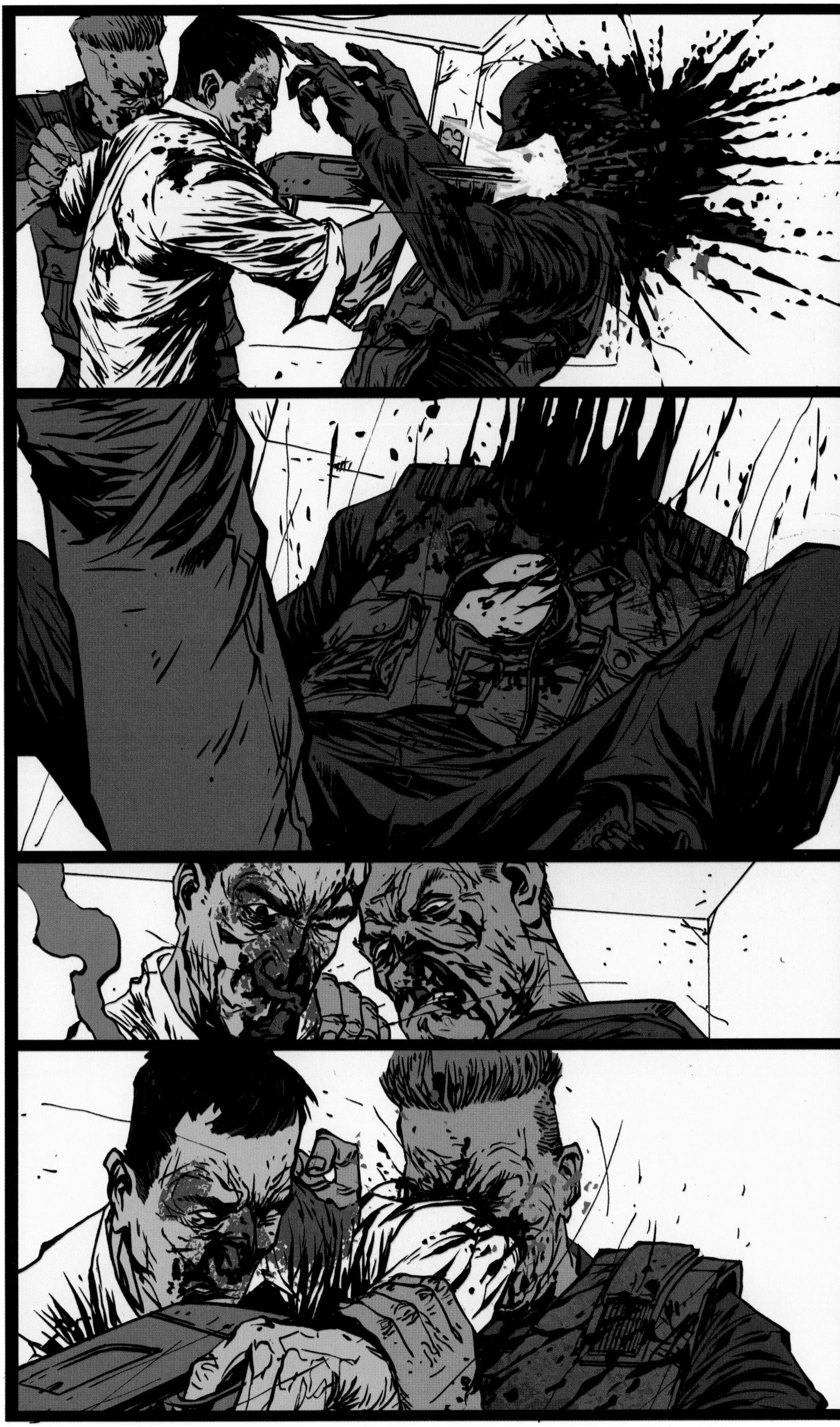

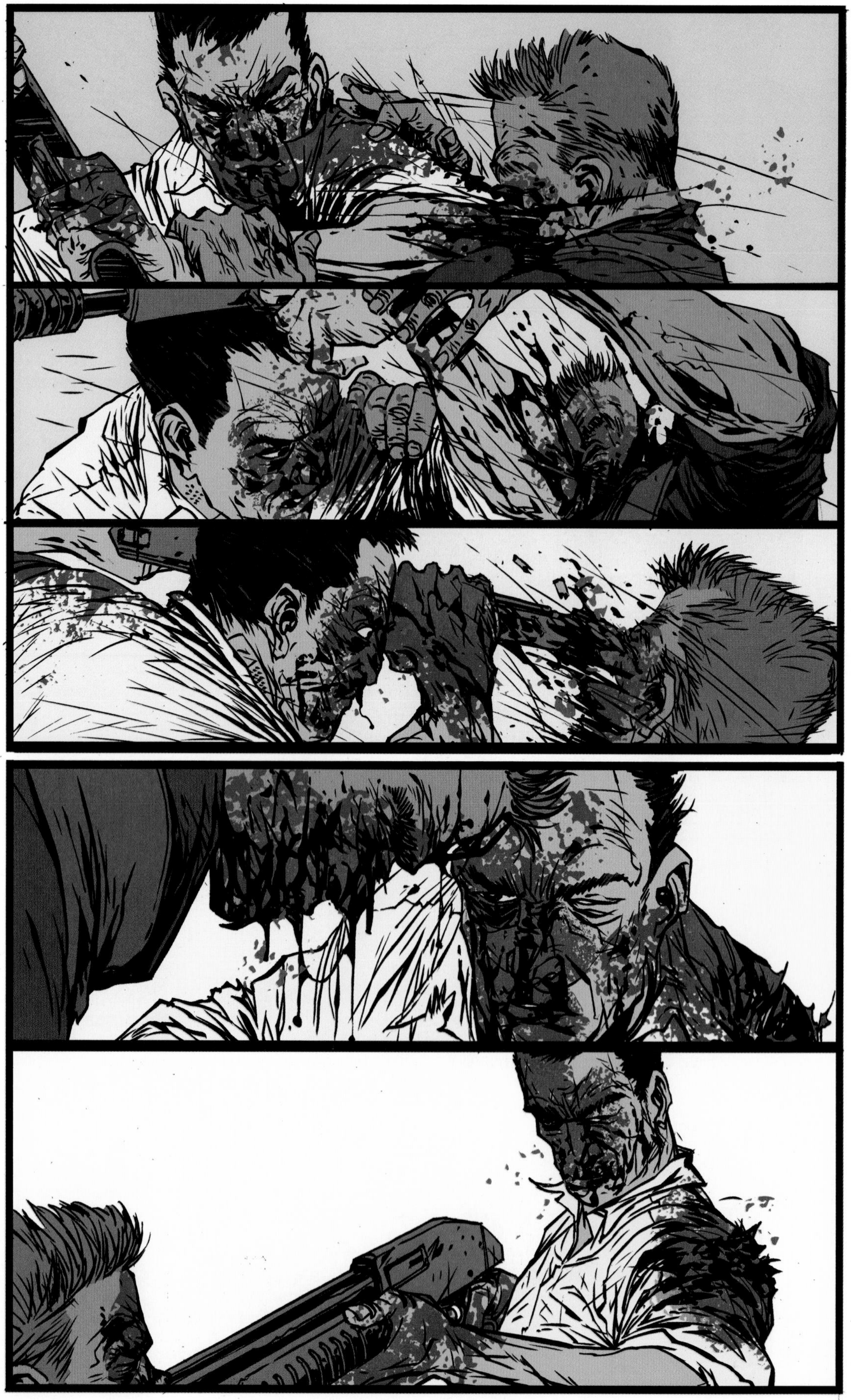

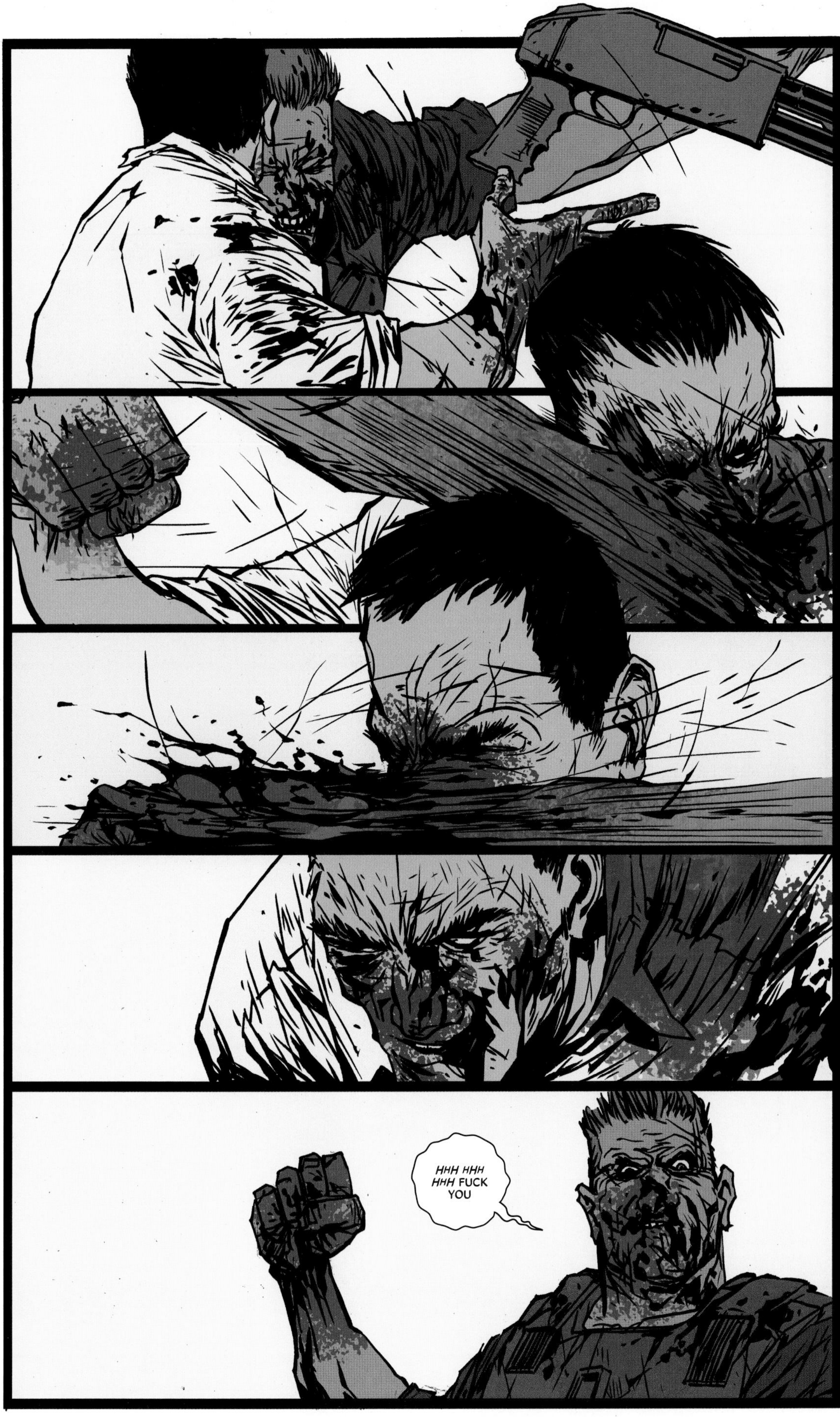
HHH HHH HHH FUCK YOU

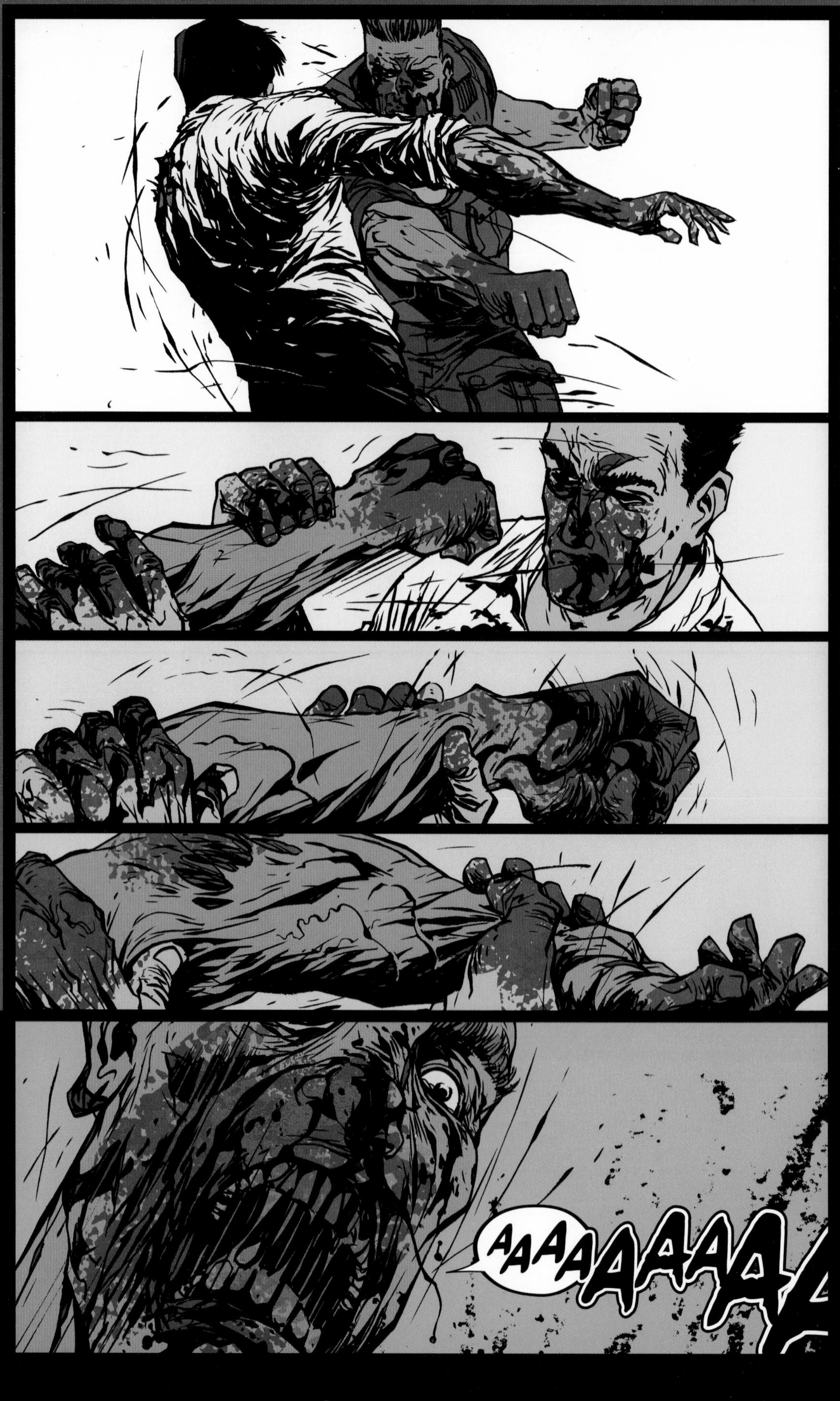
AAAAAAAA

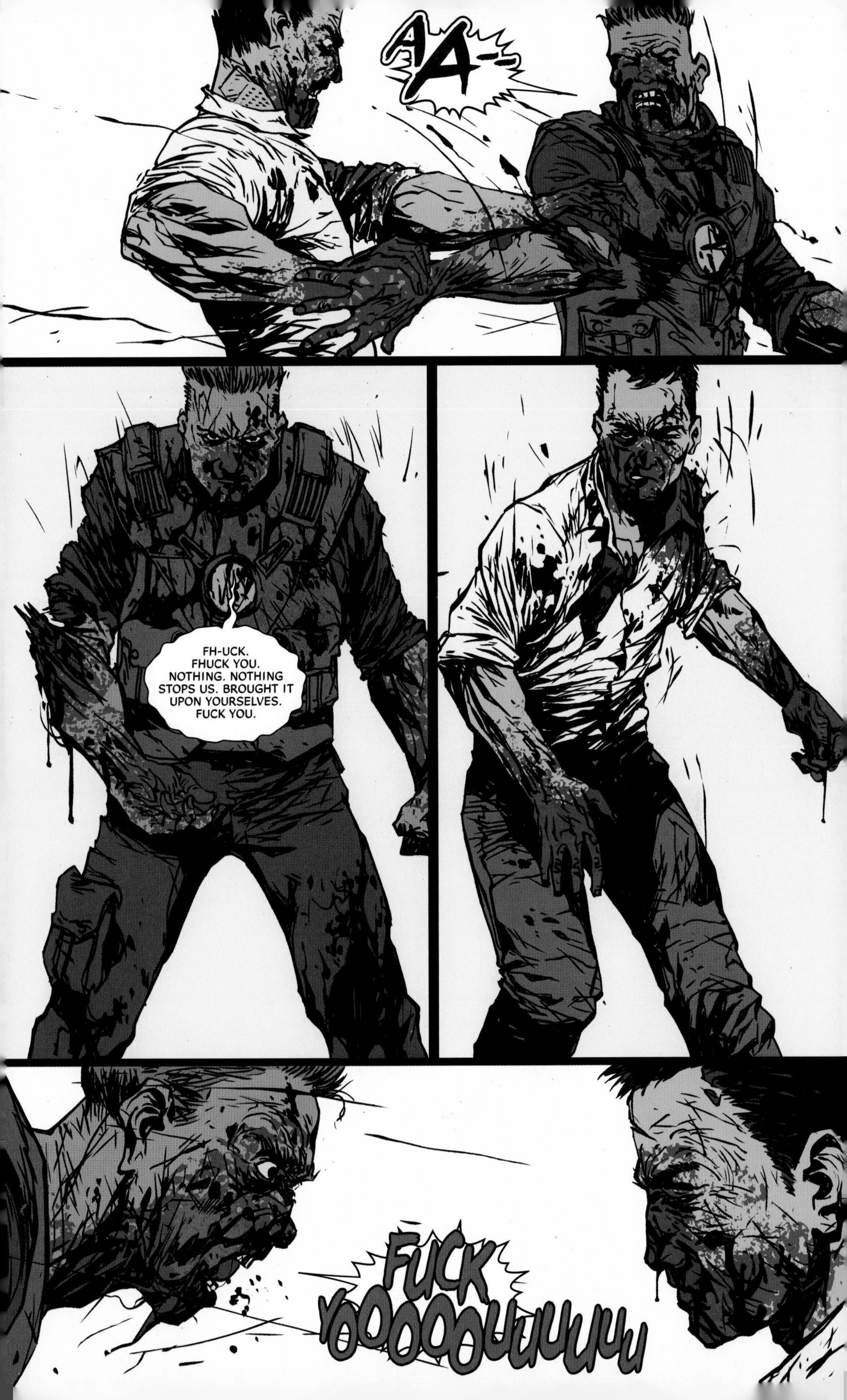
AA-
FH-UCK. FHUCK YOU. NOTHING. NOTHING STOPS US. BROUGHT IT UPON YOURSELVES. FUCK YOU.
FUCK YOOOOOUUUUUU

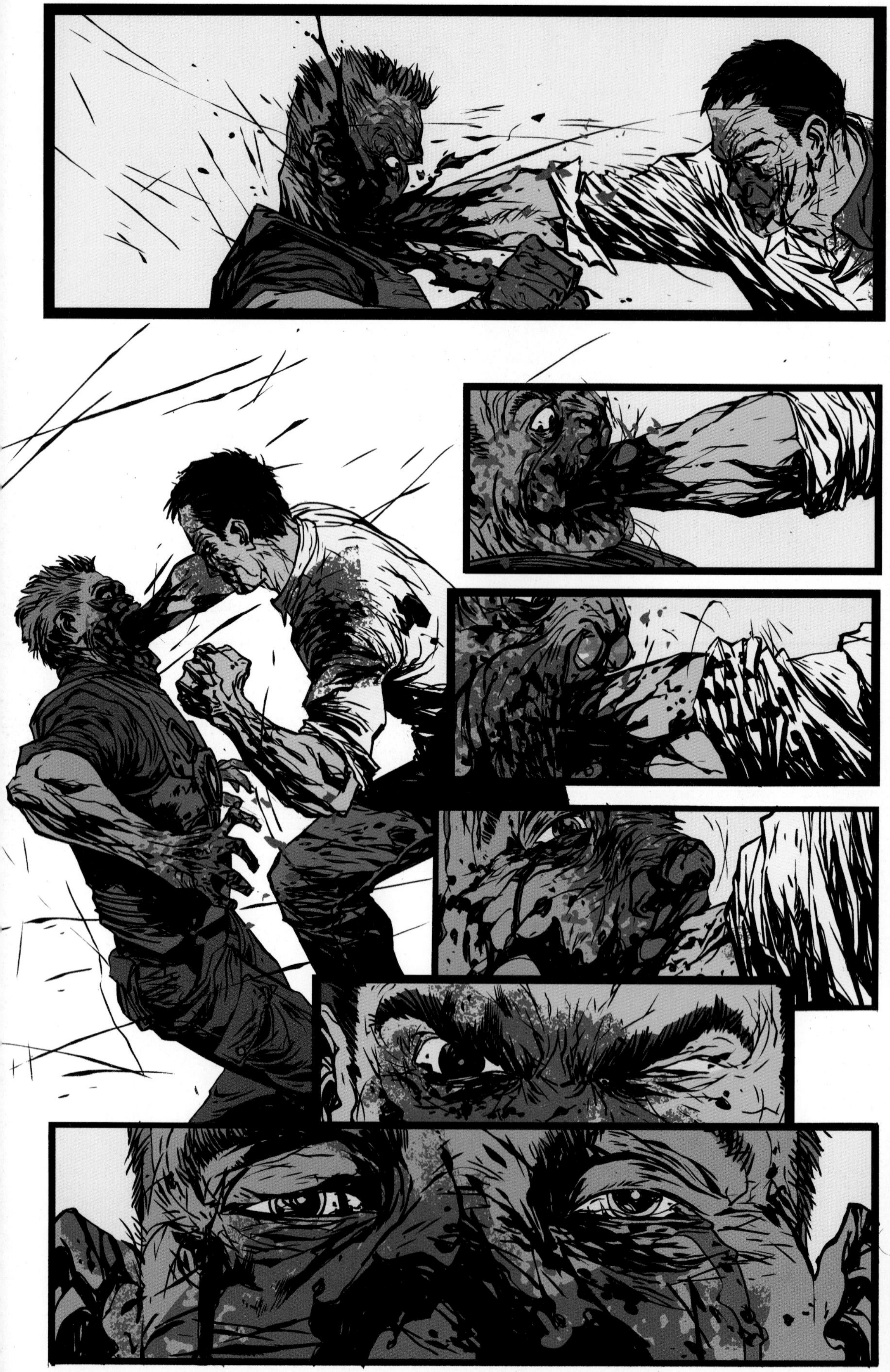

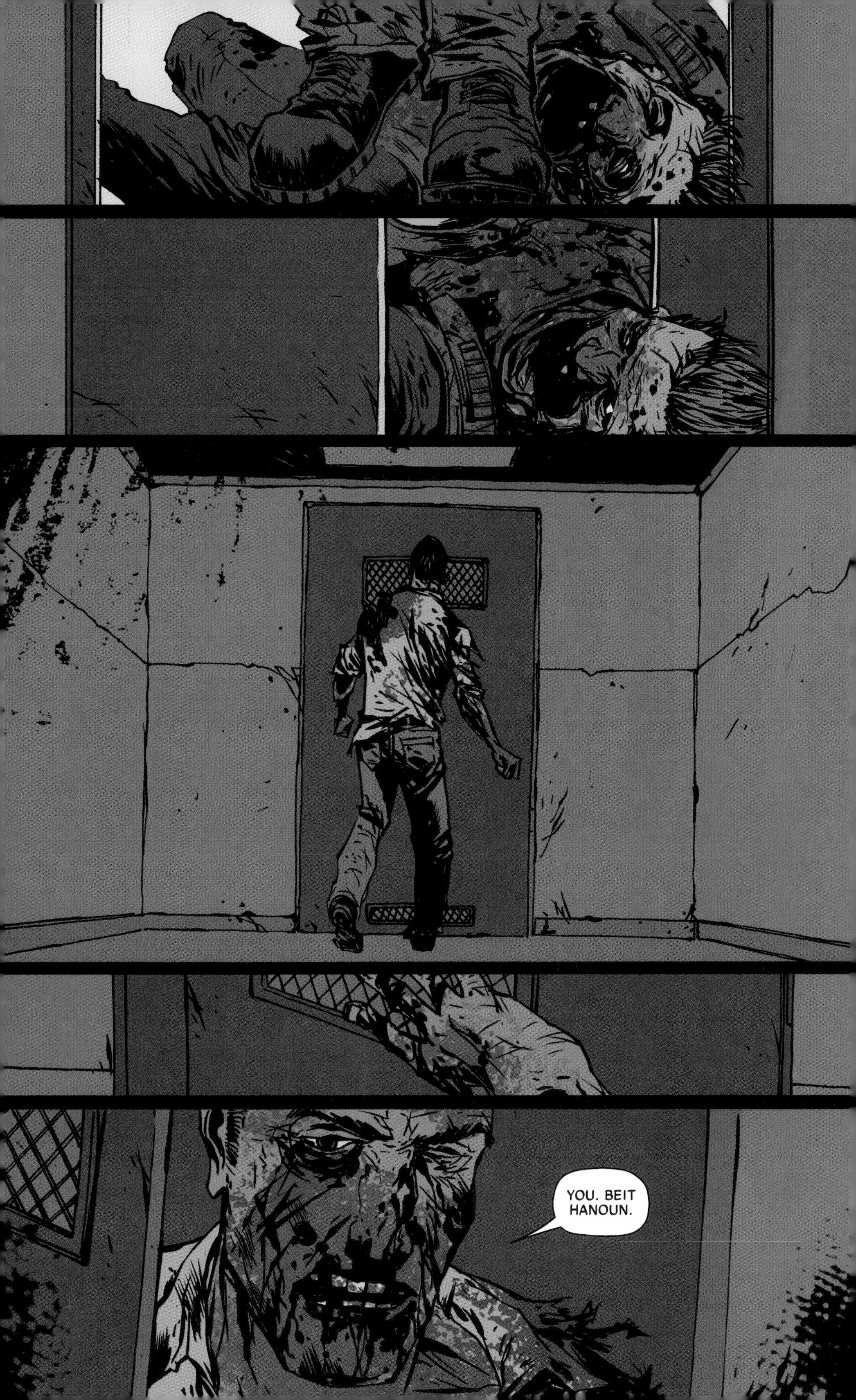
YOU. BEIT HANOUN.

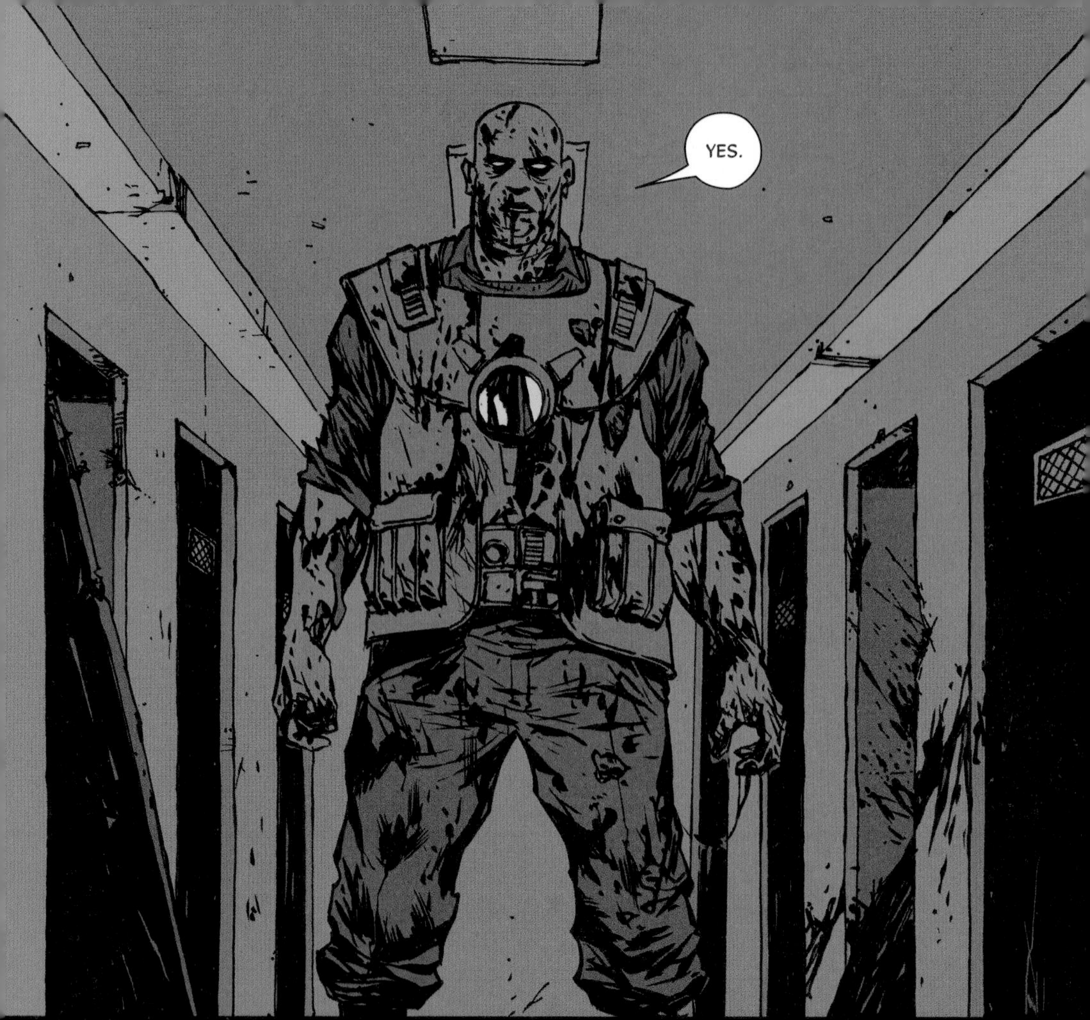
YES.

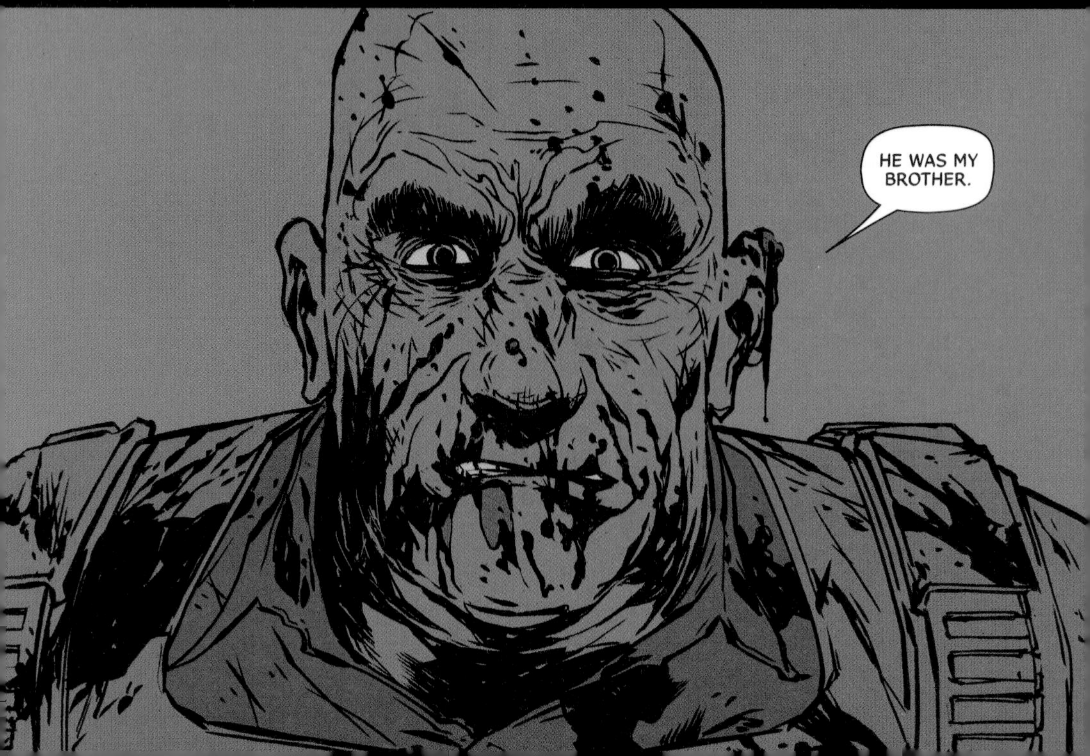
HE WAS MY BROTHER.

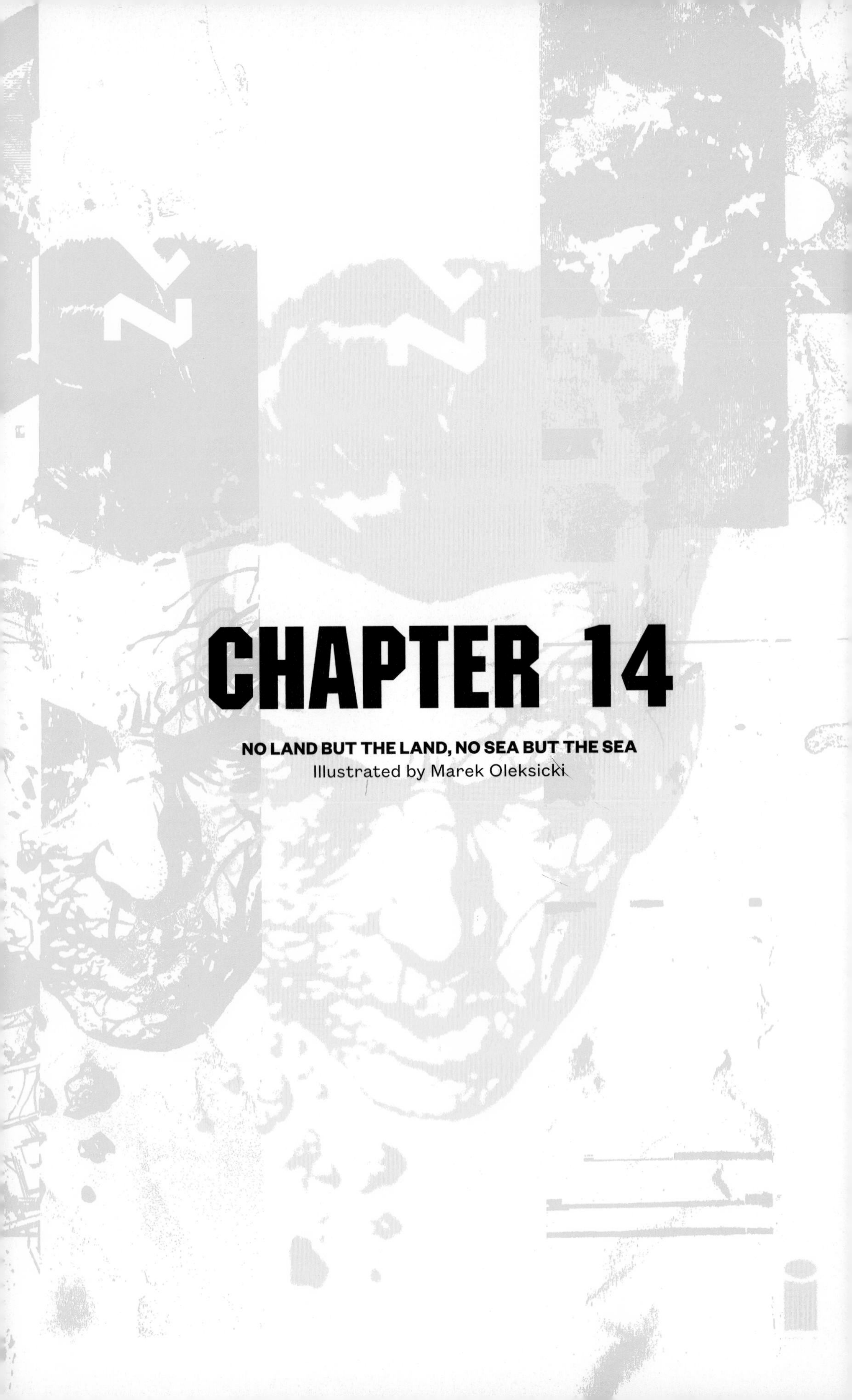

CHAPTER 14

NO LAND BUT THE LAND, NO SEA BUT THE SEA

Illustrated by Marek Oleksicki

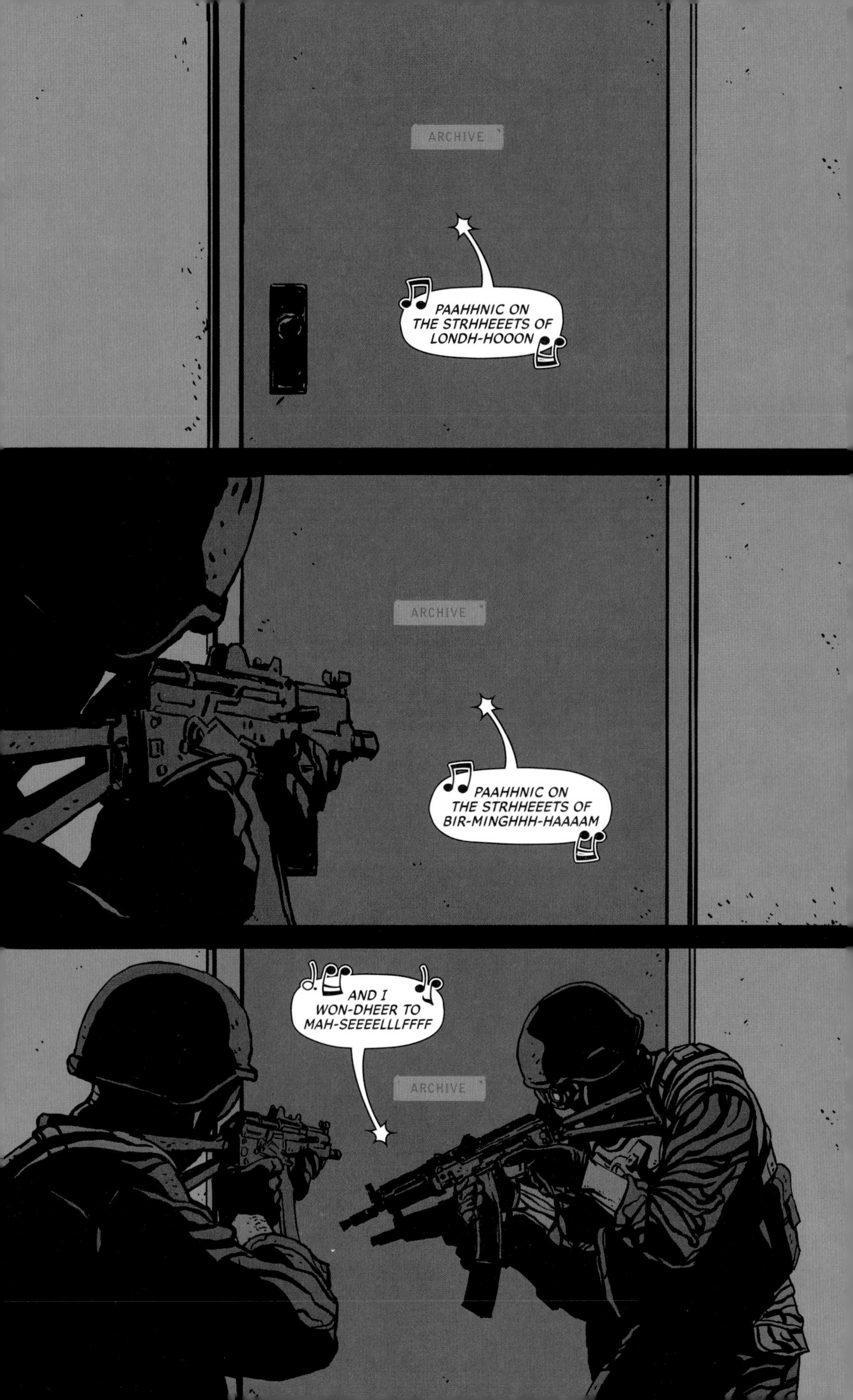
ARCHIVE
PAAHHNIC ON THE STRHHEEETS OF LONDH-HOOON
ARCHIVE
PAAHHNIC ON THE STRHHEEETS OF BIR-MINGHHH-HAAAAM
AND I WON-DHEER TO MAH-SEEEELLLFFFF
ARCHIVE

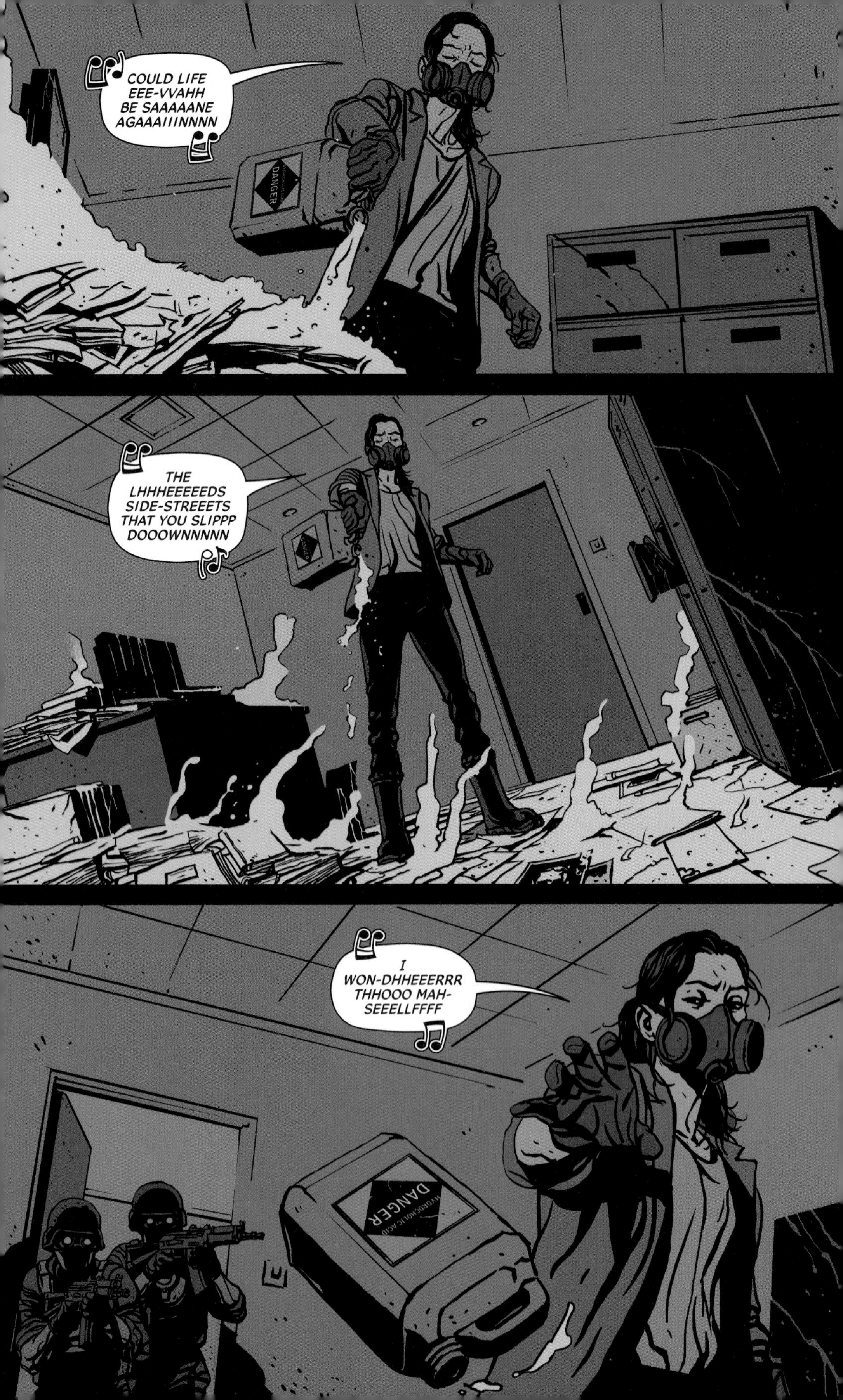
COULD LIFE EEE-VVAHH BE SAAAAANE AGAAAIIINNNN
DANGER
THE LHHHEEEEEDS SIDE-STREEETS THAT YOU SLIPPP DOOOWNNNNN
I WON-DHHEEERRR THHOOO MAH-SEEELLFFFF
DANGER
HYDROCHOLIC ACID

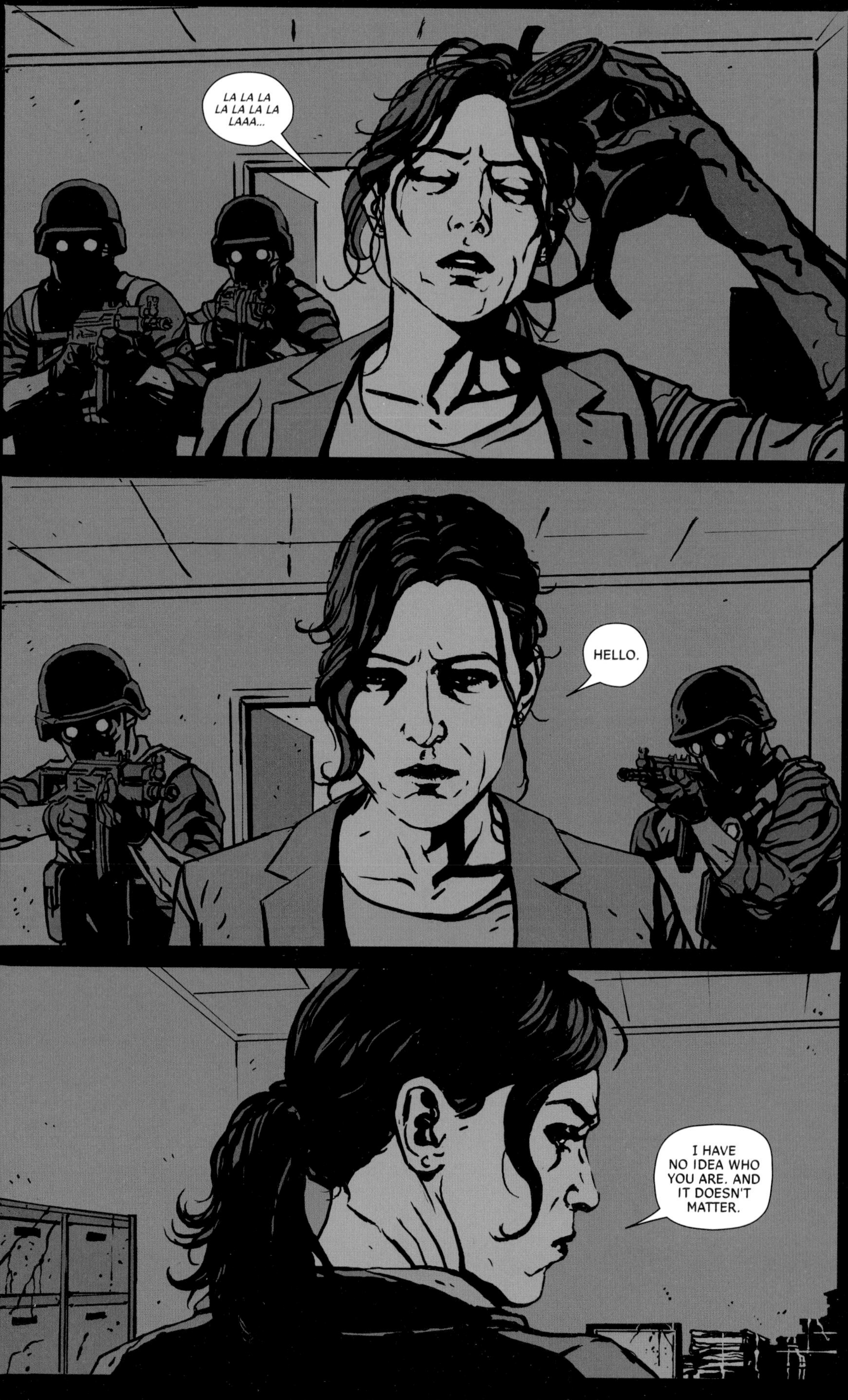
LA LA LA LA LA LA LA LAAA...
HELLO.
I HAVE NO IDEA WHO YOU ARE. AND IT DOESN'T MATTER.

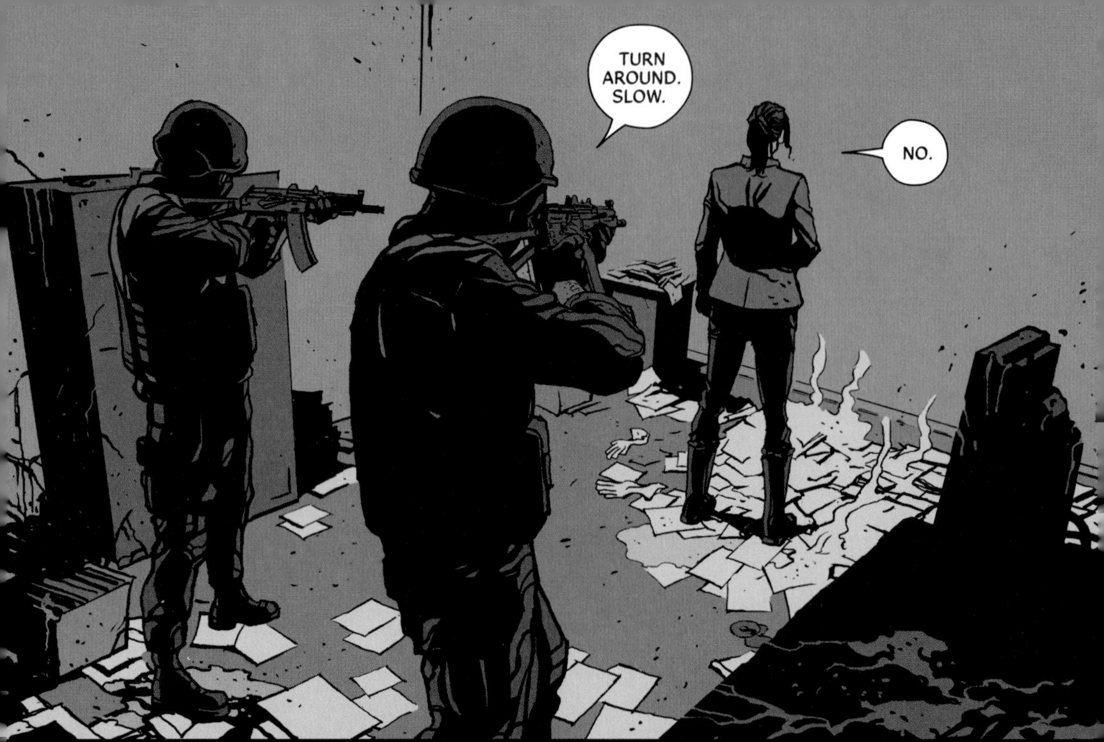
TURN AROUND. SLOW.
NO.

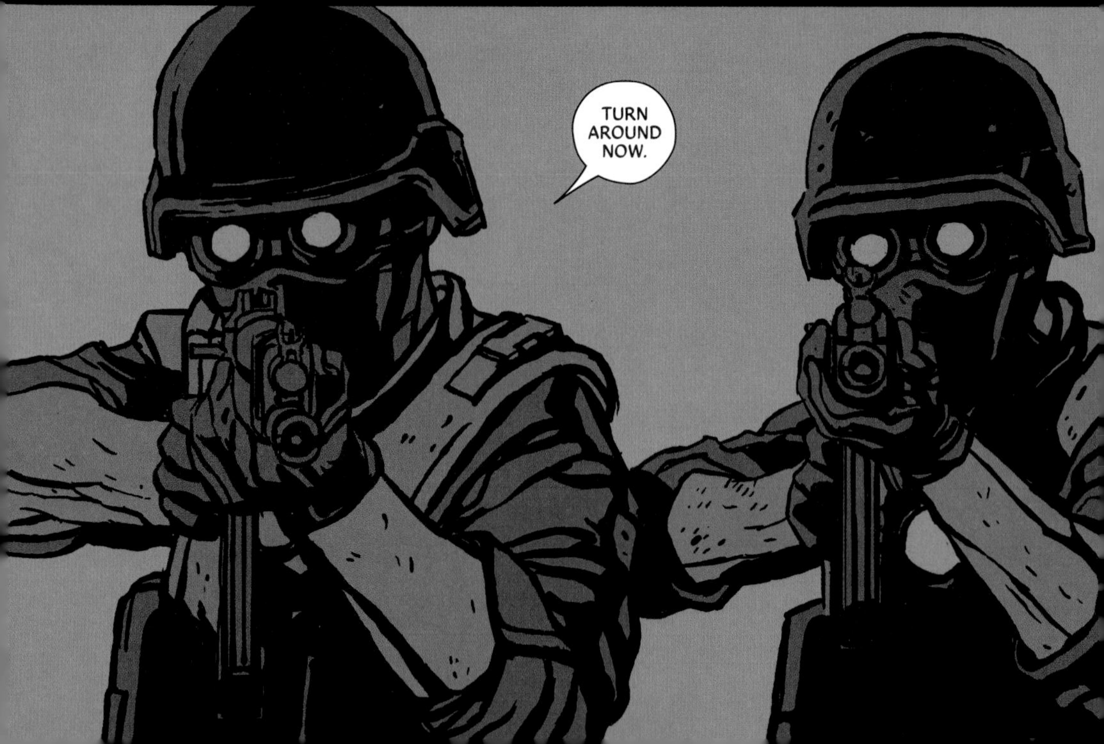
TURN AROUND NOW.

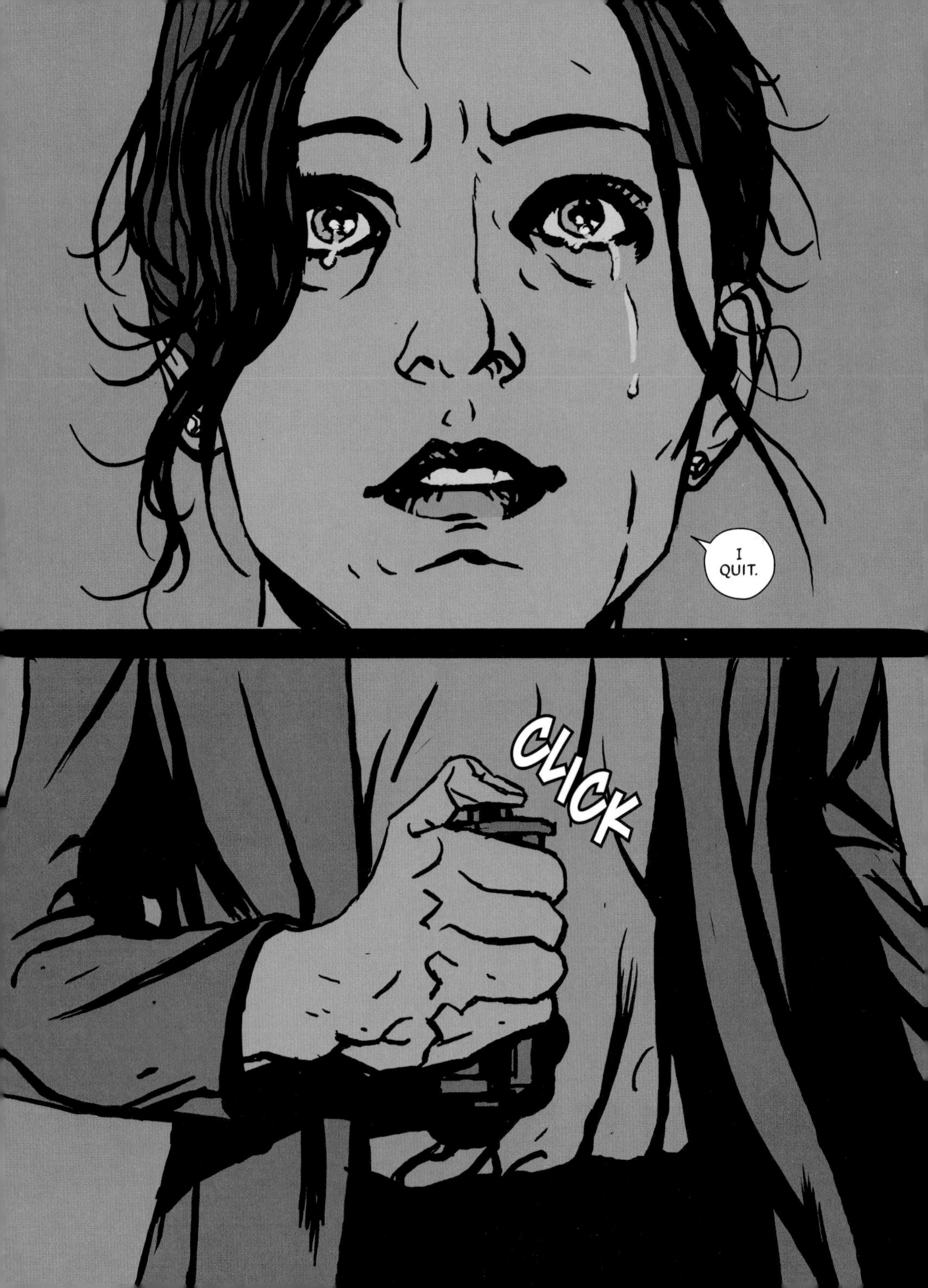
I QUIT.
CLICK

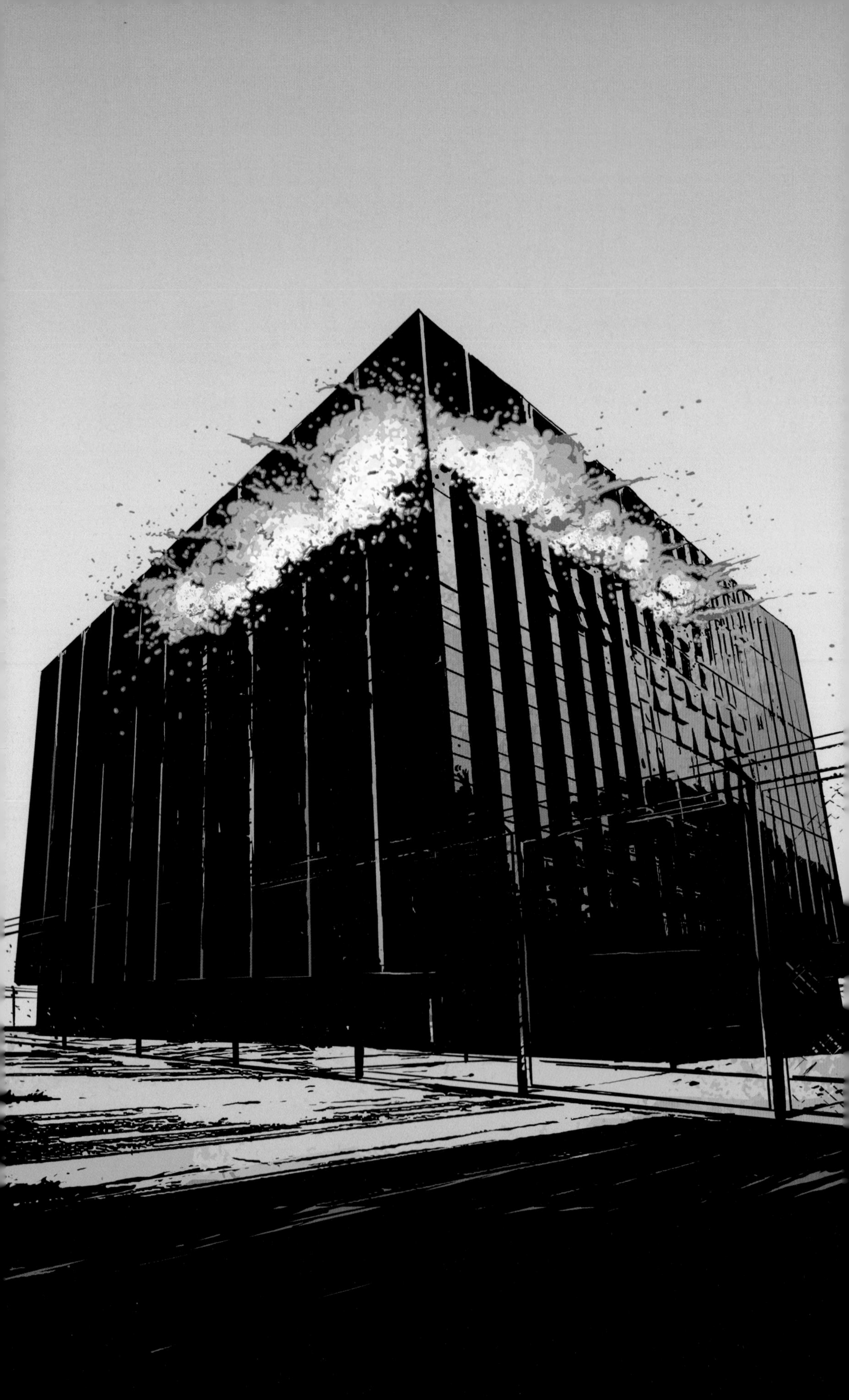

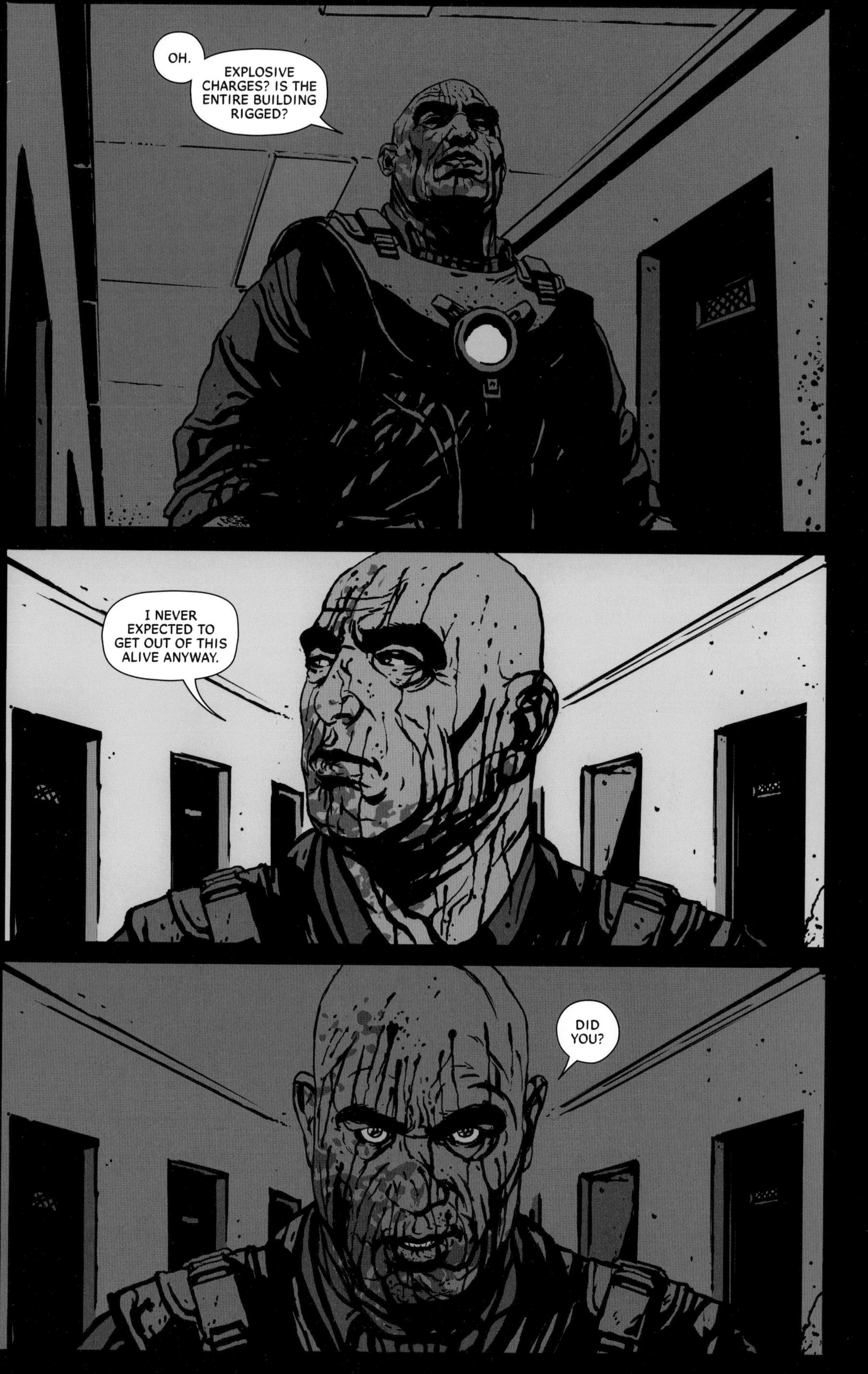
OH.
EXPLOSIVE CHARGES? IS THE ENTIRE BUILDING RIGGED?
I NEVER EXPECTED TO GET OUT OF THIS ALIVE ANYWAY.
DID YOU?

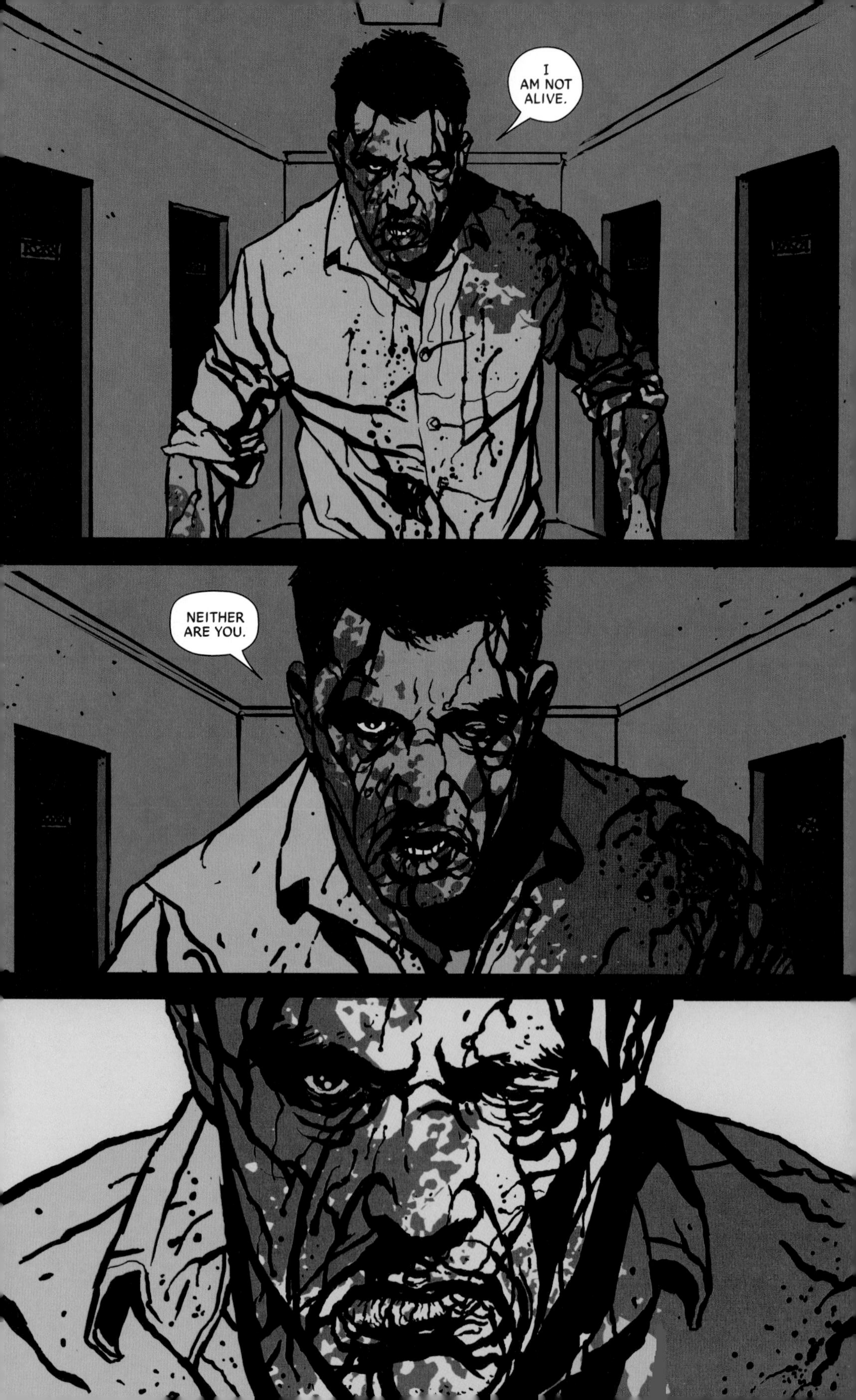
I AM NOT ALIVE.
NEITHER ARE YOU.

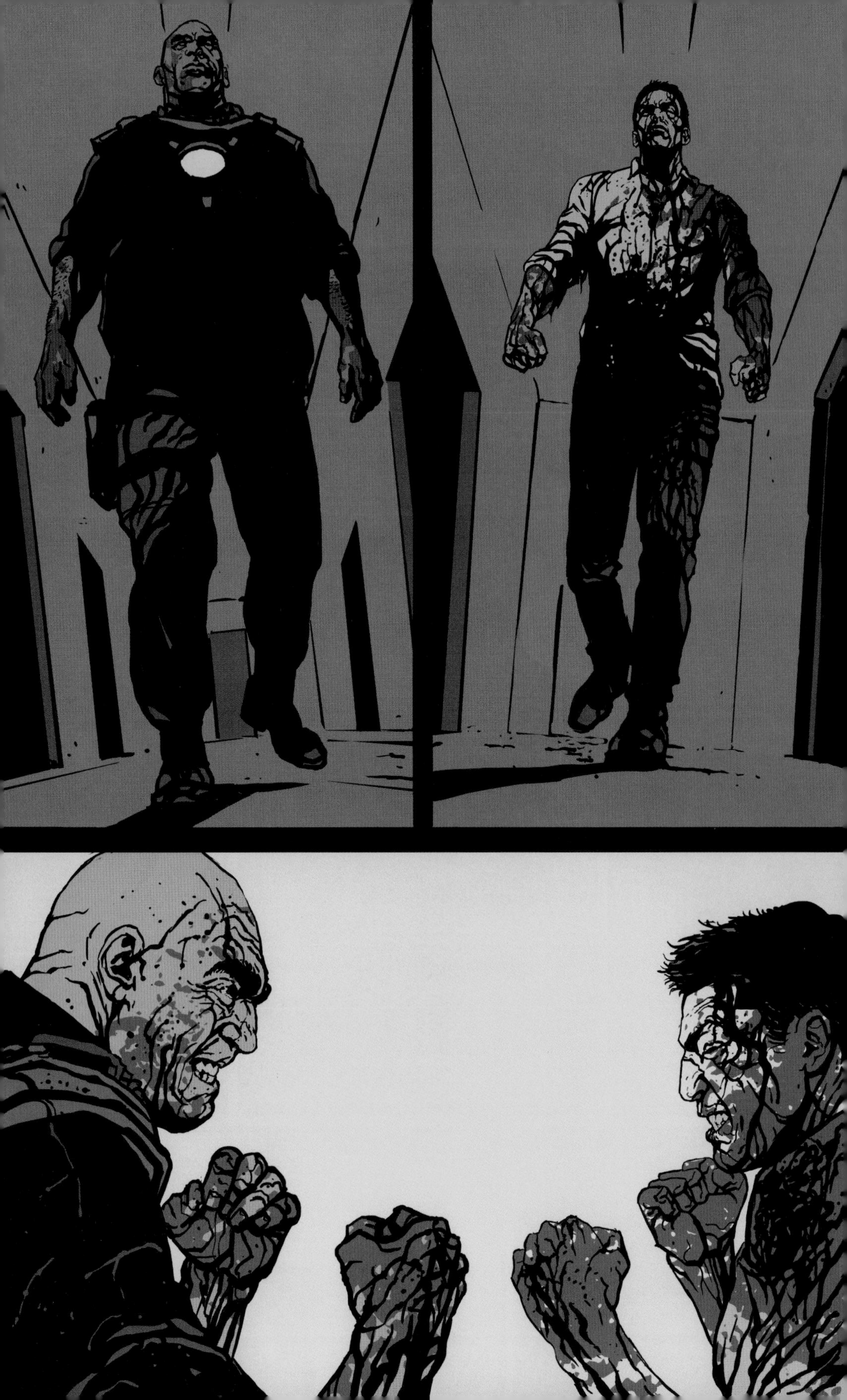

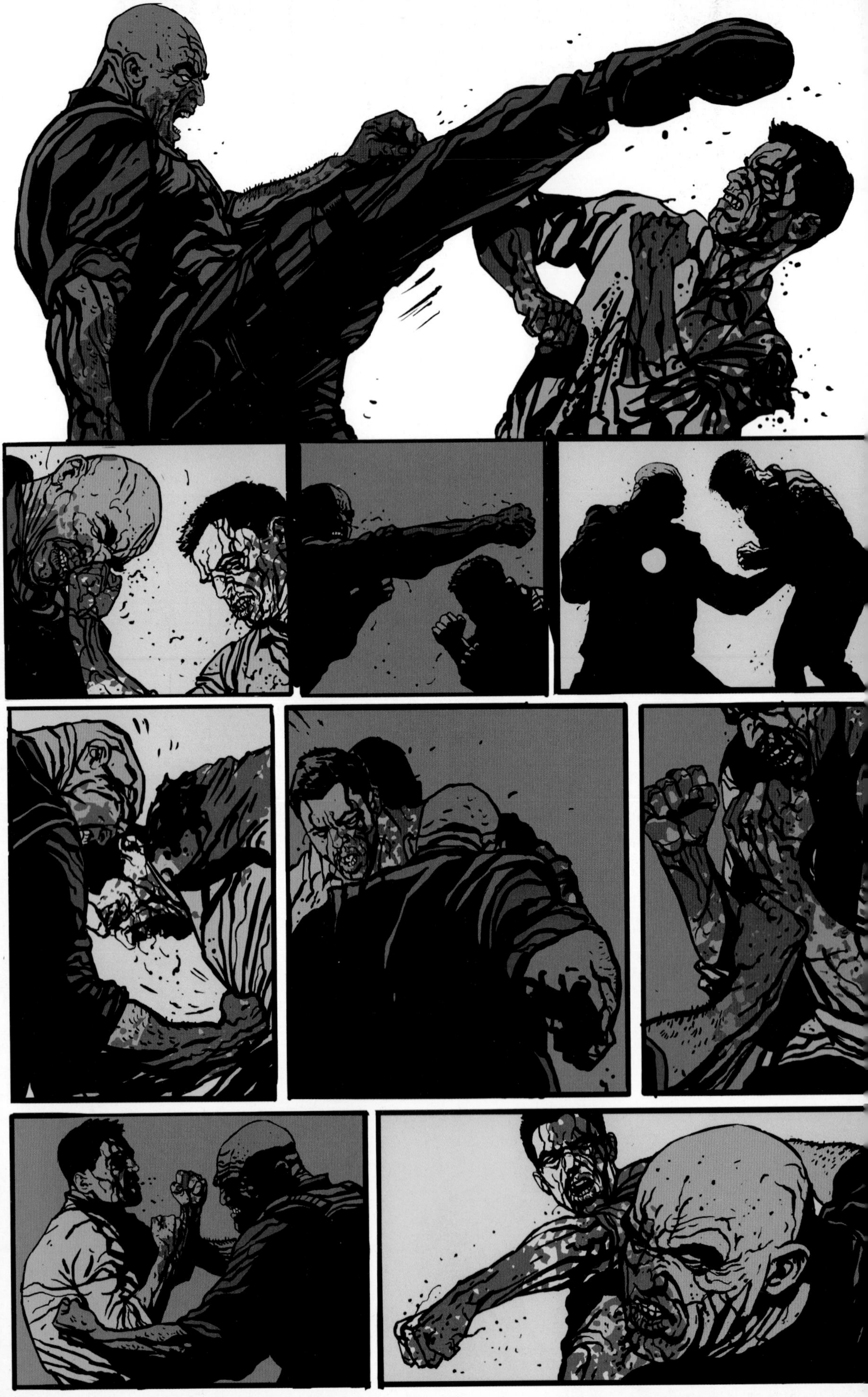

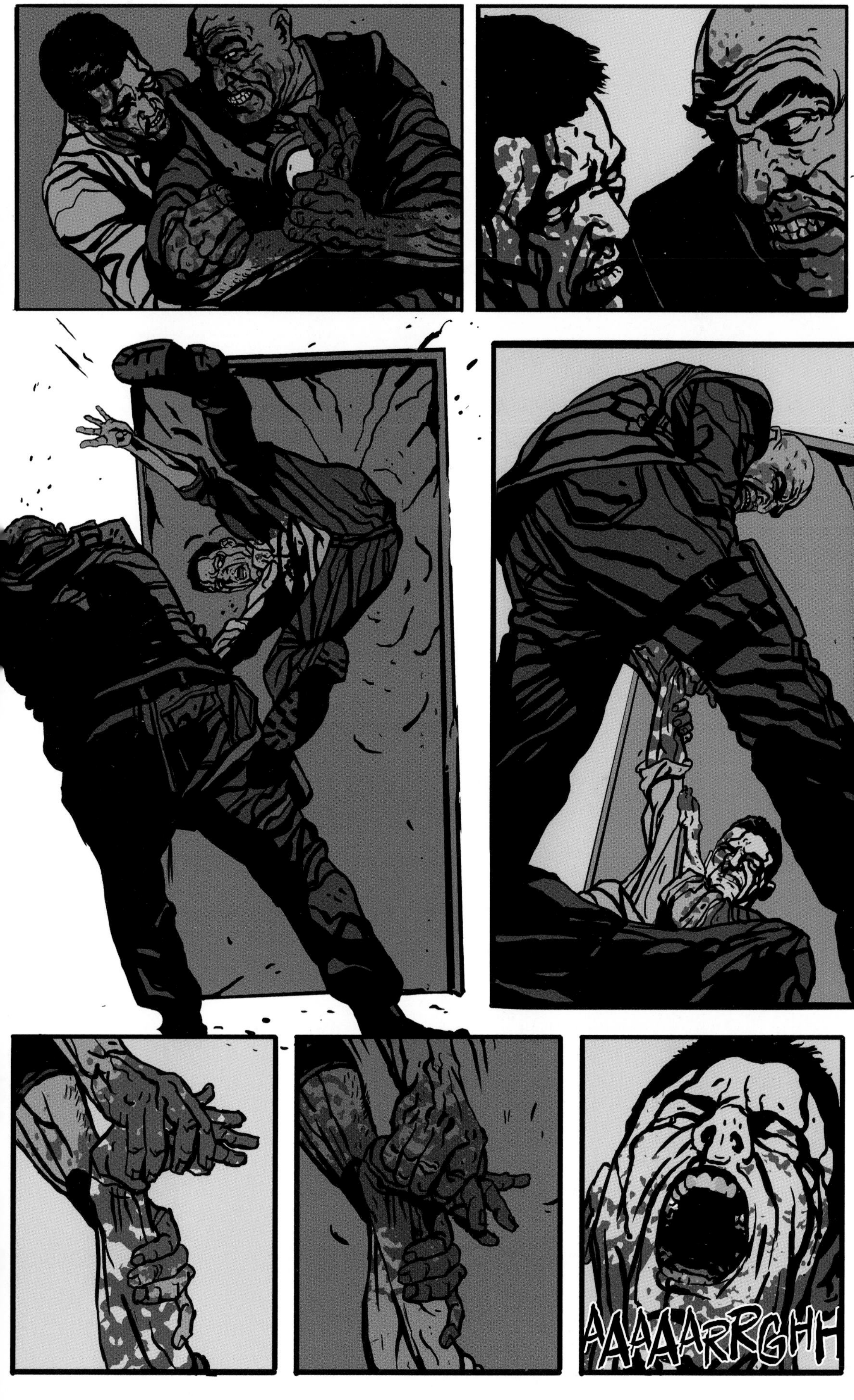
AAAAARRGHH

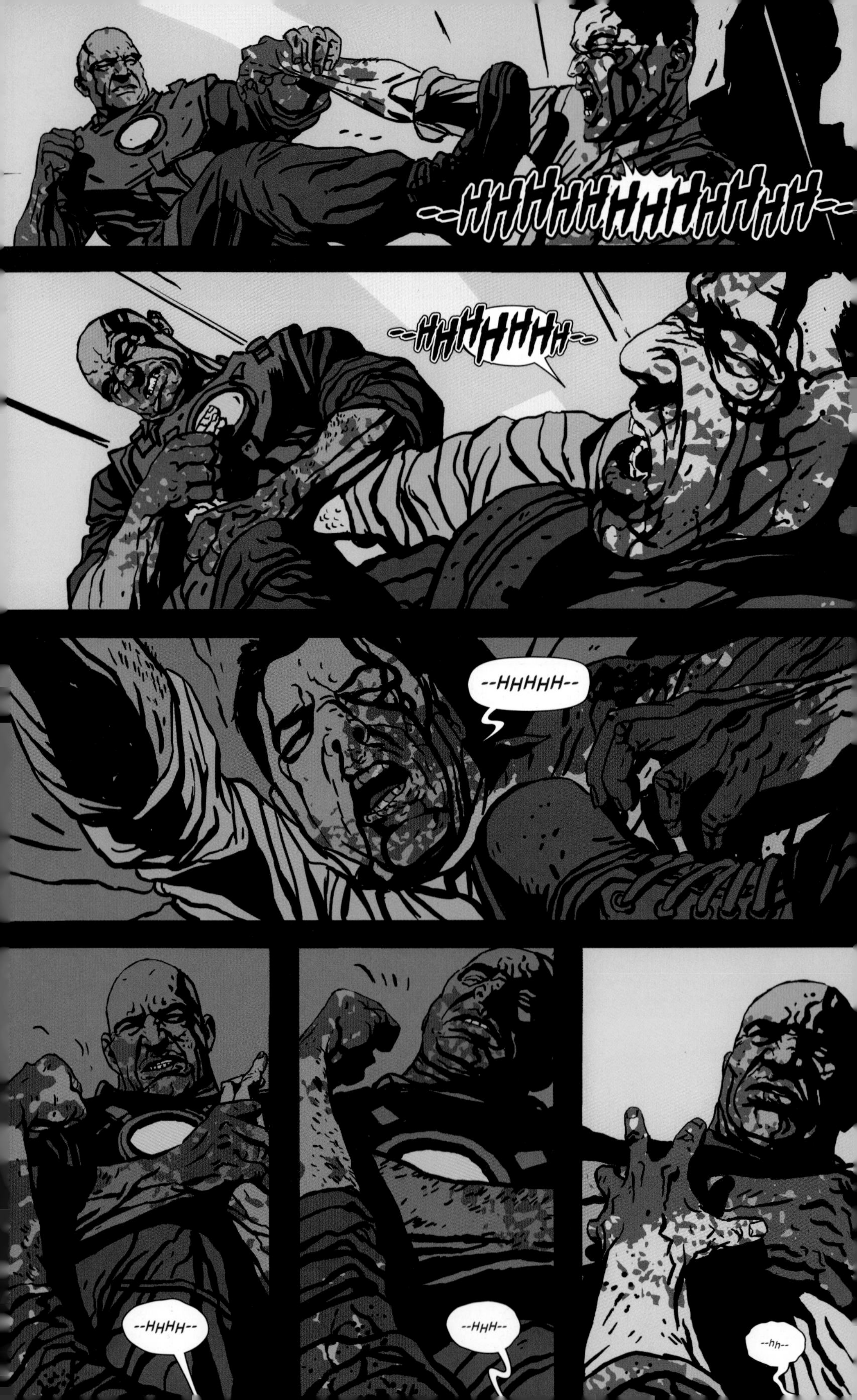
--HHHHHHHHHHHHHHHHH--
--HHHHHHHH--
--HHHHH--
--HHHH--
--HHH--
--hh--

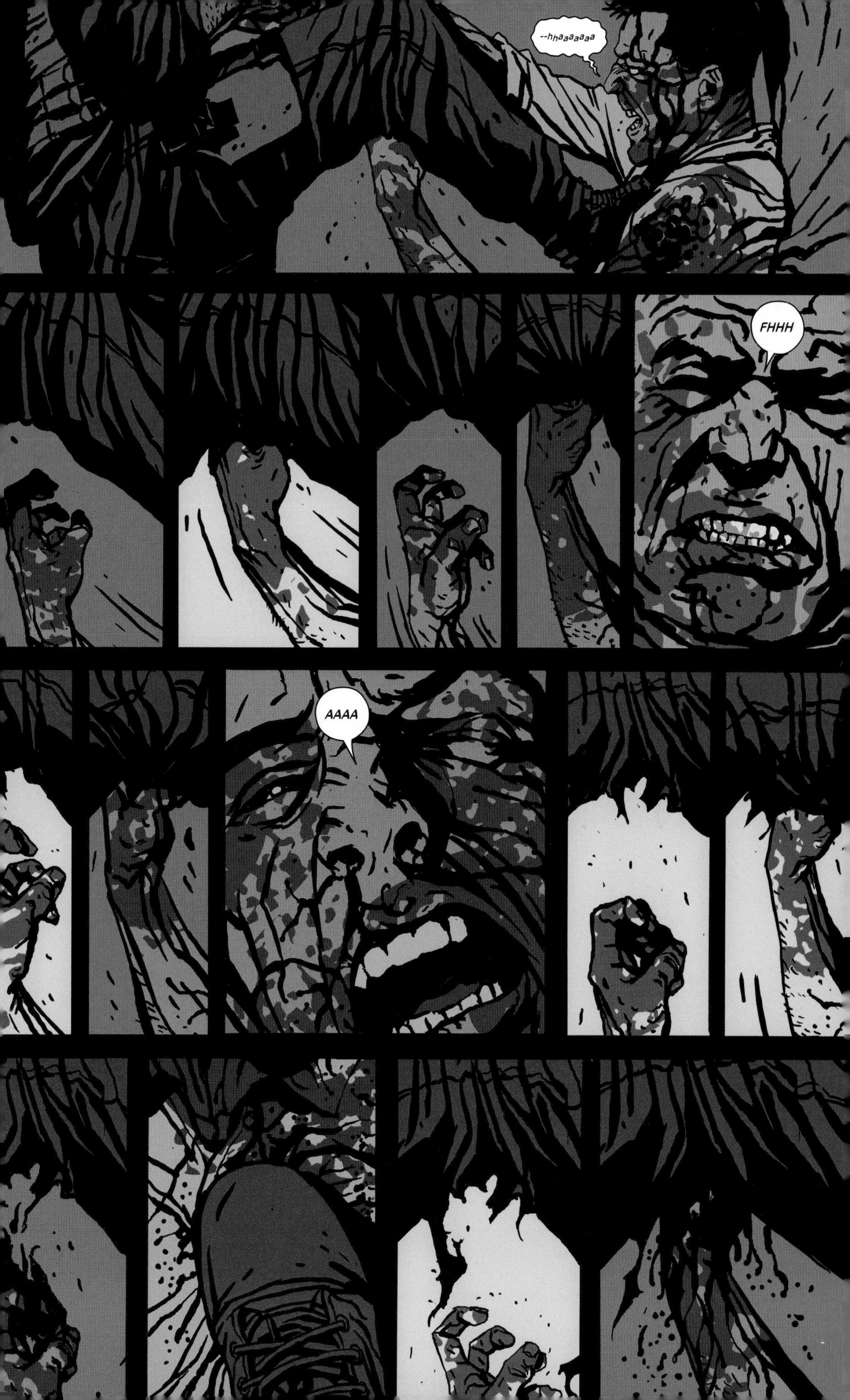
--hhaaaaaaa
FHHH
AAAA

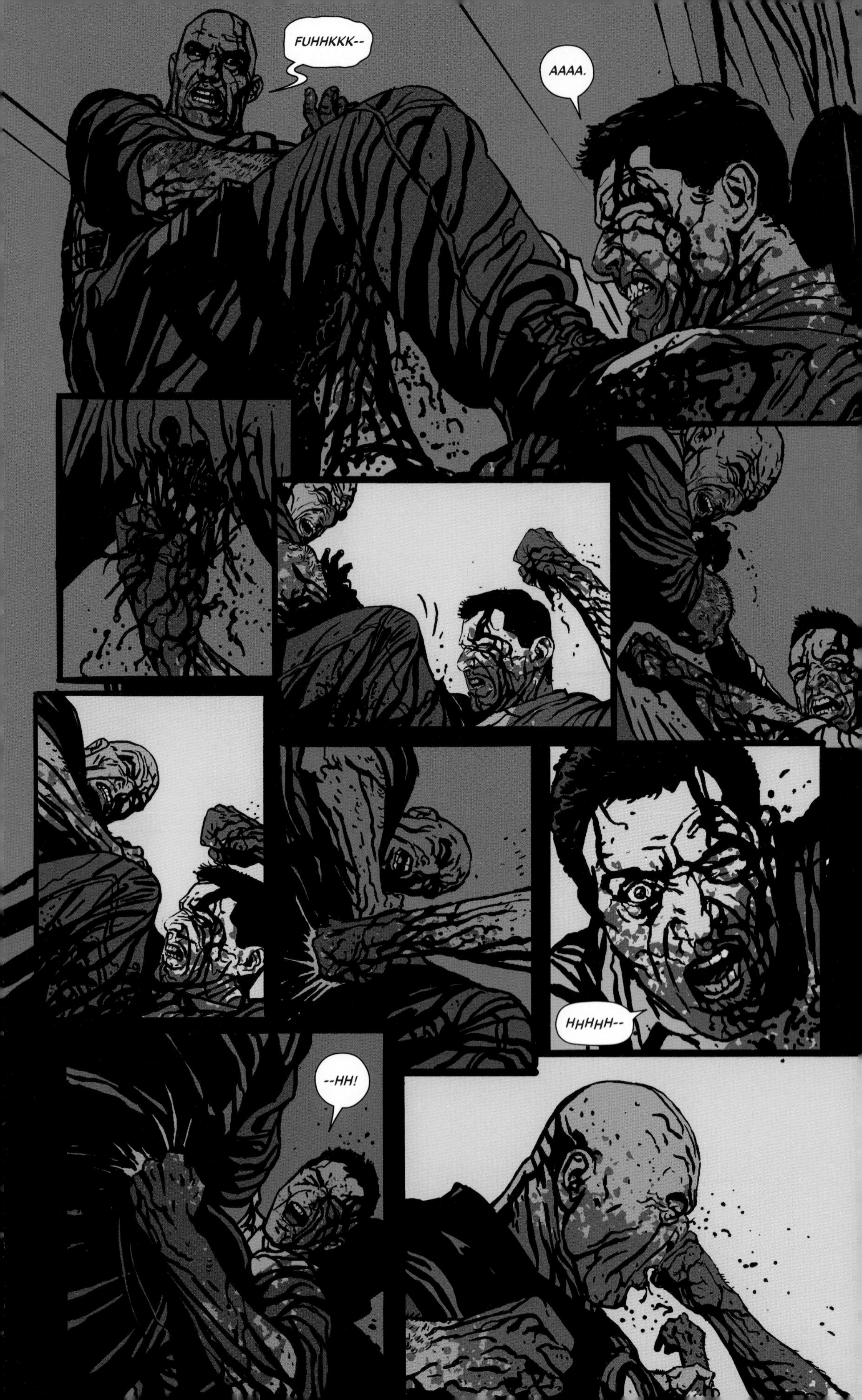
FUHHKKK--
AAAA.
HHHHH--
--HH!

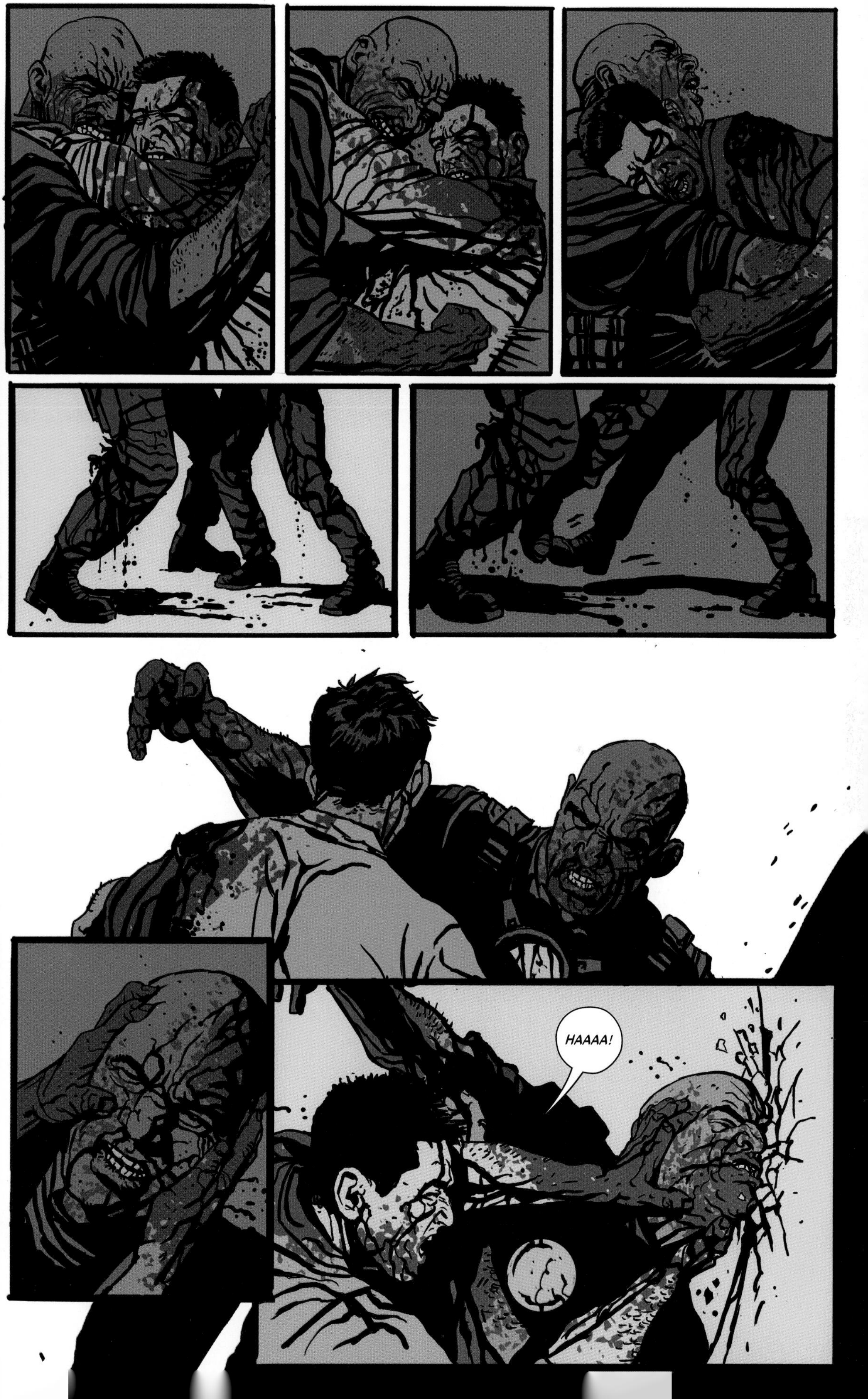
HAAAA!

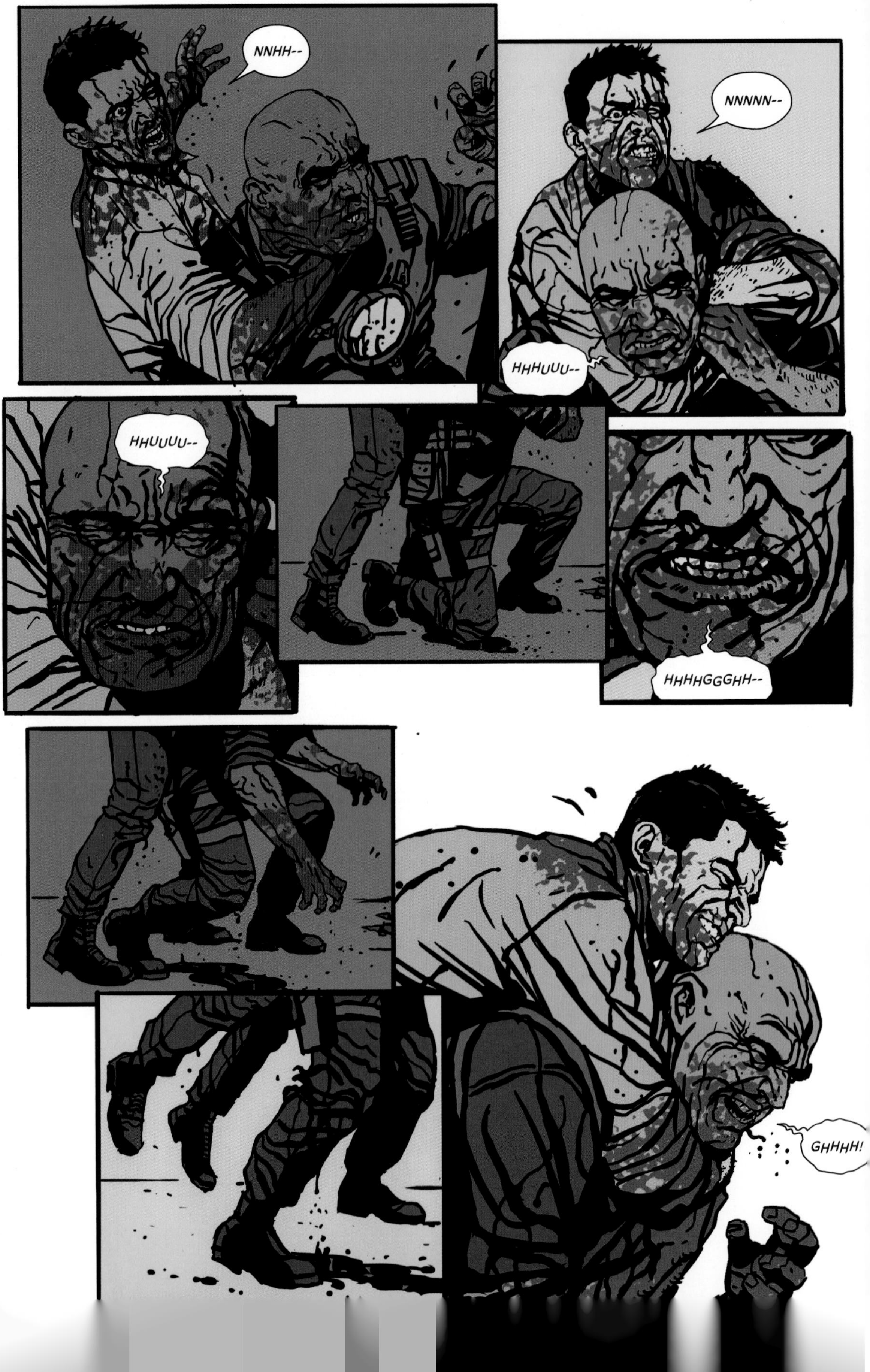
NNHH--
NNNNN--
HHHUUU--
HHUUUU--
HHHHGGGHH--
GHHHH!

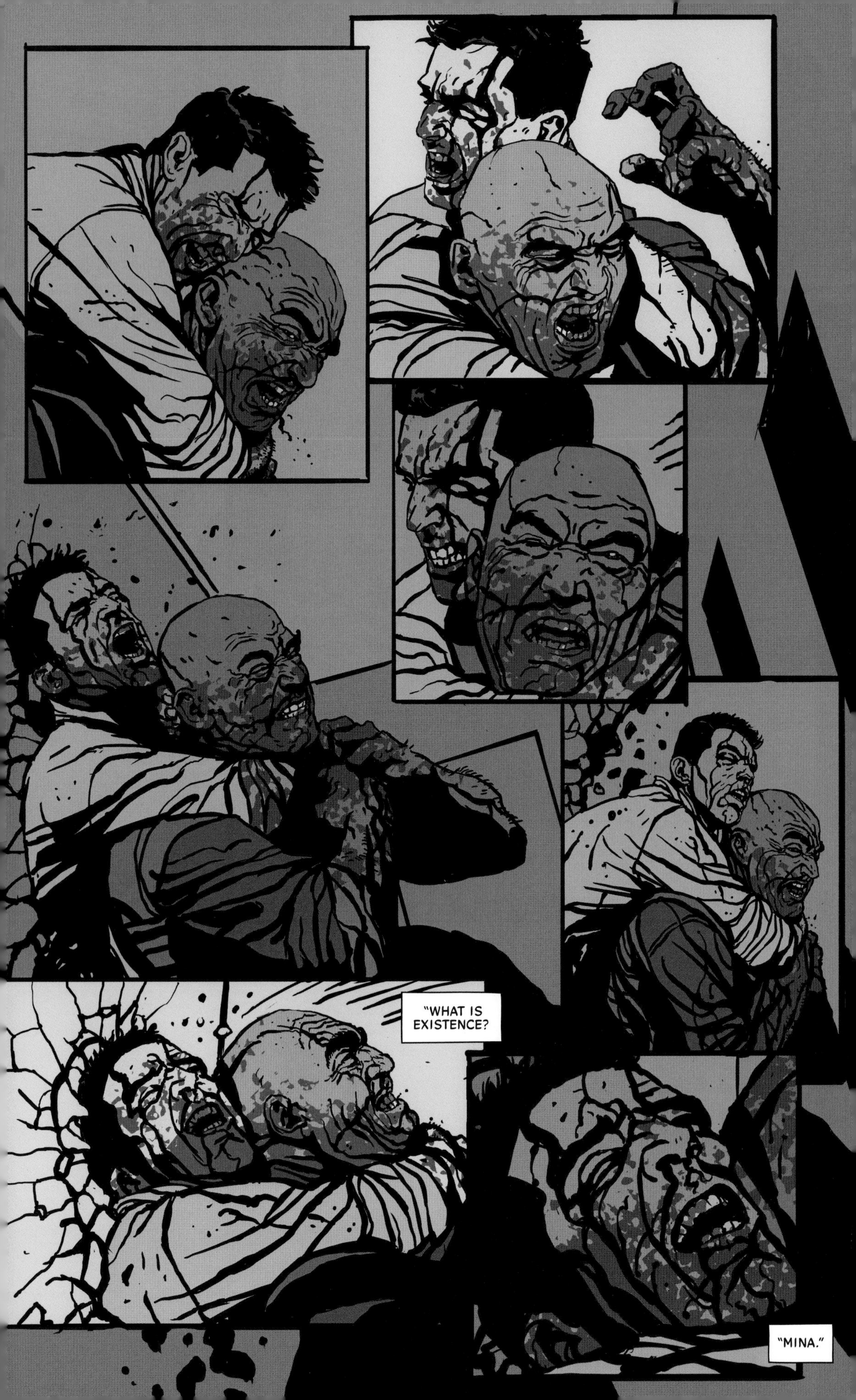
"WHAT IS
EXISTENCE?
"MINA."

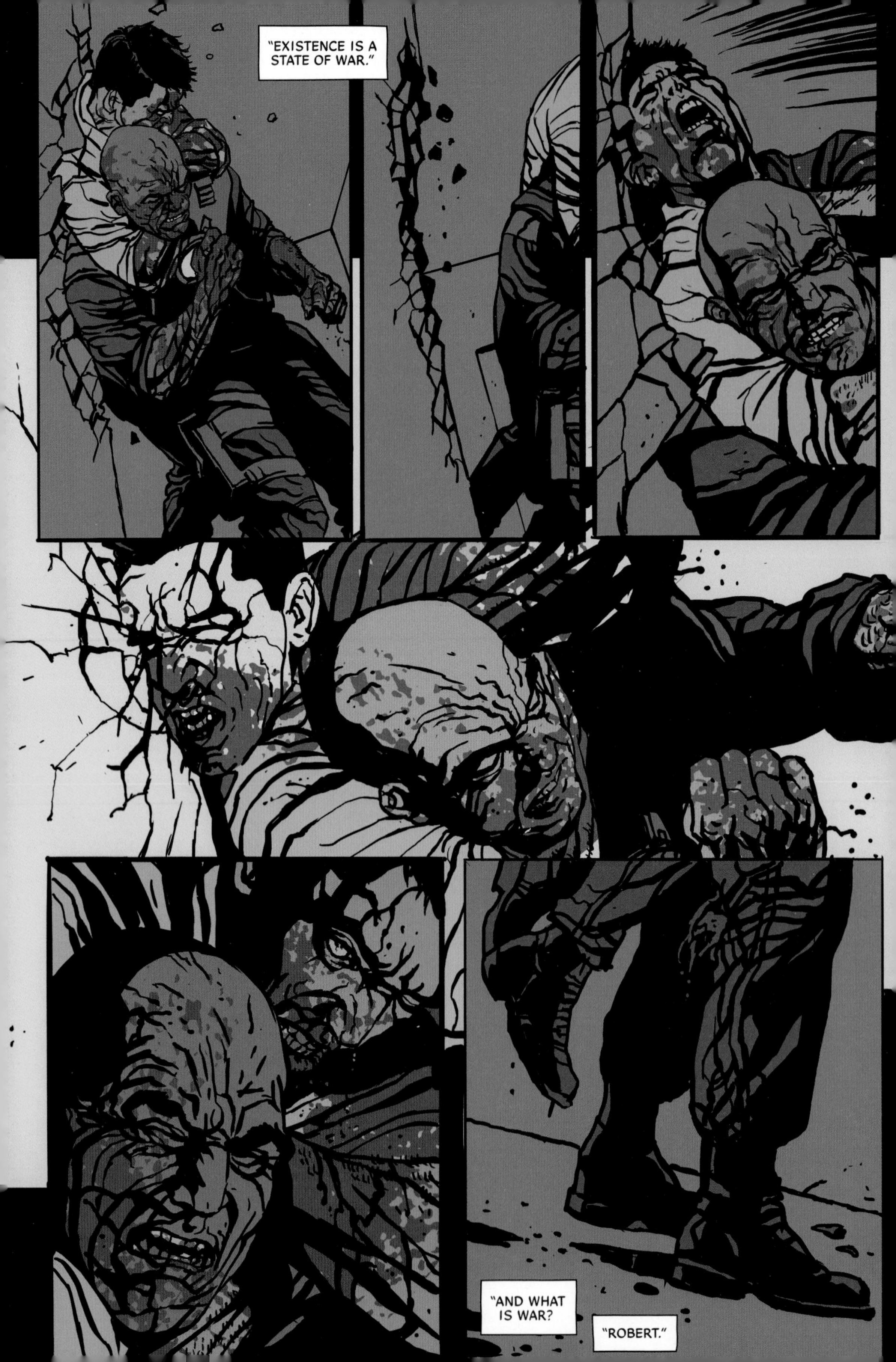
"EXISTENCE IS A STATE OF WAR."
"AND WHAT IS WAR?
"ROBERT."

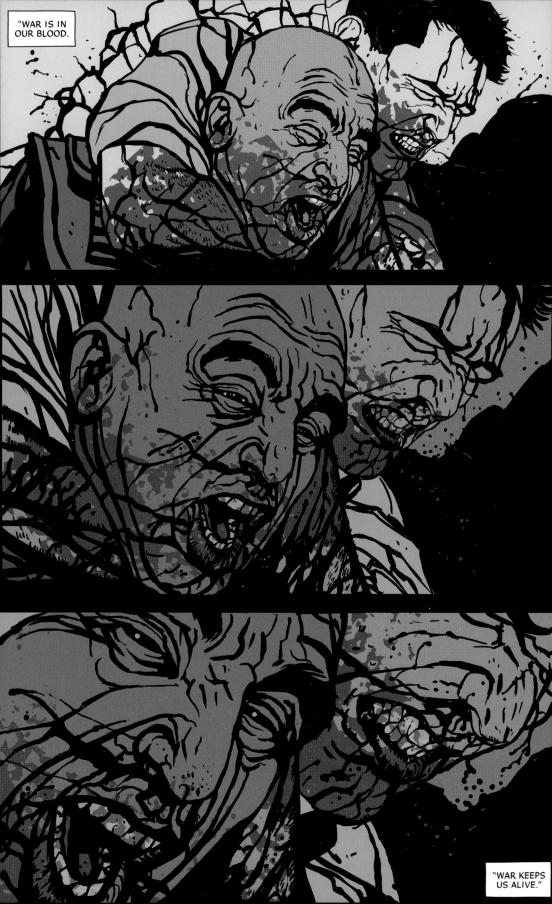

"WAR IS IN OUR BLOOD.

"WAR KEEPS US ALIVE."

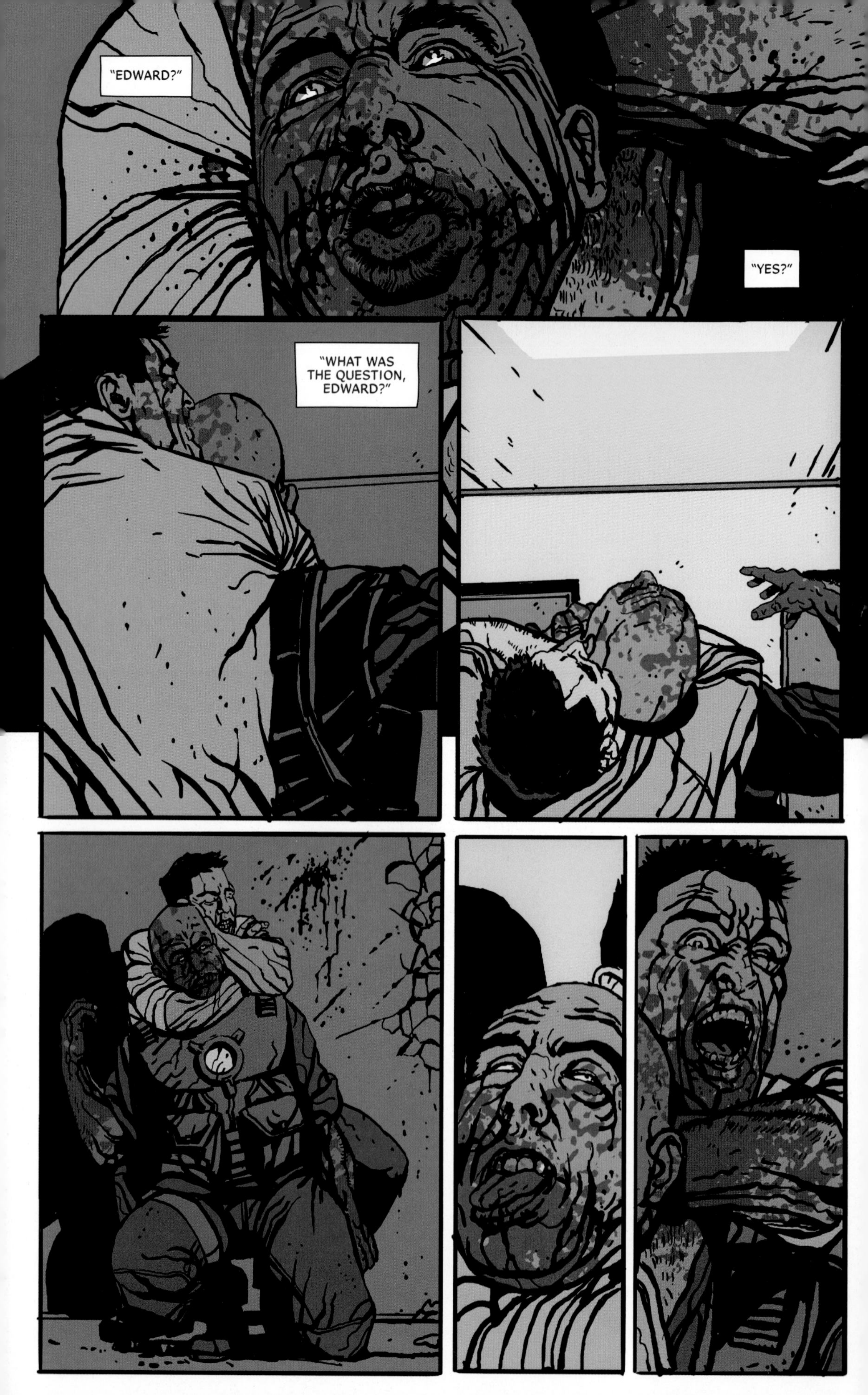
"EDWARD?"
"YES?"
"WHAT WAS THE QUESTION, EDWARD?"

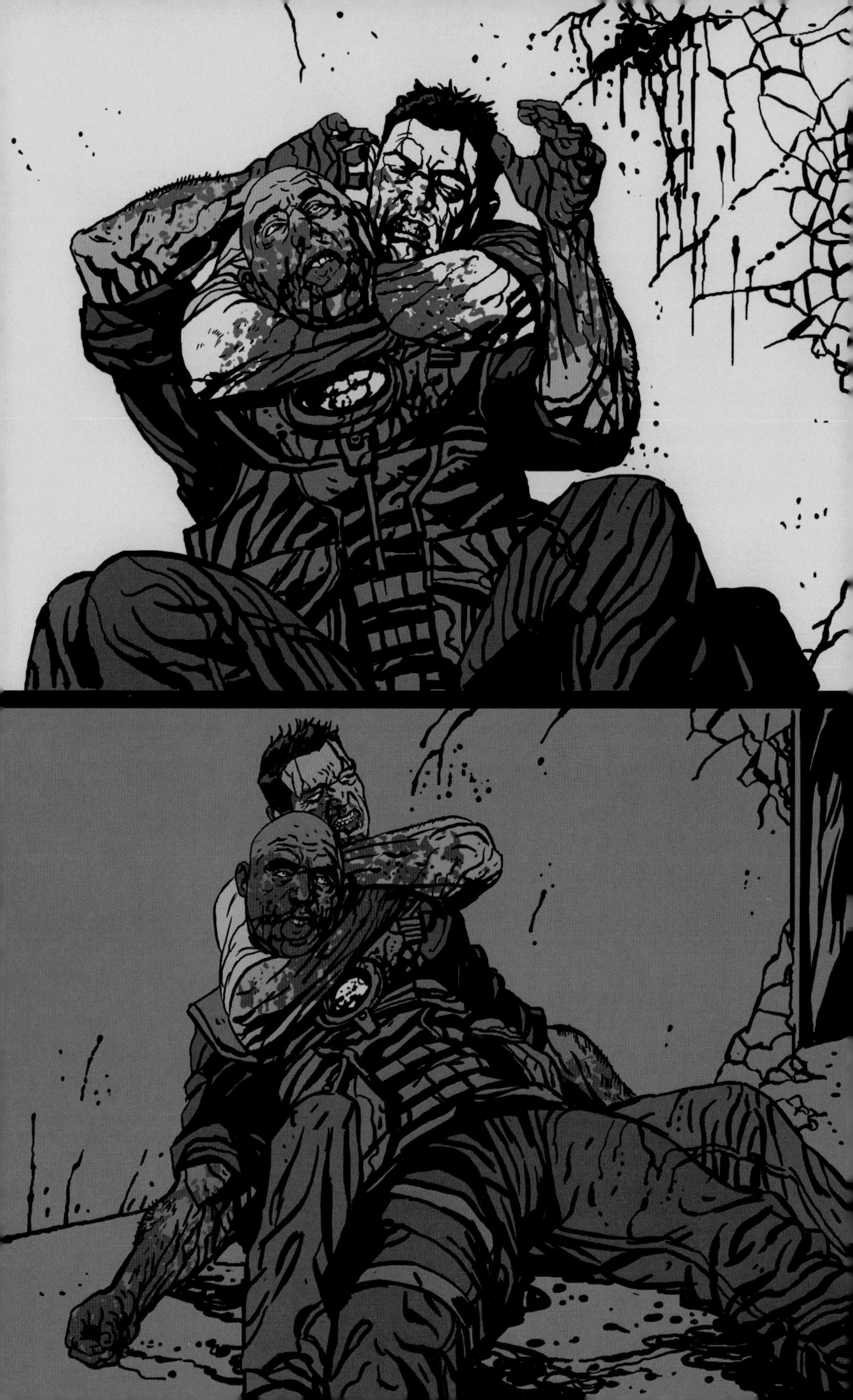

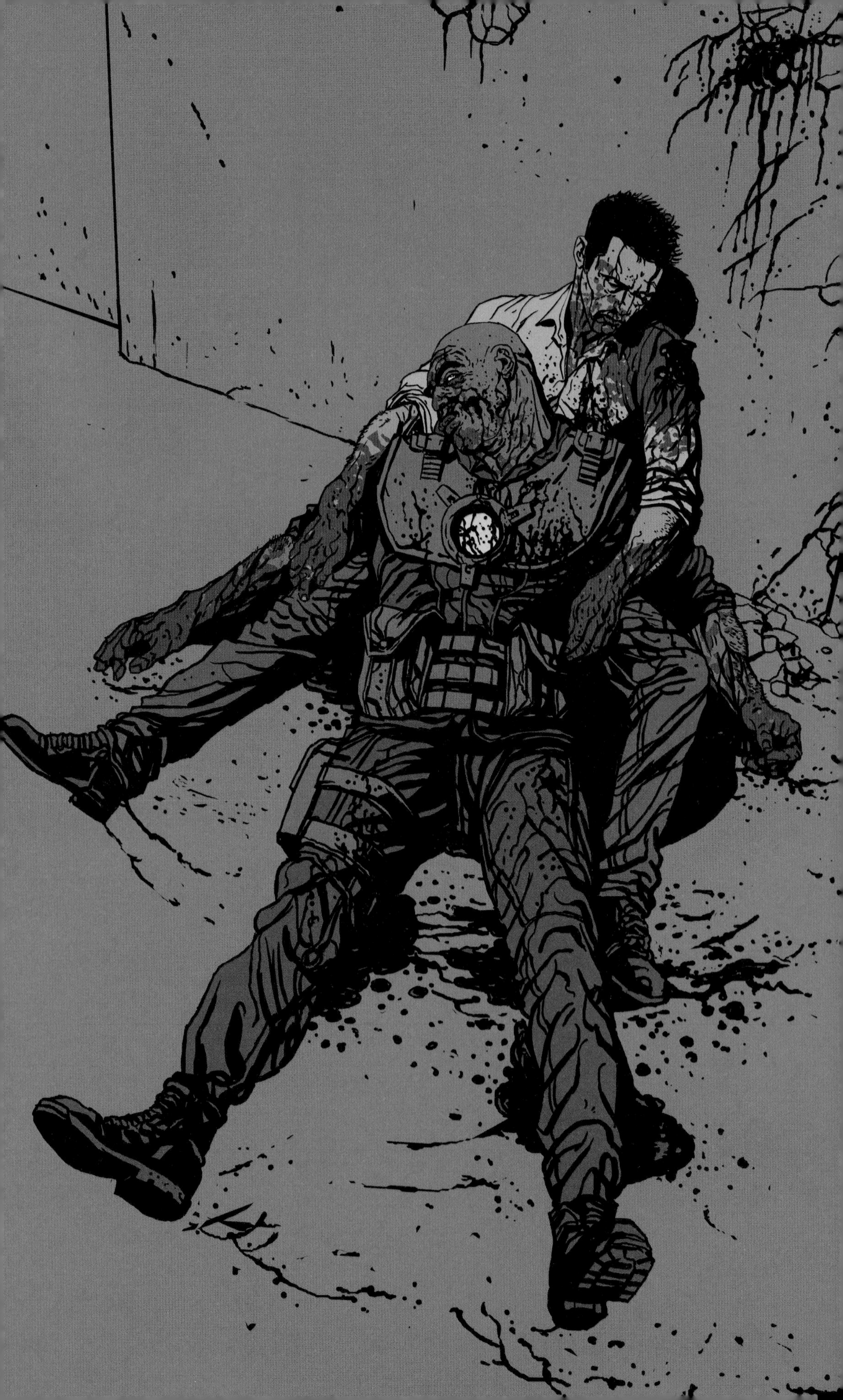

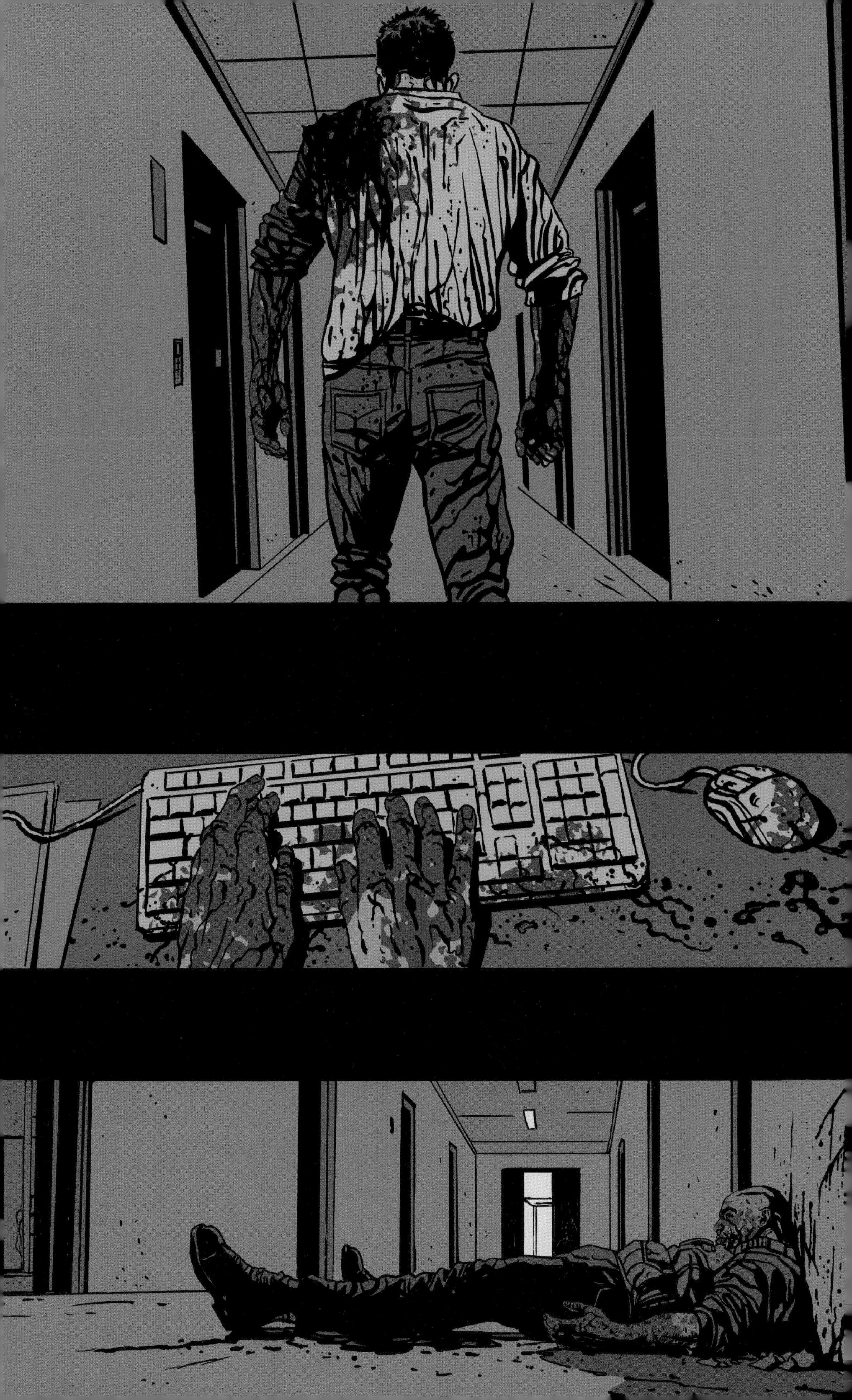

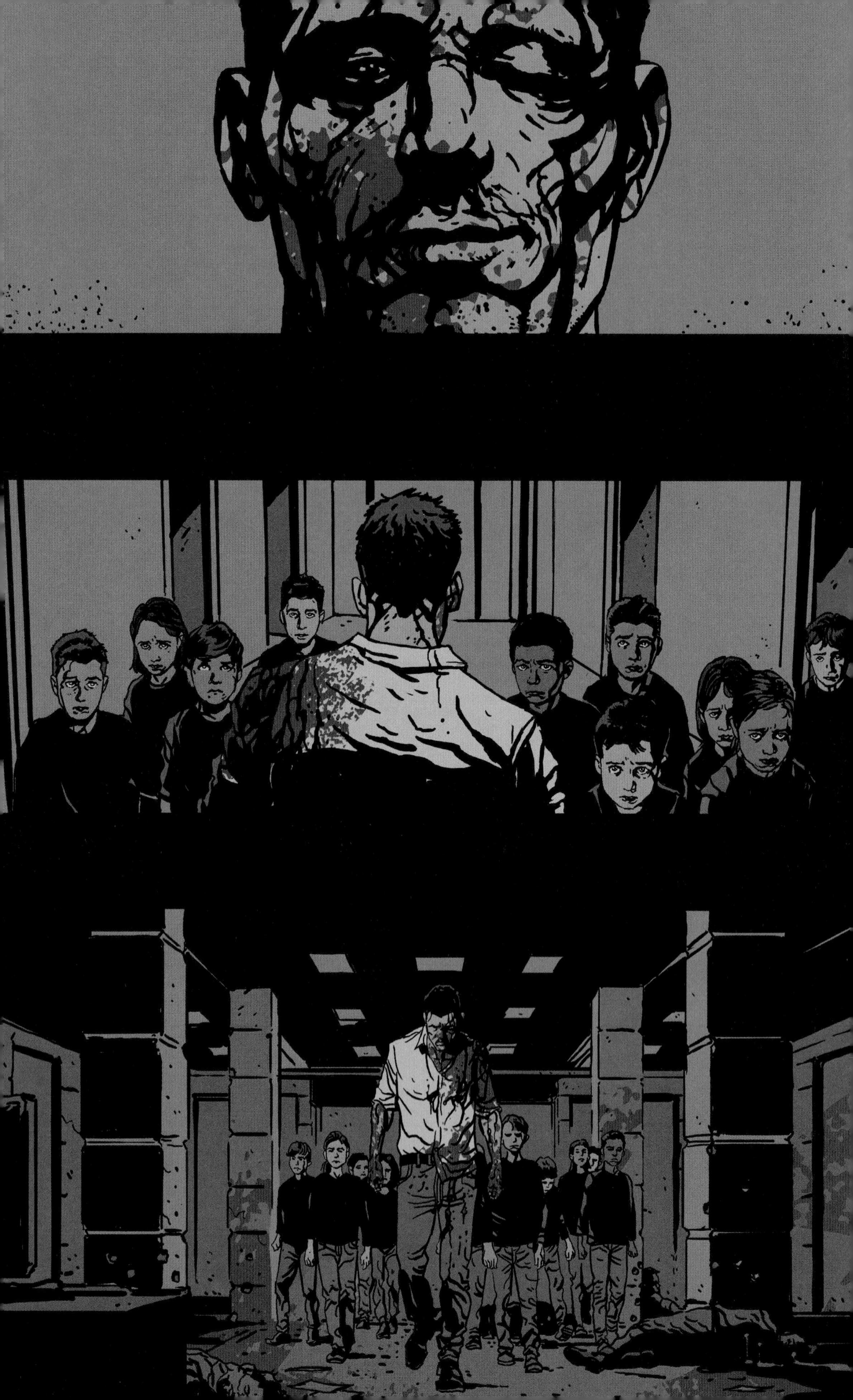

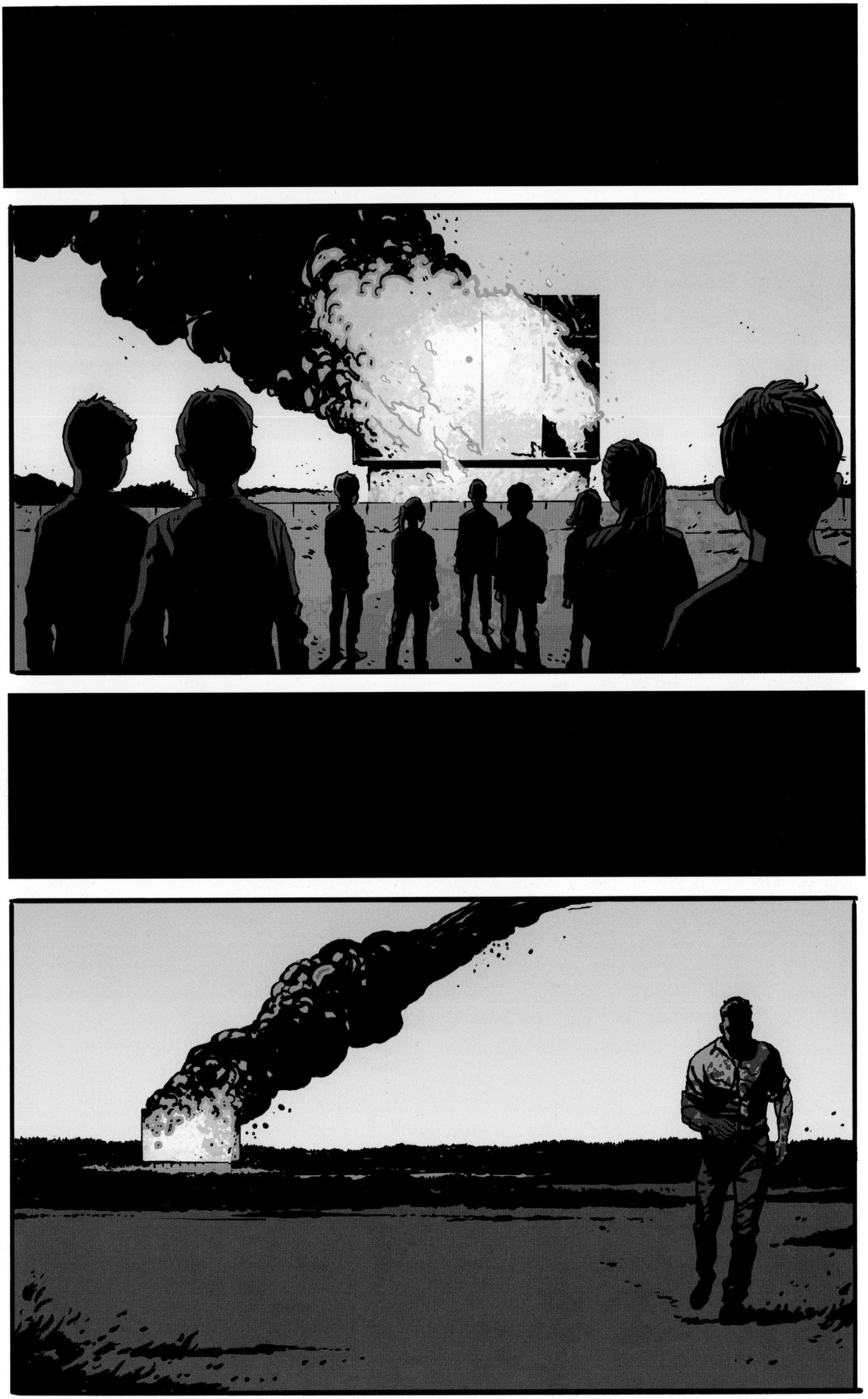

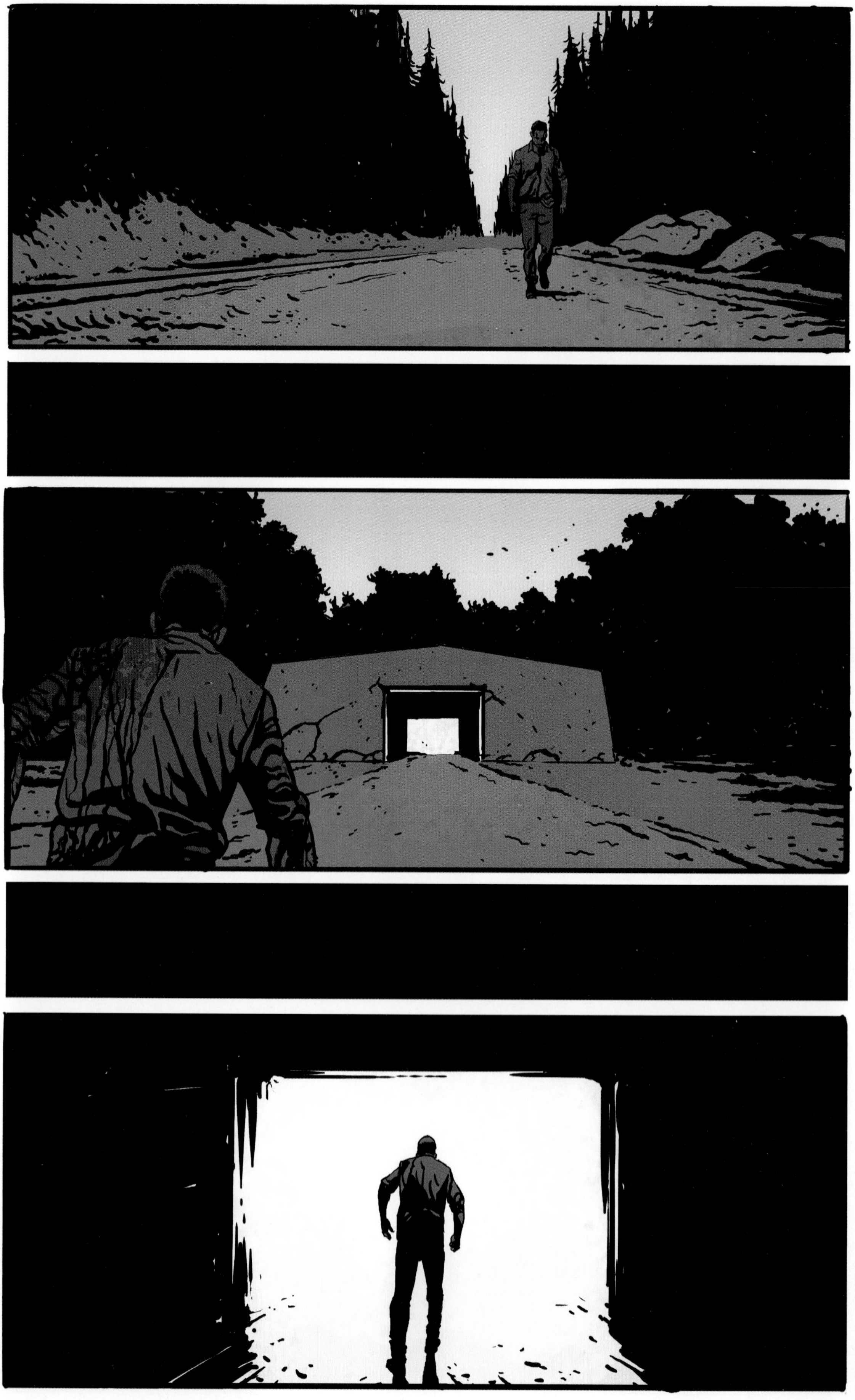

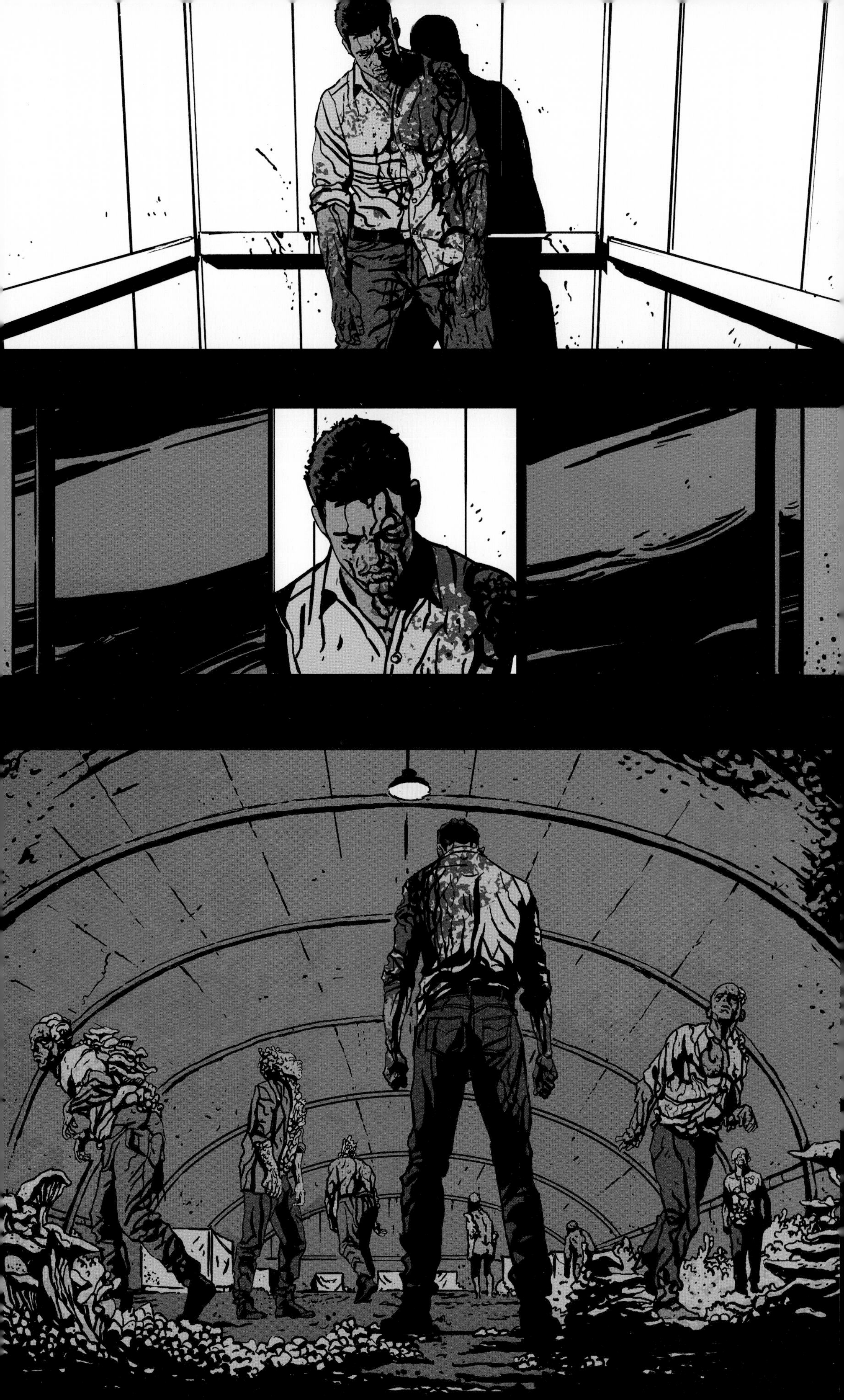

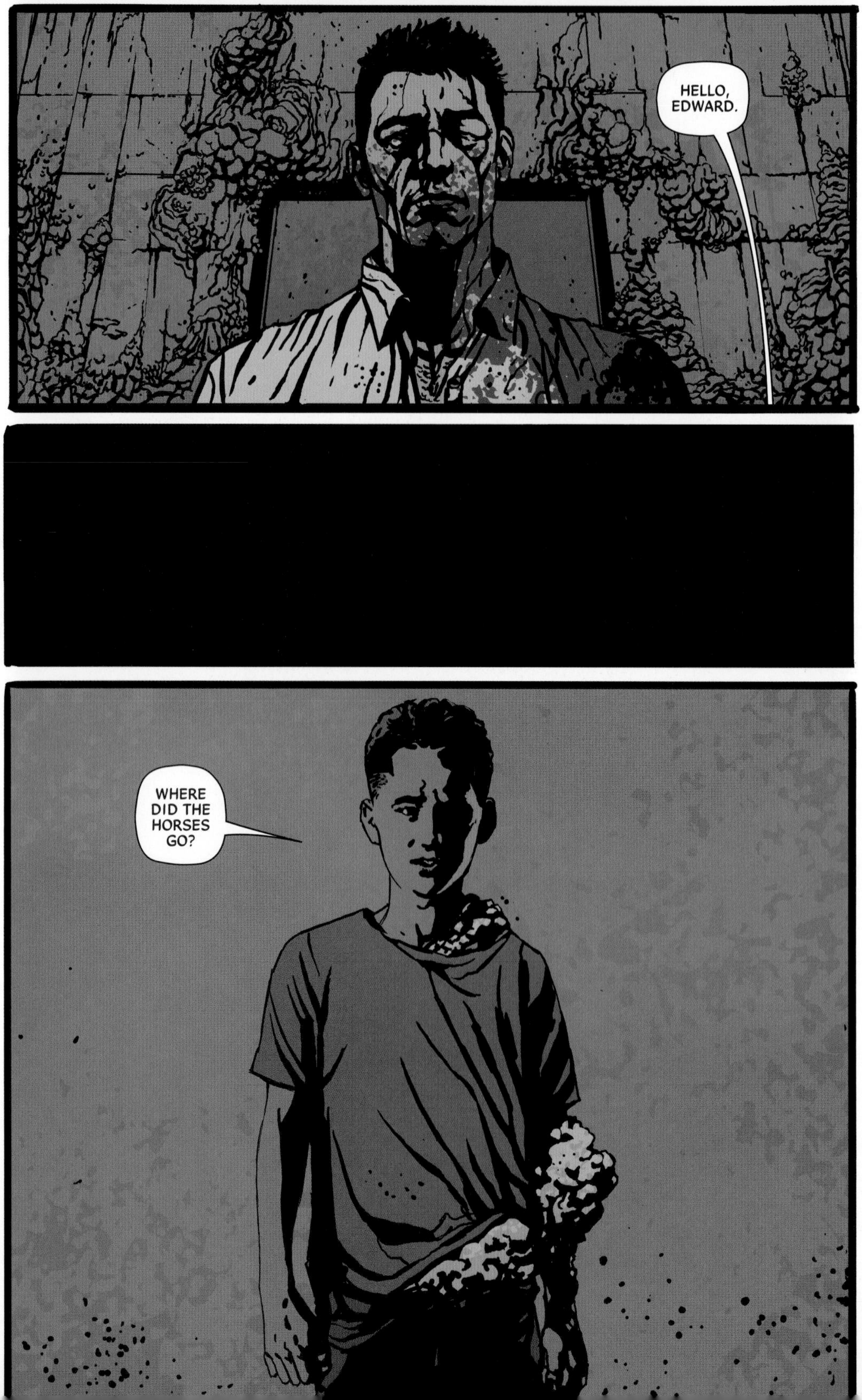
HELLO, EDWARD.
WHERE DID THE HORSES GO?

CREATOR BIOGRAPHIES

Photo by Clayton Cubitt

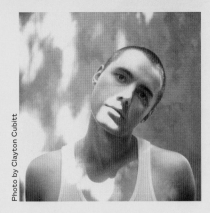

Ales Kot invents, writes & runs projects & stories for film, comics, television & more.
He also wrote/still writes: *Change*, *Material*, *Wolf*, *The Surface*, *Wild Children*.
Current body born September 27, 1986 in Opava, Czech Republic.
Resides in Brooklyn. Believes in poetry.
Twitter: @ales_kot

Ricardo Lopez Ortiz. Born and raised in Bayamón, Puerto Rico, studied Illustration at New York's School of Visual Arts. Currently living and working from his Brooklyn studio.

Adam Gorham is a Toronto-based comic artist. Since starting his career in 2008, he has completed a graphic novel trilogy called *Teuton*, which he co-created and illustrated with friend Fred Kennedy for Big Sexy Comics. He's since worked for IDW Publishing, Boom! Studios, and Image Comics.
Adam will collaborate with Ales Kot again on a mini-series from Valiant Comics in 2015.

Alberto Ponticelli began in 1997 with Dark Horse Comics (who produced the miniseries *Egon* and *Dead or Alive*). He worked with Joshua Dysart on *Unknown Soldier* (Vertigo/DC Comics), which was nominated for the Eisner Award for Best Incoming Series. His other DC/Vertigo Comics credits include *Frankenstein*, *Agent of SHADE* (written by Jeff Lemire and Matt Kindt), *Dial H* (written by China Mieville), and currently *FBP* (written by Simon Olivier). In 2008 he produced his own first graphic novel *Blatta*, which won several awards in Italy.

Marek Oleksicki
Born May 16 ,1979 in Białystok, Poland.
He is a comic book artist and illustrator.
Graduated from Academy for Fine Arts in Warsaw in 2004.
He has been working on several comics projects as well as storyboards, advertisements, magazines covers and shorts.
He debuted in the USA in 2009 as the artist for Avatar Press' *Frankenstein's Womb* graphic novel by Warren Ellis.
He worked on *28 Days Later*, *Planet of the Apes*, *The Darkness*, and several other projects.
Oleksicki currently resides in Białystok, Poland.

Jordie Bellaire is an Eisner Award winning colorist best known
for her work on *Manhattan Projects*, *Pretty Deadly*,
Nowhere Men, *Autumnlands: Tooth & Claw*, *Howtoons*, and *Three*.
She lives in Ireland with her calico, Buffy.

Clayton Cowles graduated from the Joe Kubert School of Cartoon
and Graphic Art in 2009, and has been lettering for Image and
Marvel Comics ever since. For Image, his credits include
Bitch Planet, *Pretty Deadly*, *The Wicked + The Divine*, and less than
ten others. His Marvel credits include *Fantastic Four*,
Young Avengers, *Secret Avengers*, *Bucky Barnes: Winter Soldier* and
way more than ten others. He lives on Twitter as @claytoncowles,
and spends his real life in upstate New York with his cat.

Tom Muller is an Eisner Award nominated Belgian graphic designer
who works with technology startups, movie studios, publishers,
media producers, ad agencies, and filmmakers.
In comics he's best known for working with Ashley Wood (*Popbot*,
WWR), Mam Tor Publishing, Ivan Brandon (*24SEVEN*, *VIKING*,
DRIFTER), Tori Amos (*Comic Book Tattoo*), and a myriad of logos for
Marvel and DC Comics. He collaborated with filmmaker
Darren Aronofsky on the *NOAH* graphic novel, and is designing
Valiant Entertainment's *Divinity* and Valiant Next covers.
He lives in London with his wife, and two cats that test the limits of
what they can get away with on a daily basis. Find him online most
hours of the day (and night) by Googling "helloMuller".

Sarah Horrocks is a writer, artist, critic, and podcaster.
She currently resides in Oklahoma.
Follow her on twitter: @mercurialblonde

Tonči Zonjić is the Croatian artist of comic books such as
The Immortal Iron Fist, *Marvel Divas*, *Who is Jake Ellis?* and its
sequel, *Where is Jake Ellis?*, and the critically-acclaimed
Lobster Johnson series. He lives in Toronto, Canada.

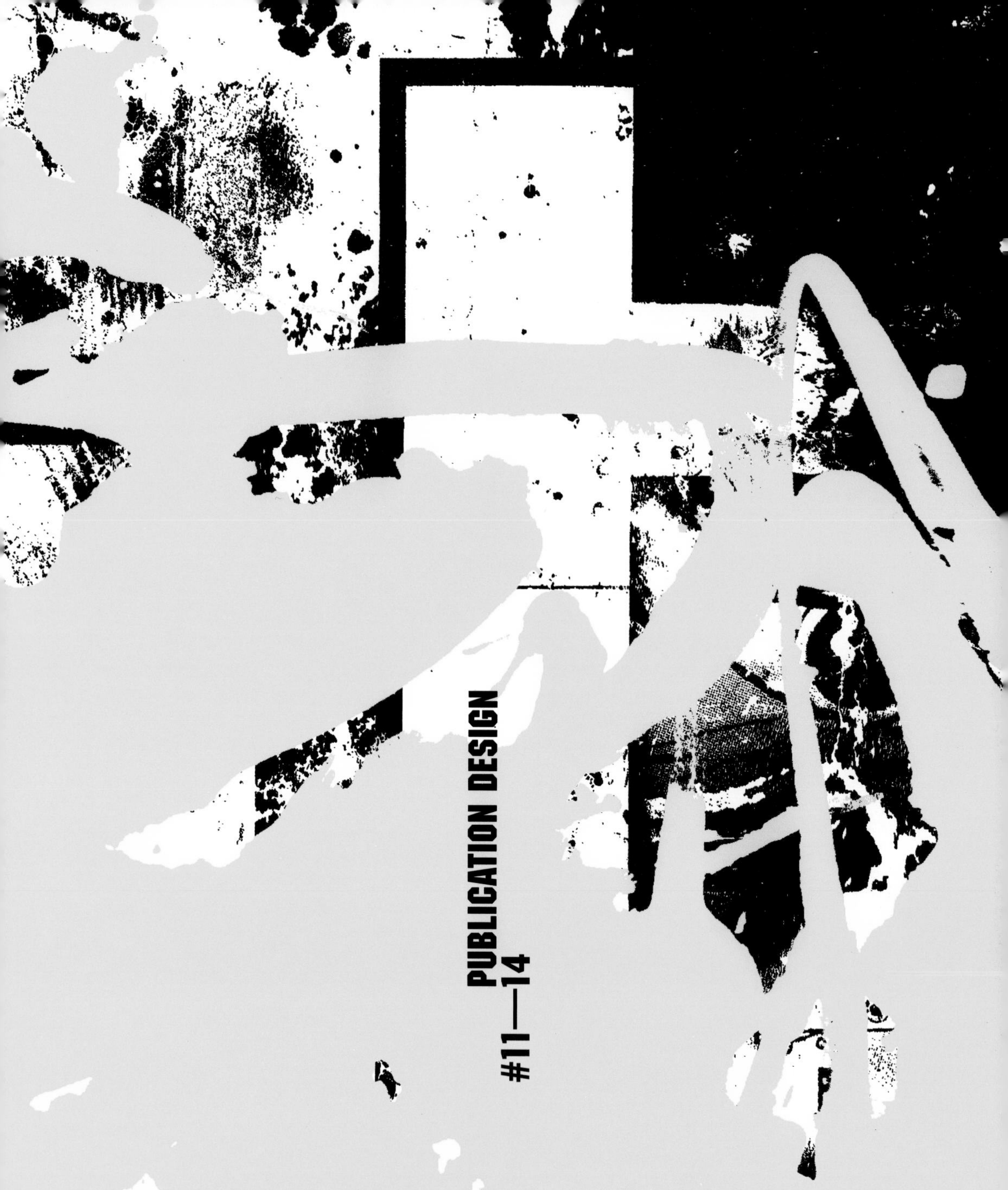
PUBLICATION DESIGN
#11—14

The original ZERO single issue publication designs by Tom Muller, with key art from series artists Ricardo Lopez Ortiz, Adam Gorham, Alberto Ponticelli, and Marek Oleksicki — and variant cover art from Sarah Horrocks and Tonči Zonjić.

Written by Ales KOT
Illustrated by Ricardo Lopez ORTIZ
Colored by Jordie BELLAIRE
Lettered by Clayton COWLES
Designed by Tom MULLER

CHAPTER 11:

KILLSHOT

ZERO #11. Lorem ipsum dolor sit amet consectetur adipiscing elit.

Cover design, graphics & color by Tom Muller with:
Cover A: Ricardo Lopez Ortiz / Cover B: Sarah Horrocks

Image Comics, Inc.

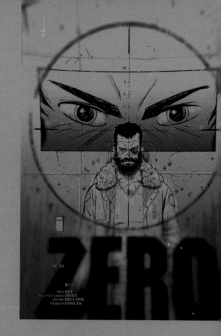

ZERO

Nº 11

$2.50

Ales KOT
Ricardo Lopez ORTIZ
Jordie BELLAIRE
Clayton COWLES

SIOBHÁN PENN

ZERO

Edward Zero was a secret agent.
He quit the Agency.
This is the story of his life.

CHAPTER 11:
KILL SHOT

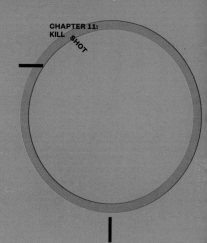

ZERO

SARA COOKE

CHAPTER 12:

FAMILY REUNION

Zero was a secret agent.
the Agency.
the story of his life.

Sara Cooke runs the Agency.

CHAPTER 12: FAMILY REUNION

Written by **Ales KOT**
Illustrated by **Adam GORHAM**
Colored by **Jordie BELLAIRE**
Lettered by **Clayton COWLES**
Designed by **Tom MULLER**.

Cover design, graphics & color by Tom Muller and Adam Gorham

RATED **M**

MATURE

Image Comics, Inc.

Robert Kirkman	chief operating officer
Erik Larsen	chief financial officer
Todd McFarlane	president
Marc Silvestri	chief executive officer
Jim Valentino	vice president
Eric Stephenson	publisher
Ron Richards	director of business development
Jennifer de Guzman	pr & marketing director
Branwyn Bigglestone	accounts manager
Emily Miller	accounting assistant
Jamie Parrano	marketing assistant
Emilio Bautista	sales assistant
Kevin Yuen	digital rights coordinator
Tyler Shainline	events coordinator
David Brothers	content manager
Jonathan Chan	production manager
Drew Gill	art director
Jana Cook	print manager
Monica Garcia	senior production artist
Vincent Kukua	production artist
Jenna Savage	production artist
Addison Duke	production artist

Media inquiries should be directed to Roger Green & Phil D'Amecourt at WME Entertainment and Ari Lubet at 3 Arts Entertainment.

ZERO #12. November 2014. Published by Image Comics, Inc. Office of publication: 2001 Center Street, Sixth Floor, Berkeley, CA 94704.

IMAGECOMICS.COM

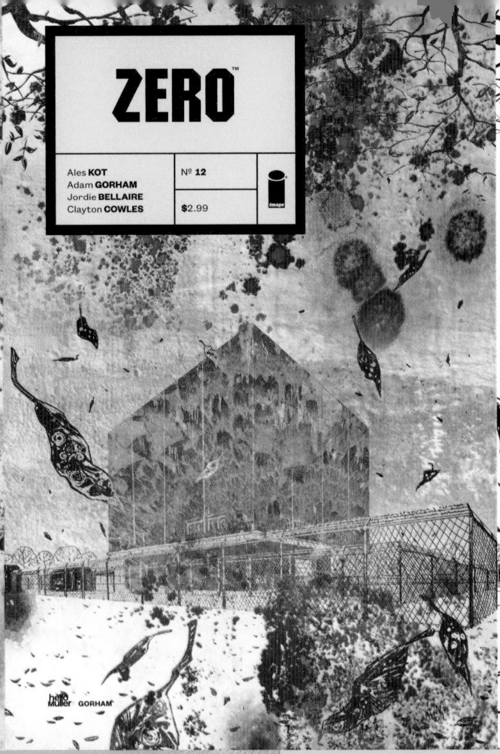

ZERO™
Ales KOT
Adam GORHAM
Jordie BELLAIRE
Clayton COWLES
Nº 12
$2.99
hello Muller · GORHAM

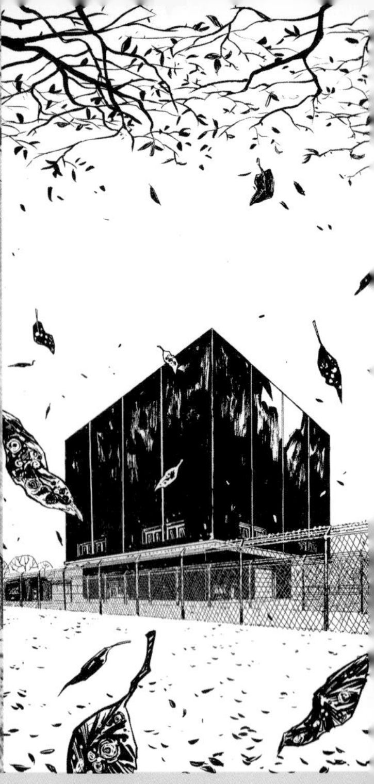

CHAPTER 13: FAREWELL

Written by **Ales KOT**
Illustrated by **Alberto PONTICELLI**
Colored by **Jordie BELLAIRE**
Lettered by **Clayton COWLES**
Designed by **Tom MULLER**.

Cover design, graphics & color by Tom Muller and Alberto Ponticelli

Image Comics, Inc.

Robert Kirkman	Chief Operating Officer
Erik Larsen	Chief Financial Officer
Todd McFarlane	President
Marc Silvestri	Chief Executive Officer
Jim Valentino	Vice-President
Eric Stephenson	Publisher
Ron Richards	Director of Business Development
Jennifer de Guzman	Director of Trade Book Sales
Kat Salazar	Director of PR & Marketing
Corey Murphy	Director of Retail Sales
Jeremy Sullivan	Director of Digital Sales
Emilio Bautista	Sales Assistant
Branwyn Bigglestone	Senior Accounts Manager
Emily Miller	Accounts Manager
Jessica Ambriz	Administrative Assistant
Tyler Shainline	Events Coordinator
David Brothers	Content Manager
Jonathan Chan	Production Manager
Drew Gill	Art Director
Meredith Wallace	Print Manager
Monica Garcia	Senior Production Artist
Addison Duke	Production Artist
Tricia Ramos	Production Assistant

ZERO #13. December 2014. Published by Image Comics, Inc. Office of publication: 2001 Center Street, Sixth Floor, Berkeley, CA 94704.

Media inquiries should be directed to Roger Green & Phil D'Amecourt at WME Entertainment and Ari Lubet at 3 Arts Entertainment.

RATED **M**
MATURE

IMAGECOMICS.COM

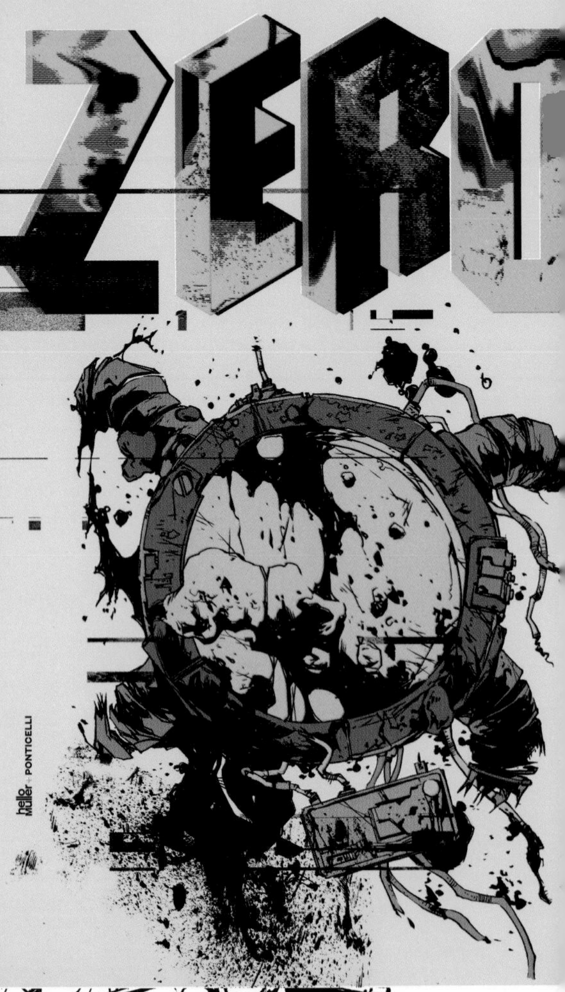

ZERO
hello Muller · PONTICELLI

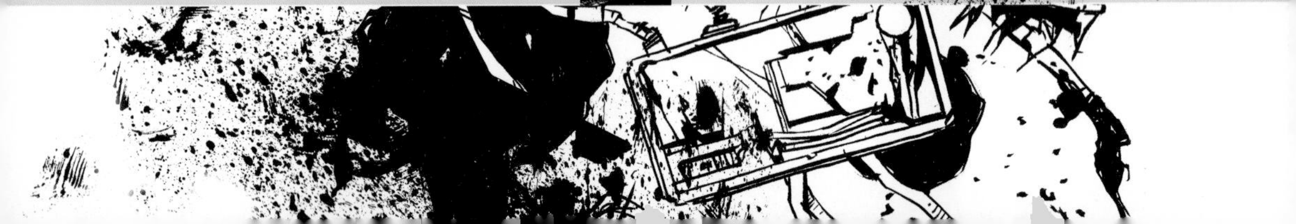

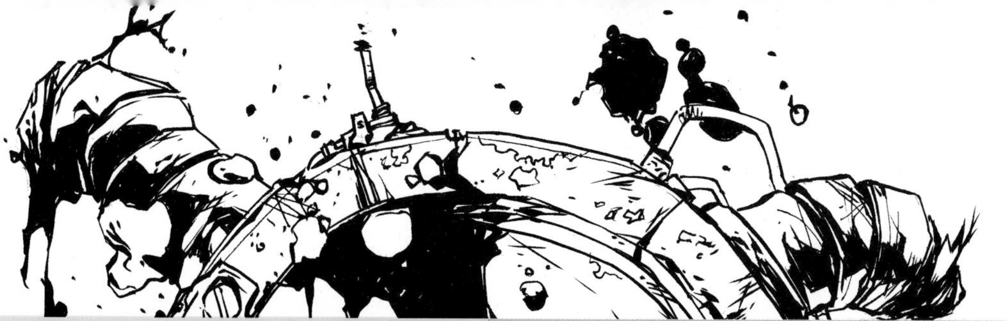

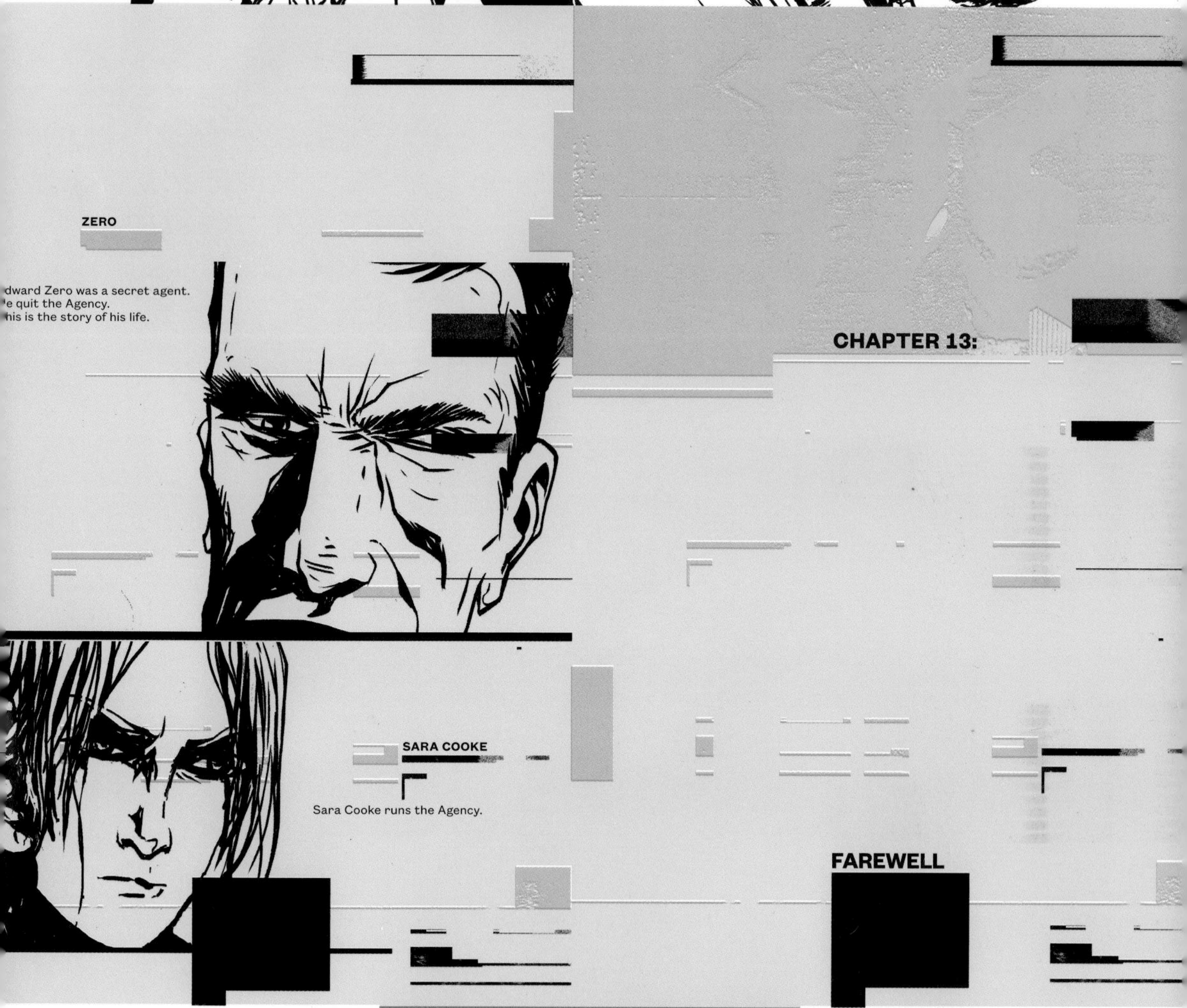
ZERO
dward Zero was a secret agent.
e quit the Agency.
his is the story of his life.
SARA COOKE
Sara Cooke runs the Agency.
CHAPTER 13:
FAREWELL

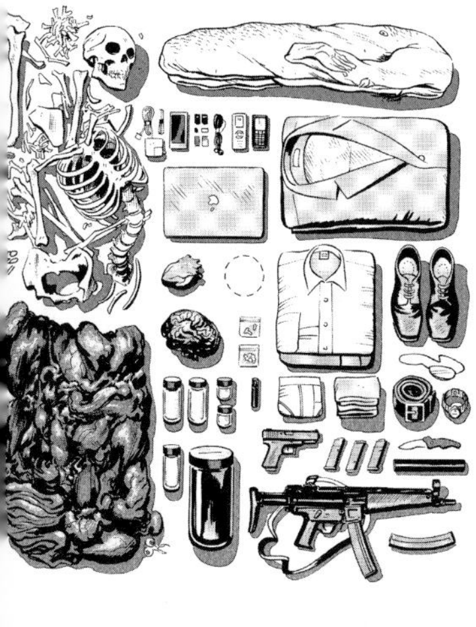

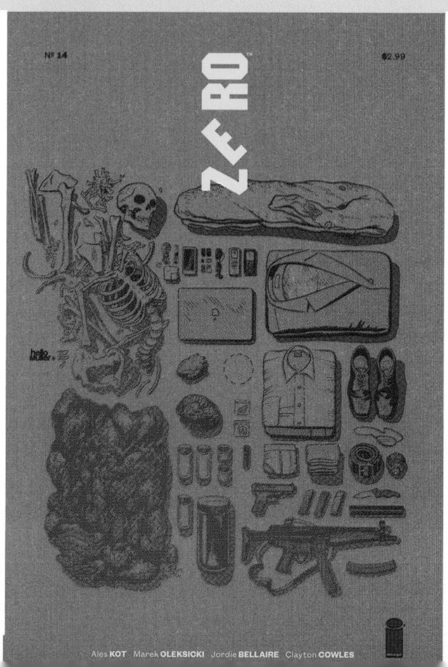
Nº 14
ZERO
$2.99
Ales KOT Marek OLEKSICKI Jordie BELLAIRE Clayton COWLES

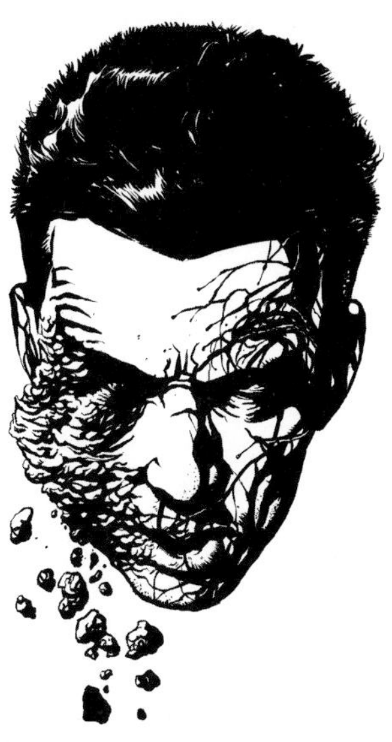

ZERO #14, January 2015. Published by Image Comics, Inc. Office of publication: 2001 Center Street, Sixth Floor, Berkeley, CA 94704. Copyright © 2014 ALES KOT. All rights reserved. ZERO™ (including all prominent characters featured herein), its logo and all character likenesses are trademarks of Ales Kot, unless otherwise noted. Image Comics® and its logos are registered trademarks of Image Comics, Inc. No part of this publication may be reproduced or transmitted, in any form or by any means (except for short excerpts for review purposes) without express written permission of Image Comics, Inc. All names, characters, events and locales in this publication are entirely fictional. Any resemblance to actual living persons (living or dead), events or places, without satiric intent, is coincidental. Printed in the U.S.A. For more information regarding the CPSIA on this printed material call: 203-595-3636 and provide reference # RICH - 558002. For international rights, contact: foreignlicensing@imagecomics.com

"Panic" copyright 1986 Johnny Marr & Steven Morrissey

Media inquiries should be directed to Roger Green & Phil D'Amecourt at WME Entertainment and Ari Lubet at 3 Arts Entertainment.

$2.9

CHAPTER 14:

NO LAND BUT THE LAND, NO SEA BUT THE SEA

Written by Ales KOT
Illustrated by Marek OLEKSICKI
Colored by Jordie BELLAIRE
Lettered by Clayton COWLES
Designed by Tom MULLER

Cover design, graphics & color by Tom Muller with Marek Oleksicki (Cover A) and Tonči Zonjić (Cover B)

Image Comics, Inc.

Robert Kirkman — Chief Operating Officer
Erik Larsen — Chief Financial Officer
Todd McFarlane — President
Marc Silvestri — Chief Executive Officer
Jim Valentino — Vice-President

Eric Stephenson — Publisher
Ron Richards — Director of Business Development
Jennifer de Guzman — Director of Trade Book Sales
Kat Salazar — Director of PR & Marketing
Corey Murphy — Director of Retail Sales
Jeremy Sullivan — Director of Digital Sales
Emilio Bautista — Sales Assistant
Branwyn Bigglestone — Senior Accounts Manager
Emily Miller — Accounts Manager
Jessica Ambriz — Administrative Assistant
Tyler Shainline — Events Coordinator
David Brothers — Content Manager
Jonathan Chan — Production Manager
Drew Gill — Art Director
Meredith Wallace — Print Manager
Monica Garcia — Senior Production Artist
Addison Duke — Production Artist
Tricia Ramos — Production Assistant

IMAGECOMICS.COM

Ales KOT   Marek OLEKSICKI   Jordie BELLAIRE   Clayton COWLES

Here again at the end
Before the beginning
So the salt will spill again
Throw it over your shoulder

Oh it's in tomorrow, fortune or sorrow
Wait, you may win
I don't mean to show that I know how this goes
Before we begin
Again

BROADCAST – 'BEFORE WE BEG

Edward Zero was a secret agent. He quit the Agency. This is the story of his life.

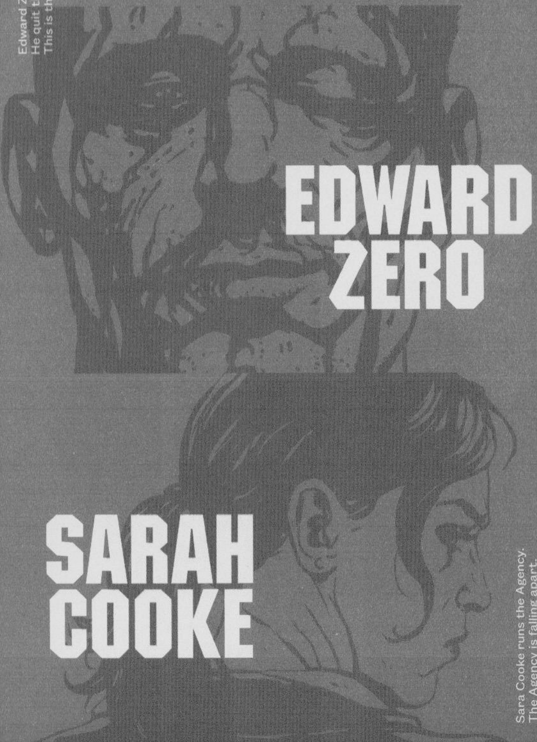

EDWARD ZERO

SARAH COOKE

Sara Cooke runs the Agency. The Agency is falling apart.

CHAPTER 14:
NO LAND BUT THE LAND,
NO SEA BUT THE SEA